Books by Robert J. Serling

Fiction

The Left Seat
The President's Plane Is Missing
She'll Never Get off the Ground
McDermott's Sky

Nonfiction

The Probable Cause
The Electra Story
Loud and Clear
Ceiling Unlimited
Maverick
Little Giant
The Only Way to Fly

WINGS

ROBERT J SERLING

THE DIAL PRESS NEW YORK

Published by
The Dial Press
1 Dag Hammarskjold Plaza
New York, New York 10017

Manufactured in the United States of America

Designed by James L. McGuire

First printing

Library of Congress Cataloging in Publication Data

Serling, Robert J.
Wings.

I. Title.
PZ4.S4854Wi   [PS3569.E7]   813'.5'4   78–3182
ISBN 0–8037–9592–0

This book is gratefully dedicated to the memory of the late William Magruder, whose contributions to aviation progress have earned him an honored place in the brotherhood of airmen, and to the following past and present airline executives:

Hal Carr, North Central
Frank Borman, Eastern
Art Kelly, Western
Harding Lawrence, Braniff
W. A. Patterson, United
Dom Renda, Western
Bob Six, Continental

WINGS

PROLOGUE

The day the Concorde flew from London to Washington in three hours and twelve minutes, establishing a new trans-Atlantic speed record, only one television station had a camera crew at Dulles Airport to meet the flight.

British Airways had alerted the news media to the likelihood of a record when the supersonic transport was halfway across the Atlantic. But it had been a hectic day in the nation's capital and no one had the manpower to spare except for WJLA-TV, the local ABC affiliate. It managed to scrape up a cameraman, a soundman, and a bored young reporter who privately considered the Concorde an environmental menace.

The reporter dutifully waited outside Immigration so he could tape quick interviews with some of the passengers, having already been promised by British Airways that he could talk to the captain later.

Two or three passengers would suffice, he decided, and he got one woman to breathe "absolutely thrilling" when he asked how it felt to set a record. The second person he approached was a tweedy, red-faced Englishman whose response to the same question was surly. The third passenger to emerge from Immigration was a big man, three inches over six feet, but with those telltale signs of withered brawn so typical of big men. Yet there was something about the old guy that commanded attention. He looked like 100-proof bourbon inside an expensive cologne bottle.

"Sir, just a minute. May I ask if you were on a business trip or—?"

"Pleasure. Took my wife over to visit some relatives. I came back early . . . earlier than we figured, you might say."

"Then, you're aware that your flight set a new speed record?"

The big man looked at him patronizingly, with just a touch of suspicion. "Sure. Captain told us when we touched down."

"Any comment, sir? How did it feel?"

"Didn't feel any different from the other Concorde trips I've made. Great airplane. If it hadn't been for those goddamned ninnies like Senator Proxmire and all those environmental freaks, we'd have an American SST. Minute I heard we set a record, that's what I thought. The crap about supersonic flight being dangerous, the phony pseudoscientific bunk. The Concorde's proved otherwise. Which is what I kept telling everybody when the stupid bastards in Congress killed our own SST program."

The reporter was mentally bleeping out the profanity, and the subject of the interview cannily sensed it. "Tell you what you *can* use, son. This flight took three hours and twelve minutes. I can remember when it took nearly that long to fly from Binghamton, New York, to Newark. That was our first route."

The reporter looked blank. "First route?"

"You don't know who I am, do you?"

"Well," the newsman hedged, "I don't quite—"

"No matter. You weren't even a gleam in your pappy's eye when we started."

He walked away before the reporter could say any more.

"Who the hell was that?" the TV man asked his crew. "Someone I was supposed to recognize?"

The cameraman looked at the tall departing figure and sighed. "If you had ever covered aviation, or knew the first thing about airplanes, you would have known. That was Barnwell Ernest Burton of Trans-Coastal. A pioneer and a pirate. The last of a wonderful breed."

"If you dig dinosaurs."

ONE

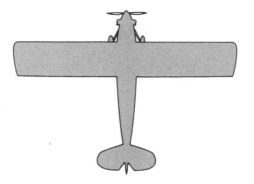

His father ran a little grocery store on LeRoy Street in Binghamton, N.Y., a small city in southern New York State close to the
Pennsylvania state line and about seventy miles south of Syracuse.
The best that could be said about Ernest Burton from the standpoint of financial success was that he made a living. The family
dwelling was a modest frame house a few blocks from the store.

His mother had been Ruth Barnwell before her marriage to
Ernest Burton, and she wanted to preserve her family name in her
first son, who turned out to be their only child. By the age of eight,
he already had gone through a dozen fistfights with kids who made
the mistake of jeering at his first name. By the age of ten he was
demanding to be called Barney.

His birthday was January 14, 1908. The previous day Henry
Farman, flying a French Voisin biplane, made the first circular
flight of one kilometer somewhere in Europe, a feat mentioned in
the primitive aviation-history books that Barney began reading
four years before he entered high school. At a time when most
youngsters worshipped the automobile, he was devoted totally to
airplanes. Typically the family's major possession in Barney's teen-
age years was a 1923 Jordan sedan which his father loved to the

point of treating it like a living creature. He washed and polished it every Sunday, religiously followed the lubrication and oil-change schedules, and his greatest joy was to take a weekend trip. "Let's drive the Jordan up to Syracuse Sunday morning," he'd tell his family.

They had relatives in the bigger city, but for young Barney the fun lay in the seventy-two-mile drive over the winding, two-lane highway marked Route 11. They would leave at first light and the trip would take almost three hours, but for Barney it was a chance to indulge in three hours of daydreaming as the Jordan was transformed from a car to the dirigible *Shenandoah*, or a giant Martin bomber like the ones Billy Mitchell led that had sunk the *Ostfriesland* off the Virginia coast in a demonstration. When Barney was allowed to sit up front with his father, the Jordan was a Spad or a Nieuport cockpit, and any car in front was an enemy Fokker caught in the radiator-cap gunsight of his twin Vickers machine guns.

His heroes were the air-mail pilots, however. So driving back to Binghamton on a rainy night the car became a DH-4 with Jack Knight Burton muttering "the mail must go through." The bumps in the road passed for storm turbulence.

Barney read thousands of words about the mail pilots and their courageous exploits but nothing about the planes being hand-me-downs from World War I. It never occurred to him that U.S. commercial aviation during his youth was light-years behind Europe's. In 1919, Britain and France were operating scheduled daily flights between London and Paris in cabin aircraft, with stewards serving food and champagne. While Barney read avidly about the exploits of American pilots, the French air-mail service surpassed America's in route length, frequency, and caliber of equipment.

Barney devoured the contents of the pulps—*Daredevil Aces, War Birds, Battle Aces*—but he never wondered why all the heroes flew British-made Camels and SE-5's or French-built Spads and Nieuports. Not for a long time did he realize that the greatest industrial country on earth had failed to put a single U.S.-designed or American-made military aircraft into combat during the Great War.

He just knew his hero worship of the Jack Knights and Hamilton

Lees and Fred Kellys was not misdirected. Their courage demanded it. Of the first forty pilots hired by the Post Office Department in 1919 to fly the mail, thirty-one had been killed in crashes by 1925. The adversities, the indifference toward aviation itself, the obsolete planes they were forced to fly, the primitive airports, and the bad airways that comprised the air-mail route system just made their achievements that much more impressive to him.

After the war, Americans regarded the airplane as an exciting but dangerous toy, to be enjoyed vicariously in movies and pulp magazines—this at a time when Germany, Great Britain, France, Hungary, Finland, Switzerland, Denmark, Poland, and Austria were operating scheduled air service, carrying people as well as mail. In the U.S., civil aviation only meant stunt flying, occasional charter or sightseeing flights, and county-fair barnstorming.

None of which bothered Barney, who, like any youngster, never looked beyond his daydream of the moment. As he grew up, he blithely ignored several indications that his ambition to become a pilot was of the pie-in-the-sky variety. Mostly, he lacked good physical coordination. When he entered Binghamton Central High School, his tall, muscular frame attracted the attention of the football coach, who talked him into trying out for the team; but Barney, while he had no difficulties mastering the duties of a single-wing tackle, had trouble performing. He was fearless and properly competitive, with all the necessary growls and snarls supposed to intimidate opposition linemen, but he was awkward and slow. Even so, Barney gave of himself, and as the coaches often privately noted, he seemed to be a steadying effect on the team. With seeming ease he would cajole his teammates out of the inevitable slumps and talk them out of their adolescent fears and jitters.

For his part, despite his general futility as a player, Barney loved football and its major fringe benefit—girls. As a varsity player, albeit a second-stringer, the letter B on his varsity sweater was a magnet. Even in the generally naïve class of '26 there were girls who Did, and the athletes usually found them sooner. Although Barney could hardly be called a legitimate athletic star, he still was a member of that exclusive fraternity, and the girls thought him more mature and experienced.

He did seem older than most of the other boys, and only part of this could be attributed to his height. Barney had an air of solemnity, an open distaste of the usual youthful frivolities, and displayed a cool indifference toward the conventional social events of a small town. It was not entirely due to any developing maturity, however. For one, Barney danced like an elephant with a hernia, his lack of physical coordination betraying him on a dance floor even more than on the gridiron. But there was something worldly about him, a quality that set him aside from youngsters his own age.

Barney worked weekends for his father, acting mostly as the delivery boy and working behind the counters when he wasn't behind the wheel of Ernest Burton's dilapidated Dodge panel truck. Actually, he operated the truck before he was of legal age for a driver's license, but fortunately he looked older than he was and the local police never stopped him. The illegality was forced on his father by sheer economics: he just couldn't afford a regular driver. The boy was required to keep the books, order stock, and work ten hours every Saturday, for which he earned two dollars a week, plus the dubious bonus of seeing his father grow old before his eyes.

Even the Saturday night before high school graduation, Barney was mopping the floor while his father emptied the contents of the cash register into an old safe.

"Almost through, son?"

"Yep. How'd we do today, Dad?"

"Oh . . . pretty good." The hesitation, the utter, futile weariness in his father's voice was not lost on the youngster.

"It's a crummy business," Barney observed. "Work your tail off and nothing to show for it."

"It's a living, young man. It's all I know how to do but I do it right."

Barney had never been intimate with his father. He liked him, perhaps loved him in a vague way, but he did not have respect for him—not since he was old enough to grasp Ernest Burton's status as a local nonentity. Now, however, he felt an unexpected urge to talk with him, know him better, glimpse the man's own unrealized dreams. He put the mop away, emptied the cleaning pail, hopped up on a counter, and observed his father for the first time in his young life.

"What did you want to be when you were my age, Dad?"

Ernest chuckled. "A rich inventor. Think up some gadget that everyone wanted and needed, draw out a patent on it, and sit back collecting royalties. I am pretty handy with tools."

"You sure are."

It was true. Ernest Burton had built for his wife and several friends beautiful little magazine racks out of metal and glass which he laboriously cut and shaped himself. Typically he gave them away, although they would have sold for twenty-five dollars if he had ever taken the time and trouble to market them. Their backyard had another of his gadgets—an ingenious sprinkling system fashioned out of old garden hoses and second-hand plumbing fixtures.

"You sure are handy," Barney repeated. He was not nearly so skilled himself, having channeled whatever such abilities he did possess into building balsa-and-fabric model airplanes powered by rubber bands. Suddenly he recalled that his father invariably had helped him build those planes, later proudly informing visitors that "Barney made this all by himself."

He felt a surge of affection for the thin, graying man in front of him. A yearning to be closer, more tolerant, more understanding, mixed with regret that he had never really tried.

"Why didn't you try inventing, Dad? How come you wound up in the grocery business?"

"Well, Barney, I never had any technical training. Had to quit high school after my second year. We didn't have much money, and after your grandfather died I had to go to work. I was the oldest in the family. I guess I kind of stumbled into this." His pale hand gestured around the store. "Old man Carruthers owned the store when I worked for him. I saved up every cent I could and when he decided to retire, he sold it to me. Along with the vacant lot next door. Then I met your mother and, two years later, you came along. I guess a son was about the only thing I had time to invent. It isn't a bad life, Barney. I'll admit there are times when . . . when . . ."

His voice trailed off.

"When what, Dad?"

"Darn it, son, I did have an idea once. A great idea. I still think

I could do something with it if I had the time and the resources. It needs a lot of experimenting."

"Why don't you work on it?"

The bright, eager glow in Ernest Burton's eyes faded. "Well, one of these days I might get back to it. Don't seem to have the gumption. I'm so tired at night."

Son and father examined each other. In Barney's face, the older man saw the ambition, eagerness, and courage he had long since surrendered. In his father's face, Barney saw defeat, discouragement, and dreams broken.

"Let's lock up and go home, son," Mr. Burton sighed. He walked toward the front of the store, then stopped as if he had forgotten something. He turned toward his son with a startled, frightened look. Barney had taken but a single step toward him when he crumpled to the floor like a deflated balloon. When Barney reached him, he was dead.

His mother insisted on keeping the store. In truth, she had little choice. Ernest Burton's life insurance was sufficient to pay off the house mortgage and the funeral expenses, leaving her the grand sum of $320.95 in a savings account. Barney wanted her to sell the store.

"What I could get for it would keep us for a year or two at the most," she replied. "Maybe I'll get rid of it later, Barney. Meanwhile, you're through high school now and you can help me full-time."

"Mom, I don't want to be a grocery clerk for the rest of my life."

"It won't be for the rest of your life. Just long enough to put us on our feet again. Then you can get a job doing whatever you'd like to do."

"I want to be an air-mail pilot," he said doggedly. "If I have to work in that lousy store, I'll never get a chance."

"Don't be a fool, Barnwell." She used his given name only when she was mad at him. "At least you'll be alive while working in your father's store. That's more than you can say for flying one of those airplanes."

Now he was mad. "I won't do it, Mom. I hate this business. It didn't give Dad a damned thing except a bad heart. You can't expect me to do something I hate."

In the end she won. He suspected it was a stalling tactic and he was right, but he didn't have the heart to make an immediate issue of her obvious procrastination over the course of the next year.

"We'll keep looking for someone," she would say, "and meanwhile, you'll have to help me like you have been."

For the first time in his life, Barney Burton glared at his mother. "Okay. But dammit, start looking! I'll give you one more month, Mom. Just one more month. If you haven't found anyone by then, I'm gonna go out to the airport and get a job there. And you can run this lousy store by yourself."

She started to cry, the tears eating into Barney's conscience. His father's death the previous spring and nineteen years of closeness to his mother were too much for his surge of independence. He ended up holding Ruth Burton closely, comforting her as she had so often comforted him as a child. "Okay, Mom. Quit bawling. I'll stay around for a while. But for Chri . . . for the love of Mike, try to get someone else. Just *try!*"

She did virtually nothing and Barney's second year in the store seemed inevitable. But on May 20, 1927, a year after Barney's graduation, an event occurred which affected Barnwell Ernest Burton in the same way it affected quite a few thousand other young Americans. That morning Charles Lindbergh took off for Paris in a tiny Ryan monoplane. When he landed, thirty-three hours and thirty-nine minutes later, the very nature of aviation was changed. Lindbergh put the word *calculated* before the word *risk* with a flight that was inherently dangerous yet meticulously planned. It gave flying a new excitement and glamor, but with it also came a new confidence in the possibility that it could be reasonably safe.

Barney devoured every word and photograph of the Lone Eagle's flight, his interest continuing through the subsequent aerial feats of 1927: Chamberlin and Levine in the *Columbia*. Byrd, Noville, Balchen, and Acosta in the *America*. Schlee and Brock in the *Pride of Detroit*. Maitland and Hegenberger in the *Bird of Paradise*. Goebel and Davis in the *Woolaroc*. Almost every week brought some new ocean-spanning attempt, most ending in disaster but with enough successes accumulating to bring home the message that the airplane could be a viable tool of commerce. While most Americans were thrilled by the exploits of these men with wings, Barney Burton was even more intrigued by that message.

More than two years before Lindbergh's flight, the nation's embryonic airline industry had come out of its womb, spanked into life by a piece of legislation known familiarly as the Kelly Act. It turned virtually the entire job of flying the mail over to private operators, who were invited to bid on the various routes.

The Kelly Act became law in 1925, and by the fall of that year the Post Office Department had awarded contracts for the first five of the twelve route segments comprising the system. All five were in operation a year before the *Spirit of St. Louis* flew into history, and the remaining segments were being flown by mid-1927. The dozen successful bidders represented an infinitesimal proportion of the more than five thousand would-be airline tycoons who had either filed actual applications or at least made inquiries to the government. A handful, thwarted in their efforts to obtain air-mail contracts, tried to make a go of flying passengers and small express items. Among them was a former Army Air Service pilot named Rodney "Bud" Lindeman.

Lindeman was a native of Binghamton and something of a local hero. He had been in Rickenbacker's 94th Aero Pursuit Squadron in France and had shot down three German planes—two short of the numerical minimum for a so-called ace, but the Binghamton papers nevertheless kept referring to him as "local war ace" after his first confirmed victory. And he still was "Binghamton's own" when in 1927 he started a small airline operating out of Bennett Field on the north edge of the town. Prior to that, he had been making a precarious living flying sightseeing and occasional charter trips.

When Barney turned twelve, his father had taken him out to the airport and paid Lindeman five dollars to take the boy on a thirty-minute hop. At the time, Lindeman flew an old but serviceable Waco-Nine biplane; Barney was put in the front seat while Lindeman piloted it from the rear cockpit. He gave the boy a helmet with goggles just before they took off. Barney never forgot it—the slipstream on his face, the wind singing through the guy wires, the engine grinding.

The half-hour ride seemed like five minutes. What had seemed so pallid from the ground took on new and exciting dimensions from the air. It was familiar terrain suddenly transformed. Lindeman flew the Waco directly over LeRoy Street and tapped Barney on the shoulder. "Your street!" he yelled above the growling engine, pointing down.

Barney looked, recognizing it from the streetcar tracks. He thought he saw his house although he wasn't quite sure, but he did spot the grocery store, which resembled a toy building, so small that Barney felt disdainful and somewhat superior. He saw people looking up at the plane and wondered if any of his friends were watching. The flight ended only too quickly, and as soon as they landed, Barney was ready to go again.

"Maybe next year, son. We don't want too much of a good thing," his father said.

"Bring him back," Lindeman had smiled.

"I'm gonna be a pilot."

His hero had grinned. "Come to see me when you're ready for lessons."

At twenty, Barney was ready. Or thought he was. He had the courage to quit the store, but not the heart; his mother's health had been declining steadily since his father's passing, for what had started out as a kind of whining hypochondria and grief became a legitimate case of high blood pressure. And so that second year he ran the store single-handedly and she was at home the day the visitor called.

"I beg your pardon, but is Mrs. Burton here?"

Barney looked up from the cash register to see a well-dressed man in his middle forties.

"She's home, not feeling too well. Can I help you? I'm Barney Burton, her son."

The man examined him curiously. Tall, well-built, smart-looking kid, the visitor mused. "Do you, ah, run the shop, Mr. Burton?"

"Well, yes, sir. That is, I run it when she's not here. Is it something I can help you with?"

"Probably not. I take it the store is in her name."

"Yes, sir."

"Would it be too much trouble for you to call her and see if she's well enough to see me? It's quite important." Barney looked mildly worried. "And it might be very advantageous to you both," he added quickly. "Suppose I give you my card."

Barney's eyes widened when he read the business card of Theodore Huntley, Director, Regional Planning Division, Amalgamated Markets, Inc. Barney was impressed. Amalgamated—a new chain of markets second only to the A & P organization in size, and growing fast. They already had a store on downtown Court Street and another on the north side.

"I'll call my mother," Barney said.

Mr. Huntley was still with Ruth Burton when Barney got home, having closed down the store fifteen minutes early. They were sitting in the living room drinking wine as Barney burst in, unspoken questions written all over his face.

"Before you explode," Huntley observed with a touch of wryness, "I expect your mother has something to tell you."

"It's wonderful, Barney," Ruth Burton laughed—and Barney suddenly realized it was the first time he had seen her smile in a long time. "Mr. Huntley says his company wants to buy our store."

"Not the store so much," the Amalgamated official corrected, "but the land it's on, plus the adjoining lot. It's an excellent location and we've made your mother a most reasonable offer."

"They're giving us thirty thousand dollars," she said excitedly. "Why, you might even be able to go to college."

Barney shook his head. "I'm too old to start college. It's been two years since I graduated high school. I'd be older than any other freshman. Besides, Mom, I'm not so sure that thirty thousand is enough."

Huntley's face wore an amused expression, but Mrs. Burton was shocked.

"Not enough? Good heavens, Barney, it's a regular fortune."

"It just sounds like a lot," Barney said doggedly. "It's not a bad price for the land, Mr. Huntley, but how about the store itself? The building's worth another ten, and we must have about three or four thousand dollars' worth of fixtures, not to mention our food inventory."

"We intend to tear down the building and build a new store," Huntley said. "As for those fixtures, I noticed them, Mr. Burton. If they're worth three thousand dollars, they would have to be in the category of valuable antiques. They're so old we'd just junk them. And I doubt whether you have more than four or five hundred dollars' worth of canned goods on hand. You can easily get rid of your perishables before you close down."

Barney ignored his mother's horrified look. "I realize neither the store nor its contents are worth much to you, but they're our means of making a living and I think we should be compensated for their loss. Mom, be quiet"—Mrs. Burton was trying to intercept her son's apparent collision course—"and let me finish. Mr. Huntley, I don't want to seem unreasonable and I'm not trying to hold you up. I just think you can do a little better."

"How much better?" Huntley smiled.

"Fifty thousand."

"You're way too high, son."

"Okay, how high were you authorized to go? It sure as hell wasn't thirty thousand. An outfit like Amalgamated wouldn't send you in here with your best offer right on top."

Huntley chuckled. "Thirty-five," he said, his eyes twinkling.

"Horsecrap."

"Barney, your language."

"Look, Mr. Burton," Huntley drawled, "any leeway I was given regarding price depended on my own appraisal of the property. I've seen your store, and that building with everything in it isn't worth three thousand dollars—and a hell of a lot less than that to us. So suppose *you* give me a figure we can discuss realistically."

"Forty thousand."

"You're still too high. But I'll come up a bit myself. We'll give you thirty-six thousand dollars and *that*, believe me, is final."

Barney glanced at his mother who nodded dazedly. "We'll take it," he said in a matter-of-fact tone that belied his excitement.

"I'll have the papers drawn up tomorrow and I'll be back with them for your signature, let's say, at seven tomorrow night. Meanwhile, if you'll sign this option agreement, Mrs. Burton . . ."

"What option agreement?" Barney asked suspiciously.

"Its gives Amalgamated a forty-eight-hour option on your property—in other words, you can't sell to anyone else during that period. Routine, my young friend. We've discovered from bitter experience that some people will use an agreed-on amount as ammunition in fast bargaining with someone else. It's a very simple, completely clear two-paragraph provision, Mr. Burton. Go ahead and read it before your mother signs. You, too, Mrs. Burton."

Barney read the neat typing on the single sheet of paper hastily and handed it to his mother. "Looks fine to me, Mom."

With the scratching of his mother's old Parker pen Barney Burton won his freedom. After Huntley left, mother and son hugged each other and Barney got a bottle of beer from the refrigerator while Ruth had a celebratory second glass of wine. For the first time in two years they talked together as friends instead of subtle adversaries.

"Don't get too carried away, Mom," Barney said seriously. "That's a nice chunk of dough but it won't last forever if that's all you're going to live on. You could invest it and maybe get yourself an easy job, something you'd really like to do."

"I've always wanted to work in a gift store. Sandy Goodman's been after me to help her out at her place—you know, the Pot Pourri. Maybe after a while, she'd take me in as a regular partner. I think that's what I'd rather do than anything else."

"Well, now's your chance, Mom. You can do anything you please."

She regarded him thoughtfully, conscious that magically their own relationship had just changed. "How about you, Barney?"

She knew the answer even before he spoke.

"I'm gonna see Mr. Lindeman tomorrow morning," said Barney Burton.

He had picked a miserable day. He drove out to Bennett Field in a heavy spring rain despite the inadequacies of the old Jordan's windshield wipers. Maybe his mother could afford a new car now, he thought, and give him the Jordan. He'd need some kind of transportation to and from the airport. It would take some persuasion on his part, for Mrs. Burton clung to the aging automobile as if selling it or trading it would be an affront to her husband's memory. Actually she was a terrible driver herself, and Barney drove the Jordan about ninety percent of the time.

Yes, he'd need a car—or would he? Once he got his pilot's license, he might not even stay in Binghamton. Maybe he'd go out West. He had read about an ex-racing driver named Harris Hanshue who had started Western Air Express two years earlier, with a mail and passenger route between Los Angeles and Salt Lake City. Western was getting ready to operate giant twelve-passenger Fokkers over a Los Angeles–San Francisco route and seemed to be the nation's fastest-expanding airline. It seemed more promising than staying around Binghamton. Tri-Cities Airlines, the name Lindeman had given to his operation—for the neighboring towns of Binghamton, Johnson City, and Endicott were known as the

Triple Cities—was pretty small potatoes. Barney knew Lindeman owned a couple of five-passenger Stinson Detroiters and a Travel Air biplane used for flight instruction. The Stinsons were operated largely between Binghamton and New York City, with sporadic trips to such unglamorous ports of call as Buffalo, Rochester, and Syracuse. It didn't seem likely that Tri-Cities would require the services of additional pilots, even of Barnwell Burton's caliber.

Barney was nervous, something unusual for him. The prospect of starting flying lessons was only a partial reason for his unaccustomed jitters, and even this was not a manifestation of fear. He was not afraid of flying; he was afraid of failure. It occurred to him, with unexpected impact even as he drove into the airport area, that learning how to fly was a pitifully small first step down a long, unmarked road. His feeling of uneasiness, of suddenly evaporating confidence, intensified when he saw one of the two Stinsons parked in front of the ramshackle building with the large sign, TRI-CITIES AIRLINES.

The plane looked so big and complicated. Sure, he could make a career piloting one of these big babies, provided he could ever acquire what seemed right then to be almost unattainable skills. And suppose he didn't have what it takes? What then? Back to the grocery business? Clerking in some department store? Was there anything he really was qualified to do? What the hell did he have going for him other than a deep love for planes and an abiding interest in every facet of aviation? Certainly no technical training.

Barney parked and stared at the plane. Slipping into his slicker, he jumped out of the car and made for the building, one hand holding his cap in place.

"Come on in, unless you're a creditor."

Barney opened the door and walked into a badly lit room, the only illumination coming from a gooseneck lamp on a battered wooden desk that squatted almost against the rear wall. Behind the paper-littered desk sat Lindeman, peering curiously at the youth standing in front of him.

The Lindeman Barney remembered had been a veritable Greek god—medium-sized but trim, muscular, and devilishly handsome with deep-set gray eyes, tousled black hair, and a small, neat mustache. The man facing him now was a caricature. The once-lean body had sagged into rolls of fat around the midriff. The eyes were bloodshot and tired, the black hair shaggy and unkempt, rather than boyishly tousled, and now streaked with a dirty gray. The mustache was still there but no longer dapper amid the sandpaper stubble on his chin.

Lindeman was alone in what passed as Tri-Cities' combined operations and business office.

"What's your problem?" he asked gruffly. Something in Barney's cold blue eyes conveyed a blend of disillusionment and disgust. Lindeman straightened up from his slumped position, fingered his bristled chin as if just discovering he hadn't shaved, and said half apologetically, "I, uh, we're not flying today. I just came in to catch up on some paperwork."

For the life of him, Lindeman couldn't figure out why it had seemed necessary to explain his sloppy appearance to a youngster who was a perfect stranger, except that there was a kind of courtly air about the boy.

"I'm sorry to bother you, Mr. Lindeman. I'm Barney Burton. We've, ah, we've met before. I don't expect you'd remember."

The pilot's eyes narrowed.

"A long time ago. It was my birthday and my dad treated me to a ride in your airplane. You flew me around Binghamton . . . in a Waco, I think. That was seven years ago."

"I flew a hell of a lot of people the past seven years," Lindeman said dryly. "You do look a little familiar. No doubt you've grown a bit since then. What can I do for you?"

"I wanna learn how to fly."

Lindeman smiled. "It's expensive."

"I've got money. Saved almost every cent I've made working in my folks' grocery store."

"I charge ten bucks an hour for dual instruction. You'll probably need at least ten hours. Does your savings account have a hundred dollars?"

"Yes, sir. Plus a little more."

"Well, how much more? In addition to the instruction fee, you have to pay for gas and oil, and there's twenty bucks aircraft rental per flight."

Barney's hopeful expression collapsed into disappointment. He had no idea flying lessons cost so much. "That's pretty steep. I think I might be able to borrow some money from my mother, though." Even as he said it, he knew Ruth Burton would rather lend him the tuition for a bartender's school than for flying lessons. On more than one occasion she had warned him not to expect any financial help if he persisted in becoming an airman. Nor could he count on getting a share of the Amalgamated check; Mrs. Burton had pointedly remarked, "When the check comes, Barney, I'm going to put the whole thing in the bank for at least six months while I decide the best way to invest it." Barney had a pretty good idea Lindeman wouldn't hold still that long.

Lindeman was studying the boy closely. "You really got your heart set on flying, chum?"

"Yes."

"It's no easy life. We've got a saying among pilots—the greatest danger in aviation is the possibility of starving to death."

"I know that, Mr. Lindeman. But I'm willing to try. I'll do anything. I'll even help you around here and you won't have to pay me much . . . maybe nothing. You can apply my wages to the lessons."

He had walked right into the trap Lindeman had baited.

"You know, that's not a bad idea. What did you say your name was?"

"Burton. Barney Burton."

"No, sir, Barney. Not a bad idea at all. I need a smart youngster around here. Tell you what, son, I'll make you a good deal. You pay me ten bucks a lesson and I won't charge you any rental. In return, you can go to work for me. I'll pay you, let's see, seven-fifty a week and we'll take the fuel out of your wages until you've paid it all back. Once you're all even with me, you can start keeping your seven-fifty."

Barney's inherent sense of caution never got off the ground. "That's great, Mr. Lindeman. When do I start?"

"Today, if you want. There's a Detroiter in the hangar that needs a wash-down."

"Where are the coveralls?"

"In the hangar." Lindeman rose wearily out of his chair, donned a bright yellow slicker, and led Barney through the rain to the barnlike structure adjacent to the operations office. A soggy windsock atop the hangar hung limply from its small pole, listlessly rising a few inches in a gust. There were no doors on the hangar entrance, and the dirt floor was a bog for ten yards inside the building.

"Not much protection from the weather," Barney blurted out. "You need some doors."

Lindeman seemed amused at the young man's audacity.

"Doors are a luxury," he explained mildly. "Little water never hurt an airplane, or a mechanic."

"But how about the winter? Must be murder trying to work in cold weather."

"We just put a tarpaulin up. Keeps the snow out. And we use a little coal stove so nobody'll freeze. Well, there she is, boy—queen of the fleet. She's about a year younger than that Stinson parked outside."

To Barney's unpracticed eye, the two aircraft were identical except in color; if anything, the blue Stinson sitting forlornly out in the rain appeared in better shape. The red Detroiter in the hangar looked shabby. However, Barney was struck by its size. Barney, who had never seen an aircraft within the distorting confines of an enclosed space, thought it absolutely enormous.

"Here's your coveralls." Lindeman's voice broke into the youth's reveries. "There's a bucket and scrub brush over by that sink. Just pour a few cups of those soap chips in the bucket and go to work. When you're finished with the plane, come on back into my office and I'll have a couple of more chores. And, by the way, be careful with that damned brush. You could poke a hole through the fabric with the handle. One dumb sonofabitch already has done that to me."

When Barney returned to Lindeman's office to inform him the job was finished, the door was locked. A note was taped just above the door handle:

Out to lunch. Be back about 1:00.

Barney would have loved to prowl around the office, peeking at the intriguing items left on the desk. He already had gotten the idea that while Lindeman must be a good pilot, he apparently wasn't much of a businessman. When it came to business matters, Barney had neat habits to go with an orderly approach; he regarded the desk as slovenly. His father had been that way, and was only too happy to let Barney take over much of his bookkeeping, send out the bills, and install a crude filing system for the store's records.

Lindeman appeared to be no less sloppy about his employees, if there were any. Barney couldn't figure out why no other Tri-Cities Airlines people were around. He had the uneasy feeling that Bud Lindeman was operating not on the proverbial shoestring but on a sewing thread.

He shrugged and went back to the hangar. Curious, he opened the Stinson's door and looked in. The cabin had a leathery smell, like a good pipe tobacco. It was filthy: dust on the window sills, a pair of coffee mugs on one of the seats. A blue rug on the cabin floor was stained and obviously hadn't been cleaned for months. The tiny cockpit wasn't in much better shape.

A half hour later, he had restored the cabin to reasonable cleanliness. At least no passenger could take offense. The rug needed some real work. He was down on his knees, trying to pick up the larger pieces of debris with his hands, when Lindeman's voice interrupted.

"Cleaning the cabin, Barney? Good boy. It needed it." The pilot sounded faintly apologetic.

"I could use a vacuum cleaner in here."

"We don't have any around," Lindeman said, "but I've got an old one at home. I'll bring it down tomorrow."

"This carpet should be cleaned before the next flight. When does the ship go out again?"

Lindeman hesitated. "Knock off for a while. I think it might help you if we had a little talk. It might even help me."

They returned to the office. Lindeman motioned him into a chair only slightly more dilapidated than his own. The pilot lit a cigar, examining Barney intently, and blew neat smoke rings like miniature gray halos.

"Well, tell me what you think of Tri-Cities," Lindeman said cautiously.

Barney looked puzzled. "I've only been here for a couple of hours, Mr. Lindeman. I haven't formed any opinions, not really. It's exciting. At least the airplanes are. But . . ."

"But what?"

Barney swallowed. "You seem to be the only one who works for the airline. And you own it."

Lindeman chuckled, no humor in the sound.

"The bank owns Tri-Cities," he said with a trace of bitterness. "And you're right. I'm the whole damned airline. I've got one other pilot, who's off today—Joe McFarland. You'll meet him later. Joe and I do all the maintenance work. I keep the books, scrounge up business, load the airplanes, and fly at least half the trips. You might as well know the truth. I owe McFarland about three months' pay, I'm behind on our fuel bills for about three thousand bucks, and every time there's a knock on the door, I figure it's somebody from Southern Tier Trust about to foreclose on the Stinsons. In other words, you have just gone to work for an airline that's about to crash."

"Why'd you hire me?" Barney asked bluntly. "I didn't even come in here looking for a job, not really. I just wanted to learn how to fly."

"Hell, I'll teach you how to fly. I could teach a chimpanzee. But then what?"

"I'm not sure what you mean."

"So you get your pilot's ticket. What are you gonna do with the damned thing? Fly for me? Christ, I can't even pay McFarland what I owe him. Fly for some other outfit? My eager young friend, as of this moment there are about five thousand trained pilots in the States and airline jobs for less than a thousand. If you were lucky enough to latch onto some carrier as a copilot, the chances are you'd be working without pay for the first three months. And once you got on a payroll, you sure as hell wouldn't get rich. You'd make a hundred bucks a month for flying a hundred sixty hours. Lemme tell you something, the future in this crazy business won't belong to the damned fools flying the airplanes. It'll belong to the guys with the guts and imagination to run an airline operation."

"Like yourself, Mr. Lindeman?" Barney was nothing if not direct. "You're running this operation and you're broke. I think I'd rather be drawing a hundred dollars regularly every month than worrying about carrying more debts than passengers."

Lindeman grinned. "That's my point. I'm just a pilot. I could fly a bathtub if you put wings on the goddamned thing. But I don't have much business savvy. Sure, I'll teach you how to fly. But I'd rather learn you more important things—like running an airline."

"Running it into the ground?" the boy asked with more honesty than rudeness.

"Yeah," Lindeman agreed amiably. "Like running it into the ground. I'd give you an idea of how tough this racket can be, and how exciting."

Barney was moved. He also was wary. "Why me, Mr. Lindeman? Besides, you've already told me this outfit's about finished. That you aren't a good businessman."

"How old are you?"

"Twenty."

The pilot's eyes suddenly did not seem bloodshot. They fixed the youth with a clear stare, like the lens of a telescope bringing a distant object into sharp focus. "The deal I offered you this morning is off."

"Off?" Barney's voice was thick with anguish.

"It was a lousy deal to begin with. I was trying to con you. I'll teach you how to fly but it won't cost you a cent. In return I want you to work for me full time, starting at ten a week. Clean up this whole bloody place. Straighten out what laughingly passes as our books, if you can. You'll be my whole ground operation. You'll make out the tickets, board the passengers, load the baggage, fuel the planes, and keep them clean. In six months you'll be a god-damned airline executive."

"If I do all that," Barney said, "when will I have time to go flying?"

"Damned if I know. Just keep nagging at me and I'll squeeze in an hour here and there."

"What kind of hours will I have?"

"Hours? For Christ's sake, you're not working for a bank. You come in at six A.M., seven days a week. You'll go home when there's nothing left to do. Eventually, when I get this airline on its feet, we can arrange some time off. Maybe even a week's vacation."

"I'll settle for getting that ten dollars a week regularly," Barney said. "You just got through telling me you owe your pilot three months' salary."

"I can pay you ten bucks easier than I can cover his back pay. Joe will wait a while longer; his old lady works. Is it a deal?"

"Deal."

3

March, 1928—May, 1928
—TRI-CITIES AIRLINES—
Binghamton—New York (via Newark)

EASTBOUND	WESTBOUND
Trip 1	Trip 3
Lv. Binghamton 8:00 A.M.	Lv. Newark 11:30 A.M.
(except Sat & Sun)	(except Sat & Sun)
Arr. Newark 10:45 A.M.	Arr. Binghamton 2:15 P.M.
Trip 2	Trip 4
Lv. Binghamton 11:00 A.M.	Lv. Newark 2:15 P.M.
Arr. Newark 1:45 P.M.	Arr. Binghamton 5:00 P.M.

EQUIPMENT: Six-place Stinson Monoplanes
FARE: $60 one-way; $100 roundtrip

Barney read the sheet with interest. Obviously, Lindeman was getting the maximum use out of the two airplanes. The two Stinsons
flew a pair of roundtrips daily except on Saturdays and Sundays,
when only one roundtrip was operated.

"I guess you fly Trips 1 and 3 with one plane and Trips 2 and 4
with the other."

"Right. I'll be taking Trip 1 out this morning. Joe will fly Trip 2 with the other, and that'll be your first job today. Thank God the weather cleared. You can wash McFarland's ship outside. When you get through, make out passenger tickets. I've got two customers booked for the eight A.M."

Barney consulted the timetable. "Hey, that's great! A hundred and twenty bucks revenue. Maybe more. Are they roundtrips?"

"We don't sell many roundtrip tickets," Lindeman said dourly. "Most people can dig up just enough courage to fly one-way. They take the train or bus back."

"Are the flights that uncomfortable?"

"When you're scared, anything's uncomfortable. Get the hell to work on McFarland's ship, Barney. I'll answer your questions later."

"Is this timetable the one you distribute around town? To prospective passengers?"

"Sure. What's wrong with it?"

"It's mimeographed. Not much class. We oughta have them printed, and it could be a lot jazzier."

"And exactly what, young airman, do you mean? *Jazzier?*"

"Well," Barney began uncertainly, his forehead creased, "you said almost everyone's afraid to fly. I was thinking we could tell a little about the airplane. How modern it is, how safe."

"Wouldn't do a damned bit of good," Lindeman said. "People fly for only two reasons. One, if they have to get someplace in a hell of a hurry and flying is the only way they can do it. Second, because they imagine they're being very brave and noble, which means the average guy gets on an airplane for the same reason he climbs on a roller coaster. Thrills—danger with a reasonable chance for survival. He likes to brag to his friends, 'flew down to New York last week,' the same as if he was telling someone, 'I took a punch at Jack Dempsey.' Flying is like name-dropping. It's also like major surgery. The operation is one big pain but the chance to talk about it—if you survive—that's the fun part."

At seven-thirty, while Barney was waging a major offensive against the cobwebs in the shoddy office, a man and an attractive woman walked in.

"Good morning. Are you folks going out on Trip 1?"

"We're supposed to leave at eight," the man said, "if that's the

Trip 1 you're talking about." He was a portly businessman in his early forties. His traveling companion—a decade or so younger— seemed ill-at-ease.

"Mr. Lindeman is out checking your plane," he informed them. "He'll be back in a minute. If you'll give me your names, I'll make out your tickets."

"Uh, Paul Smith," the man said with an air of belligerence. "This is my secretary, Miss Jones. Say, you're not the pilot, are you?"

"No, sir. You'll be flying with Mr. Lindeman today." Barney affixed the names to a pair of flight forms and handed them to the man with what he hoped was a completely impersonal smile.

"One hundred and twenty dollars one-way, Mr. Smith," he said politely. "How about coming back? Save you quite a bit on round-trip."

"We're returning on the train," the man said. "Thought we'd fly down to New York, though. Miss Jones has never been in an air-plane before."

"It's a wonderful experience," Barney assured her. She smiled at him more warmly than the circumstances called for.

"What time will we arrive in New York?" she asked.

"Ten-forty-five, Miss. You can ride an airport bus into down-town Manhattan. Takes about an hour, maybe a bit less."

"That's not much faster than a train," the man grumbled. "We should have taken the Lackawanna like I wanted, Doris. You had to insist on flying."

"It's exciting," she gasped. "Anyway, you promised."

"Okay, okay, so I promised. Still a damned waste of money. Not to mention the risk. Did you know my life insurance is suspended the minute I step aboard an airplane? That's how dangerous it is."

"I'm not the beneficiary, so I couldn't care less."

The woman was tart, and the man seemed disposed to continue the argument until he realized Barney was listening. He growled something unintelligible and lit a cigarette. There was an uneasy silence in the small room until Lindeman entered, introduced him-self to the two passengers, and announced that they might as well get started. It was only 7:40 A.M., which surprised Barney.

"You're leaving about twenty minutes early," he whispered to Lindeman.

"So what? That means we might get there twenty minutes early, which'll please the customers."

"But you're advertising an eight A.M. departure. Suppose somebody shows up at one minute to eight and wants to fly to New York on Trip 1?"

"Tell 'em their watch must be wrong. So long, Barney. When McFarland checks in, tell him I changed the plugs on '26 but he might want to bench-test the magneto. Be back a little after two. See you then."

Barney went out to watch the takeoff, feeling an undeniable throb of pride as the red Stinson snorted and coughed its way past him, taxiing toward Bennett Field's single runway. As it waddled by, Barney caught a glimpse of Lindeman grinning at him from the cockpit. Instinctively, Barney saluted. He didn't even know why he had, except it was the beginning of something.

The Stinson left the ground and roared southeast in a graceful, climbing turn. No matter what Lindeman had said about the opportunities being mostly on the ground, Barney envied the pilot of the fast-disappearing airplane. He sighed and went back to the office, where he finished the cleaning and resumed sorting out the mess on Lindeman's desk. He had no idea what to keep or what to throw away; he had a strong suspicion most of it belonged in the trash can.

He noticed an item atop the pile he hadn't gone through. It was a rather handsome sales brochure issued by the Stinson Aircraft Corporation of Northville, Michigan, detailing the virtues of its products. Barney perused it hastily, then took it back to Lindeman's desk.

WHICH PLANE SHOULD I BUY?

Ruggedness, safety, speed, efficiency, comfort, stability, beauty, low operating cost—these are vital points to be considered in the purchase of an airplane.

And they are points on which Stinson planes have built the sound reputation they enjoy today.

They have crossed the turbulent Atlantic. They have flown

over Europe, Turkey, Persia, India, China, Japan, frozen Alaska, Canada, and even into the wastes of the Arctic, north of Point Barrow. They are proving themselves daily on mail lines, air taxi lines and in the service of many corporations and private owners.

Competitive tests—such as the 1927 Ford Reliability Trophy which was won by a Stinson-Detroiter monoplane—have served only to strengthen their positions in the field.

Barney studied the brochure intently for another five minutes, then picked up one of Tri-Cities' timetables. On a rickety metal stand next to Lindeman's desk rested an ancient Remington typewriter. Barney inserted a piece of paper and began typing laboriously with two fingers. Immersed in his composition, he did not realize anyone else was in the room until a voice, tipped with just a whisper of an Irish brogue, addressed him.

"If you're bringing the books up to date, be sure to put in what our boss owes me. That is, if you're the young Mr. Burton I've heard about."

Barney looked up, startled enough to blush. He was embarrassed as he stood up and shook hands with the second pilot, a lanky, freckle-faced man about thirty, with tousled red hair, pleasant features, and laughing brown eyes framed by the crow's feet that came from squinting at too many suns.

"I take it you must be Mr. McFarland."

"The same. Except for the Stinsons and the fuel bill, Bud Lindeman's biggest debt. You *are* working on the books, I assume."

"No, sir, I was just . . . just, uh, kinda fooling around."

"With a typewriter? That's like enjoying measles."

Barney liked him immediately, and with this unspoken acceptance came an urge to confide. He yanked the sheet out of the typewriter and handed it to McFarland.

"This is what I was working on, Mr. McFarland," he said with a trace of boyish pride. "It's the timetable—but I . . . I jazzed it up a little." He watched McFarland's face anxiously as the pilot read.

" '*Luxury* Air Service . . . reliable and modern six-place Stinson monoplanes, thoroughly flight-proven in worldwide operations over five continents from Persia to the Arctic.' " McFarland shook with hearty laughter. " 'Convenient motor service to and from downtown Manhattan. SAFETY—SPEED—COMFORT.' Oh, lad."

McFarland picked up the regular timetable and read through the new one again, occasionally glancing from one to the other for comparison. He placed both on Lindeman's desk and grinned at Barney.

"Not bad," he said cautiously. "But why all the changes?"

Barney decided to answer the question by asking one of his own. "Do we do any advertising around town?"

"You must be kidding. Advertising costs money, a commodity of which we are in very short supply."

"This timetable's a form of advertising. Or could be."

"I suppose so," McFarland said. "That's Bud's department. I guess he's left a few brochures at offices. That's where most of our business comes from—guys in a hurry to get to New York for some meeting."

Barney picked up the old timetable. "I don't think this is gonna make people beat down our doors for tickets. Mr. Lindeman says everyone's afraid to fly. Seems common sense to get across the idea that it's really safe. Give 'em confidence."

"Telling people flying isn't dangerous might be construed as a form of misleading advertising," the red-haired pilot said dryly. "But I see what you mean." He picked up the two timetables again, holding one in each hand. "I didn't know we had such great equipment. Where the blazes did you get all this stuff? Sheer poetry, son." The trace of a grin flickered across his face. "You may have one heck of a time selling all this to Bud."

Barney looked at him squarely. "He may have one hell of a time paying all these debts, including what he owes you, if we don't do something to scrounge up some business. You taking anyone on your trip, Mr. McFarland?"

"Not unless somebody shows up. Nothing booked in advance."

"So you cancel?"

"Hell no. Gotta fly '26 to Newark just in case there's a customer or two for the return trip—or flight, as you've so eloquently phrased it."

"Oh, I forgot to tell you, Mr. Lindeman wants you to, let's see, I think he said change the magneto on '26 and that he's . . . no, he said to . . . to bench-test the magneto and that he changed the plugs himself. Is '26 the other Stinson?"

"NC-1126, that's my baby. Guess I'd better go out there and tidy her up a bit."

"I've already done it," Barney said with a touch of pride. Mc-Farland started to say something but shook his head instead and went out to his plane. He was back five minutes later. "Barney, that's the cleanest she's been since the day we got her. Look at her, shining like a baby's bottom."

Barney peeked outside to admire his own handiwork and suddenly realized NC-1126 was a robin's-egg blue and NC-1430 was a dullish red, almost a maroon.

"That's another thing," he announced. "Our planes are painted differently."

"So what's wrong with that?" McFarland asked, puzzled.

"It would be a lot classier if they were the same color. Then they'd look like a . . . ah, what's the word? Fleet! That's it. We'd have a fleet."

The pilot laughed. "Some fleet. Two whole airplanes."

"But it's a way for people to recognize us," Barney argued, his voice rising as the laughter got louder. "They look up and see a red airplane, and they say 'that's Tri-Cities.' We'd be identified. And we oughta have some kind of a symbol, like the bigger airlines. Like Western Air Express. All their planes are painted red, and every one carries an insignia, an Indian head."

"For God's sake, Barney," McFarland chided, "compared to us Western's like the New York Central Railroad. This is your first week and already you've spent us into bankruptcy. Printing new timetables. Painting the planes. Symbols, hell. Our symbol oughta be a red minus sign to go with the bank balance. What else is up your sleeve—free meals for the customers?"

Barney swallowed. "Maybe. Someday. A little snack and some hot coffee out of a thermos jug, or a soft drink."

McFarland sighed. "You're hopeless. I'd like to be around when you spring that idea on Bud. He'll either go into hysterics or fire you right on the spot. Probably both. I think I'll go check that mag. You didn't happen to see my coveralls around here, did you?"

"I think they're in the hangar."

"Good. Don't wanna get this jacket dirty."

Like Lindeman, McFarland was wearing indifferently pressed slacks and a windbreaker.

"You both should be wearing uniforms," the boy said.

McFarland stopped halfway out the door, and turned toward Barney. The pilot said nothing, but the expression on his face was one of disbelief.

"You and Mr. Lindeman don't look like airline pilots," the young man said stubbornly. "You might as well be one of the passengers. Only you aren't even as well-dressed."

McFarland exploded. "Now you see here, you young squirt! I don't fly airplanes with my pants and shirt. I fly with my hands and my legs and my brains. Don't tell *me* that how I dress makes one damned bit of difference to a passenger."

"I think it would," Barney replied. "An airline pilot has to be special. Someone a passenger looks up to. Someone who makes him feel at ease and not quite so afraid. A uniform would help. Nothing fancy, Mr. McFarland. A kind of military jacket with a military-type cap. And a clean shirt with a solid color tie."

The pilot leaned against the door frame. "I don't believe it," he said incredulously. "I just don't believe it. Lindeman told me you were a precocious bastard, but so help me, I don't think he knew how precocious you really are. Twenty years old and *you're* telling *us* how to run this outfit."

Barney flushed, as much in anger as in embarrassment. "Since as you'll probably tell Mr. Lindeman I oughta be fired," he said quietly, "there's one more thing. You need a shave."

The two pilots locked the door and Lindeman produced a bottle of bootleg bourbon from the top drawer of a filing cabinet behind his desk.

"Get the glasses, Joe," Lindeman said. "They're in the john."

McFarland returned, holding the glasses up to a sliver of late-afternoon light.

"God, they're clean," he marveled.

"Yeah. That kid must have scrubbed everything but my underwear. Good boy, that Barney. Lots of ambition. Lot of sense for a twenty-year-old."

McFarland poured three fingers of bourbon into his glass and passed the bottle to Lindeman. "Ambition, yes. But I swear I don't know about his having good sense."

"He was right," Lindeman laughed. "Your face looks like the topside of a boar hog."

"Well, shit, Bud, I knew I didn't have any passengers. But how about the rest of his ideas? Uniforms? Repaint the airplanes! You know what else? So help me God, he said we should have some kind of insignia. The kid must think your middle name is Mellon."

Lindeman took a large gulp of the whiskey. "Joe, be honest. Everything that boy said makes sense. This is a half-assed operation and I agree with everything he's suggesting. I should have done some of it earlier, when we started out and we had some dough to spend. Am I right?"

"I suppose so," McFarland said grudgingly. "But I hate to hear it coming out of the mouth of a half-assed kid. To tell you the truth, I kinda like his new timetable. But when he came up with that other stuff!"

"He worries me, Joe."

"Think he's really too big for his britches? If you ask me, that's exactly what—"

"No, I'm worried we won't be able to keep him. That we'll fold before I have a chance to teach him whatever I know. Before he has a chance to help us."

"Help us? How the hell is a wet-behind-the-ears kid gonna help us, Bud? Sure he has some good ideas . . . every one of them impractical. They all cost dough we don't have. Even his time-table."

Lindeman downed the rest of the whiskey in a gulp, and poured another hefty slug. "There's something about Barney Burton that gets to me, Joe. Here's a kid who in one day put his finger on just what Tri-Cities needs. Call it professionalism, a touch of class. His uniform idea, for example. I never thought of it. Or painting the planes the same color. That occurred to me when we bought '30 but I figured, why the hell bother? But dammit, Joe, we did have the dough then, or we could have bought it painted any color we wanted, only I didn't think it was very important. And let me tell you something else. The timetable he revised . . . I don't think either of us could have come up with that. The language he used.

Where the hell do you suppose he got all that stuff about the Stinson?"

"Out of a sales brochure he found in the office," McFarland said softly.

They finished the bottle between them, while Lindeman filled in his fellow pilot with the bank's negative verdict on a ninety-day extension.

"What are you gonna do, Bud?" asked McFarland.

"Keep going for another thirty days and pray something'll happen. What about you? Every cent goes to pay our fuel bill and interest on the note. I don't know if I can spare anything for you next month. Maybe a ten or twenty now and then, but that won't make a dent in what I already owe you, and it doesn't even come close to what you should be earning. And I should be paying the kid something."

"What are you supposed to be paying him?"

"Ten bucks a week. Plus free flying lessons, if I ever get around to it."

"Hell, let him work free for a while, like I'm doing."

Lindeman shook his head. "That's not fair to the boy. Anyway, I've got something to propose to you that I can't offer him. How about taking stock in place of some back salary?"

"How about taking the wings off the Stinsons so we can taxi the damned things all the way to New York?" McFarland countered. "I appreciate the gesture, but you're offering me a big, fat zero."

"If we pull out of this spin, the stock could be worth a lot of money some day."

"Like when the sun rises in the west and goes down in the east? Skip the bullshit. I'll fly for you another thirty days and if things aren't any better, I'll pull out. I hear Colonial may be hiring pilots by early summer."

Lindeman wiped the last drops of whiskey from his lips with the back of his hand. "Well, I appreciate your having gone this far with me. If I'm gonna lose the planes, I might as well lose my pilot, too. You know, if I had the guts I'd start flying bootleg booze in from Canada. There's some easy dough in that little racket."

"Also the possibility of a nice, fat jail stretch," McFarland said. "Count me out. That's a bad way to make a buck."

"Yeah," Lindeman agreed with a sigh. "I was just thinking out loud. Might as well go home, Joe. Give the lady my best. Must be nice being roped to a bread-winning nurse."

"Lousy cook but great in bed. It's a funny thing. I'd feel like a creep living off her salary if it wasn't for my doing what I love best. Even for absolutely nothing. It's not my fault, I keep telling myself."

Lindeman didn't answer, except to mutter, "G'night, Joe."

When McFarland left, the pilot sat staring at the door. He wished he had another bottle of bourbon. He wished he had enough dough. He wished he hadn't started the goddamned airline. He wished . . .

Tears fueled by the cheap whiskey spurted uninvited into his eyes. Fists clenched, he put his head down on a desk littered with the residue of failure and sobbed until he fell into a disjointed, half-drunken sleep.

Barney considered tiptoeing in and turning off the light but decided not to risk Bud's seeing that he had eavesdropped.

Things got worse. A spring snowstorm shut down the airport for three days, and even when the weather was good, passenger business was sporadic. They hit the jackpot once when the owner of a large women's specialty store decided a flight to New York would make a unique wedding-anniversary treat and took his wife plus another couple on Trip 2 one Friday morning. Fortunately, the flight was so smooth and enjoyable that they came back Sunday afternoon on Trip 4. They turned out to be the only passengers Tri-Cities flew for the next two days, but Lindeman was so pleased at the temporary affluence accorded by the merchant's $400 check that he suddenly surrendered to Barney's futile daily plea for a flying lesson.

Lindeman gassed up the Travel Air and introduced Barney to a pilot's world. Unhappily for the eager youngster, it was a disaster. Barney overcontrolled constantly, and no amount of Lindeman's patience, teaching skill, understanding, and—eventually—outright exasperation could break Barney of the fault. At first, Lindeman chalked it up to nervousness along with inexperience, but no student he had ever taught kept making the same mistakes over and over again as Barney did. The boy's coordination was poor; he lacked the grace, instinct, quick reaction, and rhythm of a natural flier. After two more tortuous hours of instruction, Lindeman was convinced Barney wouldn't ever make even a manufactured one.

During the third hour, Lindeman had him try a takeoff and Barney let the biplane stall. Only the pilot's lightning-fast recovery kept them from crashing. At the higher and safer altitudes, Barney's control work was clumsy, uncertain, and jerky. After that third hour, Lindeman reluctantly tossed in the towel.

Back on the ground, he sat the boy down in his office and gave him an honest appraisal.

"It's no use, Barney," he said. "I couldn't make a pilot out of you if I gave you fifty hours of dual. You fly like a monkey trying to screw a football. I'm sorry, chum."

Barney was disappointed but not surprised. "I'm sorry, too, Mr. Lindeman. You did your best. And I guess you're right. I just can't seem to get anything right. I know what I'm doing wrong but I keep doing it even after I know it's wrong."

"No hard feelings?"

"Why should there be?" the boy asked honestly. "You gave me a chance and I flubbed it."

"Well," Lindeman said with a trace of embarrassment, "do you still want to work around here?"

"I sure do, Mr. Lindeman. I like this job. I like working for you."

Lindeman smiled, looking five years younger in the process. He never would have admitted it to Barney, but he had been afraid the youngster might quit. Up until now, he had been figuring Barney would stay on a ground job just so long as he thought there was a chance of donning those pilot's wings. Now Lindeman was willing to admit that he had begun to rely on Barney to an increasing degree. The boy was punctual, uncomplaining, quiet, efficient, and resourceful.

Lindeman's consumption of alcohol kept increasing in direct proportion to the dwindling number of days before the bank's deadline. Seldom did he come in for the early-morning flight without an obvious hangover. Barney worried that sooner or later

Lindeman would report in no condition to fly, a fear he confided to Joe McFarland; for even as their boss withdrew more and more into the self-pitying world of an alcoholic, Barney and the Irishman became closer.

"One of these days he'll insist on flying and he'll crack up," Barney told McFarland, from behind the upside-down oil drum he used as a makeshift desk when Lindeman's was piled high with papers.

"That he will. If he ever gets that bad, better call me and I'll come down to fly his trip—providing he hasn't gone already."

"Can't you say anything to him, Joe? He'd listen to you. He wouldn't pay any attention to me."

"Wouldn't do any good. He'd just laugh at me and tell me he could fly a plane better drunk than I could sober."

"He sure needs somebody's help," Barney frowned. "And if he doesn't get it soon, we may all need help. That's all it'll take to fold us for good—one bad accident."

"Only the good Lord can help him," McFarland said philosophically. "Or us, for that matter."

Barney was in the hanger cleaning Bud's plane after Trip 3. Only seven days were left to Tri-Cities Airlines. Suddenly Lindeman came in. The pilot's face was somber, and Barney couldn't comprehend the sympathy in his eyes until Lindeman spoke, calmly but with unaccustomed feeling.

"You'd better go home, son. Your mother's ill. Very ill."

"She's dead, isn't she, Bud?"

"I'm afraid so. It was the City Hospital. She fell ill . . . at the gift shop. She passed away in the ambulance."

Barney wanted to cry; he felt he should cry. But no tears would come. Just a numbness. All he could do was nod. "I'll go," he mumbled.

"Just give me a ring here tomorrow morning and let me know how everything is. And if there's anything we can do, let me know. I'll tell Joe when he gets back from Newark. Are you okay to drive?"

"Yes, I'm fine. I'll call you soon as I can."

It was on the way to Binghamton City Hospital that what undoubtedly had been in his mind suddenly surfaced. Only two weeks before, his mother had made out a will leaving everything to her son. Barnwell Burton was now worth $36,000 plus a mortgage-free house. He cursed himself for thinking such thoughts in what was supposed to be a moment of terrible grief. He asked God's forgiveness for such greed and selfishness. He prayed for his mother's soul and asked her to forgive him. But the realization of what her death meant to his own future would not go away.

Henry McKay was a wiry, rather handsome if sharp-featured man in his mid-twenties, with a pencil-thin mustache obviously grown to make him appear older. He was an intelligent, canny young man who knew the banking business better than men three times his age and with years more experience. Closing the door of his office, he turned to his young visitor.

"Barney, it's your money you're fooling with," McKay said. "Just for the sake of argument, suppose you *did* sink some dough into that flying rathole. Exactly what could *you* do that . . . what's his name, Lindbergh?"

"Lindeman. Bud Lindeman."

"Yeah, Lindeman. From all I've heard, he's done his utmost to make a go of it. Good equipment, for example. We should know; we own it. So how are you going to operate differently? How will you drum up enough business to make a profit? You can't even vote, yet you're telling me you can run an airline better than a man who's been in aviation all his life."

"Bud Lindeman," Barney snapped, "has been a *pilot* all his life. That doesn't mean he knows how to run a business. He knows how to fly. Period."

"At your age you can make that judgment? Okay, tell me what you know about the airline business."

"Not much right now. But I'm learning. I've seen things at Tri-Cities that could be changed overnight. Lindeman doesn't go after business. He waits for it to come to him, and then wonders why he's going bankrupt."

"Elaborate."

"Spruce up the whole operation. Stress safety and speed. Establish some personal contacts with businessmen around the Triple Cities. *Sell* air travel. Because it has to be sold. People are afraid to fly. You have to make it attractive, advantageous, desirable."

McKay looked amused. "And you think you can do the selling?"

"I know I can."

"With new timetables?" McKay said with a trace of sarcasm.

"That's just the start. I've still got a lot to learn. I've already told you that. Once I learn, I'll be ready with more ideas. Like flying to cities other than New York. Lindeman seems to think that's the only place anyone wants to go. So I'd like to know when that note's due and how much it would cost me to make Tri-Cities a good credit risk again."

McKay got to his feet. "Wait here a minute." He was back a few minutes later, accompanied by an older man carrying a manila folder and wearing an expression of sheer incredulity as he stared at Barney.

"Barney, I'd like you to meet Fred Jackson, who's been handling Lindeman's account. I've already given him a brief fill-in on this . . . uh . . . situation. Fred, suppose you give us the basics on Tri-Cities."

A balding, precise man of medium height, Jackson cleared his throat rather nervously, almost as if he suspected Barney might be related secretly to the Rockefellers.

"The Tri-Cities note," he began, "is due next Monday, which is the end of the thirty-day extension we gave Mr. Lindeman, along with the warning that we would not be able to grant any further extensions. The promissory note itself is for eighteen thousand dollars—that's the principal. He also owes, in round figures, about a thousand dollars in back interest. For simplicity's sake, let's say the indebtedness amounts to around nineteen thousand."

"What has disturbed the bank," McKay added, "is that he has made no payments on the principal since he mortgaged the aircraft more than a year ago, and also has failed to meet the monthly interest payments."

"He has made only three of those," Jackson put in, inhaling the words with a sound that made it a moral denunciation. "I'm afraid foreclosure is the only recourse."

"Which will shut down the airline," Barney said.

"Regrettable but inevitable," Jackson chimed.

Barney paused, conscious that both bankers were watching him closely. "Okay, I'll make Southern Tier Trust a deal. I'll give Bud Lindeman ten thousand dollars, enough to pay off half the principal and whatever interest he owes, provided you extend the note for another six months."

"Wait," McKay cautioned, holding up his hand. "That might be a good deal for us but, according to his file, the Southern Tier note isn't Lindeman's only indebtedness. He's in hock to Standard Oil of New Jersey for three thousand in fuel bills, and the financial statement he filed with us lists more than five hundred to one Joseph McFarland, a Tri-Cities employee. That's at least another thirty-five hundred to be paid off. Frankly, unless he cleans up all these debts, I'm not sure the bank would want to extend his note, even if you did reduce the principal by a sizable amount. It seems to me you're just buying time, and in six months Tri-Cities won't be any better off than it is today."

"That's exactly what I'm buying," Barney acknowledged. "Time to do what has to be done to start making some profits. As for that fuel bill and what he owes Joe McFarland in back wages, I intend to pay those off when I sell the house. If Standard Oil wants its dough sooner, I'll still have twenty-six thousand left in my account here. The first decision you have to make is to delay foreclosure for a couple of weeks—or whatever time it takes for me to get my inheritance. And I'll sign anything—a personal note or something—promising to reduce the principal and bring the interest payments up to date as soon as the . . . as soon as my mother's money is transferred to my own account."

McKay and Jackson exchanged glances.

"You might want to consider paying off the whole nineteen

thousand," McKay suggested. "That still would leave you with another seventeen thousand."

"No. I want a good chunk of cash on hand just in case. There'll be other things I might want to do. Spend some dough on advertising, for example. We might even want to buy some bigger airplanes if business gets good." The interchangeable use of the "I" and "we" pronouns was not lost on the observant McKay.

"Barney," he said with a slight smile, "I admire your gumption but I have to question your judgment on the basis of what you've just told us. It seems to me that you're still just a hired man. Altruism is most noble, but it's not very practical."

"Altruism, hell!" Barney growled. "Rodney Lindeman is gonna have to give me something in return for the parachute I'm handing him."

Barney was at the airport at 6:00 A.M. Friday morning, so anxious was he to be there before Lindeman showed up. He felt somewhat like a prodigal son who had left home unwanted, dire predictions of a dismal future ringing in his ears, and was now back with untold wealth, success, and a sense of beneficent forgiveness. The analogy was distorted and not very applicable, he realized, but he still couldn't quench a delicious feeling of anticipation, almost of triumph. He wasn't quite sure how Lindeman was going to take it. He genuinely liked Bud Lindeman and was only too conscious of the embarrassing dilemma the loan would pose. That the pilot liked him, Barney was sure; he had been touched deeply when a floral arrangement was delivered to the funeral home from "Rodney Lindeman and Joseph McFarland." Barney knew neither could really afford that gesture—certainly not Lindeman. Anticipation suddenly turned into apprehension. He had the uncomfortable feeling he was about to hand the pilot a solution that robbed him of his pride even if it saved his airline. Maybe he should just loan him the money, keep working, and get more experience before throwing his weight around.

Then he looked at the shabby office. It was dirty, disorganized. In only five days, Lindeman—and McFarland, too—had let it degenerate into almost the sorry shape it was on the day Barney began working there. Apparently, they had done nothing but fly their trips, obviously counting on Barney to clean up when he returned. The visual proof of their carelessness and indifference stiffened Barney's resolve. Deliberately, he made no move to wipe even a single wisp of dust. He simply sat there, in the old chair facing Lindeman's desk, waiting for him to arrive.

The pilot showed up at six-fifteen, so obviously glad to see him that Barney felt a momentary stab of guilt. It dissipated quickly when Barney noticed that Lindeman's eyes, as usual, were blood-shot from drinking and lack of sleep.

"Barney! How you doing?" Lindeman asked warmly as the youth rose and shook hands. "If you're ready to go back to work, that's great. But you don't have to."

"I'm ready. And I appreciated those flowers, by the way. But I gotta talk to you first."

"Sure. What's on your mind? Anything I can do for you, just tell me."

"I think," Barney said slowly, "I'm about to do something for you. And I also think we'd both better sit down."

They faced one another across the battered, scarred desk, each nervous—Lindeman because he suspected Barney was about to offer him financial aid but wasn't at all certain of the conditions that might be attached; Barney because he knew those conditions, and that they might stir up more resentment than gratitude.

Barney went straight to the point. "Bud, my mother . . . she left me a fairly sizable inheritance, enough for me to get you off the hook at the bank. That's just a starter. Would you be interested?"

"Yeah," Lindeman said cautiously. "Yeah. I'd be interested in getting off that hook. Would it be a loan or . . . ?"

He left the question dangling in mid-air, almost as if he were afraid to voice it.

"No. I want to buy into Tri-Cities. As a partner. If I just made you a straight loan, in a few months you'd be right back where you are now. You need more than just a temporary reprieve, and I think you're man enough to admit it. Even if the thought of taking on a greenhorn partner is like eating crow. I'm young—maybe too young—but I've got some schemes and some dough to make them work."

"How much dough?"

"Thirty-six thousand dollars. And I'll be adding to that what I can get for my house. At least another five grand, maybe as much as nine. I've already talked to a real estate agent. He's going to ask ten."

"I owe Southern Tier damned near twenty thousand dollars," Lindeman said warily. "Paying my note off doesn't leave you a hell of a lot to play around with. I'd make sure the bank won't accept partial repayment, chum."

"They will," Barney assured him eagerly. "I've already talked to a guy named McKay. Henry McKay—he's a vice-president."

At least, Lindeman thought wryly, just the title of vice-president still impresses the boy. There were times when the pilot had the disturbing notion Barney Burton wouldn't have been nonplussed if President Hoover had asked him to the White House for a discussion on aviation.

"Don't keep me in suspense, Barney. How much did he recommend you spend on this sick outfit?"

"If you want to know the truth, he told me I was crazy to do anything. But he said it was my dough and he agreed to what I proposed. I'm paying off half your note, all the bank interest, and what you owe Standard Oil and Joe McFarland. It all comes to a little under fourteen thousand dollars. Let's say I only get five for the house. That still leaves me twenty-seven thousand to put into the airline."

"Okay, Barney," Lindeman said softly. "Now we get to the main ingredient of this little stew you're cooking up. What do *you* want for yourself?"

"Fifty percent interest in Tri-Cities. An equal partner, Bud. For the time being."

"What the hell does that mean—'for the time being'?"

"McKay thinks eventually we should incorporate. In Delaware. He says we can form a corporation there for practically nothing. We'd issue stock to raise some working capital—what I'm putting in isn't enough to let us expand to the point where we could bid for a mail route."

"A mail route? For God's sake, we can't keep our heads above water flying passengers and express between here and New York, and you're getting pipe dreams about a mail contract! Barney, the demand for air-mail service over our route wouldn't pay for the oil we use, let alone the gas. Look, chum, I appreciate what you're willing to do for me, but be practical."

"I am being practical," Barney retorted. "You're the one who can't see two feet beyond a bottle of booze." Lindeman glared but his angry protest died on his lips as Barney uncoiled from his chair and slammed a big fist down on the desk. His voice had the deceptive softness of oil mixed with a thousand abrasive steel shavings. "Sometimes I think you're the one who's twenty, Bud. All my life, ever since I was old enough to read about pilots and airplanes, I thought guys like you were gods. You could do something not one man in fifty-thousand could do—fly. You had skill and you had guts. But just as important—maybe more important—you had vision . . . a kind of faith in what aviation's all about. But not you. Sitting there with unpaid debts up to your armpits, and telling me *I'm* the one who's impractical because I think the only way we can save Tri-Cities is to get a mail contract. Lemme finish." Lindeman, his face pale, had started to say something. "Where the hell is *your* vision? Only a damned fool would think he could make money flying the mail between this fleabite of a town and New York. That's not what I mean by a mail contract, *Mr.* Lindeman. I mean flying between cities that don't have air-mail service *or* passenger service—routes that haven't even been proposed yet. Routes we can get if we expand, improve, experiment, try—*try*, goddammit, try! If you had spent more time looking at a few maps, like I have, instead of just flying your trips and getting smashed in between, you could have seen the potential. Buffalo and Syracuse down to Washington." Lindeman's eyes widened. "Yeah, Washington. That's where I want this airline to go. Right into the nation's capital—carrying people as well as postal envelopes!"

"Jesus Christ," Lindeman muttered, blasphemy his only recourse to Barney's evangelistic fervor.

Barney sat down again. "It's still your airline. You're still the boss. I'll still sweep this goddamned floor and clean out the Stinsons after every trip. But not as a hired hand, not as a flunky. As a partner. I've already got you a two-week extension on that note."

"How the hell did . . . ?"

"In two weeks, I'll have my inheritance. McKay gave me his

word the bank won't foreclose on the Stinsons until my money comes through. What do you say?"

Lindeman took a deep breath, like a man about to go under, and when he exhaled it was as if all the fight, all the authority, drained out of him. It was a gesture of surrender and relief. He leaned across the desk and put out his hand.

"Let's shake on it—partner," he said.

And as he felt Barney's firm handclasp, and looked into eyes far older than the face in which they were imbedded, he realized that in saving his airline, he also had lost it.

"You might consider spending a few dollars on yourself."

Henry McKay was looking at Barney's only decent suit, now three years old and decidedly approaching the threadbare stage. Barney's face reddened as the waiter ushered them to a large table. McKay smiled tightly and motioned for a menu. Lindeman and McFarland had not yet arrived. He looked at Barney.

"I assume you'll be meeting quite a few businessmen, trying to convince them to fly."

"I'll buy a new suit this afternoon," Barney promised.

"How many do you own?"

"This is it," Barney confessed laconically.

"Then go out and buy at least two. Three would be better. And while you're at it, you could also use a better car. That Jordan of yours belongs in a museum. Appearances, Barney, appearances. You can have five cents in your pocket, but dressed well and driving a good car, people will assume you're an intelligent, reliable young entrepreneur."

"A new car," Barney repeated. "That's not a bad idea." Being young, he actually was more intrigued with this recommendation than with the prospect of buying a new suit. "I suppose if I traded in the Jordan it wouldn't cost me too much. Except . . ."

Lindeman and McFarland sauntered in and approached the table. To their obvious surprise and curiosity, Barney had also invited Henry McKay. Barney had sensed that the banker's presence would provide him with an ally when he dropped a few of his reform ideas on the other two-thirds of Tri-Cities Airlines. They were hardly in their seats when he began.

"I hope what I'm about to say doesn't spoil anyone's meal, but I think I owe it to you, Bud, and Joe too, to let you know what I think is essential for our company to make money. And first off, we're gonna have to spend some to make some. If anything sounds too wild or crazy, now's the time to speak up. That includes you, Henry." Barney glanced at his partner. "We're still in hock to his bank and I invited him along to protect that stake, if it needs protecting. Okay?"

Lindeman and McFarland exchanged glances. McFarland figuratively shrugged his shoulders with his eyes, and Bud bore an I-told-you-so expression. McKay managed to look both amused and interested.

"You guys know how I feel about those different paint schemes. We can decide tonight on a single color and also on a kind of symbol or insignia."

"Let's tackle the color first," Lindeman proposed. "I wouldn't recognize a good symbol if one flew down and parked on my front steps."

Barney's face brightened. "You're on the right track, Bud. The symbol should be some kind of a bird. Like an eagle, for example."

"For this operation," McFarland observed sourly, "a mosquito would be more appropriate."

McKay cleared his throat rather pontifically. "As far as I know, there are no eagles in this area. If you want some kind of bird as a corporate symbol, I'd suggest a feathered friend who's native to southern New York State."

"A native bird," Barney agreed. "Robins or sparrows, I guess. Except I was thinking of something strong and fast—really representative of an airline."

"Hell of a lot of chicken hawks around here," Lindeman said.

McFarland laughed. "Tri-Cities—fly with the chicken hawks."

Barney shook his head. "Drop the 'chicken.' Try 'hawk.' "

The others were considering this when Barney had another inspiration. "Red."

"Red?" Lindeman asked.

"The red Stinson's newer, right?"

"Yeah, but—"

"So we paint the other plane red, too. And that gives us a symbol—a red hawk."

"A red hawk on a red fuselage is gonna be the best camouflage job in aviation history," Lindeman pointed out. "Nobody'll be able to see the damned bird."

"Jesus, I didn't think of that," Barney muttered.

"It's still not a bad idea," said Lindeman. "A red hawk. Look, it won't cost us much more to paint both planes with a color that'll make a red hawk stand out like Braille. White maybe?"

"Too hard to keep clean," McFarland put in. "How about blue? Blue weathers pretty good, and—"

Barney snapped his finger. "Silver."

Lindeman and McFarland looked dubious, but McKay nodded.

"Silver," Barney repeated. "It's not only bright, but it contrasts with red and it looks . . . well, strong. Like it was metal."

McKay nodded again. "Exactly what I was thinking. It gives an impression of strength. And I also like that red-hawk insignia. It gives me an idea for a kind of slogan. How does this sound, 'Route of the Red Hawks'?"

"A pretty fancy slogan for a two-city route," said Lindeman.

"It won't be a two-city route for very long," said Barney. "I think we should start service to other places: Buffalo, Rochester, Syracuse maybe. Or"—he could have sworn Lindeman was bracing himself for something he didn't want to hear again—"Washington."

"With two planes?" Lindeman's voice was almost hostile.

"Yep, at first. Besides, we don't have the traffic to justify two roundtrips a day between Binghamton and New York. We'll send Flight 1 out an hour later and schedule it back from Newark an hour later and drop Flights 2 and 4 and use Joe's Stinson as a Buffalo–Rochester–Syracuse–Binghamton route. I haven't worked out the scheduling details yet, but it's feasible."

McFarland was grinning. The kid already was tossing his weight around, and Joe, for one, found himself liking it, especially the prospect of flying to different cities.

"I agree we could get better use out of the second Stinson," Lindeman said amiably enough, "but what are we gonna use for this Washington pipe dream of yours?"

Barney stared down at his plate. "A Ford trimotor."

Lindeman rose half out of his chair. "You're out of your mind! That bird's going for damned near sixty thousand!"

"Fifty," Barney said matter-of-factly. "I've already checked.

Keep your shirt on, Bud. I know we don't have it right now. But if
we can start showing some black ink around here, I figure Southern Tier would be willing to refinance that note and lend us enough
for a sizable down-payment—" Barney paused as McKay's eyebrows lifted skyward. "—and if we can make a go of it flying just
passengers between here and Washington, we'll stand a better
chance of getting a mail contract for the whole route system."

"I can't give you any cast-iron promises as far as the bank's
concerned," McKay warned.

"We may not even need the bank. It might be better to incorporate, like you've already suggested, and get some capital by selling stock. I don't need or even want an immediate decision on a
trimotor, Bud—it's something I want you to think about. Our first
priority is to start showing a profit with what we have. You and Joe
will be flying tomorrow and I'm gonna get things rolling on the
ground. I'll be asking you to countersign a few checks, and you
might as well know tonight what I'm spending money on."

All Lindeman could manage was a feeble nod as Barney sailed
on unmolested. "Jim Hill, the Ford dealer, has a mechanic named
Aroni who's supposed to be damned good. I'll find out from him
what it would cost to turn that Jordan into an airport limousine.
And from the way Hill describes him, I have a hunch he might
even be able to paint the airplanes for us . . . if we don't do it
ourselves. Then I'll have new timetables printed and I'll distribute
them to every first-class business establishment in the Triple Cities
—stores, offices, car dealers—wherever there's a potential passenger. Tomorrow afternoon, when you're both through flying, I'd like
you to go to some tailor and get fitted for uniforms. They don't
have to be fancy, with a lot of braid and brass buttons. Something
simple but trim and military-like. I've written away for a catalogue
from an outfit in New York that makes metal insignia to order. By
the time you get your uniforms, I'll have wings for the jacket and
some kind of insignia for the visored caps. Probably just a variation
of the jacket wings. I don't wanna put any Tri-Cities identification
on the caps."

"Why not?" McFarland wanted to know.

"Because," Barney explained calmly, "if things go right, I think
we'll have to face up to changing the airline's name."

5

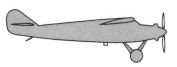

With the day's work finished, Barney had settled back in Bud's chair to check the bookkeeping.

"You work here?"

She was stunning—black-haired, ivory-complexioned, eyes like small dark stones.

"Ah, yes. Yes. I'm Mr. Tri. Mr. Cities is away on business."

"What?"

She looked mildly annoyed.

"Nothing. Nothing at all, ma'am. What might I do for you?"

"You could tell me if the plane from New York is in. Joe Mc-Farland is carrying a parcel for the hospital. I'm Nurse Kyle."

" 'Fraid you're out of luck. The flight is stuck in Newark. Bad weather."

"Shit!" She bit her lip.

"Pardon?" Barney had never heard a woman curse before.

"Shit," she repeated absently and tossed her shoulder bag on the desk between them. "Any chance of it coming in tonight?"

Barney glanced outside at the quickly fading daylight and shook his head. "Not unless Mr. McFarland pulls in sometime within the next twenty minutes. Sorry. Was it real urgent?"

Nurse Kyle looked mildly exasperated. "Not quite life or death, but important enough."

"The storm is between Ossining and the Connecticut line so I don't think there's any way he'll get around it, but it should be past us by midnight. So your parcel will be in the air at first light and landing here by nine-thirty, I expect. We'll be happy to deliver it to the hospital as soon as it lands."

"I suppose that will have to do." She looked beautiful in the twilight, but also exhausted. "In the meantime I need to call the cab company in town for another taxi."

Barney nodded, smiling. "You're welcome to use the phone. Or, if you like, I could drop you off on the way home. I'm just about to close up. It'll save us both having to wait for the cab."

She looked directly at him for a second. "Okay, I'll take you up on that."

She lived on the northeast side of town, she said, on Bellow Street, and then fell silent.

He told her she looked all-in. She said it was just her age showing, and he laughed and quickly protested. Nurse Kyle lit a cigarette without offering him one and said she was thirty-two and at least a decade older than he was. About three miles out of town he got up the nerve to introduce himself and learned that her first name was Rosina. A mile later the left rear tire blew out and put the car into a roadside post that knocked the fender back against the front left tire and banged him hard against the windshield.

It took him the better part of an hour to change the tire and bend the bumper back from the wheel. By then the bump on his forehead had turned into a blinding headache aggravated by every rock in the roadbed. And by the time he pulled up in front of the big frame house where she lived, Barney could hardly see straight and was feeling nauseous.

He felt her fingers touch his throat feeling for a pulse, and he suddenly realized he had fainted. Nurse Kyle ordered him out of the car and led him up the back steps, holding his elbow with obvious expertise as she guided him inside and up to a large porcelain sink. She slapped a cold compress on his forehead and over his eyes, and led him on, ordered him to stop, turn, sit, and lie back. There was a slight pain in his temple as he slid back, but then it was cool and peaceful and black as night.

He smelled smoke—cigarette smoke—and opened his eyes. Rosina Kyle was sitting curled up in a wing chair, a small circle of light illuminating the newspaper in her lap. The smoke drifted from her nostrils, then blossomed from her pursed lips as she exhaled.

"Jesus," he mumbled, trying to roll up into a sitting position.

"Wait."

"Wait?"

"Wait." She rose and bent over him and efficiently pulled back an eyelid while flashing a light into his eye with a small mirror. His eye began tearing.

"You're okay, but you may have a mild concussion."

"Feels like a championship hangover. Funny, I feel a bit giddy, too. Even—Hey!" Barney frantically groped around under the quilt. "My clothes!"

"Yeah, I rolled you out of them. You were in a cold sweat when you slipped off. Relax, Mr. Burton. You're about the twelfth male Caucasian I've disrobed this week. There are few surprises remaining for me in that department, young man."

At first he had thought he was in the living room but now realized he was neatly hospital-cornered into a bed. "Well, I hope you weren't too bored," he said, trying to sound nonchalant.

"I've seen worse. And your not being circumcised was mildly interesting. Not too many specimens left with that particular feature."

Barney felt the color rise in his cheeks.

"All right, Mr. Burton. I'll stop teasing. No, don't close your eyes. For the next day or two you'll have to sleep no more than three or four hours at a time."

"Why?"

"So that you don't wake up with your brains set like concrete. Or worse."

"I appreciate the concern."

"Don't mention it. Here, read the paper. I'll be in the next room if you relapse." She glanced at her watch. "It's one-thirty. You can sleep in an hour. I'll wake you at six. Good night." She rose from the chair and moved toward the door.

"Good night, Miss Nightingale. And thanks. I hope I can return the favor one day."

"Good evening, Mr. Tri. You're most welcome. And don't be a wise-ass."

By their second cup of coffee, Barney had joked his way through his life story. It was the first time he had joked or laughed that hard in a long while and it seemed easy to do around her.

Rosina Kyle was even more beautiful in the morning light, her dark features and eyes set off by the dazzling white of her uniform.

"Think you can drive?"

"Sure."

"Good. Get out of here. I have to get to work by eight."

"Jesus, me too." Barney jumped to his feet, finished off his coffee in one gulp, and slipped past her at the door.

"Don't forget to get your head examined today."

"I won't." He paused in front of her in the doorway. "Say."

"Yes?" She held the door open with her back while adjusting her white nurse's cap, tucking the edges into the dark hair wound tightly back in a French roll.

"Can a concussion give you a fever?"

"Not usually." She touched his forehead with the back of her hand. "Are you feeling warm?"

"Very."

"Don't, Barney," she said, suddenly serious.

"Sorry."

"That's not what I mean."

He nodded, not at all certain what he was agreeing to. "Maybe we'll run into each other again. Soon?"

"You never know."

He didn't have the faintest idea why he did it, or why he thought she would tolerate it, but he slowly stepped toward her and, without touching, kissed her.

She puffed her cheeks and exhaled. "You are warm. Maybe I had better take your temperature before letting you out of the house." She motioned him back inside with a tilt of her head, and he responded like a puppet. Rosina Kyle knew something about animating people, something she had learned in hospitals about quietly exerting her will.

The door squeaked shut. She walked to the low counter next to the sink and leaned back against it, one hand over her eyes.

"Listen. Barney. Are you sure?"

He stood in front of her, saying nothing. She lowered her hand and took him by the shoulder, but there was none of the clinical confidence in her touch.

"Please," he said very quietly.

She sighed. "Listen. I'm a responsible medical technician. In an hour and ten minutes I'll be staring into someone's abdomen in an operating room. So why . . . so why don't I shut up, since there isn't very much time at all for this sort of thing."

"Yes, why?"

She chuckled, then drew him toward her and, staring straight into his eyes, she undid his belt and trousers, touching him freely while he stood there startled, as if at attention.

"If you wrinkle this uniform I'll brain you," she said, and stepped easily out of her underwear.

Leaning back against the low counter, she brought him forward and into her, her skirt like a tablecloth between them.

"And please don't be virile," she whispered. "Not today."

"I won't be," he said, feeling vaguely faint, astonished to be inside her, she ever so gently gripping him and releasing him with her muscles and all the while motionless.

He kissed her, or half kissed her, their shaky breathing making it difficult. Her lips felt cold as she gasped in air between clenched teeth and tightened around him.

"Jesus," he mumbled.

"What?" she whispered back, her eyes closed.

"It's better than flying."

"It's better than anything except a banana split."

"What's . . . what's your favorite . . . flavor?"

She made a sound in her throat and he felt her pulsing. Her hand tightened on his shoulder and she seemed to quiver.

"Did you?"

"What do you think? Yes." She opened her eyes. "Don't just stand there. Fuck me."

She wrapped her legs around his waist, opening wide to him.

"Now, Barney," she said, "it's your turn."

Barney sat patiently waiting in the offices of School Superintendent Jerome Shaefer, a chubby-cheeked man with a seemingly friendly smile but one that gave Barney the impression it could be turned on and off like a faucet. Shaefer hadn't become school superintendent until last year, but he had already acquired a reputation for toughness. Which was fine, Barney figured. If he could sell Shaefer he was halfway around the track.

"Henry McKay speaks very highly of you," Shaefer confided. "Says you're one of the city's most promising young businessmen. You're with that little airline out at the airport, aren't you?"

"Yes, sir. Which is what I want to talk to you about. My partner and I believe that commercial aviation has a tremendous future. It's a young industry, and a young industry needs young men and women. We want to get young people interested in aviation. We want to get their parents interested. With that in mind, we'd like to set aside a special day at Bennett Field for your students. We want to introduce them to flying. Not in some old barnstorming biplane like the Jenny, but in one of our modern luxury airliners. We want them, and their parents, to experience what aviation is really like today."

"A commendable goal," Shaefer said, "but while I can endorse it in general terms, I need more details. Exactly what do you require of me—or rather my school system?"

"Just read this, Mr. Shaefer. I think it will answer your questions."

The superintendent put on his glasses and read aloud. " 'School Aviation Day . . . Bennett Field, 9:00 A.M. to 5:00 P.M. Ride the modern air transports of your hometown airline, fast-growing Tri-Cities! A free thirty-minute flight for any child between eight and sixteen if accompanied by an adult paying a nominal charge of $3.00. Your pilots will be Binghamton's own war ace, Captain Rodney "Bud" Lindeman, and former Army pilot Captain Joseph McFarland. And that's not all—A special acrobatic flight of Captain Lindeman, recreating the maneuvers that brought him combat fame! . . .' Hmm. 'The Route of the Red Hawks,' eh?"

Shaefer handed back the paper. "I must say, Mr. Burton, I had no idea Tri-Cities had such growth plans. While I normally would refuse to allow the schools to become involved in any commercial venture, this seems to have certain values."

"I don't think it could be called a commercial venture, sir," Barney said in his most earnest voice. "Frankly, Mr. Shaefer, we'll be losing money on School Aviation Day, and we'll lose it gladly. It's the price we're willing to pay to develop interest in our industry. Incidentally, sir, may I also take the liberty of inviting you and Mrs. Shaefer to be our guest on a flight to New York and back next Saturday?"

"I'll have to ask Mrs. Shaefer, of course," the superintendent beamed, "but I certainly appreciate the invitation. And under the circumstances you've presented, I see no reason why we can't get these flyers around all our schools." Shaefer rose to his feet and extended his hand.

After the superintendent had ushered him out with great flourish, Barney headed for the airport to finish painting the office, since the new furniture was scheduled for delivery by the end of the week. He was still in paint-splattered overalls when Lindeman brought Flight 3 in with three passengers aboard. The pilot stomped in, whistling happily. He headed for the filing cabinet containing the whiskey, then stopped short, conscious that Barney was watching him.

"Little too early for a drink," he said. "Unless you'd like to join me, partner."

"Pour me just a shot," Barney surprised him. "Got some good news for you, and we might as well celebrate a bit."

Lindeman got out the bourbon with alacrity but exercised enough willpower to hold his portion down to the same level he poured Barney.

"Good leads today, Barney. Took one guy down to New York this morning, and I guess you saw what I had on the return trip. Plus some freight. Things are picking up."

Barney gave him the flyer. Lindeman read it and frowned.

"This supposed to be a big deal? A full day of sightseeing flights, and you've got me and Joe both working them? What the hell happens to the New York trip that Saturday?"

"We cancel it. This is more important."

"Important, my ass! We won't take in enough to pay for the gas, and you're giving away food and drinks and those pictures. Where do we get pictures of the Stinson?"

"I called the factory. They're sending me a couple hundred glossies. The hot dogs Southern Tier will pay for. I also might be able to work out the same deal with the Coca-Cola plant here. I'm gonna try, anyway."

"Did McKay say the bank would furnish the food?"

"No, but I think they will. Good advertising. Henry'll go for it. Take my word."

"You hope. Goddammit, Barney, you know we use Saturdays for maintenance on whatever plane's not flying the one roundtrip. You can't have both of us for that sightseeing crap, even if we cancel the schedule. And according to this"—he waved the flyer—"I'm supposed to do acrobatics, too. What with—an umbrella? Do you expect me to loop a Stinson?"

"The acrobatics will be in the Travel Air," Barney said calmly. "We'll even put on some War insignia—the red, white, and blue bull's-eyes. In water-colors, to save dough. Look, Bud, you're right about maintenance. I didn't think about that angle. I'm sorry." His tone was so apologetic that Lindeman curbed his indignation. "If we just had a mechanic around here, it would free you from responsibilities you shouldn't have to worry about."

"Yeah," Lindeman agreed. "I suppose we should think of hiring one someday."

"Maybe we oughta think about hiring one right now," Barney suggested. "You know something? I think reducing your workload, and Joe's, too, is really important. It's false economy to make you guys do your own maintenance. What would you say to my looking around for a good mechanic who'll work cheap?"

The pilot was thinking. "I'm a little worried at the way we've been spending money."

"There are two things we *can* afford." Barney stabbed the air with his finger for emphasis. "One is anything that produces efficiency and the other is anything that pays dividends in the long run. Say, there's the kid who works for Hill's Ford; he's supposed to be a crackerjack mechanic. I'll have him drive out here tomorrow so you can talk to him."

"He may know automobile engines, but that doesn't mean he'd be a good airplane mechanic," Lindeman said.

"Maybe, but I have a hunch you could teach him all about Wrights in about two days."

"Hunch, hell," the pilot snorted. "You had him all lined up before you brought up the subject of a mechanic, didn't you?"

"Yeah," Barney admitted. "I knew you'd raise hell when I showed you that flyer, so I had to make sure you'd want a mechanic before I told you about him."

Lindeman had to laugh. "You sly . . . you really trapped me. Okay, have him come see me. Now this—what the hell do you call it—'School Aviation Day'?"

Barney set down his glass. "By the end of the week I'll have nearly a thousand of these flyers distributed in every school in the city. I made a deal with the superintendent of schools. When he gave us his blessing, it was like handing us free advertising space on the front page of the Binghamton *Press*."

Lindeman looked at him with a mix of consternation and awe. "When do you aim to put on this circus?"

"Three weeks from Saturday. That'll give us plenty of time to repaint the Stinsons, finish decorating these offices, build a refreshment stand and a few other odds and ends. Such as a big map I'd like to hang somewhere so all the parents will see it."

"A map?"

"Of what our route system will look like. A good sign painter could put a map on a big piece of plywood. We'll hang it over the office entrance where people can't miss it. By the way, what would you think of selling the biplane?"

Lindeman's face went tight. "Absolutely not, Barney! I got to draw the line there. I love that little bird. And she's all paid for. Besides, what'll we use for instruction flights? Not the Stinsons?"

"Bud, how many students have you taken up in the Travel Air since I came to work here? Not counting me?"

Defiance deteriorated into dejection. "One. And he lasted only two lessons more than you. Goddamn you, Barney, you still gotta give me a good reason for selling it."

"Easy. If that route map comes true, we'll need every cent we can raise for more equipment. Not just one trimotor but two, maybe three. Be sensible, Bud. You don't even fly the Travel Air once a week."

"It's a good thing to have around for emergencies," Lindeman muttered. "And suppose we do get a mail contract. She'd make a great mail plane."

"This is 1928, Bud. Every airline in the country is adding cabin planes, aircraft that can carry people as well as mail. Have you seen pictures of that new Boeing Model 80? Hot and cold running water. Upholstered seats with reading lamps. We can't hang onto any airplane strictly for sentimental reasons, including the Stinsons."

"The Stinsons belong to *us*," Lindeman said stubbornly. "The Travel Air is mine."

"I won't argue that point," said Barney, "and I'm not gonna press the matter. But I would like you to think about it, just in case we need some fast cash and don't want to go into hock anymore."

"Fair enough," Lindeman said, mollified. "Anyway, we couldn't sell it right away. We need it for that school day of yours."

They sat in McKay's study, Barney sipping a cordial for the first time in his life.

"Henry, you've been telling me that we should incorporate, sell stock to raise capital, and then apply for a mail contract—right?"

"Yes."

"I have the feeling we're building the wings of an airplane before we have a fuselage to put them on."

McKay patted the collie dozing at his feet. "That's an interesting analogy. Continue."

"Well, wouldn't we attract a hell of a lot more investors if we had the mail contract first?"

"Probably. But you won't get any mail contract with that route system of yours and a couple of Stinsons to operate it."

"What would impress the Post Office Department most, or that guy you told me about, Walter something Brown?"

"Folger. Walter Folger Brown. And in answer to your question, solid financial condition first. Second, a proposal to bring air-mail service to points which could use it but don't have it yet. And third, modern equipment, capable of providing good passenger service as well as carrying mail. The latter is high on Mr. Brown's priority list, from what I hear. He happens to think the airlines can't grow up if they keep depending entirely on mail revenue. Unfortunately, no airline can exist without it, as you've demonstrated yourself."

"That's just my point, Henry. Go back to those three standards by which you say the Post Office Department judges a mail bid. We don't have decent equipment. We don't have a decent route system. But with the right equipment Tri-Cities can start flying to Washington from four cities in New York State. And once we go into Washington, we'll qualify for the mail contract."

"Barney, if you were in Brown's shoes, would you consider anything less than two hundred thousand dollars solid financing?"

"Western Air Express started out with three hundred sixty, and they're now the biggest airline in the country."

McKay's eyebrows shot up.

"They raised that dough *after* they got a mail contract. What the hell does the Post Office Department want from us? They gave Western a contract before it had a single plane or pilot, or even an office."

"Walter Folger Brown was not the Postmaster General of the United States when Western got started," McKay said. "Things have changed. Brown has seen too many airlines go under simply because they *were* undercapitalized."

Barney rubbed his eyes.

"Barney, when are you thinking of getting service started on the Buffalo route?"

"I hope within weeks. I'm gonna drive to all three cities starting the day after tomorrow. I've already arranged to meet with guys at the Buffalo, Syracuse, and Rochester airports. We need someone to handle our flights at each city—sell tickets and all that. Until we get our own personnel in there."

"Good. One of these days, I want you to hire yourself a lawyer —I'll get you one if necessary—and let him incorporate the airline in Delaware. This partnership business is minor-league stuff. Once you're incorporated, you can float a stock issue and raise some capital. With capital, you can buy a couple of bigger airplanes. With bigger airplanes, you can expand down to Washington. And when you go into Washington, you can apply for a mail contract."

McKay paused to light a cigar and puff meditatively. "Remember the first day you came in to see me? One of the things I advised you was *not* to play around in the stock market."

"I remember. You said the bottom was gonna drop out inside of a year."

"I still think it will. But in the meantime, it's possible to make a killing, provided you make it fast and then get the hell out. Interested?"

"Yes."

"Last night I talked to my father about you. He's a tough, smart old pirate and he thinks playing the market right now is strictly for damned fools. But he got a tip on one stock that's priced low. He advised me to buy a few thousand shares, let it go up about twenty-five points, and then sell. Mind you, he said twenty-five points. It'll probably go as high as thirty but Dad says don't take chances. He's putting twenty-five thousand into it and I'm adding another ten grand. And Dad says to let you in on it."

"How much of a plunge, Henry? I don't think I should be playing games with the airline's money. We could lose the whole damned thing."

"You've kept five thousand in your own checking account. Use that."

"Jesus, that's all I've got to my name."

"I'm well aware of that. I'm also only too well aware that today's market is built on sand. It's risky and it's always a gamble. But this is inside information—from someone who owes my father a very large favor."

"What's the company?"

"Caldwell Manufacturing. It's a small outfit in Ithaca. The president is a former Cornell professor who has a patent on some new kind of thermostat that's adaptable for use in automobiles and in refrigerators, too. My father lent him the money to get the company started. He called Dad last week and told him he's about to sign royalty agreements with General Motors, Ford, and Chrysler, plus three companies making refrigerators. When that news gets out, Caldwell stock will head for the moon. Now do you see what I mean?"

"Yeah," Barney nodded. "How much is the stock now?"

"One dollar a share."

"Count me in."

"On one condition. I want your solemn promise that when the stock reaches twenty-five, you sell."

"Will you sell? And your father, too?"

"Damned right."

"Who do I make the check out to—you?"

"We'll deal with a legitimate broker, John Chase and Company. Write the check out to them. There will be a buying-commission fee but I'll take care of that. You can reimburse me later."

Barney took out his checkbook and wrote a check for $5,000—leaving him, he noticed, with a balance of $26.50

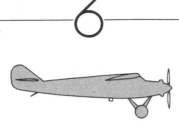

6

Barney had optimistically counted on about a hundred children showing up with their parents, which was about double what Lindeman and McFarland were predicting.

No actual head count was taken, but Henry McKay—who by 11:00 A.M. was dispatched hastily for more hot dogs and soft drinks—estimated the attendance at well over a thousand.

The two hundred photographs of the Stinsons disappeared in the first hour, but there were few complaints, largely because Barney had been foresighted enough to buy several hundred small balloons. The new mechanic, Larry Aroni, found himself running the refreshment stand, while Barney worked at arranging the airplane rides, the most hectic task of all because the demand outstripped both the planes and the time available for the flights.

Lindeman finally resorted to shaving the advertised thirty-minute hops down to twenty minutes, but even this didn't take care of all who wanted to go. By 5:00 P.M., the two Stinsons had carried more than two hundred passengers—nearly half of them paying parents—and another two hundred were clamoring for their rides. Barney argued briefly with Lindeman and McFarland, then grabbed the cheerleader's megaphone he had borrowed from the high school and announced that the sightseeing flights would be resumed the next day. This produced loud applause and cheers and sent everyone home happy.

All day Bud Lindeman seemed to be having a ball, joking with parents and small fry alike and getting an obvious kick out of climbing into his old flight suit, donning helmet and goggles and traditional white scarf, and taking off in the Travel Air for acrobatics. He had been superb, a skyborne virtuoso, with loops, barrel rolls, and Immelmann turns delighting the crowd. His finale brought gasps. He completed a loop and then spun earthward, pulling out only a few hundred feet from the ground.

It was after he landed and was sipping a fast Coke before resuming the sightseeing flights that Barney noticed he was pale and seemed worried.

"Anything wrong, Bud?" Barney asked solicitously.

"Naw. A little tired. Guess I'm getting too old for those stunts."

But later, when it became apparent they couldn't handle everyone who wanted to fly in the Stinsons, Lindeman snapped at Barney for suggesting they continue the next day.

"What the hell do you want, my blood?" he had snarled. "I'm too goddamned tired."

McFarland backed him up, but when Barney said, "Okay, I'll tell everyone we're sorry but we just didn't anticipate the demand," Lindeman had relented.

"No, don't tell 'em that," he grumbled. "Shit, let's do it again tomorrow. I'll get a good night's sleep. You, too, Joe."

Barney still suspected that there was something wrong, but in the flush of the day's success he had put it out of his mind. He was bursting with pride, and justifiably so. The two freshly-painted Stinsons fairly gleamed in their silver coats with the fierce, blood-red hawks on each side of the fuselages. The operations office couldn't have been recognized as the same shabby room Barney had first entered a few months before; not a few adults tried out the new lounge chairs, and Barney heard such comments as "I didn't know Tri-Cities ran such a classy operation." Like an anxious playwright hovering around the back of the theater, he got in as much eavesdropping as possible.

The Binghamton *Press* had a reporter and photographer there to cover the event, and a terrific guy named Frank Loudermilk had come up all the way from Newark to write up the story for the *Ledger*. Barney treated them like visiting potentates, and even slipped the photographer a fivespot to take a picture of the five-foot route-system map.

Like Barney, McKay spent as much time as possible wandering through the crowd, listening to the various comments. He admired Larry Aroni's paint job on the Stinsons and the spotless interiors. Until School Aviation Day, he hadn't seen the results of Barney's office redecorating either—the light-brown walls contrasting nicely with the cheerful orange-colored lounge chairs and Lindeman's new walnut desk with a black leather swivel chair behind it. Every vestige of untidiness had been removed, including Barney's oil-drum desk. Except for the dozen or so airplane pictures Barney had hung on the walls, it could have been any attractive business office.

What our boy hath wrought, McKay thought to himself. And he had accomplished all this virtually alone. McKay especially liked the way Barney had called on businessmen personally, extolling the virtues of air-travel, handing out timetables, and emphasizing ever so subtly how important it was for civic-minded executives to support not only Tri-Cities but commercial aviation in general. McKay had sat in on a couple of sessions, having arranged the appointments himself, and marveled at Barney's smoothness and self-confidence. He was articulate rather than glib, personable without being pushy.

McKay also found himself admiring the way Barney handled Lindeman. He had been with the two of them on enough occasions to observe the boy's skillful deference that was still dominance. It was a difficult, precariously balanced relationship deftly handled—an eager, enormously skilled rookie drawing know-how and teamwork out of a fading veteran without making him feel like a has-been.

And now this Aviation Day. Nothing but smart, adroit promotion on a gnat-sized budget. The first time he had met Barney, he had the impression of a headstrong, impulsive, rather impractical novice who was getting into the dangerously deep waters of an adult world. Now he was convinced Barnwell Burton had skipped some intermediate stage and grown up overnight, as far as business was concerned, anyway.

But the boy would need some formal coaching on the finer points of finance. Toward the end of the day, McKay managed to get him alone for a few seconds. "Barney, how about dinner tonight?"

"I'd better not. Larry Aroni and I—you met our new mechanic? —we're gonna grab a fast bite and come back here to clean up the airplanes for tomorrow. Larry's gonna check the engines out, too. Wouldn't want anything to go wrong on Sunday's sightseeing flights."

"Perhaps tomorrow night?"

"Same thing. We'll be resuming our regular schedules Monday and we'll be working here most of Sunday night. How about Monday?"

"Don't kill yourself for dear old Tri-Cities," McKay warned. "Maybe you could drop in at the bank sometime Monday. I've got some business to discuss with you."

"Airline business? Or personal?"

"Both, you might say."

"Let's see. I'll be working here all morning and I'm taking the vice-president of Spaulding Bakery to lunch. Guy named Marty Boykin. You know him?"

"Slightly."

"Well, the other night I got this great idea. When we start going into Buffalo, Rochester, and Syracuse. I'd like to start serving snacks—just sandwiches and a beverage. So I'm gonna see Boykin about working out a deal with his bakery. We'd get the bread free in return for wrapping the sandwiches in paper that'll have some plug for Spaulding bread printed on it."

"Plus a free trip for Boykin and all the little Boykins."

"Huh?"

"Just kidding."

"Yeah. Anyway, what do you wanna see me about Monday? I could get to the bank around five-thirty if that's not too late."

"Five-thirty will be fine, but make it my house. I'll tell you all about it Monday. Just some general business points I'd like to review with you. Oh hell, Aroni's waving at me. I hope we didn't run out of hot dogs again . . ."

The sightseeing flights tapered off by mid-afternoon Sunday, after another $225 had gone into Lindeman's cash box. There were only a half-dozen people still around and Lindeman wearily tossed in the towel.

"I'll give you fifty bucks to take up two more loads," he told McFarland. "If anyone else shows up, our friend Barney here can fly 'em. I've had it."

Barney didn't have the heart to argue. When two men drove up, each with a small boy, Barney apologized to them.

"We just got a call from New York to get one of our Stinsons down there for a special emergency charter," he lied. "Rushing medicine to some hospital in Pittsburgh. And the plane that's up sightseeing now needs some engine work as soon as Captain Mc-Farland lands."

"Will the repairs take long?" one father asked.

"The rest of the day, I'm afraid. I hate to disappoint the boys. I really do. Tell you what, fellas, you come into the office with me. There are some framed pictures of airplanes on the wall and I'll give one to each of you. Any one you pick. And Captain Lindeman will autograph them."

He marched the kids toward operations, let each select a photograph, and they departed reasonably happy after Lindeman signed "best regards from Rodney 'Bud' Lindeman" on both shots.

"Nicely handled," Lindeman said after they departed. "I couldn't fly that goddamned plane another twenty feet. Matter of fact, I'm gonna ask Joe to trade our flights tomorrow, so I can get a little extra sleep. I'm just bushed."

"You also seem worried about something," said Barney.

Lindeman looked at him sharply. "Being tired isn't being worried."

"I never said it was. But you still look worried. If something's bothering you, Bud, get it out in the open. No secrets in this partnership."

"You see that spin yesterday—the curtain act?"

"God, yes. It was sensational. I thought—"

Lindeman turned around. "It damned near was a final curtain, Barney. I blacked out during the topside of that loop. I never meant to spin in. When I came to, I was only a few hundred feet from the ground. I thought I'd bought the farm for good. How the wings stayed on when I pulled out, I'll never know."

Barney was stunned. "Jesus, Bud. Go see a doctor. Tomorrow. We'll cancel your flights."

"Don't have to see a doctor. I already have. High blood pressure. Not as high as you told me your mother's was. But no more acrobatics for Captain Lindeman. From now on, just straight and level."

"Maybe you shouldn't be flying at all. What did the doctor tell you?"

"Oh, nothing to worry about so long as I take it easy. Cut down on the drinking and all that crap. But in a way, it's a break for you. I'll sell the Travel Air soon as I can. You always manage to get what you want, don't you, partner?"

He didn't mean to sound bitter but it came out that way.

"I'm not trying to run this show," Barney said quietly. "But most of the decisions have to be made on the ground, and you're flying half the day. It would be fine with me if we hired another pilot so you could work with me more. And if you want the truth, I think we should hire one anyway. This high blood pressure business scares the hell out of me. If something happened to you in the air, you'd kill not only yourself but our passengers. One crash would ruin us. You know that as well as I do."

"Gonna ground me?" Lindeman asked in a strangely gentle voice.

"You've got too much sense for that. I think, if necessary, you'll ground yourself."

Lindeman slumped back into his new chair. "As usual, you're right. I could sure use some relief. Be honest with me, though. We aren't in good enough shape yet to take on another pilot, are we?"

"Not exactly, but if there's one thing we can't cut corners on it's engines. Hiring pilots is your department, Bud. I'd say go ahead and hire one, even if we have to use him on a part-time basis for a while. Maybe you could teach Larry how to fly."

"I probably could," Lindeman frowned, "but I won't. He's a

natural-born grease monkey, the best mechanic I've ever seen. I loaned him all my technical manuals and I swear he must have memorized them in one night."

"Good boy, Larry," Barney nodded. "Okay, start looking for our third pilot, but he's gotta be good. Damned good. I guess we could promise him at least a couple of days' work every week."

By noon the next day, it was apparent that Lindeman was going to have to find his man faster than anyone suspected, Barney included. The office phone started ringing shortly after 9:00 A.M. In the next three hours Barney had booked future space for no fewer than twenty-three passengers.

He leaned back into the fine leather of the armchair, completely exhausted and completely happy. He could barely hear Henry McKay's explanation of buying on margin but hoped he could at least keep his eyes open. He realized what Henry was doing. It had started with books being pressed upon him. Now, under the guise of a business meeting, McKay was tutoring him in the finer points of finance and what little he could recall of administration principles from two courses at college.

McKay sat up. "Barney, you look all in."

"Yes." Barney leaned forward, rubbing his face with both hands. "It was quite a Monday."

"Not to mention the weekend. When are you going to take some time off?" said McKay.

"Tomorrow."

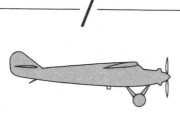

7

He picked her up at sunup and they drove north to Lake George, spent the morning swimming, took a tour boat around the whole lake in the afternoon, and had an early supper on the veranda of a little inn overlooking the waterfront.

With coffee ordered, Rosina Kyle slouched back in her chair and stared at Barnwell Burton finishing his steak.

"You look as red as that side of beef," she teased. "And your nose looks like a strawberry."

"Mmmmm." He pushed the plate away. "I'm still famished. Maybe we should have dessert with our coffee."

"You're looking at it, chum. So don't dawdle over the java."

"Listen," he whispered into her bone-white shoulder, "that was very nice, but hardly dessert."

"Still hungry, eh?" she said, her face close to his on the pillow. She was stretched out lazily next to him, the whiteness of her body luminous in the half light. Nearly asleep, she lifted herself on her elbows and kissed his chin, then slumped back onto her stomach.

Barney smiled. "What I wouldn't give for a banana split," he said, lacing his hands behind his head, feeling the telltale warmth invade her body that he knew was sleep.

"I'll see what I can do," she mumbled and languorously slid down along his body and suddenly enveloped him with her lips, her warm tongue flickering like a candle. He gasped. It was the first time anyone had ever—

He struggled to pull her away. But she pushed his hand away and only moved faster. And he came.

After a moment she looked up, her face glistening with moisture, and smiled, happy and proud of herself. And he realized just how much he was in love with this wanton, brazen angel, and just how empty he had been without her.

They slept late the next morning, took a bath together, got dressed for breakfast, changed their minds, and got undressed and made love.

It was well after midday by the time they finally ordered breakfast at a roadside diner. They were completely and pleasantly exhausted by sun and sex and began devouring the eggs and bacon practically before the waitress put the plates down. Finishing first, Rosina purloined some of Barney's toast and began eyeing his bacon.

"I'm on to you, so watch it," he said, his mouth full.

Rosina made a face at him and withdrew from the vicinity of his bacon.

"Hoarder."

"Sticks and bones . . ."

"You look wonderful, Barney."

He broke into a huge grin.

"When are you going to let yourself have some time for you? I know you're liking the flyboy business, but you need more time like this."

"Look who's talking. She works for fifteen days straight, takes two days off, and suddenly I'm hearing lectures on recreation."

"Do I hear a complaint?"

"Yes. Why can't I see you on a regular basis? Why do you have to spend so much time at that hospital?"

"The same reason you're practically living in that airplane hangar and staying up nights reading those tomes Henry McKay lent you."

"I've got a lot to learn and a lot to do."

"Such as—?"

"Such as becoming a mogul."

She laughed, the sound full and uninhibited.

"Why are you laughing?"

"Because . . . because you're completely serious!"

"Yes," Barney said, looking completely serious.

Barney was to meet the third pilot before he left on another trip to line up more business.

It was a strange introduction.

"This is my partner, Barney Burton," Lindeman said. "Barney, I'd like you to meet Alonzo Davenport."

"Jesus," Barney blurted out with his usual honesty, "you're small."

The little man with the frogface glared. "I fly the goddamned airplanes, not carry 'em!"

"He's got nearly a thousand hours logged," Lindeman interceded hastily, "and he used to work at Ford as a test pilot."

"Sounds good," Barney said. "Sorry about that crack, Alonzo."

"Hate that goddamned name," the pilot growled. "Call me Al. Anyway, I'd rather be undersized than underaged."

"We're even," Barney laughed. "Welcome to our little aerial asylum."

This time they shook hands with considerably more warmth, and in another five minutes all four were rejiggering the schedules. They quickly agreed on establishing one daily roundtrip between Binghamton and Buffalo via Syracuse and Rochester, cutting the New York service down to a single daily roundtrip—which Davenport would fly Fridays, Saturdays, and Sundays, taking over McFarland's Binghamton–Buffalo schedule Mondays and Tuesdays. Barney left within the hour for Syracuse, taking Bud's Model A. He was half inclined to drive the modified Jordan because it was an advertisement on wheels, but this would leave the airline without its courtesy car. Aroni had already volunteered to handle the embryonic limousine service; the burly young Italian put driving only a shade behind sex and eating on his scale of personal pleasures.

Barney was back three days later with Buffalo and the two intermediate airports lined up; in each case, he had offered the airport manager ten percent of every ticket sold as compensation for handling reservations and aircraft servicing. Service began July 15, 1928, with as much fanfare and publicity as Barney could dredge out of local newspapers, and traffic held up for almost a month—mostly because of the novelty. When it began to slacken, Barney resorted to promotion stunts and bargain fares, even a special "Happy Honeymoon" rate, with free bus service from Buffalo to Niagara Falls as part of the package. This, too, attracted some new business, but faded all too quickly.

By September, Barney was dipping into the cash reserves to meet the airline's payroll. Neither he nor Lindeman drew any kind of salary. Both occasionally took small sums out of whatever current cash influx was available, Barney limiting this erratic source of income to his rent and food plus gas for the Model A, which he used solely on business.

Barney was only too well aware of where the trouble lay. Using Binghamton as the hub city on an air transportation route was like locating Yankee Stadium in Poughkeepsie. It was tough enough to sell people on air travel, but convincing them to fly on a route system that contained only one major city made it even harder. In 1928 train service was too good, and the family automobile too convenient, for the airplane to make much of a dent in the transportation market. Carrying the mail, Barney knew, was the only way to stay afloat until passenger traffic could be developed. And that would never happen without attractive destinations—centers of business, industry, government.

As Tri-Cities' once-fat checking account dwindled, Barney made increasing inquiries as to the status of his Caldwell stock. Henry McKay had to report a hitch in the signing of the royalty agreements, and when two months went by with no encouraging word, Barney gave up hope. Now, for the first time, he understood Lindeman's inner tortures and recourse to the bottle. The two of them drew close. Lindeman suggested that they dismiss both Aroni and Davenport. "I'll start flying all the trips, and Joe and I can go back on maintenance," he proposed.

"No," Barney said stubbornly. "Hold on for another month."

"Chum, we're using our cash up so fast we won't be able to buy bigger equipment even if we get a mail contract. There won't be enough for a decent down-payment. And the way we're going, the bank won't lend us another cent."

"I'll talk to McKay again about the mail situation," Barney said gloomily.

Without newer and larger airplanes, they could not expand to Washington. With their evaporating resources, they could not afford to enlarge the fleet. And with their worsening financial status, obsolete aircraft, and unviable route system, they were not likely to qualify for a mail contract. The circle was vicious and inescapable.

The harsh clang of the telephone jarred him out of his gloom-drenched meditation.

"Tri-Cities Airlines, Mr. Burton speaking."

"Barney. Henry McKay."

"Yeah." Barney's heart began pounding. Something in McKay's voice—

"Caldwell Manufacturing. The roof just blew off their stock. It opened at twenty-five this morning and it's still climbing. I'm selling mine, Barney, and so's Dad. And *you*, you rich young sonofabitch, you'd better sell with us or I'll—!"

"Sell," Barney said quietly, and hung up.

McKay called him back thirty minutes later, his own voice unsteady.

"By the time we put in the sell order," he rasped, "it was heading toward forty. We ditched it at thirty-eight. You've just made yourself a hundred and eighty-five thousand dollars."

"Well, now what do you want me to do? Put the money in your bank and let the cobwebs gather?"

"A fair question. What I'd *really* like you to do is get out of the airline business, go to college for four years, and then come into the bank with me. By the time you get out, I'll probably be its president."

"No dice. Thanks, but I still think there's a future in this crazy business."

"That's what I figured you'd say. All right, what do you want *me* to do?"

The blue eyes were as cold as steel. "I want you or your father to get me an appointment with the Postmaster General—inside of the next thirty days. By the time I see him, Tri-Cities will be ready to fly from Buffalo, and three other cities, into Washington. Meanwhile, I think me and Bud Lindeman will be taking a little trip."

"I don't even want to guess where," McKay sighed.

"You shouldn't have to guess. We're going to Dearborn, Michigan, to buy a couple of Ford trimotors."

They fidgeted uncomfortably in the hard, upright red-upholstered seats on an Erie Railroad coach car heading west. Barney had wanted them to fly with McFarland to Buffalo and catch a train or even a Great Lakes steamer from there to Detroit, but the weather was foul and McFarland's return trip was scrubbed halfway, forcing Tri-Cities to issue railroad tickets to the passengers, as was the custom.

"Our worst enemy: the damned weather," Barney was grousing as he squinted through a soot-streaked window at the gray landscape flashing by. "Can't fly half the month in the winter and never passengers at night. No wonder people won't use airplanes."

"Well, it won't be like that someday," Lindeman philosophized. "An old Army buddy of mine was telling me the other day about a young lieutenant who's been fooling around with a blind landing device. Kid named Doolittle, Jimmy Doolittle. He's supposed to flight-test it next year."

"No kidding? How does it work?"

"Damned if I know. Something about sending a radio signal from the ground to an instrument in the airplane which lines the pilot up with the runway."

"Took an American to come up with an invention like that," Barney said. "Just like the Ford trimotor we'll be seeing. It took an American to design the first all-metal airliner."

Lindeman was amused. "Chum, your reading glasses must be painted red, white, and blue. A German named Hugo Junkers built an all-metal plane in 1915. It had an aluminum skin and a cantilever wing with internal bracing to do away with struts. And if you'll glance once more at that Ford come-on letter you've read twenty times since we left Binghamton, you'll see that's how Uncle

Henry builds his trimotors. Junkers also designed an all-metal transport and then built a bigger version carrying nine passengers. It went into service in '21. If memory serves me, our own Post Office Department bought six of them to use on mail runs between New York, Chicago, and Omaha. The old Junkers even had a corrugated fuselage like Ford's. Matter of fact, Hugo Junkers had a trimotor operational in 1924—a low-wing, ten-passenger job— and that was three years before the 4-AT flew. Bill Stout would be the first to admit he got more than one idea from Junkers."

"Bill Stout? The one who designed the Ford trimotor?"

"The same. Only he really didn't design the airplane we're gonna see. Stout is an eccentric little guy—skinny, with thick glasses and a mustache like that crazy Broadway comedian, Groucho Marx. I first met him years ago at an air show. Anyway, Bill Stout sold Ford on the idea of building all-metal transport planes. Henry was one of a handful of industrialists Stout solicited for money, or rather his son Edsel was. Stout's letter said something like, 'I want a thousand dollars and I can only promise you one thing—you'll never see the money again.' Edsel took the letter to his father and they each sent a thousand bucks. Interested in hearing the rest of the story?"

"Yes," Barney said.

"Well, Ford later financed the Stout Metal Airplane Company and built a factory on Ford property in Dearborn. Stout's first try was a failure. I think he called it the 'Air Pullman.' But then he came up with the 2-AT model, which looked a hell of a lot like today's trimotor except it had only one engine. They had a falling out after Stout built the 3-AT. It was a trimotor but it flew like an oversized rock. Henry finally bought out Stout's company but kept the name."

Barney caught himself fondling the letter from the Ford company inviting him to Dearborn for a first-hand look at the trimotor. Bud was right—it was becoming dog-eared. To him, it was like a government clerk getting an invitation to a White House dinner; the salutation, the phrasing, seemed to imply that it was addressed to a Captain of Industry, and Barney, for all his new-found success, still could wonder if it had really happened. Suddenly embarrassed, he took his hand from his pocket and the letter.

"If—" Barney yawned. "—if the 4-AT we're seeing wasn't designed by Stout, who did design it?"

"From what I hear, several people—including this guy Mayo, his chief engineer. He's supposed to have a pipeline right to Henry Ford himself, and when Mayo tells him something about aviation, Mr. Ford listens. Nobody knows how much credit Mayo should get, though. The fuselage is strictly Stout's. And the 4-AT's wingfoil is almost identical to the Fokker F-10's. Which reminds me, maybe we shouldn't commit ourselves to anything this trip. We'll take a good look at the 4-AT, I'll test-fly it, and then we'll discuss it between ourselves before signing anything. It might be a damned good idea to investigate Fokker's trimotor after we see Ford's."

Barney frowned. "It's made of wood."

"It's also lighter, faster, and the payload's greater. I didn't get a chance to show you this yet, Barney, but look it over. I got some performance specifications from Fokker for their F-10 and compared them to the 4-AT." He handed his partner a piece of paper on which he had typed three columns.

	Ford 4-AT	Fokker F-10
Passenger Capacity	12	12
Payload	2,000 lbs.	2,500 lbs.
Ceiling	16,000 ft.	18,000 ft.
Rate of Climb	900 FPM	1,400 FPM
Cruising Speed	100 MPH	120 MPH
Empty Weight	6,500 lbs.	2,000 lbs.
Price	$50,000	$70,000

"See what I mean?" Lindeman asked. "That's the penalty for the metal construction. The Ford weighs two and a half tons more, and look at what this does to rate of climb, maximum ceiling, cruising speed, and payload. The Fokker'll fly circles around the Ford."

"But it can't be as strong, Bud. Wood just isn't as safe as metal."

"The Fokker's fuselage is built of tubular steel," Lindeman said, "and its plywood wing is stressed like a bridge girder. You're overemphasizing the advantages of metal construction. Hell, I'll bet a wooden airframe is cheaper to maintain over the long haul. You'd probably run into metal fatigue before you'd ever have wood rot."

Barney said with a tight smile, "But you're ignoring the most important specification—price."

"There's only a twenty-thousand-dollar difference," Lindeman argued. "Personally, I think the F-10 is just that much more airplane and worth the dough."

Barney shook his head impatiently. "We could buy three Fords for what two Fokkers would cost. And it's my money, anyway." He saw Lindeman wince almost imperceptibly and was sorry he had said it. "Hell, Bud, we won't make any decision until you fly the 4-AT. You're the expert, not me. If you don't like it, we won't buy it."

His partner brightened. "I'll give the bird a fair shake, Barney. I promise you I won't go in prejudiced against it."

They checked in at a small hotel not too far from the factory, guests of the Ford Motor Company.

They were in the room having a quiet drink out of the bottle Lindeman had brought, discussing where they might have dinner, when their phone rang and Lindeman answered.

"It's Schroeder, Ford's chief test pilot. Shorty wants to take us to dinner tonight."

"Swell. You know him?"

"Only by reputation. And according to said reputation, he was born with wings, weaned on high-octane fuel, and teethed on a Liberty engine cylinder. I think you'll like him."

Barney did. Schroeder had been an Army pilot with the rank of major who specialized in high-altitude flying. Feisty and likable, he entertained them all evening with aeronautical anecdotes. Barney, in fact, felt a little ill-at-ease, sandwiched between two such members of the close-knit airmen's fraternity. At times, their jargon sounded like a debate in Chinese and Barney was too embarrassed to ask for a translation. In the early stages, Lindeman tried nobly to bring his young partner into the conversation but succumbed to the lure of Schroeder's repertoire. Barney was content just to listen.

"And so help me, Shorty, there I was with a goddamned Pfaltz on my tail, both my guns jammed, and my wingman was off chasing . . ."

"Major Schroeder," Barney wedged in, "we'd sure like to have an honest opinion of the 4-AT as it applies to our route structure."

Schroeder's eyebrows arched, as if he had just heard a kindergarten student recite the firing order of a Wright Whirlwind ignition system. "Well, Burton my boy, I don't think it makes a goddamned bit of difference what kind of route you fly. Our Tin Goose will do the job for you. It's the only airplane of its size in the world, for example, that'll take off in three plane lengths, which is roughly the equivalent of lifting yourself up by your own bootstraps."

Lindeman smiled benignly, wearing the expression of a man who has been ignoring his wife all night and suddenly discovers that she not only hadn't gone home but wants to get into the party. "I can't wait to fly it, Shorty, and I want Barney to go up with me. He's the one who'll be writing the check. He, uh, he's done some flying himself."

The last was a sop to Barney's pride, and for a moment Lindeman wondered if he should have referred to the aborted flying lessons; Barney merely grinned in silent understanding.

"Hell, of course we'll take him for a ride," Schroeder said jovially—although he came close to verbally underlining the word *ride*, having guessed that Barney was no pilot. "I won't give you any guff, either. A test pilot who's not honest about his factory's product is a damned fool. We have an airplane jockey around here named Larry Fritz. Few years ago, Western Air Express sent Fred Kelly, their number-one pilot, out here to test-fly the 2-AT. It wasn't a bad airplane, but it was underpowered for Western's mountain routes. Western already had agreed to buy the airplane but Fritz warned Kelly they were making a mistake. 'It'll never get over the Rockies,' he told Fred. So they went out and bought the Douglas M-2 instead. Same thing happened with me back in '25 when Bill Stout handed me that trimotor monstrosity of his, the 3-AT. Lemme tell you, that was probably the ugliest airplane ever built and it flew like it looked. Stout mounted the outboard engines on the wings and all they did was destroy the airflow; you couldn't use the center engine to swat flies. All it did was turn the prop." Schroeder chuckled, shaking his head. "Ford had just hired me out of the Army and old Henry himself came out to see the first flight. It almost turned out to be the last. She took off okay, but when I tried to land with normal power, it dropped like a brick from about thirty feet up. I can't remember how many times it bounced on me, but I finally got into the air again and then landed using about as much power as I did on takeoff. I climbed out, walked over to Henry, and said, 'Forget it.'

"Henry couldn't believe it. He insisted on another test, and the next pilot came back with the same verdict, only more detailed. Said it couldn't be operated commercially even with a payload as low as eight hundred pounds. And he also told Ford the damned thing couldn't maintain altitude on two engines. That was one of the boss's safety standards. Worse still, the test pilot reported that it wasn't even safe to land at a field as large as Ford Airport. And remember, the airport you're seeing tomorrow is about as big as they get.

"Well, that did it. About a month later, the whole factory was gutted by a fire and the 3-AT was one of the three or four planes inside. There wasn't enough left of Bill Stout's ship to fill a garbage pail. Even the aluminum had melted to ashes. Stout wasn't seen around the place after that. I think Bill Mayo told him Mr. Ford wanted him to go on a nationwide lecture tour. Stout left plans for another trimotor, but it was pretty much a bum like the 3-AT. When he got back from his tour, some new engineers Mayo had just hired already had the blueprints done for the 4-AT. There was some talk about the fire being arson, but it was just that—talk."

"Okay," Barney said, "tell us about the 4-AT."

"What is there to tell? Bud, here, has to fly it to appreciate it. We're using a new alloy—'Alcad,' it's called. Combines the corrosion-resistance of pure aluminum with the strength of Duralumin. She uses Wright J-6's with two-bladed metal props."

"Horsepower?" Lindeman asked.

"Two-twenty-five on each engine. Noisy little beast, by the way, but you kinda get used to it. You gotta cup your hands and shout to be heard in the cockpit, and the cabin's almost as bad. I'll show you the control setup tomorrow, but there's one thing you'll get a kick out of—the steering wheels. Came right off the deluxe Model T. Mr. Ford doesn't miss a trick."

"I'd sure like to meet him," Barney sighed. "Read a lot about him. Must be a character."

Schroeder grinned. "I heard one of his executives say once, 'I never had a boss who treated me better, or who treated me worse.' "

"I was telling Barney about the Fokker F-10 on the way here," Lindeman chimed in. "You ever flown one?"

"Negative. But I know guys who have. Frankly, they love it. But nobody can tell me wood spars are as safe as metal ones. That F-10 will outperform the Goose, sure, but it'll never outlast it. Tony Fokker keeps saying our 4-AT is a carbon copy of his trimotor, and strictly between us, externally it is. And not by accident."

His audience listened intently.

"It happened a few years ago when our engineers were still working on a trimotor design and knew they had to come up with something better than what Stout had dumped in Ford's lap. One day Admiral Byrd flies into Ford Airport in his Fokker F-7—a little smaller than the F-10 but basically the same design. Ford rolls out the red carpet and insists that Byrd stay the night. He does. And while he's being wined and dined, his Fokker goes into our hangar. Our boys spent all night inspecting every inch of it, especially the measurements and shape of the wing. Nobody dared tell Henry Ford about it, but that, gentlemen, is why our trimotor's wing looks like it came right off a Fokker. However, like I said, the metal structure is really the big difference."

Lindeman looked pleased because his Fokker story had just been confirmed; Barney looked even more pleased because Schroeder was so convinced of an all-metal plane's superiority.

"I don't suppose there's much chance of meeting Mr. Ford," Barney said.

"Who knows? He's liable to pop up anytime, anywhere, or we won't see him for weeks. I'll tell you one thing, though: the airlines owe one hell of a debt to Bill Stout just for getting Henry Ford interested in aviation. Funny, but Ford hates to fly himself. I think the only time he ever went up was when Lindbergh talked him into taking a short flight. Yet once he was sold on commercial aviation, he went whole-hog. Take Ford Airport. Wait till you see it! Beautiful, with a snack bar and fireplace, special busses for passengers, concrete runways nearly three thousand feet long. First paved runways in the country, matter of fact. We even have radio beacons . . . developed right here at Ford. And I suppose you guys know about the Ford Air Transport Service. It was the first private contractor to fly the mail in 1926, between Chicago, Detroit, and Cleveland. Classy operation, too. Our pilots wore snappy blue-and-gold uniforms, and every trip had what we called a Flight Escort, a uniformed attendant just to make passengers feel comfortable. Hell, we had all this *before* Lindy crossed the Atlantic, when most people thought flying consisted of a bunch of barnstormers hopping around.

"Well," Schroeder glanced at his watch. "Time to go home, kiddies. Bill Mayo wants me to bring you to his office at 9 A.M. sharp."

They met Mayo the next morning, the chief engineer being a deceptively nondescript man of short stature. His bland features could not hide, however, the incisiveness that lay coiled underneath.

"I'll talk to you fellows after you've had a chance to see what the airplane can do," he said. "We're willing to let the ship speak for itself."

Barney, envying Lindeman's privileged cockpit status with all his young heart, enjoyed the demonstration flight nonetheless. He stood behind Schroeder and Lindeman, listening as Mayo gave his partner a short but thorough pre-takeoff briefing.

". . . here's your altimeter, rate-of-climb indicator, turn-and-bank indicator, airspeed indicator, magnetic compass, gyroscope, and clock."

"Where the hell are the engine instruments?"

"Look outside. They're on the inboard side of the wing engine nacelles."

"For Christ's sake, you need twenty-twenty vision to see 'em."

"Yeah, I think the design team forgot to include 'em on the instrument panel and hung 'em outside as an afterthought. You'll get used to them. These big pedals here aren't brakes; they're the rudder pedals. The brakes work off this gearshift lever next to my right leg. And if it looks familiar, it should. The knob is right off a Model A. These three starter buttons are the same ones you'll find on a late Model T. She's self-starting, by the way."

"How about trim control?"

"Just twirl that small crank above and behind us. That's why we say you can always tell a Ford pilot, because he's grown a third arm. Now to start up, we . . ."

Barney felt so out of place and useless on the fringe of the tiny cockpit that he went back to the cabin.

It was the biggest aircraft interior he had ever seen, with six seats on each side of the aisle. They were made of wicker with thin leather cushions. Barney scribbled into his little black notebook: *must get pillows for seats.*

He was pleased at the six-foot height of the cabin. He had to stoop a little himself, but for the average passenger it provided the unusual opportunity to stand up in the aisle. There were curtains on the windows, individual reading lights, and polished plywood paneling on the walls. The overall impression was one of luxury.

During the twenty-minute demonstration ride, he found out Schroeder hadn't exaggerated the noise level. The plane vibrated enough to shake teeth fillings, and Barney was startled by a jarring, unfamiliar sound that turned out to be the exterior control cables slapping against the fuselage. But the discomforts were minor compared to the feeling of security Barney had. The throaty growl of the Wright Whirlwinds, the knowledge of those metal sinews stretching throughout the great frame, the stability of the giant wings. This, Barney knew, was real air transportation.

When they landed, Schroeder suggested that Lindeman go up a second time on a more stringent test flight. "Try a couple of take-offs and landings, get an idea of her stall characteristics, give her the works, Bud."

Lindeman agreed with alacrity, inviting Barney to go along but with such half-heartedness that Barney would have said no even if he had wanted to. After the two pilots took off again, Barney walked back with Mayo to his office for a cup of coffee.

"I might as well tell you, Mr. Mayo," he said, "as far as I'm concerned we'll sign for two airplanes. I'd still like a final okay from my partner after he lands but from all I've seen, I'm impressed."

Bill Mayo studied the earnest young man intently before replying. The boy sitting across his desk could have been his son, yet he was about to buy $100,000 worth of airplanes. Did he really know what he was doing? Did he have the experience, judgment, and managerial ability to spend that kind of money? Mayo had the uncomfortable feeling he should be discouraging him, yet he also had the even more distinct feeling that Barnwell Burton was not just play-acting the Young Executive.

"I'm delighted you could reach a decision based on a short demonstration flight, Mr. Burton."

Bill Mayo stopped in the middle of a word as a tall, lean, stern-faced man opened the door to his office and entered. The chief engineer jumped to his feet.

"Mornin', Bill."

"Good morning, Mr. Ford."

Barney's eyes widened. Henry Ford in the flesh. Recognizable even if Mayo had not addressed him by name. The slightly stooped shoulders, the wiry frame, the deep-set eyes that were almost cadaverous, with bushy eyebrows that looked like miniature awnings. An expressive face with the unique quality of reflecting several emotions simultaneously—inquisitiveness, stubbornness and ruthlessness, a touch of gentleness. There was an old-world aura about the man, a kind of quaint Victorian courtliness that was an anomaly in Henry Ford's world of impersonal mechanization, insatiable assembly lines, and dictatorial authority.

He didn't just look at Barney; he impaled him with a searching stare. "Good morning, young man. I'm Henry Ford."

Barney got to his feet and realized his legs felt weak. But his handshake was firm and his voice clear although, for a fleeting moment, he was afraid it would splinter to a falsetto.

"Mr. Ford, this is Barnwell Burton of Tri-Cities Airlines," Mayo said. "They're considering buying the trimotor."

"This is a privilege, sir."

"Sit down, son, sit down. You, too, Bill. Just dropped in to see how the Aircraft Division was doing. Haven't checked up on you people for some time. Tri-Cities Airlines? Don't believe the name is familiar."

Barney's smile was boyish without being obsequious. "We're small potatoes. We operate a pair of Stinson Detroiters just in New York State, out of Binghamton. But we have plans to expand, which is why we're here."

The bushy eyebrows lifted. "We?"

"My partner's with me. He's out flight-testing the airplane. I just came back from a quick hop but he wanted a longer look. He's the pilot in the family, so to speak."

Ford pulled a chair from a corner and sank his lanky frame into it, positioning himself so he could face Barney. "And what was your opinion of it?"

"I'm no aeronautical engineer, Mr. Ford. I tried to look at it from a passenger's viewpoint. And I have to give it high grades, with one exception. Those wicker seats don't seem very comfortable. The leather cushions are too thin. And she's awfully noisy, but what airplane isn't?"

Ford grinned, and the smile on his craggy features made Barney expect to hear the sound of tinkling glass. "About those seats, Mr. Burton. I don't believe we're putting those on many planes anymore. Am I right, Bill?" Mayo nodded. "The newer models have upholstered seats. And our new 5-AT, coming out shortly, will be quite luxurious. A much better airplane all around. What are the specs on the 5-AT, Bill?"

"Four feet more of wingspan. Two feet longer in the fuselage. Space for thirteen to fifteen passengers and a thirty-eight-hundred-pound payload with ten miles an hour greater cruising speed. FOB Dearborn, fifty-five thousand dollars—five thousand more than the 4-AT and worth every penny."

At the last statistic, Barney shook his head ruefully. "We're very small, with limited resources. We want the best airplane we can buy for the least amount of money. I think the 5-AT might be a little too big for us. Maybe—"

"What's your capitalization?" Ford cut in.

A few months ago, Barney wouldn't have known what the word meant, but now he was benefiting from the crash courses taught by Professor Henry McKay. "We're strictly a partnership at present, Mr. Ford. But we intend to raise capital by incorporating. The trimotor will give us a chance to expand and make our stock more attractive."

The auto magnate recrossed his long legs and stroked his chin. "And where are you planning this expansion?"

"To Washington, sir. I . . . we figure there's no direct air service between western and central New York to the capital. Once we can get some passenger traffic moving, we intend to bid for a mail contract."

"I see. I'd have to assume you have some political connections." Ford's inflection indicated he actually assumed just the opposite.

"Yes, sir, we do. Our, uh, financial adviser is the vice-president of Southern Tier Trust in Binghamton. His father will intercede with the Postmaster General. We're hoping to see Mr. Brown in the near future—after we get the kind of equipment needed to operate a Washington route."

Ford uncoiled out of his chair, rose, and shook Barney's hand. "It's been a pleasure, Mr. Burton, and I wish you luck. Bill, if this young man buys our airplane, I think we should give him a little helping hand. Install the deluxe seats at no extra cost."

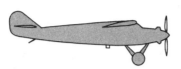

Nineteen twenty-nine was only twelve days old when Barney, on McKay's recommendation, hired a lawyer, who filed incorporation papers in Delaware. There was a flurry of debate in McKay's office over what to name the new corporation, Lindeman not wanting to change it and Barney arguing that the name no longer fitted their route system.

"Trans-Continent Airlines?" McFarland offered.

Barney shook his head. "No, but we do need a name that would be easy to change if we get bigger. Like . . . Trans-East. No . . . wait . . . what was your suggestion, Joe?"

"Trans-Continental. But—"

"I got it!" Barney's eyes were bright. "Coastal Airways."

"Wait a minute," Lindeman protested. "That's just as confining as Trans-East."

"But it's easy to change, Bud."

"Change to what?" His partner was scornful.

"Maybe Trans-Coastal, some day when we go all the way to the Pacific."

"We won't be around to see it," Lindeman grumbled.

McKay was staring at Barney. "I wouldn't be too sure," said the banker.

The meeting broke up and everyone left, except young Mr. Burton. He clearly had something on his mind, McKay thought. Barney was standing at the window, his back to McKay.

"Henry, how about your becoming an officer of Coastal Airways?"

"You want officers who'll be active," he said. "I've got too much to do at the bank."

"I need some brains around me," Barney argued. "Lindeman and McFarland are strictly pilots, when you come right down to it."

"So go out and hire yourself some brains when you can afford to recruit talent. Meanwhile, you can run a one-man operation. What the hell, that's what you've been doing almost from the day I met you. Anyway, my contribution to Coastal Airways will be far more practical than acquiring a meaningless title. I haven't gotten around to telling you yet, but I'd like to buy some stock in the outfit. And so would my father, though under duress, I'll admit."

Barney was pleased. He knew that in money matters, Henry McKay was wary. The banker's willingness to invest was a welcome indication of faith as well as friendship.

"This, Mr. McKay, is going to be a busy month."

McKay's confidence ran into five figures—he bought $25,000 worth of stock and talked his father into acquiring another $10,000 worth. At his suggestion, they had offered the stock at $10 a share, and there were a surprising number of takers, mostly in the Binghamton area. Within two weeks, Coastal Airways had been capitalized to the tune of nearly $500,000—a happy development which nevertheless gave Barney some twinges of conscience. The stock sales pitch was based largely on an appeal to "support your home-town airline," and Barney knew that Coastal's days as a Binghamton-based air carrier were numbered.

Actually, McKay wound up as the majority stockholder. Lindeman's holdings were almost token: he had to borrow money to buy one hundred shares and McFarland invested the same amount. Barney himself purchased only five hundred shares, a decision which McKay questioned.

"You should have more of a share in your own airline than that," he told Barney.

"It's just for a starter," Barney assured him. "I can pick up more stock later if things go all right. Maybe a few thousand of yours. Dammit, Henry, I want enough ready cash on hand to meet any emergency, like a payroll, if we hit a really bad period."

"What payroll?" McKay laughed. "You've got a corporation with exactly three officers, if you count McFarland, and two employees with a few shares of stock themselves. I know that Aroni kid bought two hundred. I never saw a company with so many chiefs and so few Indians."

"That's going to change," Barney promised.

It did.

By March 1, he had hired another pilot, a mechanic to back up Aroni, an office secretary, and a full-time eager-beaver traffic salesman named Cal Motts who had been working as a ticket agent for Colonial Airways in Syracuse.

Ford delivered the second trimotor March 28, and the very next day Barney was in Washington concluding arrangements for ground facilities at Hoover Airport. After acquiring some gate space for Coastal from the airport manager, he wandered around the facilities of the two carriers already serving Washington. There was the Washington–New York Airline, with a single roundtrip between the capital and Newark daily, and Pitcairn Aviation.

On May 1, 1929, Coastal Airways' trimotors—carrying the red hawk on their corrugated fuselages—began flying between Buffalo and Washington via Rochester, Syracuse, and Binghamton. That evening Barney and Henry McKay met for a drink to celebrate.

"Come on, Barnwell. Look like you're pleased, at least."

"Oh, I am. Really. And I appreciate all your help more than I can say. But there are a couple of big unfinished items still to be taken care of."

"Like marriage, maybe?"

Barney was caught off guard.

"I've heard about that raven-haired doll you've been dating." McKay smiled at Barney's stony expression. "Why don't you bring her by one night for supper? My wife and I would be happy to have you over."

"Hmm. And I thought we were so discreet about it. Yes, I have been seeing a lot of her lately, but no, I hadn't yet thought about our settling down. Actually, I had something else in mind—getting to see the key person in Washington."

McKay nodded. "The Postmaster General."

On May 14, Barnwell Burton and Henry McKay were ushered into the Washington offices of Walter Folger Brown, Postmaster General of the United States.

"Don't be nervous," McKay whispered.

"I'm not," Barney said and he wasn't. Yet on first sight, Barney found Brown a rather imposing figure. Tall, spidery-thin, and extremely well-dressed, he wore steel-rimmed glasses that accentuated the glint in his expressionless eyes. He looked tough as a wire.

Brown greeted them cordially enough, asking McKay about his father, and motioned them into a pair of black leather chairs. He got right to the point.

"I'm told you're interested in obtaining an air-mail contract, Mr. Burton."

"Yes, sir."

"From where to where?"

Barney outlined Coastal's route system, pointing out that there was no direct air-mail service on the Buffalo–Washington segment, nor between Binghamton and New York City.

Brown shook his head. "You couldn't carry mail between New York and Washington. That's part of Civil Air Mail Route 19, which Pitcairn operates."

"I know that, sir."

"And frankly, I don't really see any great need for direct mail service from places like Rochester, Syracuse, and Binghamton to New York and Washington. Buffalo, perhaps, but the others are rather small cities."

"Granted," Barney said quickly. "But we're planning to extend that Buffalo–Washington leg further south, all the way to Atlanta."

"I understand you're operating only two Ford trimotors. You can't do much expanding with just a couple of airplanes."

"No, sir. But we'll shortly start negotiating with Ford for another aircraft and possibly two." McKay's eyebrows arched at the announcement; it was news to him. For that matter, so was Barney's projected plan for operating as far south as Atlanta.

Brown was frowning slightly. "Any expansion to Atlanta, Mr. Burton, would seem to put you in direct conflict with Pitcairn. CAM Route 19 runs from New York to Miami through Washington and Atlanta."

Barney reached into his briefcase and brought out a map. "If you'll look at this, sir, CAM-19 starts running inland between Washington and Richmond. It goes to Atlanta via Greensboro, North Carolina, and Spartanburg, South Carolina. We'd like to expand via a coastal route from Washington to Norfolk, down to Raleigh, and directly south to Wilmington, North Carolina, and Charleston, South Carolina, *then* swinging west to Atlanta."

"Still not much of an air-mail market," Brown said. His stern face, however, was mirroring curiosity that was almost interest.

"Sir, Coastal Airways has no intention of acting primarily as a mail carrier. Our entire expansion plan is based on our belief that the areas we'd like to serve want passenger service as well as air mail."

Brown could not keep a smile from wrinkling the corners of his thin mouth. "I suspect Frank McKay has been rehearsing you on my own beliefs in commercial aviation's future, Mr. Burton."

Barney allowed himself a tight smile. "Henry's father did tell me you have strong convictions about passenger traffic. But if I didn't share those convictions, I wouldn't have brought up the matter. I know you're only too well aware that mail revenues are needed to support passenger business, until more people are sold on air travel. That's our sole reason for filing a mail-contract application. I only wish we didn't have to. Personally, I'd be happy if we could make a decent profit just carrying people."

"Have you filed a formal application yet?"

"No, sir. But one is being drawn up. It should be ready in about a week."

Brown rose to his feet. "Send it through the proper channels, Mr. Burton. But meanwhile I'll alert my staff to let me know when it comes in. I'd like to take a close look at it. Henry, say hello to Frank for me. And Mr. Burton, I appreciate your coming in to see me. I wish Coastal good luck."

Outside the Postmaster General's office, Barney found himself sweating.

"How do you think it went?" he asked McKay.

"I think," said his majority stockholder, "that I might buy a few more shares in this nutty company of yours."

It was almost time for their new office secretary to arrive for work and Bud Lindeman had some correspondence for her. Unused to dictating, he had gotten into the habit of typing out letters for the girl to transcribe with more acceptable neatness, and he reached into a drawer for some blank stationery. As he did so, his eyes fell on the new business letterheads Barney had ordered. *Coastal Airways* in red lettering. And on the left side, in smaller, discreet black type: *Rodney Lindeman, President.*

Rodney Lindeman, President, he thought.

"Bullshit," he said aloud, and put aside the paperwork to think about the problem he and Barney would have to face that morning.

The only way to operate a four-hundred-mile leg between Buffalo and Washington with just two trimotors was to base one of them at Buffalo and the other in the capital. Both flights left their respective cities at 9:00 A.M. With the three stops at Rochester, Syracuse, and Binghamton, each aircraft was flying a seven-hour daily schedule. During the fall and winter months, Lindeman had warned, the departure times would have to be moved to 8:00 A.M. to assure daylight arrivals.

The Stinsons were relegated to flying between Binghamton and Newark: two roundtrips daily, just as they had been when Lindeman first hired Barney. Because there were one-pilot trips, Lindeman assigned the two most experienced of the new men, Jerry Stephenson and Tim Latte, to the Stinsons, although he had some misgivings at first.

Barney walked in and they picked up without preamble where they had left off the night before. "Their logbooks each show more than five hundred hours' flight time," he said to Barney, "but I figure there isn't a log in existence that hasn't been padded a bit. Funny, but damn near every application we have on file claims five hundred hours."

Barney looked worried. "You know there can't be any compromises, and no cutting corners. I hope you didn't turn Stephenson and Latte loose on those Stinsons too soon."

"Relax, chum. I've been working with them almost every day. They were good when we hired 'em and they're getting better."

"How about the other two new guys? I can't remember their names."

"Bert Costin and Mark Culbertson. Good prospects. Greener than the hills of Ireland, both of 'em, but they're eager. And they'll learn a hell of a lot flying with Joe and Al on the Fords. I figure in about six months, we can switch 'em over to the Stinsons and put Stephenson and Latte on the trimotors. If the guys last. Nobody likes the idea of flying seven days a week."

"I don't like it either. We could use a relief crew on the Fords, and if business stays the way it is, I guess we'd better hire us a couple more pilots."

Lindeman cleared his throat. "Uh, Barney, suppose I flew a Washington trip every weekend. Give Joe and Al some time off. Until we add a reserve crew."

Barney's expression darkened. "I thought we had an agreement —no more line flying for you, just training. By the way, how's your blood pressure these days?"

"Fine."

Barney gave him a look of pure suspicion. "When did you see your doctor last?"

"Couple of weeks ago."

"What did he tell you?"

Lindeman hesitated. "Well, it's still a little high, but not as bad as it was."

Barney grimaced. "No dice, Bud. You might as well realize you're president of this corporation, not just an airplane driver. It won't kill any of the guys to work a little harder and longer until we really get going."

Lindeman shrugged. "Okay, but I think we're gonna get some static from McFarland. His old lady's always raising hell about his being in Buffalo all the time. It's nearly done 'em in."

"So why doesn't she move to Buffalo?"

"Don't ask me. He just says, 'You don't know her.' Shit, I don't know *any* woman. But that gal of McFarland's is strong-willed.

He's been really tight-lipped lately . . . always is when they're on the outs. I hope she doesn't cause us any trouble." Lindeman stretched stiffly. "I, ah . . ."

Barney had come to know his partner's moods and knew he was disquieted for a reason. "What?"

Lindeman looked downcast. He had recounted McFarland's dilemma badly. "I have a pretty strong hunch Joe is going to want out of the Buffalo run."

"How soon?"

"Soon."

Lindeman waited, anxious to hear Barney's reaction. Only Barney had none. He just kept doodling on a scratch pad.

"Well, you got any suggestions?" Barney finally asked.

Lindeman was a little surprised. "I suppose we have to hire someone who can fly a trimotor, and damned fast."

"Any prospects in that batch of applications on your desk?"

"Not a one. All single-engine jockeys, and nobody with more than a couple hundred hours."

"Call Shorty Schroeder. See if he can recommend somebody."

"Yeah," Lindeman agreed, thankful that Barney was not making an issue out of McFarland's demand. "He should be able to help us. And we'll keep Joe happy—not to mention that dame of his."

Barney finished the doodle and started another. "Just in case Schroeder can't find us someone in a hurry, who's the best of the new guys?"

"Well, it would be a toss-up between Stephenson and Latte. Jerry's a more natural pilot—flashier, you might say. Latte is more mature. Steadier, I guess."

"I think you'd better pull Latte off the Stinsons. When Davenport comes through today, assign Latte to him as his copilot and tell Al to give him as much training in the next two weeks as he can. Who's Davenport flying with now?"

"Costin."

"You can start checking him out on the Stinsons, as Stephenson's eventual replacement. I want Stephenson trained on the Fords as soon as possible."

Lindeman smiled happily. "Well, that seems to solve everything.

Even if Shorty comes up with somebody, it won't hurt to have 'em ready for the Fords; like you've been saying, we'll be adding a third trimotor one of these days. And after I break in Costin on the Stinson, we'll have him and Joe for the New York trips."

"I don't think so, Bud." Barney's voice was mild but with a cold undertone.

"And what's that supposed to mean?"

"It means I don't intend to pay McFarland top dough for flying a half-assed trip. We need him on the trimotors and he refuses to fly them. That's his privilege. Our privilege is not having to waste Coastal's money on flights that don't require pilots of his experience. In plain language, they don't earn enough to warrant his salary."

Lindeman sucked in his breath. Barney looked up from his scratch pad and their eyes collided—Lindeman's concerned, disbelieving, pained; Barney's a pale blue that was almost white, like ice reflecting.

"You'd better elaborate a bit, chum," Lindeman said quietly.

"I don't think I really have to."

"I'd still like to hear you say it."

"Say what?"

Lindeman's temper reddened his cheeks. "Don't get coy with me, *Mr.* Burton. If you have any intention of ditching Joe McFarland, you'd goddamned well better come right out and say it! And not just to me—to Joe's face. Provided you have the guts, which I doubt. Because you know he'll punch those teeth of yours right down your throat!"

Barney's only sign of anger was a slight tightening of his jaw. "I'm not ditching him, he's ditching himself. He's making his own choice. This airline's going somewhere and Joe McFarland can go with it, but it can't be on his terms. It has to be on ours."

"Ours? Yours, Barney. I'm not laying down any terms for a guy who's been with me since the day I started this fucking airline."

"Not mine, either. Coastal's terms. *Coastal's.* Get it through your skull, we're all working for a company now. We don't make one decision, we don't spend one lousy cent, we don't move one inch in any direction unless it's for the good of Coastal Airways. Nobody is bigger than the airline. That includes you, me, Mc-

Farland, and anyone else living off its operations. We have one job to do—move people and packages and someday mail pouches between cities. We have one goal—to earn some dough while our airplanes fly their schedules. We have two responsibilities—the passengers we fly, and the people who invested their money in this company. I am not going to sit still for anything or anyone who gets in the way." Now he was on his feet, looking even taller than he was. "You put aside the sentimentality and misplaced loyalty and just give me one honest, logical reason how letting McFarland beg off would be anything but detrimental to the airline."

Lindeman didn't answer.

"And while you're trying to dream something up, let me tell you *we're* the ones getting screwed, not McFarland. He's forcing us to hire a pilot higher-priced than we want. He's asking us to pay him a trimotor salary for flying a single-engine airplane, which makes it impossible to show a profit on what's a marginal route segment at best. And now you want to hold his hand, pat him on his head, and tell him, 'It's okay, Joe. Your life comes first, we understand.' Well, maybe you understand. I don't!"

"It's a question of loyalty—" Lindeman started to say, but Barney cut him off with a withering glance.

"Whose?"

Lindeman exhaled. His anger was beginning to fade even as his resolve sagged.

"I see your point, but I can't hurt Joe." He looked up at Barney. "Why are you being so hard about this? You want to fire him? Is that your solution?"

"Not necessarily. We could use him—but only as a reserve pilot. And not at the scale we're paying him now. If he insists on staying in Binghamton, fine. But with a twenty-five percent cut in pay, his resignation as treasurer, and absolutely no guarantee as to how long his reserve status will continue."

"I don't get that last part," Lindeman said, frowning.

"It's simple. Binghamton's no place to base an airline. I'd like to move our headquarters to Washington. And don't look so surprised. You knew damned well I was gonna take off in that direction sooner or later."

"You'll raise quite a few hackles in this town, chum."

Barney shrugged. "In the long run a few stock dividends will make up for ruffled civic pride. Anyway, let's solve this McFarland thing before we worry about moving. I'll tell Joe how things stand, and if he wants to take a poke at me he can go ahead and try. Only you might tell him beforehand that I'll do my best to return the favor. Agreed?"

"Agreed," Lindeman said sullenly.

"Okay, while we're discussing Mr. McFarland's unquenchable desire to fly only out of Binghamton, I might as well dump another unpleasant thought on you. Let's drop one of the Binghamton–New York trips."

"Hell, Barney, I know traffic hasn't been holding up, but it's better than it used to be and . . ."

"We're losing money on the two daily trips. If we cut down to one, we might at least break even and maybe show a small profit. That's another reason I can't buy this whole McFarland business. I want the younger pilots to fly the New York run. It'll be good training for upgrading them to the Fords. Then we can use Joe as a backup on the trimotors. I can't see his sweetheart objecting to his being away one or two nights a week at the most."

"I have a sneaking hunch," Lindeman said with a reluctant smile, "a hunch you are about to make one of your equipment decisions. So I'll ask the obvious: do we need both Stinsons with only one roundtrip a day?"

"No. We'll sell the older one. Whatever we can get for it will go toward a down-payment on another Ford."

"That's what I figured." Lindeman sighed. "Where are you going now?"

"Downtown to have breakfast with Henry. Then I'm picking up the mail-contract application. Should be back in a few hours."

Lindeman scratched his chin. "Listen, maybe you could do something for Joe. I'd try it myself but I know I couldn't pull it off. But you—"

"Try what?"

"Talk to Joe's dame. Maybe you could get through to her."

Barney rose and turned away. "I don't think so." He stepped out of the plywood-enclosed office he shared with Bud Lindeman. "What could I tell her?" He shook his head. "No."

"Tell 'er if she wants Joe she's gotta go along with his flying. If she doesn't, everything he's put into this half-assed outfit will have been for nothing."

Barney pursed his lips. "I don't know."

"Know, hell! We owe it to him."

"All right. Maybe."

"Terrific."

"Are you sure Joe isn't going to be awfully put out?"

"He'll never know, if you do it right." Lindeman hurriedly scribbled on the back of an old envelope. "Here's her address. Rosina" —he said it slowly as he wrote it—"Kyle."

"Listen, Barney. I care for you a lot. Probably more than is good for you."

"Are you married to Joe McFarland?"

She glanced down, absently kneading the small stub of a candle on the kitchen table. "I was trying to tell you that he and I had lived together for a long time. We were on the outs when you and I . . . Barney, I fell in love with you. It wasn't the most sensible thing I've ever done, but it happened, slowly. Anyway, I was irresponsible, and disloyal. Not to Joe, but to you. You're ten years younger and . . . *shit*."

"Does it matter? Does it really matter?"

She pressed the lip of the candle in toward the wick. "I'm not exactly proud of getting you tangled up in this." She looked up at him sitting across from her, the late-afternoon breeze bending the tree outside the window just behind him. "I also know I'd do it again. Probably. Honest to God, I couldn't help it, and I wouldn't have wanted to if I could have."

"But."

"But I'm thirty-three. And you're not. And Joe is a pig-headed shit and I owe him some things. I didn't used to think so; we weren't married, I used to tell myself. But it doesn't have anything to do with it, I've since found out. License or no, I'm responsible . . . to him."

"More than to me?"

"Yes."

All evening he had expected her to cry, especially when he confronted her. Now he found himself turning away to hide the tears sliding along his own cheek. Perhaps sensing this, she got up and went over to the cabinet to get a cigarette, then over to the stove for a match from the box she kept on one end of the brown iron top.

"Look, Barney. You'll find all this out for yourself one of these days. And you'll think back to this and maybe understand."

"Sure." He wondered if she could see that his breathing was jagged.

"Joe is pushing forty. He's done what he wanted to do. Now he wants something else. And so do I. There's one more rung up that I can go at work, and I want the satisfaction of that, but afterward I want something else. And for all intents I might as well be there now, Barney."

"I thought you loved me."

"Oh, honey, I do. But that's not everything. Where do *you* go from there? You can't not be young and wanting everything! Are you going to stay here in Binghamton just because you're in love? Of course not. But Joe is, and so am I. We're very similar, very close in some way. I don't know if we're precisely right for one another, but there's something pretty durable between us, and I guess we've got to follow it out. Just like you have to with your life. And you're way ahead there. This town has never seen anything quite like you, Mr. Burton. And won't again for quite a while after you leave it."

"What makes you so sure?" He turned back toward her. "What makes you so sure I'm going to leave it?"

"Because you have to. Because you're headed places few of us in this town could even imagine."

Barney sat quietly looking at the ivory-skinned woman with the jet black hair.

"Barney? Say something."

"I'm going to miss you, Rosina."

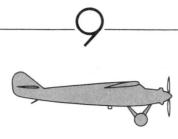

9

McFarland got right to the subject.

"You firing me, Barney?"

Barney tossed the pencil onto his desk and stood up, pretending to stretch.

"Let's say I'm demoting you."

"Demoting me to *what*?"

"Reserve pilot, with a cut in pay."

"The hell you are. I'm an officer of this company."

"You won't be for much longer. I'm asking you to resign as treasurer."

"By whose authority?"

"By a majority vote of the board of directors, as soon as I can convene a special meeting."

"You sonofabitch. *I'm* a director myself and I'm not voting myself out. And don't tell me Bud is gonna go along with you."

"He will, Joe. And even if he didn't, the by-laws of this corporation specify that any officer can be ousted by a majority vote. The other directors are Henry McKay and his father, and they'll vote with me. At best it's three-to-two against you. That's assuming Lindeman would be on your side. Only he won't. The reason I'm offering you a job as a reserve pilot is because of Bud. He figures he owes that much to you."

McFarland's face was lobster-red. "He owes me a hell of a lot more than that," he snarled. "How about all those months I worked without pay just so he could keep his crummy airline operating?"

Barney's face softened. "Bud appreciates your loyalty, Joe, and while you may not believe this, so do I. But you've put yourself in the position of becoming expendable. I don't want to see you leave Coastal Airways; you're a damned fine pilot. The trouble is that we don't really need you in Binghamton and that's where you insist on staying."

"There's a lot I could do," McFarland argued.

Barney shook his head. "If you were sitting behind this desk, instead of me, you'd never pay a pilot what you're making just to fly a Stinson from here to Newark and back once a day. Your salary's pegged to the trimotor. Be honest. Is it fair to the airline?"

"It seems more important to be fair to someone like me, who's been with Bud Lindeman right from the start, than to some two-bit corporation, or a Johnny-come-lately who got lucky."

"Meaning me." It was a statement, not a question. Barney's voice had turned cold again. "If it wasn't for this Johnny-come-lately, there wouldn't be any airline."

Larry Aroni picked this moment to stick his head inside the door. "Ship's all refueled and checked, Joe. Ready to roll. Oh, and I fixed the gyro you complained about. Mornin', Barney."

"Morning," Barney muttered. McFarland just nodded an acknowledgment. Aroni started to say something else but saw the tense looks on their faces, and backing out, closed the door. But the brief interruption had dissipated some of the anger.

"Sorry I said that, Barney. Oh, shit. Why the hell am I arguing with you? You know how I feel. Unfortunately, I know it isn't gonna change your mind."

"I'd be perfectly happy to wait a couple of days to see if you can change yours."

"I couldn't. I couldn't change Rosina's mind if you gave me a year. She's barely talking to me now."

"Suppose you told her that within a year—and maybe a lot sooner—we'd be moving the whole operation to Washington? And

I'll promise you right here and now I'll base you there. There must be some good hospitals in Washington."

For just a second McFarland smiled, looking reprieved. Then his face fell. "Binghamton's her home town. She doesn't want to leave. And in about six weeks, she expects to be made head surgical nurse."

"Yeah?"

"Well, it's a hell of a promotion for her and she has her heart set on it." McFarland puffed his cheeks. "It's the Stinsons or nothing."

Barney nodded as if he was agreeing to something. "That was the best I could do for you, Joe. I think it was a fair offer."

"From your standpoint, I suppose it was. Tell me something: why the sudden haste to make me the ex-treasurer? The cut in pay I can understand."

"Because we *are* moving to Washington within the year and all the officers will be based there. Also because your title as treasurer is strictly honorary. The lawyer who drew up the incorporation papers said we had to have a treasurer and Henry McKay didn't want the job. To put it bluntly, Joe, I don't need you as an officer, any more than I need an experienced trimotor pilot flying Stinsons."

"Right." McFarland rose to his full height and, spinning on his heels, he walked out.

Barney sat motionless for a few seconds, then eased into the small lounge area outside his door, nodding with forced pleasantness to the three passengers waiting to board the Washington-bound trimotor. He also managed a handshake for McFarland's copilot, who arrived to escort the customers to the plane.

"All set to leave, folks," Culbertson called out.

It had been Barney's edict that the copilot must greet boarding passengers before every departure, as well as visit the cabin at reasonably frequent intervals during the flight. An ancillary duty involved serving ham sandwiches and coffee after leaving Binghamton, the halfway point on both the northbound and southbound schedules. Barney still hadn't gotten the local baker to supply the free bread, but decided to serve the food anyway to justify his optimistic advertising: "Enjoy a delicious complimentary snack while relaxing a mile above the earth."

He watched Culbertson herd the passengers out to the sturdy

trimotor and waited outside Operations until the Ford bounced
down the runway, its Wright engines growling. Only to himself
would Barney ever admit that he both loved and hated to watch a
takeoff; each was a triumph, and also a reminder of a dream that
had ended in failure. He always would tell himself that each flight
was merely the climax of what he had made possible with personnel
selection, training standards, route development, advertising, selling, hard work. Which was perhaps true, except that it didn't
help.

Pilots, he thought. Pilots.

Not until the trimotor disappeared from sight did he turn and go
back into his office. When Agnes Jaffe returned from lunch, he
remained in a morose mood that was not improved by the arrival
of the mailman.

"Probably nothing but bills and complaints," he said to the secretary. "I'll finish dictating before I—"

The third envelope from the top of the unopened pile was just
visible enough for him to see the return address: *Office of the
Postmaster General.* Barney stared at it, unable to move.

"You were dictating 'relative to the new fuel contract we discussed on the phone Tuesday . . .' " Miss Jaffe wet her lips impatiently.

Barney didn't answer. He was opening the envelope, hands
trembling.

"Mr. Burton, what did you want to say next?" Miss Jaffe inquired.

"Jesus Christ," Barney said hoarsely, his eyes skimming over the
letter.

"I beg your pardon," she said as Barney kissed her and let out a
whoop.

On October 1, Coastal had taken delivery on a new Ford 5-AT
costing $55,000, with a second one scheduled to go into service
early in 1930; and, with the new mail contract, they had been
efficiently delivering mail for months. Yet it was a trying period for
Barney. On one hand, he had committed the company to expansion that more than doubled its route mileage and payroll, just as
the entire industry was beginning to feel the oncoming Depression.

It had cut Coastal's mail revenues nearly in half, and all Barney's promotional efforts had failed to increase passenger traffic enough to make up for the suddenly thinner mail payments. He rejiggered schedules to get maximum use of the enlarged fleet, sold a Stinson —Bud Lindeman went on a two-day mourning binge when it was signed over to an aircraft broker—and most employees found themselves working a seven-day week without overtime. They had no choice: there were no unions and they realized the airline's survival was at stake.

Barney was at the airfield by 7:00 A.M. and sometimes earlier, and he seldom got home before ten at night. On what was supposed to be his vacation, he spent the entire time working in Washington, taking one day off to find a one-bedroom apartment in Alexandria, just across the Potomac River and not too far from Hoover Airport, that their pilots could use and that he would eventually occupy.

Most of his employees looked forward to the move. Larry Aroni and Cal Motts were both bachelors. Al Davenport, who at Barney's suggestion Lindeman had named chief pilot and already assigned to Washington, had hated Binghamton.

Toward the end of the winter Henry McKay hosted a dinner party at which Aroni and Motts got mildly drunk. Lindeman stayed surprisingly sober; McFarland pointedly stayed away. When everyone had left, Barney and Henry McKay took their brandy snifters into the oak-paneled study.

"I'm not one to engage in corny sentiment," McKay said, "but I don't mind admitting I'll hate to see you go."

"I could lie and say I wish I wasn't going, but I'm not. There's no future here for me or Coastal. The only regret is that I won't have you around to lean on, Henry. But, hell, we haven't gone yet."

"True. And I'll be as close as your telephone, or as far away as your next flight to Washington. And I want to remain a part of your airline as long as I'm needed."

Barney grinned. "Does that include a loan anytime we need one?"

"Well, I'll always recommend one, and so will my father. Take my advice, though, Barnwell. Establish some credit contacts with a sound Washington bank now. Riggs, for example. They're conservatively managed and have an excellent reputation. Set up an account there. You don't owe Binghamton, Southern Tier, or me personally one drop of gratitude. You've been good for all of us."

"Any other pearls of wisdom, Henry?"

"I guess not. Everything all set in Washington?"

"I think so. We've leased a hangar and office space at Hoover, and we've got some downtown quarters in the National Press Building—a ticket office on the ground floor and offices on the third floor."

"The Press Building? Fourteenth and F Streets, I believe—right smack in the center of the business district. That's one hell of a location, and the building's only a few years old. You're not over-reaching yourself, are you? That's prime space."

"They gave us a good deal. What with the economy so lousy, they were having trouble finding tenants."

"Sounds great."

"Yeah. Funny thing though, while I was looking around for office space, I noticed that all the airlines have separate ticket offices. Seems like a waste of money. Wonder why they all don't get together and lease some large central location? Be more convenient for the public and more economical for the airlines. They could do this in every large city."

McKay looked at him with frank admiration. "That brain of yours never stops, does it?"

"Well, you boys certainly look pleased with yourselves."

"Dad, we didn't hear you come in." Henry McKay rose from his armchair.

"Good evening, sir." Barney shook hands with the elder McKay.

"Barney," the old man crooned. "So how was the self-congratulatory shindig my son lavished upon his sterling investment?"

"A great success, sir."

The old man smiled and nodded, waving Barney back to the comfort of the sofa as he accepted the armchair offered by his son.

Henry McKay poured his father a brandy. "Dad has some information. I can tell from that noncommittal expression of his."

"Smart-ass generation," snapped Mr. McKay. After sipping the brandy, he examined the amber liquid and chuckled to himself.

"But, yes, you're right. I do have some news. There will shortly be introduced in Congress legislation to be called the McNary-Watres Act," Frank McKay looked up, his eyes suddenly serious. "The sponsors are Senator Charles McNary of Oregon and Representative Lawrence Watres of Pennsylvania, but the real author is Walter Brown. Briefly, the bill is aimed at squeezing out some of the smaller, marginal, less efficient air carriers." He tasted the brandy again. "It has three main provisions. First, any air-mail contractor with two years' operating experience would be able to exchange his present authorization for a new route certificate good for ten years."

"Jesus," Barney said, "we haven't been flying the mail for two years. We'd be dead."

"Theoretically, that would seem to eliminate Coastal. But not entirely. The measure would recognize so-called 'pioneer rights,' which means no airline would be given the right to fly mail over a route started by another company."

Barney looked puzzled. "Then I don't see how the smaller carriers could be squeezed out."

"The fly in the ointment, Barney, is the bill's definition of pioneer rights. Namely, an airline with such rights is the lowest bidder who has operated a fixed daily schedule over a route system at least two hundred and fifty miles in length for not less than six months prior to the advertising for the new air-mail bids. I believe, in fact, that the low bidder also has to be what the bill terms 'responsible'—which gives the Postmaster General quite a bit of leeway in determining what makes a carrier qualify."

"Well." Barney pursed his lips. "We'd qualify under that definition. Our route system totals nearly seven hundred miles and we've been flying it since last May. We're near the six-month minimum and this bill hasn't even become law yet."

"True, but I haven't finished," the elder McKay cautioned. "The McNary-Watres Act also would completely change the government's system for making mail payments. What are you getting now—three dollars a pound?"

"That's right," Barney said.

"Under the new system, the maximum rate would be a dollar and a quarter per mile regardless of how much mail is carried. The space available for mail—in other words, the number of mail flights you operate daily—would be the criterion for the payments. You can see what this does to the smaller airlines with relatively few flights, and I'm afraid Coastal falls into that category."

Barney and Henry McKay glanced at one another. "We're in the soup," said the latter glumly.

"Not necessarily," Barney argued. "Not if we go ahead with our expansion plans, add more flights and more cities."

"That's one solution," Frank McKay agreed, "but your mail revenues are still going to decline under that new rate. But that's not the whole story, gentlemen. What I'm about to tell you is not in the McNary-Watres Act. This is strictly the brainchild of the Postmaster General, and I got it from him personally. When this legislation becomes law—and it's going through Congress, believe me —Brown is going to specify that no operator will get a mail contract unless he has compiled at least six months of nighttime flying. That would eliminate Coastal."

"The hell it will," Barney said. "We'll start flying at night immediately."

"What airports do we serve that have lighting facilities?"

"Buffalo, for one. Washington, of course. And Newark. Syracuse will have lights in another month. But not Binghamton and Rochester."

"How about lighted airways?"

"Buffalo–Washington's okay. Binghamton–Newark wouldn't qualify. But okay." Barney slapped his thigh. "We'll revise our schedules beginning next week, so at least one trimotor will be landing at Buffalo and Washington after dark. By the time this bill goes into effect, we'll have our six months' operating experience. I take it we have that much time, Mr. McKay?"

"I would anticipate the McNary-Watres Act will be signed sometime next April."

"I don't quite get it, Dad," Henry said. "Why is the Postmaster General doing all this?"

The elder McKay looked at Barney. "I'd like to know if you can guess the reason."

"It seems obvious, Mr. McKay. He wants the airlines to encourage passenger business and he figures if he can cut down the portions at the air-mail trough, they'll be more aggressive in the passenger market."

"Precisely what Walter Brown told me. So it'll be up to you, Barney, whether Coastal survives."

Barney put aside his brandy snifter. "We have to, Mr. McKay. We don't have any choice."

Barney followed the progress of the McNary-Watres Act along its tortuous legislative path. When its passage became inevitable, Barney summoned Cal Motts.

"You and I are taking a trip," he told Motts. "We'll start in Buffalo and work our way down through the entire system. We'll visit every big office building, all the travel agents, department stores, factories, and hotels in each city, and we'll deliver a sales pitch they're not going to forget. We'll even talk at schools if we have to—give the kids stuff to take home to their parents."

"Sure, Boss," Motts agreed amiably. "What are we selling—the advantages of air mail?"

"Partially. Mostly we'll be pushing air-travel. I want our passenger business up by at least twenty-five percent within the next two months. More. And sooner, if possible."

It wasn't easy. The Depression had made passenger traffic erratic, but Barney and Motts worked hard. Barney liked Cal, a lanky tow-headed youth with an ingratiating smile. He was more glib than articulate, shrewd rather than intelligent, but he was the essence of a good salesman—he gave the decided impression that he believed in the product.

Barney's own little black notebook was in constant use during the trip as he jotted down criticisms, suggestions, and fresh ideas relating to service both in flight and on the ground. He also made a point of talking to every one of Coastal's employees and was obsessed with a newspaper article concerning Boeing Air Transport's plans to hire registered nurses as cabin attendants. "Stewardesses," BAT called them, after considering such titles as "couriers" and "hostesses." They would be tried out on the San Francisco–Chicago route, and if the public liked the idea, more would be assigned to Boeing's flights.

Barney decided that as soon as the sales trip was over, he would sit down and figure out exactly how much it cost Coastal to operate per mile flown. If the ten-cents-a-mile fare could be cut to eight cents, perhaps the greater percentage of seats occupied would more than make up the supposed revenue loss.

On the last evening of their trip, Frank McKay phoned Barney's hotel room. "My boy, I just got a call from the Postmaster General. He's setting up a series of meetings with top airline officials in Washington starting May nineteenth. I think you or Lindeman should be there—as a matter of fact, you'll be getting an invitation by mail."

"All airlines, sir?"

"Definitely not. Just a few carriers—those selected by Mr. Brown himself. Coastal's included—and I don't mind telling you, if it weren't for me, you'd be out in the cold. Brown is asking Western Air Express, the Aviation Corporation, Transcontinental and Western Air, United Aircraft, Eastern Air Transport, and the Stout Line, plus a few others."

Barney was excited but puzzled. "Those are the big boys, Mr. McKay. We aren't in their league."

"I know that. Brown's including you because I asked him to. He notified me mainly because he wanted to explain why he *wasn't* inviting Coastal. Walter Folger Brown is going to rewrite the air map of the United States, Barney. By the time he's finished, he'll have revised all the air-mail routes and divvied them up among a handful of carriers. I asked him where Coastal fitted into the picture and frankly he said nowhere. At first, that is. I told him that in another five years, you'd have Coastal competitive with any airline in the country and you don't deserve to be left out of a major route realignment. You must have impressed him that day in Washington, because after he hemmed and hawed a while, he said he'd include Coastal. Said you seemed to have a lot of moxie and the right attitude toward the industry's future."

"May nineteenth, you said?"

"May nineteenth. But frankly, I think Lindeman should go."

Barney hesitated. He didn't want to disparage Bud but he was no hypocrite, either. He knew he could do a better job of representing Coastal's interests than Lindeman. Besides, he couldn't trust Bud Lindeman to stay sober, and Walter Folger Brown, Barney had gathered, was not the type who would tolerate a frequently intoxicated airline chief.

Frank McKay might as well have been reading his mind. "I realize you'd be the logical one to go, Barney, but Lindeman after all *is* the president. I think if we all had a talk with Lindeman beforehand, gave him a good briefing and so forth"—a diplomatic way of saying they had to warn Lindeman to keep away from booze, Barney thought—"well, I expect he'll do a fine job."

"I guess so," Barney said grudgingly, and wondered if it wasn't his age that McKay was concerned about.

He laid it on the line when he returned to Binghamton the next afternoon and told Lindeman about the Washington meeting. "I want your word you'll lay off the heavy drinking, Bud. The whole future of this airline depends on what we get out of Brown. He's straitlaced, Frank McKay says. We're finished if you botch this up with so much as a hangover."

"I won't let you down," Lindeman promised. "I wish you were going instead of me, though."

"Frankly, so do I. You worry the hell out of me. I wish Henry was going along with you, but his old man wouldn't let him take time off from the bank. I gotta trust you—and, so help me, I'll quit you if anything goes wrong."

"I promise I won't touch a drop while I'm in Washington. But I can't guarantee what'll come out of the meetings."

"Nobody else can, either. All I can do is send you there with a general idea of what we'd like to wind up with. Write this down." Lindeman got out a piece of paper. "We want our present route system left intact, plus an extension running from Washington down to Norfolk, Raleigh, Wilmington, Charleston, and Atlanta. Now that'll come as no surprise to Mr. Brown—I told him that's what we were planning the time I met him in his office. But I want a further extension—Atlanta northward to Pittsburgh, and from Pittsburgh to Buffalo via Binghamton. In effect, that gives us a circular route that starts from Buffalo, runs south all the way down the coast to Charleston, South Carolina, swings west to Atlanta, and then goes north up to Pittsburgh and Buffalo."

"I don't get it, Barney. Why Pittsburgh?"

"Because nobody is serving it on a north-to-south basis yet. It's virgin territory and we stand a good chance of getting our foot into the door. It's a major industrial center, and once we're established there . . . it's a kind of gateway for westward expansion."

"You're an ambitious young bastard," Lindeman said. "But suppose the Postmaster General doesn't go for this, or let's assume other carriers at this meeting will oppose it. What do I ask for as an alternative?"

"You'll have to play it by ear," Barney said. "I have a hunch there won't be much opposition. Basically, what we're seeking is a north-south expansion, and almost everyone else will be grabbing for east-west routes. East-west is supposed to be the potential money-maker. If you do run into trouble, start fighting for something we don't really want or couldn't hack at this stage, anyway— like a transcontinental route from Atlanta to the West Coast. Give yourself some bargaining room, Bud. It might be better to start out with some grandiose expansion plan that'll step on practically everyone's toes. Then you can pull back and tell 'em you'd settle for the circle route I've just outlined."

"I see what you mean. Nuts. You *should* be going, not me."

"You'll do just fine," Barney said, but even as he spoke the reassuring words, he didn't mean them.

For a solid week, he went over various route plans with Lindeman, not only the ones he had drawn up for Coastal but those he figured the other carriers would be seeking.

The Postmaster General had gone to considerable pains not to publicize the meeting, so Barney knew he wouldn't be reading about developments in the press.

"Keep me informed," he told Lindeman when he saw him off. "Don't hesitate to call me at any hour—at the office or at home."

"You want information or reassurance?" Bud asked with a grin. "Don't worry, chum. I'll be good, like I promised."

"Where will you be staying, in case I want to reach you?"

"At the Raleigh Hotel. Listen Barney, why the hell don't you just come along with me?"

"Somebody's gotta run the store while you're away, and there's no telling how long you'll be gone."

On the third night after his departure, Barney still hadn't heard from him and couldn't stand the suspense. He called the Raleigh, and somewhat to his pleasant surprise, Bud was in his room and seemed completely sober.

"Glad you called, Barney. Everything okay at the shop?" His voice was brisk, almost too brisk, Barney realized. It was pitched an octave higher than normal, as if Lindeman was nervous.

"Everything's fine here, Bud. I was wondering what's happening at your end."

"Nothing much to report so far. Brown spent the first day outlining what he wants to accomplish. Generally speaking, he'd redivide the present routes among the carriers present at the meeting. The most controversial thing that's come up involves Western Air Express and Transcontinental Air Transport. Brown wants them to merge. TAT's all for it but Pop Hanshue from Western told Brown to go to hell. I thought for awhile they were gonna throw punches at each other."

"What about our route proposal?"

"Well," Lindeman said doubtfully, "it hasn't really come up yet. I'm just standing by waiting for the major fireworks to end."

"What major fireworks?"

"Two new transcontinental routes, one central and the other southern. Brown wants to hand out the central route to TAT and Western, provided that they merge first."

"The hell with a transcontinental route," Barney growled. "Bud, I'll leave it up to you when to make our move, but the first chance you get put our proposal on the table."

"I will, son, but it's hard to decide when to jump in. I don't want to be premature."

"You don't want to be late, either. I wish to hell I was there."

"So do I," Lindeman said with feeling.

Barney felt a chill. "You're over your head, aren't you, Bud?"

"Way over, chum."

Barney sensed the relief in his voice now that the admission was in the open.

"I'll catch the first flight out tomorrow!"

"I'm sorry . . . You should have come in the first place."

"Don't apologize. Just keep your eyes open until I arrive."

As soon as he hung up, he called Frank McKay, breaking the

news that Lindeman needed help. McKay's reaction surprised him.

"I don't disagree that you should be there," he said, "but I think you should stay away from the sessions themselves. Let Lindeman represent Coastal with Brown, while you stay out of sight and call the shots."

"I don't understand, Mr. McKay. If I go there, I should be sitting in on the discussions."

"Generals work better directing a battle from the rear, not exposing themselves on the front lines."

"I still don't follow you."

"Barney, I have the utmost respect for Walter Folger Brown, but I think he's inviting future trouble with these meetings. He's making himself vulnerable to possible charges of collusion, secret deals, and a great possibility of political backlash. Mind you, everything he's doing is perfectly legal. The Watres Act is virtually a blank check for restructuring the whole airline industry. But sometime in the future, it could boomerang and become a political issue. When and if that happens, I wouldn't want your name connected with these conferences in any way. Let Lindeman front for you. Stay away from the spotlight."

"Have you talked this over with Henry?"

"No, I haven't. Until you called just now, we didn't know how things were going. I'll fill him in, if you want me to."

"I think you'd better, Mr. McKay."

The conference went on for days. Barney, chafing under the restrictions the elder McKay had imposed, spent the first five in the hotel room he was sharing with Lindeman. The double occupancy was Barney's idea. He wanted to make sure Bud stayed away from the bottle, and somewhat to his surprise Lindeman walked the straight and narrow. He reported by phone every time there was a break for coffee or lunch. Barney weighed the developments Lindeman recounted and sent him back into the next session with whatever advice seemed appropriate. Actually, there was little either could do at the moment; the heated debate swirling around the Postmaster General largely involved the two transcontinental routes up for grabs. Barney knew Coastal was like a distant cousin listening to the reading of a fat will, hoping against hope there would be something left when the immediate family had received their shares.

This status was changed on the sixth day, when a tired but suddenly cheerful Lindeman returned to the hotel around 5:30 P.M. and told Barney the Postmaster General had inquired about him.

"He asked me if you were coming to any of the sessions. Said he'd like to see you if you came into town."

"Into town? Then he doesn't know I'm here?"

"No. I wanted to check with you first. You wanted to stay low and I didn't know if I should tell Brown you're already here. Should I have?"

"No, you did just right. But I'll be damned if I'll stay submerged forever. I'm gonna call Henry's father."

It took him an hour to reach Frank McKay. "He's asking to see me, Mr. McKay, and I think I should. I'll stay away from his office as you advised, but would you happen to have his home telephone number?"

McKay allowed that he didn't think it would do any harm and gave Barney the number. Brown was not at home but Barney left word for him to return the call, and shortly after 10:00 P.M., the Postmaster General reached him. Brown suggested that Barney come to his office the next morning at eight o'clock—"I'd like to talk to you before the other participants arrive," he explained.

"I'd like to bring Mr. Lindeman with me, if that's satisfactory to you."

"Lindeman. Oh yes, Coastal's president. I've seen him at our conferences. I have no real objections, Mr. Burton. However, I do think it would be best if I saw you alone. If any of the other airline officers showed up earlier than expected, I wouldn't want them to know I had been discussing matters with Mr. Lindeman privately."

Barney arrived at eight sharp, alone and nervous. The secretary showed him right in.

"I half expected *you* to represent Coastal," Brown said as they shook hands and Barney sat down. "Somehow, I got the impression you were running the airline. Your president hasn't said two words since the meetings began."

"I'm the vice-president," Barney said. "Mr. Lindeman and I share responsibilities. Your invitation was directed to airline presidents and we felt Mr. Lindeman would be an able delegate." It was funny, Barney thought, how stilted and almost pompous his vocabulary became in Brown's presence.

"I see. Well, are you aware of what's transpiring?"

"Yes, sir."

"Frankly, young man, I don't see any sense in the government handing out its money to every little company flying around and calling itself an airline. Air transportation is the coming industry and I think it's high time the marginal operators, the small fry so to speak, are weeded out. As of today, there are forty-four airlines operating in the United States, and that's about forty too many. The future belongs to carriers with solid financial backing, imaginative development of air-travel markets, far less reliance on federal handouts for carrying the mail, and sound technical operations. Do you agree?"

"Wholeheartedly, Mr. Brown."

"Then can you give me any reason why an airline as small as Coastal deserves to take part?"

Barney's jaw tightened so hard he was almost gritting his teeth. "If you're speaking of the present, there is no reason whatsoever for our being here." Brown's eyebrows arched. "But if you're talking about the future, I can give you far more than one reason."

Walter Folger Brown leaned back in his black leather swivel chair and looked at Barney, a half-smile on his lips. "Now *that's* a very interesting answer, Mr. Burton. So interesting it deserves some elucidation."

"The size of an airline has nothing to do with its marketing practices, its operational efficiencies, and its vision. You cited financial status. We operate only five airplanes, but four of them are new Ford trimotors, and every aircraft in our fleet is owned free and clear—not one penny of indebtedness. Our cash flow from both mail and passenger business is sufficient to more than meet all operating expenses including the payroll. You ask for imagination in developing the market for air travel . . . I'll tell you something I haven't even told our board of directors or even Bud Lindeman, for that matter. I have a study underway to determine how much we can cut air fares to encourage more passenger traffic. I believe, sir, that fear and fares are the major obstacles to the development of air travel. If my study of Coastal's own fare structures shows we can put more people on our airplanes by charging less, and still make money, we're going to do it. Also we've been flying since 1927 and we haven't so much as scratched an airplane. We're paying our superintendent of maintenance as much as our pilots—and that's a decision I made personally. Yes, we're small. Our annual revenue wouldn't equal the monthly payroll of a company like Western or United Aircraft. We're minor-league compared to some of the others you're meeting with daily. But we're major-league in everything else *but* size—imagination, guts, ingenuity. And *that's* my answer to your question!"

The thin smile blossomed into a full-scale grin. "Mr. Burton, what does Coastal want?"

Barney handed him a map of the proposed expanded route system as he had explained it to Lindeman. "What we want and need is on this piece of paper, Mr. Brown. If you'd like, I'll leave it here so you can study it further."

The spoils conference ended six days later. The whole thing had taken twelve days. Only one participant went away empty-handed, and that was Western Air Express, which had been ordered to turn over most of its routes and equipment to a newly organized carrier called Transcontinental and Western Air—TWA.

At the same time, Coastal Airways was granted a ten-year certificate to carry mail and passengers over the "circle route" Barnwell Burton had envisioned. It was a victory for which he deserved most of the credit. Long before the actual award became official, he knew he had clinched it, and he planned accordingly. His first major decision was to buy three more Ford trimotors—one a brand-new 5-AT and the others used 5-AT's he picked up from Eastern Air Transport for the bargain price of $20,000 each. Lindeman opposed him, cornering Barney in the hangar the moment he heard about it.

"I don't like the idea of acquiring used transport planes," he argued. "The chances are that they're pretty beat up and it'll cost us almost as much to put them in shape as it would to buy us a new plane."

"They're in good shape," Barney said.

"How the hell do you know that?"

"I sent Aroni to New York last week to look them over. He says all they need is a good cleaning plus a couple of engine overhauls."

"If they're so good, how come Eastern's dumping them?"

"Because they're buying those new Curtiss Condors and their Fords are surplus."

"I didn't know that," Lindeman admitted.

"If you spent more time keeping up with industry news instead of burying your nose in the nearest bottle, I wouldn't have to make all the equipment decisions." Lindeman visibly twinged. "Sorry I said that, Bud, but it's true, dammit. For a guy who's president of this company, you sure don't act like it."

Lindeman decided to change the painful subject. "Maybe we should look at that Condor instead of putting all our eggs into the Ford basket. That's one hell of a plane—it's fifty knots faster than the Ford, the cockpit visibility is unbelievable, it's ten times quieter, and for comfort you can't beat it. Curtiss actually put sound-proofing into the cabin and they're using three-bladed props to reduce noise."

Barney nodded. "It's a great airplane, but not for us. It's twice as expensive as the Ford and it's a biplane, and, for my dough, biplanes are obsolete. And it's got a wooden airframe. I think the days of wood-built transports are over. Nope, I figure we'd better stick with the Fords until we can really afford to buy a better airplane."

Lindeman shrugged; he was used to losing his arguments with Barney and he had long since passed the point of resenting his figurehead status. He couldn't even get himself to hate the younger man for his cocky confidence and occasional arrogance. There were times when he actually feared him, knowing that Barney had the muscle to oust him from Coastal completely at any moment. From that fear sprang almost total subservience—and more drinking. He had no way of knowing the fear was unjustified, that Henry McKay had been urging Barney to dump Lindeman for weeks.

"He's doing you absolutely no good whatsoever," the young banker had pointed out over lunch at the businessmen's club. "The salary he's making is pure charity. You told me yourself you've got Davenport doing most of the training and check-riding, because Lindeman half the time isn't sober enough to fly. Why the heck do you keep carrying him on your back?"

"Because he carried me on his—a long time ago," Barney shot

back. "He'll be president of Coastal as long as he wants the job."

"Give him some honorary title. Make him president-emeritus or chairman of the board or—"

"You're the chairman of the board."

"Which makes about as much sense as calling Lindeman the president. You're the whole damned airline, Barney. You should be president *and* chairman. You'd be doing Bud a favor if you retired him. Hell, he's a laughingstock. Everyone knows who's running the airline. I can't understand why the man's own pride won't force him to quit."

"He hasn't much pride left. Being president is all he has."

McKay eyed him amusedly. "I thought once you had the guts to do it."

Barney looked squarely into the banker's eyes. "I'm about to be tough, Henry. Coastal is moving in thirty days to Washington."

TWO

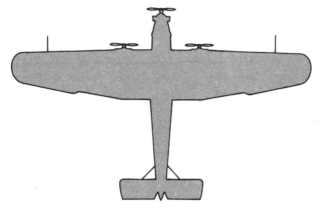

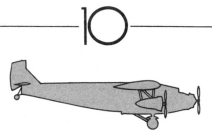

10

"Good morning, Mr. Burton."

"Morning," Barney nodded as he passed his secretary's desk. "Get me Cal Motts—better yet, ask him to come up. I'd like to see him."

Barney left the door of his office open and, pulling several folders from his briefcase, he tossed it onto the small two-seater couch. A plane's engines revved up somewhere outside, causing Barney to glance at the windows. In the distance a trimotor was lining up for takeoff.

The move to Washington had probably saved Coastal Airways from extinction, he thought. By concentrating the bulk of his manpower in the pivotal city on the airline's system, he was far better able to dictate its operation. His decisions were implemented faster; he could control expenditures; he was closer to the center of things and had a much better chance of anticipating economic shifts that would affect the airlines, not to mention the levers of political influence now within reach.

Barney opened the top folder containing the weekly status reports and began his habitual morning review. Pilots, mechanics, sales personnel, clericals—he flipped through quickly. Four pilots in Buffalo, two in Atlanta, the rest in D.C. Washington had given him a centralized command post.

"Morning."

Barney looked up as Cal Motts and the D.C. station manager, Ben Shub, walked in.

"Have a seat," he said as the two men made themselves comfortable in chairs facing his desk. Barney got up and came around to the front of it, propping himself on a corner of the desk top. "I got an idea. Cal, I want you to draw me up a list of all employees who work in the Press Building, including such items as their marital status, if any, and whether they have kids, how many, and so on. Ben, you do the same for everyone who works at Hoover."

Motts and Shub glanced at each other.

"Sure, Boss," Motts said. "What do you have in mind?"

"Free weekend flights over our system. For a whole family."

His traffic manager and his station manager looked puzzled. Motts smiled. "Well, I guess they'll appreciate it, Barney. It'll make for good employee relations."

"Screw good employee relations. An awful lot of people come out to the airport Saturdays and Sundays, just to watch the planes, including our employees. So I decided we could use a little psychology on these sightseers. When they see a Coastal plane ready to leave, they'll see people like themselves getting on that plane—just as casual and matter-of-fact as if they were boarding a train or bus. In other words, gentlemen, they'll get the idea that air-travel can be routine. That other families actually fly. That Coastal carries not just businessmen, but ordinary Americans who are intelligent enough to recognize the advantages of traveling by air."

"But they aren't 'ordinary Americans,'" Motts pointed out. "They're our own employees and they're flying on free passes."

"Sure," said Barney, "but those spectators won't know it."

"Not bad," Motts said, Shub nodding in agreement.

Barney rubbed his eyes. "Post some notices announcing the availability of the family passes. We might even have a name for them—we would call 'em 'familiarization flights.' But when we get this thing rolling, I want some simple ground rules followed. Every employee should dress neatly, and that includes children.

Ties and jackets are a must. Anyone who looks like a slob will be denied boarding. And one more thing—under no circumstances is anyone to reveal he or she is not a legitimate, fare-paying passenger. That applies to what's said either on the ground or in the air. That clear? Good. When you put up notices, you'd better suggest that anyone planning to take a familiarization flight should check our reservations office on the day of departure to make sure there's space available. And, Ben, tell your people at the airport if a customer shows up at the last minute and the flight is full, whatever employee is riding should be bumped." Barney snapped his fingers. "Maybe we should offer newsmen free passes too."

Shub seemed embarrassed.

"You got problems, Ben?" Barney demanded. "That order on priority should be very clear."

"It's clear, Mr. Burton," Shub replied calmly. "But I think now would be a good time to establish some kind of policy for *any* employee riding on a pass—including company officials." He spoke the last two words with an inflection approaching bitterness.

"The policy already *has* been established," Barney snapped. "If the last seat in the airplane is occupied by anyone from Coastal and a paying passenger needs a seat, the employee or officer gets the hell off. There are no exceptions; that includes me."

"Does it include Mr. Lindeman?"

"It includes Lindeman. I said no exceptions. And if anyone gives you trouble, call me."

"Someone's already given me trouble," Shub mumbled.

"Okay—who?"

"I'd rather not say, Mr. Burton." Shub looked nervous.

"I'd rather you did. Except I've got a pretty good idea. Lindeman?" The station manager hesitated. "Come on, Ben. Even if he knew you told me, your job's safe. I can handle Bud."

"It was Mr. Lindeman," Shub admitted reluctantly. "Dammit, Mr. Burton, what the hell was I supposed to do? He's the president of the airline!"

"What happened?"

"It was last Friday. Flight 12. Mr. Lindeman was going up to Binghamton for the weekend. Believe it or not, he was the twelfth passenger—we were using a 4-AT. I even kidded him about how lucky he was to get the last seat. We were just about ready to call the flight when some guy comes up and wants a ticket on Flight 12 all the way to Buffalo. I asked him wait a minute, ran down to the gate and caught Mr. Lindeman just as he was boarding. I told him we had a revenue passenger and would he give up his seat. He . . . well, he asked me if I was kidding. I said no, that I assumed anyone from Coastal would have to give priority to a ticketed passenger. Mr. Lindeman said my assumption was wrong and he started to get on the plane."

Shub paused.

"Go ahead. What happened next?"

"Well, I guess I got a little mad, because I grabbed his arm. I don't remember exactly what I said then but I was more or less pleading with him to change his mind. Grabbing him was my big mistake. He really chewed me out. Called me about six dirty names, reminded me he was the president and if I wanted to keep my job I'd better get the hell out of his sight. It was embarrassing. Most of the other passengers heard the whole argument, if you could call it an argument. It didn't last more than a few seconds."

"What did you tell the guy who wanted to go to Buffalo?"

"That the flight was full and that I couldn't get anyone on the plane to relinquish his seat. I said I was sorry and I offered him space on Flight 10 Saturday morning. He told me no thanks, he'd take an overnight train."

"I'll take care of the matter," Barney said wearily. "Meanwhile, you both can go to work on those lists. We're gonna make people think this is the best-patronized airline in the country if I have to drag our employees out to the airport weekends and carry 'em on board."

"Is that all, Mr. Burton?" asked Shub.

"Yes. Thanks, Ben."

Shub rose quickly and left. Cal Motts, Barney knew, was hanging around for a reason.

"What's the problem?" Barney asked.

"You mentioned free rides for newsmen. I can see that we might be headed for some trouble if we're too lenient about giving away tickets to members of the press. There must be five hundred newspapermen in this town. If we start offering free transportation to every news hound in the Congressional Directory . . . This isn't Binghamton."

"Good point." Barney paced along the window.

"How about limiting the passes to guys who actually write about aviation . . . cover it on a regular basis."

"You know any? Personally, I mean."

"Only the ones Bud has introduced me to, but they seem top-notch. Bud took me along to see a little guy, Ernie Pyle, who lives on N Street. He seemed to know every pilot in the country. He loves flying, writes a column on the side about aviation for the Washington *Daily News*, and believes in the business."

"I should meet him." Barney stopped pacing. "He could probably give us names of other reporters who would qualify."

"Okay. I'll get Bud to take us over to his place some night." Motts glanced at his watch. "Jesus, I've got to get going."

After Cal Motts left, Barney buzzed his secretary and asked her to order delivery of the *Daily News*. Being in the habit of reading only the morning editions, he had never seen the afternoon paper. When the first issue came, hours later, Barney flipped to Pyle's column and read intently. Frugal with his words, balancing them casually but precisely, Ernie Pyle was obviously good at his job. So when Cal Motts called late in the day to say that Bud had wangled an invitation from Pyle, Barney Burton immediately accepted.

As it turned out, the host was "having a few friends over," as Bud explained when the cab pulled up at 456 N Street Southwest. Cal Motts, Lindeman, and Barney Burton walked up to the second-floor apartment and were greeted at the door by Pyle's wife, Jerry, who greeted them like old friends. Even after a few moments of conversation with her, Barney realized that she knew little about planes and flying but simply welcomed anyone in whom her husband expressed interest.

"Ernie collects friends like some people collect stamps," she said, smiling. "Last week a mob of pilots came over and there was a new face in the crowd, a very distinguished man with white hair. Turned out to be a patrolman Ernie had run into somewhere. But enough of this. I'm being a terrible hostess. Come in, come in," she ordered cheerfully and led the way back into the apartment.

There were four people in the living room: a Navy lieutenant; a tall, attractive young woman with cropped brown hair and boyish features; and two young men in shirtsleeves sitting on the floor, their backs propped against the sofa. Pilots from the look of them, thought Barney. Ernie Pyle appeared from the bedroom: a thin-faced pixie of a man in a moth-eaten pullover and a grin that would have melted an iceberg.

"Hi, Bud!" he said. "Cal. And this must be Barney. I'm Ernie Pyle. Come meet our other friends."

Two of the other "friends" turned out to be TWA pilots. The Navy lieutenant, to Barney's surprise, was Apollo Soucek, who had just set a world altitude record of 43,166 feet, as Ernie Pyle was quick to announce. Catching the young woman by the elbow, Pyle turned back to Barney.

"I'd like you to meet Amelia Earhart."

Barney looked dumbstruck.

"Amelia, this is Barney Burton, Coastal Airways."

"My God," Barney finally managed to say. "This is a great pleasure. I was just reading about your new speed record. A Lockheed Vega, right?"

"Yes," she said, smiling warmly.

"Must be a great airplane. I wouldn't mind having a few on our system, except we're pretty much committed to multi-engine equipment."

"Fords, I've heard," said Amelia Earhart. "I flew in one of the first, but only as a passenger. But Ernie here has logged a lot of time in the Tin Goose."

"My, yes," exclaimed Pyle, rolling his eyes. "I covered the first coast-to-coast trip in '29. That was a TAT Ford trimoter. What a trip! Took the train from New York to Columbus, then the tri-motor to Wanoka, Oklahoma, where we had to get on the train again. Then we picked up another Ford at Clovis, New Mexico, and flew it on into Los Angeles. It took us . . . forty-eight hours."

"Hon," Jerry Pyle interrupted, "why don't you ask folks to sit down and make themselves comfortable while I fix up some drinks and stuff."

"Okay, right. Please." He motioned people toward armchairs and the sofa. "Anyway, today you can do it in thirty-six hours by plane alone."

"It should be less than that," Soucek broke in, then turned to the blond TWA pilot slumped against the sofa. "You guys have to overnight in Kansas City, don't you?"

"Yeah," the pilot answered. "Because the darn government won't spent the money to light enough airways. Amelia here flew across the Atlantic nearly *three* years ago—the Atlantic—and we still can't fly transcontinental without that hotel stop."

"It isn't lack of lighted airways so much," Barney put in. "We need faster planes. The Ford is just too slow. I've heard rumors Boeing is designing a new transport—a low-wing job with two engines—supposedly faster than a pursuit plane."

"Son, those rumors are a dime a dozen," Lindeman scoffed. "I've heard that about the Boeing, too, but it's supposed to be another trimotor. It'll probably wind up with six engines and won't get off the ground."

Amelia Earhart leaned forward into the conversation. "Lockheed will build a multi-engine transport one of these days. Combine the Vega's speed with the payload of a Ford, and you'd really have quite an airplane. By the way, have any of you heard about the new transport Ford's building?" Nobody had. "It's another trimotor," she continued, "but about three times bigger than the Goose. Bill Mayo told me about it when I was in Detroit a few weeks ago. He showed me the prototype. It's huge! It has two engines mounted in the wings and the third on top of the fuselage with four-bladed props. Mayo told me it'll carry up to forty passengers. He called it the 14-AT."

"Sounds too big," Bud Lindeman groused. "I'm with Amelia, Barney, I wish we'd sell all seven trimotors and buy Lockheeds."

"We'll unload the Fords someday," Barney sighed, "but you can't sell today's passengers on single-engine ships. They want the security of multi-engined equipment; the problem is fear."

"What was the name of that pilot who flew your Atlantic trip, Amelia?" Soucek asked.

"Bill Stultz. A wonderful person, God rest his soul. About a year after our flight, he landed a half-mile short of the runway at Roosevelt Field."

The talk shifted to high-altitude flight, and Soucek was telling about his own experiences.

"After the first flight, I landed at the Naval Air Station and as soon as I climbed out of the plane, I asked for a cigarette. Ernie was the first to hand me one. The next time I went up—I think it was the record flight—I came down and damned if he wasn't there handing me another cigarette."

"Then you landed one day and asked where the hell I was," Pyle laughed. "You wouldn't smoke until I got there. I had to rush over from Hoover Airport to the Air Station just so you could bum another cigarette."

"Ernie gave me my nickname," Soucek said proudly. " 'Soakum,' everyone calls me."

"You had that long before I met you," said Pyle, his eyes dancing. "And they'll call you that even when you make admiral."

Barney leaned back. He had been accepted. Meeting Pyle, Amelia Earhart, Apollo Soucek—it was like being introduced to royalty, which in a way they were. They were as obsessed with flying as he was. What meant most to Barney was that he felt a special kinship with them, a natural camaraderie. He had been accepted by these fliers; he was a member of the fraternity and they had made him feel welcome and wanted as a new friend. And this he treasured. That second-floor apartment was an aviation mecca, and there he was, in the middle of it, loving it.

Barney bent forward and whispered, "Miss Earhart, would you like to have lunch with me tomorrow?"

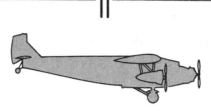

11

It was the most posh speakeasy in town, numbering among its patrons several congressmen and senators and a distinguished cabinet member. Barney arrived a half hour early, tipped the maitre d' generously for the best table in a secluded corner with an excellent view, and left to pace the street and wait. Promptly at noon he reappeared; Amelia Earhart arrived a few moments later and they were seated immediately with much flourish.

The corner table, as it turned out, afforded little privacy, with waiters materializing every few minutes to adjust the flowers, refill the full water glasses, spin the wine bottle chilling in the ice-bucket . . . and every time it was a different waiter, each come to steal a glance at her. Barney couldn't blame them. She really was quite beautiful, he thought, but wondered how much of her effect was due to her irresistible accomplishments. How could anyone separate the person from the special aura of growing fame—that tingling sense of her inevitable and exciting place in history? Amelia Earhart, he caught himself repeating in his mind. Amelia Earhart.

"Is something wrong?"

Barney shook his head emphatically. "On the contrary. Everything is wonderful."

She smiled that radiant smile of hers and it was like basking in sunshine. "You mustn't work so hard, Barney. You're too young to be devoting yourself so totally."

Barney shrugged. "There's not much choice at this point. The company is young and it's been a rough year. Rough on managers, and even worse for pilots."

She nodded, looking sympathetic.

"I know. Ernie is pretty worked up about it, too—seven thousand qualified transport pilots and only fifteen hundred jobs. Captains flying a hundred twenty-five hours a month for two hundred fifty dollars, and copilots flying a hundred sixty hours and drawing half what the pilots do."

"Yes, it's pretty bad at the moment."

"A lot of copilots that pass through Ernie's place say that airlines aren't paying anything for the first six months, on the theory that they're receiving valuable training for free."

"It's true, I'm afraid. And one of these days the pilots will form a union and the industry will suddenly realize how important those guys are."

"I think it has already happened," she said, sipping the wine and making a pleasant face at him. "That *is* good."

"You were saying."

She put down her glass. "Yes, though I'm not sure I should be." She paused. "Well. If I can tell you off the record, as they say in Washington . . . Six guys—pilots from United, American, and Northwest—Ernie says met very privately last month in a Chicago hotel to discuss the formation of a union."

"There have been other attempts," said Barney. "Air Mail Pilots of America, National Air Pilots, Professional Pilots . . . they all faded."

"True enough. But there wasn't a Depression then. I think this one may stick."

"You may be right."

"More wine, monsieur?" the waiter broke in.

"Please," Barney said, trying not to sound annoyed.

"And what about you, Mr. Burton? When are you going to organize a union for the managers?"

"I'd be too young to qualify," Barney chuckled.

"Don't be so self-conscious. The industry is young, too. And the personnel has to be; present-day equipment requires a lot of physical coordination."

"I'm sorry to say you're right." Barney looked chagrined. "Unfortunately I haven't got any. Barnwell Burton, world's worst pilot."

"What's this?"

"It's true. I couldn't pilot a plane for love nor money."

"What's the problem?"

"The hands and feet won't do what the instructor says they should. I overcompensate like crazy. Bud Lindeman didn't have a single gray hair until he took me up one day. By the time we landed he looked like a polar bear."

"Well, the answer may be simple."

"Simple?"

"Yes." She leaned forward on her elbows. "Listen, Barnwell, I think I know what your problem is. It's not going to solve anything for you so far as becoming an airline pilot. But it might help your ego to know why you're so bad in a cockpit."

Barney felt dumbfounded. "Go on."

"It's simple. You need glasses."

"Glasses?"

"That's what I said."

"Glasses."

"Yes." She took out her compact and held its mirror toward him. "Look at the lines in your forehead." Barney self-consciously erased them, and doing so realized he couldn't see himself in the mirror any longer.

"I've been squinting."

"Correct." She smiled at the self-discovery. "I was sure you wore glasses, but were being vain about wearing them when you were reading the menu."

"What do you mean?"

"You had it about six inches from your nose."

"You're right!" Barney felt ecstatic.

"And while we're on the subject, Mr. Burton, I do wish you would weigh the importance and future of those who are going to command the air-transportation industry . . . from the ground. You can only do so much about it at seven thousand feet. The tough part, the major part will be down here. This is where it will have to happen first, before it can happen up there."

"Miss Earhart."

"Yes?"

"Would you like some champagne?"

She smiled back at the beaming Barnwell Burton.

"I'd love some," she said.

Bud Lindeman didn't wait to be announced. He stormed right into his partner's office.

"Why in blue blazes did you cut captains' pay to two hundred a month?" Lindeman half-shouted.

"Good afternoon, Bud."

"Well?"

Wait till he hears I've cut copilots' pay to $100, thought Barney. He sighed. "Bud, we either prune overhead or we go in belly-up. As soon as things improve, I'll restore the cuts, but the pilots have to go along with me for the time being."

"And what—*what* are those card slots about? Those things Aroni is installing above the windows of the trimotors?"

Barney held his chin in his hand. "They're for advertisements."

"No!" Lindeman roared. "I won't stand for it." He crossed his arms in defiance. "Absolutely not."

"Why not?" Barney said calmly.

"Because it's . . . it's . . ." Lindeman sputtered with anger. "It's goddamned undignified, that's why."

"Agreed. But it's also lucrative—pure gravy."

"You want our ships to look like streetcars?"

"Bud, I'd put advertising messages on the underside of the wings if it would mean additional income."

"So what the hell are we gonna call our pilots—airborne motormen? Christ, Barney."

"Look, I agree. The messages aren't very dignified. But business is bad enough right now to make pride something of a luxury."

"We'll lose passengers."

"Maybe. But I'm surprised at your being so concerned about that."

"What are you referring to?"

"Not giving up your seat to a paying customer when asked, and giving Shub a really hard time about it, too."

"Well," Lindeman said weakly, "I'll admit I was something of a prick. I suppose I should apologize to Ben."

"That might be nice. In the meantime, how does this pass priority system strike you?"

Barney shoved the notice toward Lindeman, who picked it up and scanned it quickly.

"I see my signature is required," said Lindeman.

"You're the president and this is a major policy."

"Hmm—Looks good, Barnwell." Lindeman gathered himself upright to better look the part. "Where's a pen?"

Barney smiled and unscrewed the cap of his Parker, then handed the pen to his partner. "By the way," he said with studied nonchalance. "We're averaging only six passengers per flight . . . only slightly above the break-even point with a load factor of fifty percent." Barney rose from his chair and began packing his briefcase with the evening's work.

"Yeah," said Lindeman, concentrating on signing the document in his best hand. "What the hell's a load factor?"

"The industry's measure of occupancy on each flight." Barney snapped the briefcase shut. "Six passengers on an airplane seating twelve is a 'load factor' of fifty percent."

"My, how fancy. You mean our planes are flying half-empty."

"Yes, and we're barely breaking even. And I don't see us increasing the percentage the way things are in the country with this lousy Depression."

"Yeah," Bud said absently as he reread the policy notice he had just authorized.

"Right now we're taking in ten cents a mile per passenger and it costs us six cents to operate. A ten percent reduction in fare, for instance, would give us nine cents per mile, or a profit of three cents per."

"I think I'm with you."

"If we could increase the load factor to seventy or eighty percent, that would more than make up for it."

"Make up for what?" Lindeman looked up. Barney was standing by the door, his briefcase in his hand and his jacket slung over his shoulder.

"I'm going to cut the fares by ten percent."

"The hell you say." Lindeman slapped his thigh. "We're still taking in more from mail than from passengers. A fare cut won't get us as much new business as you think, but I suppose I should let you try it and get some experience at landing on your ass."

"How much would you like to bet?"

"A hundred bucks," snapped Lindeman.

"Three months?"

"Done."

"Good night, Bud."

"Good riddance."

Barney timed the advertising campaign for the new fares for the spring of 1932, planning it without the help of an agency so as to save money. With Cal Motts helping, he composed the copy slogans himself.

" 'Bringing air fares down to the level of train travel.' That's good, Boss. But how about 'down-to-earth air fares'?" Motts looked expectantly at Barney, who had his nose buried in the copy. "Where are your glasses?"

"Oh, yeah—my *reading* glasses." Barney mumbled, feeling around his vest. "Ah, here they are." He picked up the wire-rimmed spectacles and slipped them on.

The ads were good, each one tailored to the city where it appeared and listing Coastal's fares to the other cities in the system. The first morning the new fare ads were run, Postmaster General Brown called to express his "delight," as did Jack Frye, TWA's vice-president, who called from Kansas City.

"That's a great campaign," he said. "I heard all about it from our station manager in D.C."

"Thanks," Barney said. "I just hope it works out, or I'll be loading baggage soon."

"I wouldn't worry. We cut our transcontinental fare a lot more than fifteen percent in January last year and traffic jumped four hundred fifty percent. By the way, how tight are you locked into that puddle-jumping airline of yours?"

"Fairly tight," Barney said cautiously. "What do you have in mind—or are you just fishing?"

"Fishing for a good man, frankly. I'd like to talk to you about joining TWA. I think we could make it worth your while."

Barney was intrigued and flattered. He was aware that he already had acquired something of a reputation as a business prodigy —and so he had thought about what he would do if he were offered a chance to go with another airline. His ego, he knew, was against him. A vice-president of Coastal at twenty-four, he didn't expect to be offered the equivalent title or authority on a larger carrier, but he decided to test Frye, an extremely forthright executive.

"If you're thinking of a vice-presidency, I'd be interested in coming out and talking to you," Barney said. "Otherwise, we'd both be wasting our time."

"Well, you sure as hell wouldn't be loading our baggage," Frye chuckled wryly, "but I honestly couldn't promise you more than a reasonable management position—with promotion to a vice-presidency contingent upon how things worked out."

The connection suddenly became bad and crackled with static. "I think I'd better stay here," Barney shouted. "Big-frog-in-a-small-pond syndrome, I'm afraid. But I appreciate your interest."

In less than two months Barney cut fares by fifteen percent, not ten, spent $3,500 advertising the reductions, and was interviewed by newsmen from most of the Northeast's papers, large and small. Four times he made page one. Confident young Mr. Burton made for a good story.

Bud Lindeman paid off the bet after Coastal's load factors soared to a daily average of seventy-eight percent by mid-April of 1932, and profits rose accordingly—enough to permit abandonment of the "streetcar ads." Barney's latest success, however, triggered the president's abdication of responsibility. Suddenly Lindeman was drunk almost daily, taking three-hour lunches and returning to the office in mid-afternoon in a stupor. Barney pleaded, scolded, and threatened—going so far as to arbitrarily remove all the whiskey bottles Lindeman had in his office. Bud was relatively sober when he discovered this transgression and stormed into Barney's office.

"You have no right to interfere with my private life!" he yelled.

"You have no right to get smashed in front of employees!" Barney roared back. "You're nothing but a goddamned disgrace to the company and to yourself."

"So be it, chum. You don't give me anything to do around here, so I might as well get drunk."

"I'd give you plenty to do if you stayed sober long enough to do it."

"Well, I'm sober now. So give me something to do. Let me make a decision. Set a policy. Take some action. Go ahead, Barney—what'll it be?"

"The hell you're sober. Look at your clothes—you must be sleeping in them. You look like a sink full of unwashed dishes. You haven't shaved for two days. Your eyes are so bloodshot I could drain them for a transfusion. You clean yourself up, stay off the bottle for a week, and I'll let you start making like a president."

Lindeman glared, muttered "shit!" and stomped out, passing Cal Motts and Larry Aroni on the way.

Aroni pursed his lips in a silent whistle. "Not good, Barney. You're in for some trouble."

"*We're* in for some trouble, Larry. *We.*"

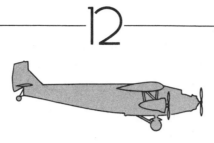

12

Bud Lindeman did not attend the small ceremony at Hoover Airport held in honor of Ernie Pyle's being named managing editor of the *News*. Amelia Earhart presented him with a truly handsome wristwatch and presented Jerry with a beautiful jewel box. Everyone congratulated them both and smiled broadly. It was a step up for him, to be sure, and he wasn't exactly moving away, yet everyone knew it wouldn't be the same—not really. Ernie would have to give up covering aviation; earlier that morning he had turned in his last column for the afternoon edition.

After the little ceremony, Barney invited them all back to Coastal's facilities at the field, where food and refreshments were waiting in the corner of a hangar. Pyle sought him out at the gathering to thank him for his thoughtfulness, and they talked for some minutes and watched the guests partake of the sandwiches and salads arranged with obvious care atop the freshly cleaned workbenches.

"Incidentally," said Pyle, "some of the Postmaster General's work may be coming unglued soon, now that Roosevelt's been elected."

"You really think so?" asked Barney, much concerned.

Ernie Pyle shrugged. "Brown meant well, I suppose, but I've heard rumors that some of his dealings might not have been exactly kosher."

Barney nodded, all too aware of how vulnerable the Postmaster was on that score. There was a roar of laughter at the other end of the room, where Amelia Earhart had been encircled by admiring young airmen.

"Marvelous, isn't she?" Pyle said.

"Yes," said Barney, softly. There was something so alive and fresh about her.

"Come on," said Pyle, putting down his drink, "let's see what they're up to," and took Barney by the shoulder and steered him through the crowd.

Barney did not need to actually hear the small group's conversation to know that the inevitable topic was flying and the machines that fly.

"So there's Pop Hanshue," one of the pilots was saying, "Mr. Western Air Express, looking very proper. And this twit asks him when he is going to try a new Curtiss Condor. And Pop says, 'Not until they build a tunnel through the Rockies.' "

The small circle convulsed again, Amelia coloring with laughter.

"Oh, God," said the pilot, wiping away a tear. "It was incredible. What would Pop Hanshue do with it anyway? Western has ordered this gigantic Fokker."

"The F-32?" asked Barney.

"Yes. It's so big and luxurious there's one model with a private smoking lounge."

"Yeah," Larry Aroni broke in, "it may have a lot of fans because it's the first four-engined job, but it's a plumber's nightmare. Those air-cooled rear engines on the tandem-mounted power plant just won't get enough air."

The blond young pilot was shaking his head. "I think you're wrong. They've engineered it very carefully. It even has an extinguishing system for in-flight fires."

"So does the Condor," said Aroni, sounding unconvinced. "And it's just as bad. I wouldn't take either one of 'em over a Ford Tin Goose."

"Yeah," said the pilot, suddenly assuming a winged stance with arms outthrust. " '*Smooth as a yacht, swifter than the wind.*' "

Even Aroni laughed at the dramatic rendition of Ford's latest advertisement.

"Gentlemen," Amelia said, as the flasks came out and drinks were poured. "It's time for a toast," and everyone murmured their consent. "To the best friend a flier ever had," she said. She raised her glass toward Ernie, as did everyone else, and the mood of the gathering shifted in that silent moment as people clicked glasses and flasks with the Pyles and sipped. Barney suddenly realized she was looking at him expectantly and that as the host he should be saying something. He cleared his throat.

"I, ah, want to thank you all for coming. It's a happy yet also sad occasion for us who have come to know and love these two people." He suddenly remembered the paper wedged in his pocket and took it out. "I don't know if we will ever have such an understanding heart among us again. As I have often said, Ernie Pyle's head is clearly in the clouds." The warm laughter rippled back through the circle of friends. "And it is only his skill as a typist that has saved him for the greater rewards he is now about to reap. Ernie's last aviation piece will be in this afternoon's paper. I asked him about it earlier and he let me read the corrected copy, which I have here. Aside from being a classic example of bad spelling . . . I think it is its own tribute to what he has given us all." Barney put on his glasses and read: " 'This column has tried to feel with those who fly. It has recorded the surprised elation of those who have risen rocketlike into renown, has felt despair with those who have been beaten down by the game, has shared the awful desolation of those who have seen their close ones fly away and come back only in the stark blackness of the newspaper headlines . . . This is the end of what to me has been an epoch.' "

The crowd applauded. Barney looked up to see Amelia looking misty-eyed at Ernie. It was strange. Parts of this last column of his had a significance for each of them, but the entire thing could have been written for her alone, almost as if it were a personal letter to and about her.

The guests turned back to one another and resumed their conversations. The Pyles began saying their farewells; the party would soon break up. Barney offered to drive Amelia back into town and twenty minutes later they left.

"I'm going to miss him," said Barney, glancing sideways at her as he drove.

"Yes," she said quietly and turned away to look out at the passing landscape.

Ernie was right, he thought. It was the end of something for all of them. Afflicted and frightened, the country awaited the New Deal, and the airlines were as jittery as everyone else. It was a miracle that they kept operating at all with fifteen million people unemployed and the disintegrating economy sapping confidence. Yet he sensed what Ernie did—that they were approaching a point where air-travel was about to be revolutionized in every phase, even though its present primitive state was all too apparent despite the industry's reassuring statements.

Twenty-five airlines; seven hundred daily flights all told. The biggest outfit now was United, formed with Brown's blessings by the consolidation of Boeing Air Transport, Varney, National Air Transport, and Pacific Air Transport. Seven hundred flights flown by four hundred fifty ships. Impressive, except for the fact that eighty percent of all the airline planes were single-engined and the average seating capacity in this mighty fleet was six. And the pilots numbered less than six hundred, a disturbing drop from the fifteen hundred there had been two years earlier, before the Depression was fully felt. Not an easy business. Each of those men stood a fairly good chance of not reaching retirement age what with a hundred and eight airline crashes that year, six of them fatal. Fifteen deaths for every million passenger miles flown, and little wonder. There were no such things as reversible propellers, de-icers that were any good, fire-extinguishing systems that worked, no complete network of ground-to-air radio beams for navigation, instrument-landing systems, approach lights, or even scientifically reliable methods for testing the structural integrity of an aircraft.

There *were* nearly 18,000 miles of lighted airways on the 27,000 miles of air-mail routes, but only because the airlines had paid for beacons themselves, the government not being sufficiently interested, given the more pressing economic problems. On some

routes there was a beacon light every mile, and an airline radio
station every three hundred miles, the maximum distance even the
biggest and heaviest transports could make on one load of fuel.
Coast-to-coast flying time was down to twenty-seven hours, with
only twelve refueling stops. There were good signs—all the airlines
were beginning to install two-way radios in their planes, which
pleased the crews far more than the latest government edict requiring all airline captains to pass a special test for instrument flying.
Flying by sheer instinct, most pilots insisted, was safer than flying by
a bunch of gauges. It was an opinion fashioned from the same logic
that had pilots objecting to closed cockpits because they wanted to
feel the wind on their faces.

Meanwhile every airline manager in the country was trying to
embellish his operation with whatever would make it seem more
sophisticated and attractive to the traveler: soundproofing, radio
receivers so that passengers could hear the World Series that year,
public-address systems aboard each ship, and restaurant conces-
sions at airports, the best one naturally being at Newark, the busi-
est airport in the country. Barney wondered if perhaps Coastal
shouldn't have moved there instead of Washington, what with one
out of every five passengers leaving from Newark. But the competition was too great, and with Roosevelt trying for the White House
a lot might change. After all, FDR had flown from Albany to
Chicago in an American Airways Ford trimotor to accept his
party's nomination, choosing this means to counter the whispers
that a polio-crippled man was too frail for the Presidency. Barney
sighed. It was an accurate commentary on the status of air-travel
that Roosevelt's flight was seen as something of a publicity stunt, a
breathtaking defiance of the safe and conventional, even given the
sturdy trimotor's sterling reputation. And then those pictures of
Roosevelt deplaning, the notable grin barely camouflaging the
unmistakable look of sheer misery on his face. The trimotor was
indeed safe, but obsolete.

"Barney."

"Huh?"

"We just passed my hotel," she said.

"Sorry. I'll take us back around the block and up to the front
entrance." He made the next right turn sharply. It started to rain

and he snapped on the wiping blades, then took the next right again to bring them back to Connecticut Avenue, where he stopped for traffic and turned toward her.

She tilted her head to one side. "Why are you looking at me that way, Barney?"

He turned back to concentrating on the road, holding the clutch depressed as a car chugged past. "You reminded me of someone I once drove back from an airport on a day like this."

"What was her name?"

"Rosina," he said, releasing the clutch and turning the corner and into the hotel driveway, then pushing the lever into low gear for the uphill ascent to the hotel entrance.

"Were you in love with her?"

The car eased to a stop alongside the long, sheltered walkway that ran along the front.

"Yes," he said, nodding slowly. "Very much." The wipers swished back and forth, erasing the droplets. "And why are you looking the way you are, Amelia?"

"What do you mean?" She tried to smile, her freckled cheeks curling round.

"What's his name?"

The smile vanished and she fixed him for a moment with those steady, deep eyes, before turning away to stare at the windshield.

"Are you in love with him?"

"Very much," she said, softly, and opened the door on her side. "Does he know?"

She shook her head no. "You're a good friend, Barnwell."

"So are you. Let me know if ever you need some bad advice."

"I will," she said, nodding. She bit her lip, nodding again, quickly kissing him on the cheek and springing out of the car with the grace of a pilot. And she was gone.

No one was prepared for United's coup.

Larry Aroni was the first to hear the news at Coastal Airways and immediately drove in from Hoover to see Barney at the company's offices in the Press Building, the young vice-president's official but infrequent business residence.

"He's waiting; go right in," said the secretary, as Aroni flew past, vaulting the wooden-railing divider.

Barney was leaning against the window, half-sitting on the sill, half-standing. He looked back at Aroni.

"Well?"

"Four *million* dollars. A four-million-dollar order for fifty-nine of Boeing's new Model 247."

"You know the exact specs?"

Aroni caught his breath. "Most of 'em. It's an all-metal, low-wing job; cruises at one-sixty MPH; carries ten passengers."

Barney toyed with the shade. "Who made the deal?"

"A family affair, this one. The Boeing Air Transport piece of the United group worked the deal. Boy, it's left everyone else out in the cold, even the big guys. American and TWA right away asked Boeing if they could handle more orders. But of course United's huge order will have the assembly lines tied up for a year at least."

"What's the price?"

Aroni thought for a moment. "Ah, sixty-eight thousand apiece."

Barney huffed. "We would need at least two and that comes to too much. Besides, we probably couldn't get them for two years." He looked at Aroni. "This is going to take some doing."

Barney thought of asking Henry McKay for a loan through Southern Tier and went so far as to sound out Riggs, where he had opened a company account as Henry had urged. When the Riggs loan officer candidly indicated that his bank could not help until the banking industry as a whole stabilized, Barney decided not to bother Henry McKay. Besides, he reasoned, if TWA and American couldn't buy assembly-line positions for another year, an airline the size of Coastal wouldn't stand much of a chance. Yet the idea of any other carrier having the fastest and most modern ship annoyed him profoundly.

Boeing was the only aircraft manufacturer committed to multi-engine transports. Certainly Fokker trimotors could be had for peanuts after Knute Rockne's ship lost a wing and crashed into a Kansas wheatfield. The plane's reputation had never recovered, however, and now, two years later, Barney was sure it was all over for large wood-constructed airliners. But that did not solve the problem of just where to obtain metal-bodied, multi-engined aircraft. Indeed, when Aroni had asked him what Coastal might do, Barney had simply said, "I haven't the slightest idea." Yet less than a week passed before the answer arrived in Washington and appeared at Barnwell Burton's downtown office.

"A Mr. Frye of TWA is here to see you," his secretary announced.

"Show him in."

He had never met the TWA official in person, but there was immediate rapport between Jack Frye, a round-faced, husky, and handsome man in his forties, and Barney.

"The boy wonder of the industry," Frye chuckled. "Burton, I'm glad to meet you in the flesh. Heard a hell of a lot about you."

"The feeling's mutual. What are you doing in Washington?"

"Seeing some politicians. Took a chance you'd be in—wanted to chew the fat a bit. How's Coastal doing?"

"So-so. We're holding our own, anyway. If you're considering a merger, the answer's no."

Frye laughed, but not with much humor. "You don't have anything we'd be panting for, Barney; certainly not those seven Fords you're operating. Matter of fact, that's what I wanted to talk to you about. Equipment. You heard about that United 247 deal? Well, they really pulled a fast one, gotta give them credit. That new Boeing will cut transcontinental travel time down to under twenty hours with only seven stops. United will be putting them in service next summer and, when they do, they'll murder us and American. Unless we do something fast. There's just a chance we can. Ever heard of Donald Douglas?"

"Sure. He built the World Cruisers the Army flew around the world in '24, observation planes for the military, and mailplanes. I think Western operated a fleet of Douglas M-2's and M-4's for a while. But all he's produced so far is a biplane. As far as I know, he's never built a large transport type."

Frye reached into his briefcase, pulled out the copy of a letter and handed it to Barney. "Read this."

Sept. 12, 1932
TRANSCONTINENTAL & WESTERN AIR, INC.
10 Richards Road
Municipal Airport
Kansas City, Missouri

Douglas Aircraft Corporation
Clover Field
Santa Monica, California

Attention: Mr. Donald Douglas

Dear Mr. Douglas:

    Transcontinental & Western Air is
interested in purchasing ten or more trimotored
transport planes. I am attaching our general
performance specifications covering this
equipment and would appreciate your advising
whether your Company is interested in this
manufacturing job.
    If so, approximately how long would it take
to turn out the first plane for service tests?

                Very truly yours,

                Jack Frye
                Vice-President
                   in Charge of Operations

JF/gs
Encl.

N.B.   Please consider this information
       confidential and return specifications if
       you are not interested.

Barney handed back the letter. "Interesting. What are your requirements?"

"Briefly, an all-metal trimotor grossing a maximum fourteen thousand pounds with a top speed of at least one eighty-five at sea level and around one fifty cruising speed. Range—about a thousand miles. A service ceiling of twenty-one thousand feet minimum and ten thousand feet on any two engines. Seating capacity of at least twelve with a payload of twenty-three hundred pounds or higher. And a landing speed of not more than sixty-five miles an hour."

"Is Douglas the only manufacturer you've approached?"

"Hell, no. Our specs went to everybody. But Douglas came back to us in less than a week. They're not only interested, but they've already started preliminary design work. Only they're opposed to a trimotor—they want two engines because they think people will shy away from anything that even remotely resembles a Ford or Fokker. And they may be right. Anyway, they've come up with some tentative plans for a twin-engine job that'll clobber the 247. Colonel Lindbergh—he's now technical adviser for TWA, as you probably know—well, Lindy's seen the sketches and he's impressed."

"The final product doesn't always live up to the blueprint promises," Barney said cautiously. "Look at Ford's 14-AT. It looked like the airliner of the future. The damned thing never even flew and I've heard Ford is scrapping it. By the way, did you send those specs to Bill Mayo?"

"I did. I might as well have asked him to design a moon rocket. Confidentially, Barney, Ford's canceling *all* airplane production next month. It seems Henry got tired of losing money on the trimotors. And he wants no part of competing against established airframe companies like Boeing and Lockheed."

"Or Douglas?"

"Yes, Douglas." Jack Frye arched his eyebrows. "For my dough, Douglas could wind up as the biggest of them all. They've got a team of young designers with a lot of imagination and guts. Personally, I think the Boeing 247 has an Achilles' heel. If I'm right, United has just tossed the biggest boomerang in aviation history."

"You're calling the 247 a boomerang? But Jack, it's airborne revolution. There's never been another plane like it."

Frye smiled with an air of triumph. "It's a revolution that didn't quite go far enough. I've talked to some Boeing people on the airline side. They're unhappy. Originally, the 247 was supposed to be at least a twelve-passenger plane with a top speed of two hundred and grossing sixteen thousand pounds. But United's pilots raised hell when they saw those specs. They claimed a sixteen-thousand-pound plane was too heavy to land safely. So Boeing had to scale down the design. They reduced passenger capacity to ten and they're using Pratt & Whitney Wasps instead of the new Hornet engines they wanted to install. That cuts down the performance. Sure, the 247 is revolutionary. But the one Douglas is building will be bigger, faster, and more comfortable. And once we get it into service, it'll make the 247 a has-been overnight. United will have four million dollars' worth of obsolete airplanes trying to compete against the DC-2."

"DC-2 is that what Douglas calls it?"

"The prototype will be the DC-1. The production aircraft will be the DC-2. Listen." Frye leaned forward. "I know it's pretty early in the game, and I don't want to commit you to anything, but I'd like to tell Douglas that Coastal is interested."

"Sure, we're interested. What's the price tag?"

"We're paying a hundred and twenty-five thousand for the prototype, but the production model won't run nearly that high. We're figuring on around sixty grand—about the same as the 247. That's a ballpark figure, of course."

"Did Douglas give you any idea when you can take delivery?"

"They hope to start test flights by July of next year, just about the time United puts the 247 into service. They'll smack us good for about a year but then watch out! The thing is, Barney, the sooner you commit Coastal to the DC-2, the better break Douglas will give you on price. Way I see it, this could be the first airplane built that can make money just carrying passengers. If I'm right, and Douglas builds the kind of bird they're promising, *long* lines will be forming in Santa Monica. Douglas figures to lose money on the first twenty or thirty planes, but from then on they could have a seller's market."

"How many is TWA buying?"

"We're considering an initial order of twenty-five."

Barney whistled. "Twenty-five! The way things are right now, I'd have trouble raising funds for a down-payment on two."

"Well," Frye shrugged, "I'm just letting you know which way the winds are blowing."

"Yeah. And I appreciate it, Jack, but I'm just a bit curious why you're letting Coastal in on this Douglas project."

"Heck, you guys aren't any competitive threat to us. Frankly, I'm trying to do Donald Douglas a favor, as well as you. The more airlines that show serious interest, the more encouragement he'll have for going ahead full steam."

"It's still a gamble," said Barney. "The DC-1 could be a turkey."

"Maybe. But I don't think so. I'm a pilot. I used to have my own little airline, Standard Airways, before Pop Hanshue bought in. We were flying between Los Angeles and Tucson via Phoenix, and later to El Paso. Then TWA was formed and I wound up behind a desk. But I still fly occasionally and I've still got a pilot's feel for a beautiful airplane. I swear you can tell from almost the very first drawing whether the bird's gonna hack it. I felt that way about the DC-1. It just looked right—clean, honest, graceful, powerful. A kind of symmetry . . . My God, Barney, an old air-mail jockey like me getting absolutely poetic. Sorry. It's just that I've never been so excited about an airplane."

"Don't apologize," Barney said warmly. "You can tell Mr. Douglas that Coastal Airways definitely is interested. One of these days I'll fly out to the West Coast and talk to him. Any lunch plans, Jack?"

"Yeah, with a couple of guys at the Bureau of Air Commerce. But give me a rain check. Meanwhile, when you decide to see the Douglas people, let me know and I'll fix you up with a pass. I'd like you to try TWA."

"I've heard you run a first-class operation. I'll take you up on that offer."

After Frye left, Barney sat there meditating, conscious of his office's shabbiness and wondering if the TWA vice-president had thought less of him because of those second-class surroundings. They were luxurious compared to the office he had at Hoover, but the furniture still was second-hand, the drapes obviously cheap and poorly hung, and the off-white paint on the walls looked paltry. He was proud of the prestigious address, but, he glumly concluded, it was akin to placing mail-order furnishings into the Taj Mahal.

Why the hell am I worrying about what Jack Frye thinks of this crummy room? He isn't the kind of guy who judges a man by the condition of the chair he's sitting in. Someday I'll fix this place up, by God, but right now I've got more to think about than office furniture—airplanes. The Fords have had it. I wish Frye hadn't raved so about the DC-2. Christ, we gotta have that goddamned bird. There's going to be some competition in this industry. It's coming as sure as the sun rises. And when it does, a carrier with inferior equipment might as well be flying World War biplanes. Frye's right. If we ordered the DC-2 now, we'd get a break on the price. No airframe manufacturer ever knows what to charge for a new model, not until he gets production costs in line and figures out how to amortize development costs. Maybe I *should* talk to Henry McKay about a loan.

He flew to Binghamton the next day. Regretfully, Henry turned him down.

"I couldn't get it past our loan committee. Banking is on the verge of collapse. You're asking for fifty thousand, but it might as well be fifty million."

"You know we're good for it, Henry. Coastal's not a poor risk."

"Sure, I know it, but it doesn't help. Banks are failing all over the country; the panic is on. Comparatively speaking, Southern Tier's in good shape. We're in no immediate danger of going under. But we're not making any loans, not until we see what a new administration might do. No hard feelings, I hope. I'd loan you the fifty grand myself if I had it to spare, Barney."

"No hard feelings. I understand. I got the same story from Riggs. Chum, you bankers are in worse shape than the airlines."

"There's one possibility, Barney. Have you thought about borrowing from the Reconstruction Finance Corporation? You'd probably qualify for an equipment loan."

"Yeah, I thought about the RFC," Barney said. "But I'll be damned if I'll borrow from a government agency."

"Why not? Other companies have."

"It's against my principles, that's why. Put yourself into hock with those fucking government vultures, and the next thing you know they'll be telling you how to run the airline. I'll fly the Fords till the wings fall off before I let a bunch of bureaucrats in the back door."

"Well, it was a thought. You might keep it in mind in case things get really desperate."

"They never will," Barney promised. Rashly, as it turned out.

Coastal's system just was not conducive to profitable operation in the late fall and winter months. There were too many delays and cancellations because of weather, and this compounded by a sharp decline in traffic as a disillusioned nation drifted aimlessly toward the demise of the Hoover regime and the unknown policies of the smiling man whom Walter Lippmann had written off as "a pleasant man who, without any important qualification for the office, would very much like to be President."

Christmas of 1932 was gloomy for Barnwell Burton. From childhood, he had relished the trappings of the Yuletide. The tinseled tree with its fresh smell of forest pine, an aroma that became part of his memories like a delicate perfume. The carols, a kaleidoscope of carefree joy and a kind of sweet sadness. This particular Christmas got to him more than ever before. He was at the airport one day in late December when Ben Shub approached him. "Mr. Burton, could you loan me three bucks?"

"I guess so," Barney said, reaching for his wallet. "What's it for?"

"See that old lady standing by our ticket counter?"

"Yeah." She could have posed for Whistler's Mother. "Why?"

"Some lousy pickpocket lifted her handbag. She was flying to Pittsburgh to spend Christmas with her son. The old gal comes up to the counter sobbing her heart out. Wanted us to trust her for the ticket. I had to tell her no. She was quivering, she was so unstrung. Anyway, a few of us got together and chipped in some dough for a roundtrip ticket—me, Mr. Aroni and a couple of his mechanics, and whatever pilots were in Operations. Except we're three bucks short. I'll pay you back when I get my next check."

Barney took out a twenty-dollar bill and gave it to the station manager. "Forget the three bucks. This'll make up the difference and give her a little spending money."

Barney left hastily so he wouldn't have to face the old woman's tearful gratitude. Old ladies were bad enough to deal with, without having to endure their sniffling. He knew there was not one person on Coastal's payroll who wasn't having financial difficulties. Ben Shub had a wife and three kids and he wasn't exactly prospering on what Coastal was paying him. Larry Aroni was sending at least a third of his pay home to his parents, the elder Aroni having been laid off at Endicott-Johnson.

That afternoon, he made out checks for $25 to every employee and had them distributed throughout the system, along with a little note expressing his personal thanks and those of Rodney Lindeman for their loyalty and performance under adverse conditions. The money came from his personal savings, which he had transferred to the company's account.

He spent Christmas Eve at home, alone, stretched out on the couch, staring at the little tree on the coffee table, its bright ornaments and tinsel casting a lulling pattern on the far wall.

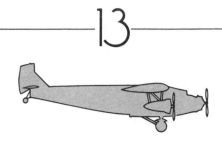

13

His name was Fulton Lewis. Back in 1932 he had been a young Washington reporter for the Hearst papers. One afternoon Lewis lunched with Bill Briggs, a friend who worked for the Ludington Line, the passenger carrier operating between New York and Washington via Philadelphia, where the company's two wealthy owners resided. In business since 1930, it held the distinction of being the only airline in the country that operated without the benefit of an air-mail contract. As Briggs casually explained over coffee, the profits were slim and operating costs high for their tri-motor Stinsons, Lockheed Vegas, and Consolidated Fleetstars that departed each hour. Mail revenue would have helped greatly, but the contract for the Washington–New York route was held by Eastern Air Transport.

"I really thought we would be flying the mail by now," said Briggs. "My God, we only bid twenty-five cents a mile. I suppose Eastern must have underbid, but I don't know how they could have managed it."

A few weeks after his lunch with Briggs, Fulton Lewis was examining a Post Office news release reciting the dry facts of the New

York–Philadelphia–Washington mail contract that years earlier Eastern had been awarded for *eighty-nine* cents a mile.

For the next several months Lewis had dug into the Post Office Department records and unearthed the whole story of former Postmaster General Walter Folger Brown's closed-door negotiations and of the twelve-day conference he had conducted. Fulton Lewis compiled a full report and turned it over to his boss, William Randolph Hearst, only to have the publisher decide against publishing it. However, Hearst did finally consent to turning the material over to someone who could use it—Hugo Black.

Black was from Alabama and the chairman of a Senate committee investigating ocean-mail contracts, the chief method by which the government subsidized the U.S. Merchant Marine. The investigation had been droning on with little public attention when Lewis's report was delivered to him. Senator Black recognized its potential instantly and quickly extended his committee's probe to include air-mail contracts.

Black scheduled hearings for March 4, 1934, but did not wait for the hearings before igniting the political dynamite in his possession. Late in January he met with President Roosevelt, informed him that existing air-mail contracts had been obtained through fraud and collusion, and urged FDR to cancel them all and let the Army Air Corps fly the mail until new ones could be awarded.

Roosevelt promised to consider the proposal. In the meantime the Senator turned over his files to Carl Crowley, Solicitor General of the United States, who condensed the voluminous material into a hundred-page report which he personally delivered to Postmaster General James A. Farley.

"I can't wade through all this," Farley growled. "Just tell me about it briefly."

"There seems to be ample justification for canceling all air-mail contracts on the grounds that they were obtained through collusion."

Farley was shaken by the implications. "It would wreck the airlines," he muttered. "I have to think this over."

"You don't have much time," Crowley warned. "Senator Black already has told the President about this."

"I'll set up a meeting at the White House tomorrow," Farley

promised. "We'll both talk to the boss. But frankly, Carl, it scares the hell out of me."

After Crowley left, the Postmaster General called in a trusted aide. "I want to talk to someone from the airline industry, and I want to talk to him fast and completely off the record. Is there anyone right here in Washington who'd be available immediately, this afternoon?"

"I suppose Eddie Rickenbacker could fly down from New York," the aide suggested.

Farley snorted. "Not him, for God's sake! He's five miles to the right of Calvin Coolidge. What's the name of that young guy at Coastal? I've been told he's capable and doesn't think Hoover should be enshrined."

"Barney Burton. Fellow named Lindeman is the president but Burton runs the show."

"Call him and tell him I want to see him in my office as soon as he can get here."

It was a mystified Barnwell Burton who showed up fifty-two minutes later and was ushered into the office of James A. Farley, to be greeted with disarming warmth by a man of consummate skill in the art of making friends.

"I'm not one to stand on ceremony, Mr. Burton," Farley began, "so if you don't mind I'd like to call you Barney and I'd appreciate your using 'Jim.'" Barney, still bewildered, nodded. "Barney, I need some advice. Frank, honest advice. I can't even tell you what this is all about; all I can do is ask you some questions. What I ask and what you tell me is completely off the record; I don't want it to leave this room. I will say one thing: the future of the airline industry may be at stake. Those are the ground rules. If you have any doubts, any reservations, you can walk out of here right now and forget I ever sent for you."

"Start asking," Barney said promptly.

"Okay. Was Coastal Airways represented at a meeting my predecessor held with a number of airline officials in 1930?"

"Yes, sir. Bud Lindeman, our president, was there."

"That's where you got your present air-mail authority?"

"Correct. Or rather, shortly afterward."

"How did Lindeman happen to get invited? As I understand it, Coastal was pretty small potatoes at the time."

"One of our directors knew Postmaster General Brown. Well enough so that he wangled an invitation for us."

"You knew about the meeting?"

"Sure. It wasn't exactly secret."

"No," Farley observed dryly. "Just not very well publicized. Did Lindeman ever tell you what went on at those sessions?"

"He briefed me almost every day. Matter of fact, I came to Washington shortly after they began. I didn't go to any of the sessions myself but Lindeman filled me in every night."

"Did he give any indication of illegality? Shenanigans? Under-the-table dealings?"

"No, sir. He . . . he just told me the gist of what was talked about each day. Who wanted which routes—things like that—what Brown himself thought the route structure should be. Bud was more of an observer than a participant, frankly. I wound up telling Brown myself what Coastal wanted."

"At the conference?"

"No, sir. I saw him privately before one of the sessions. He asked me why I thought Coastal deserved an expanded air-mail route and I told him. I had met him before and I guess he liked my views on the future of the industry; I always thought the airlines should try harder to increase passenger business so that they wouldn't have to rely on mail pay so much. I still think so. A few weeks later, we got our present route system."

"So as far as you're concerned, neither you nor Mr. Lindeman saw anything shady or crooked?"

"No, sir. I've since heard rumors that the whole business wasn't entirely open, but I sure couldn't testify under oath to that. Not so far as the meeting involved Coastal. We were invited, we showed up, we asked for route expansion, and eventually we got it. What happened with the other carriers I couldn't say. Frankly, I kind of doubt if there was anything really illegal going on."

"Why do you say that?"

"Because I think I got to know Walter Brown's views fairly well. I suppose there were a few ripe plums handed out, but you have to understand that Brown was primarily interested in developing a prosperous, efficient airline industry and he didn't think this could be accomplished by letting everyone into the act. We were lucky to get what we did; we were small, and we didn't fit his conception of an airline. He used size and stable financing as his yardsticks for a successful carrier."

Jim Farley suddenly frowned. "I don't have much precise data or facts on hand, but one case has been cited to me as typical. Ludington bid twenty-five cents a mile for a Washington–New York mail route and the award went to Eastern for a bid of eighty-nine cents. Something smells, Barney."

"Not if you understand Brown. I know something about that Ludington-Eastern business. In fact, I once talked to Brown about it. He told me he felt Eastern was offering a major north-south network that covered almost the entire eastern seaboard from New York to Florida. Ludington wasn't bidding twenty-five cents a mile for a route that long—only the New York–Washington segment. Eastern got it because its application fitted Brown's idea of what a route system should entail—one airline serving a large region, not a lot of little airlines operating small segments. Anyway, Brown also told me something I don't think is generally known—he gave Eastern its mail contract on the condition that it buy out Ludington at a fair price. From what I've heard, Ludington got a very generous chunk of cash."

Farley leaned back in his chair, brow furrowed in thought.

"I'll confess to a great deal of curiosity," Barney finally couldn't resist saying. "I have to assume you're sitting on what means to be a major scandal, only you're not quite sure to what extent."

Big Jim Farley laughed. "No guessing games. Even if you guessed right, I couldn't confirm it. No, son, about the best I can do is to promise you I won't forget your being so honest with me. I'd like to ask you one more question, though."

"Shoot."

"Could your airline exist without mail pay?"

Barney hesitated before replying. "It would be touch and go. A lot would depend on the ability of our new planes to develop more passenger traffic. We've ordered three new DC-2's but we won't be taking delivery until next fall, and we have to come up with the money to pay for them in the interim. Without modern equipment, we wouldn't stand a chance, nor would any other airline. Could we survive without a mail contract? I'd have to say not for long. It would be a race between when mail pay ended and when we could put new planes into service. And even with the new equipment, we couldn't expect anything approaching reasonable profits. It's a sad thing to say, but there is no airline that can make a profit just carrying passengers. Not yet, anyway."

Farley nodded without further comment; it was impossible for Barney to tell whether the Postmaster General was agreeing with him or merely acknowledging what he had said. Barney left after Farley repeated his admonition: "This discussion is strictly between the two of us. You'll know why soon enough."

Barney learned why at four o'clock on the afternoon of February 9, 1934, the hour that James Farley, speaking from the White House, announced the cancellation of all air-mail contracts effective midnight, February 18. Three days after Farley's announcement, FDR himself decreed that the Army Air Corps would begin flying the mail on February 19.

What Barney did not know was that Farley had argued with Roosevelt against outright cancellation, urging the President not to take such drastic action until the Post Office Department had issued new bids for all air-mail routes.

Normally, Barney never would have had the temerity to decide to ask Farley to see him privately.

Men of far greater political clout than the young vice-president of Coastal Airways had already spoken their minds. Lindbergh's reaction had been an angry telegram to Roosevelt, charging that the cancellation "condemns the largest portion of our commercial aviation without just trial." Captain Eddie Rickenbacker told the press the Army wasn't prepared to fly the mail. "Their ships aren't equipped with blind-flying instruments, and their training, while excellent for military duty, is not adapted for flying the air mail," the crusty vice-president of Eastern added. "Either they're going to pile up ships all the way across the continent or they're not going to be able to fly the mail on schedule."

The White House bombshell sobered up Lindeman in a hurry. He rushed to join other airline presidents, who were issuing statements as fast as their public-relations people could compose them.

Barney, who had never gotten around to acquiring a PR man, had just about agreed to write his under Lindeman's name when he had decided he could at least try to see Farley.

"You couldn't get into a Post Office toilet at this point," Lindeman muttered.

"I can't lose anything," Barney said, "and it might do a lot more good than denouncing him in print. Besides, I have a hunch this whole mess wasn't Jim Farley's doing."

"That's ridiculous," Lindeman scoffed. "He made the announcement, didn't he?"

"Yeah," Barney agreed, "but . . ."

"But what?"

"Nothing. I'm still gonna try. So don't go issuing any statements until I give you the word."

He called Farley's office, was asked to leave his name, and somewhat to his surprise the Postmaster General called him back in less than five minutes.

"Come on over in an hour," said Farley pleasantly. "But don't be alarmed if you're searched before they let you in. I seem to be persona non grata with most of your colleagues."

"The only thing I'm armed with is a few questions," Barney said.

"Can't say that I blame you. See you later."

"Thanks for seeing me," Barney said. "I know you're busy."

"Least I could do. You gave me your time some weeks ago."

"That's why I'm here. I told you I couldn't see any evidence of fraud in the so-called Spoils Conference. You must know a hell of a lot more than I do or those mail contracts wouldn't have been canceled."

"Actually," Farley sighed, "I doubt if I *do* know much more than you do. The Solicitor General told me there's reason to believe there was fraud, so I went along with the shutdown. I didn't have time to go through all the actual data Crowley had, but he gave me a condensation and it didn't look very clean for your side."

"Guilty until proven innocent," Barney said quietly. "That's what it amounts to. I know Coastal wasn't involved in any crooked dealings with Brown, and I'd be surprised if the majority of the other airlines acted illegally. That cancellation slapped all of us, regardless of how clean we were."

"Off the record, Barney, I have to agree. I argued against cancellation, but the President had his dutch up, as he loves to say."

"So now what? I don't know about the rest of the carriers, but Coastal could go bankrupt without that mail pay. TWA's already announced they're furloughing all employees indefinitely. United says they won't lay anyone off but that'll cost them about three hundred thousand a month. Is it fair to penalize the innocent along with the guilty—assuming there *are* guilty parties?"

"No, it's not fair," Farley said quietly. "All I can tell you is keep your shirt on and—this is a personal request—keep your mouth shut. Things'll work out. The Army can't fly the mail indefinitely."

"It says it can."

The Postmaster General uncoiled his tall frame from his swivel chair and began to pace up and down behind his desk. "Barney, you're not to repeat this to anyone. The President called Benny Foulois to the White House—he's chief of the Air Service. Well, the President asked Benny pointblank if the Army could do the job. The general said, 'Yes, sir.' And that's all the boss needed. But you have to realize the spot General Foulois was in. He's been under constant attack from Billy Mitchell, who says the Air Corps couldn't lick a South American banana republic, or words to that effect. Just between the two of us, I'm scared to death. I'm not sure the Army *is* ready. And if we have a few crashes, I'll be the guy catching all the hell."

Farley's normally good-natured Irish face was flushed and his eyes showed genuine concern. Barney felt sorry for him.

"Well," he said slowly. "I guess all I can do is what you asked—keep my shirt on and my mouth shut. Only it'll be hard to keep my mouth shut if I'm losing the shirt."

"I realize that," the Postmaster General said sympathetically. "But I think things will work out. Your industry needs some changes, Barney. Too many carriers are in bed with non-airline companies. General Motors owns Eastern and Western Air Express. American is part of a big holding company. Then you have United with an engine manufacturer under the same roof as the airline itself. Even if Brown and the industry come out lily-white, there's going to be legislation to restructure the airlines. All I can ask of you is patience and a promise not to make waves. If the Army falls down, I'll be the scapegoat and it'll help to know there are a few guys like yourself who aren't running with the wolves."

"Jim, I can't promise you anything. I'll be under pressure, too. But I understand your situation and I'll at least try to stay neutral as long as I can."

Farley smiled, but simultaneously his eyes narrowed. "I can't make any promises, either. But I'll remind you that Jim Farley has a long memory."

Barney issued no statement, much to Lindeman's annoyance, who threatened to issue one himself but was too afraid of Barney's wrath to defy him openly. He also lost his argument that Coastal should follow TWA's example and shut down temporarily. Barney wasn't willing to go as far as United's W. A. Patterson, who refused to furlough anyone, but he instituted stringent economy measures. Two days before the February 18 deadline, he furloughed virtually all Coastal employees except those working at the major stations. Excluded from the layoffs were station managers and a single mechanic in each of the smaller cities. He ordered an immediate twenty percent cut in all salaries—including those of officers—and took himself and Lindeman completely off the payroll until further notice.

Barney silently cheered the industry's last act of defiance. At 10:00 P.M. on the eighteenth, two hours before the mail contracts expired, Jack Frye and Eddie Rickenbacker took off from Burbank in the brand-new DC-1 carrying the last load of privately contracted mail. They landed in Newark eighteen hours and four minutes later—a new transcontinental speed record. It was a flight that contrasted dramatically and tragically with what followed in the next few months.

A dozen Army pilots lost their lives either on mail-flight training missions or on actual mail-carrying operations. The last fatal accident occurred March 31, the safety record improving as the Army pilots gained experience and the weather improved. But as far as the Roosevelt administration was concerned, the damage had been done; Farley's scapegoat prediction was only too accurate and he was more embittered toward FDR and Hugo Black than the airlines themselves. He kept in occasional touch with Coastal's youthful executive. Barney, in turn, made a point of reminding him how comparatively inefficient the Army's operations were.

"It's costing the government about two dollars and twenty cents a pound to fly the mail," he pointed out one evening, "and the airlines were doing it for less than sixty cents. Fifty-four cents, to be exact."

"I'll pass that statistic onto the White House," Farley said sourly, "plus any other tidbits that devious mind of yours can concoct."

"Sure. It took about seven thousand airline employees to run the air-mail service for that fifty-four-cent figure. The Army has to charge more than two dollars with only five hundred men assigned to the operation, and the airlines were serving twenty-seven thousand miles of routes compared to only sixteen thousand for the Army. That's simple arithmetic, even for someone like Senator Black."

"You don't know the honorable Senator from the sovereign state of Alabama," said Farley.

The hearings generated a lot of headlines and a lot of smoke but no fire. They ended with absolutely no evidence of skullduggery in Brown's administration of the Post Office Department, but Black, seething with frustration, got his revenge. He introduced legislation, the Air Mail Act of 1934, reopening all airline routes to competitive bidding and requiring the separation of air carriers from all aircraft-manufacturing companies, and banning all executives who had attended the Spoils Conference from holding office in their respective airlines.

The minute the Act was introduced, smaller carriers, hungry for routes long denied them, began applying pressure on the administration and the Congress. It was Jim Farley who placated them by convincing administration supporters on the Hill to introduce a special provision forbidding all airlines which had been represented at the Spoils Conference to bid on new routes.

Barney heard about the amendment from Ernie Pyle and went charging over to Farley's office.

"What the hell are you trying to do to us?" he demanded. "That amendment would kill us and nearly every other airline as well. You're opening up the whole air-transportation system to a bunch of cheap marginal operators with no experience, no modern equipment, and absolutely no right to fly routes we've pioneered."

"Sit down and calm down. I've already heard from United, Eastern, American, and a few others. I'll tell you what I've told them. That provision is strictly a technicality—it's worded so all an airline has to do is reorganize its corporate structure under a different name. Eastern Air Transport will become Eastern Airlines, American Airways will be known as American Airlines. United Aircraft and Transport turns into United Airlines. All you have to do is change the name of Coastal Airways to something else— like Coastal Airlines. That's just four letters, son. Understand?"

"Yeah," Barney sighed. "My God, I thought school was out. Tell me, will that bill pass?"

"I wouldn't try betting against it."

"With all its present provisions?"

"I could give you a buck for every word or comma that will be changed by the time it reaches the White House. Barney, you look worried."

"Not worried. When you said that bill is going through Congress, I suddenly realized that Bud Lindeman can't be Coastal's president."

"You're a little late reaching that conclusion," Farley remarked dryly. "The provision ousting from office any Spoils Conference attendee has been in the legislation for weeks. Seems you would have grasped the implications before this."

"I didn't really believe it would be left in the bill," Barney said soberly. "That's gonna boot out a hell of a lot of good airline men—Pop Hanshue at Western, Brittin of Northwest, Phil Johnson over at United. My God, the list reads like a Who's Who in commercial aviation. They weren't crooks, Jim. Those goddamned Black hearings didn't produce one iota of wrongdoing on anyone's part. Including Lindeman's."

"How will he take it?" Farley asked.

"Badly, I'm afraid."

Barney broke the news to Lindeman that afternoon, as gently as he could.

"It's not certain," Barney added in an unconvincing tone. "The amendment still could be eliminated before it reaches Roosevelt."

Lindeman was calm, but his pale face gave him away. "You don't really believe that, do you?"

Barney puffed his cheeks. "No, I don't. Of course, anything could happen between now and the final vote, but I think we should talk about your future. Just in case. For example, I'd like you to remain on the board of directors. There's nothing in the Act that forbids it. And there's nothing to prevent you from going over to another carrier. I've heard Hanshue's going with Eastern."

"I doubt if another airline would take me on as president," Lindeman said, with a wry smile.

"I suppose not." Barney looked across the desk at the man who had given him his start. "You really liked being president, didn't you?"

Lindeman's eyes glistened and his voice was low, hoarse. "It's all I had, chum. The only semblance of dignity and decency a lousy alcoholic could hold on to. Thanks to you, Barnwell. Anyone else would have tied the can to me long ago. Why didn't you?"

"You know why. You gave me a chance to get into this business. I pay my debts."

Lindeman grinned, and for one startling second he looked like the man Barney had first met on that rainy day six years ago. "That's all I've been to you the last two or three years, isn't it, chum? A debt. A liability you've carried around on your shoulders like Christ carried the cross."

Barney was silent, embarrassed. He changed the subject. "We don't have to decide anything right away. But I want you to know I'll arrange for as liberal a bonus as we can afford. Hopefully enough to keep you going until you latch on somewhere else."

"I'd appreciate that, Barney. I'll leave the amount up to you. There won't be any argument or bickering. I know you'll be fair."

Barney went back to his own office and sat down wearily. He had left a Bud Lindeman who had suddenly seemed ten years older, an expression of defeat and total resignation added to the tired, bloodshot eyes and sagging jowls. Barney felt miserable.

He can't get a decent job, Barney thought. He can't fly anymore and that was all he was good for anyway. Funny, but the only time Bud really stayed sober was when he went to Brown's conference

—and that's what did him in, finally. And I was lucky. If Henry's father hadn't told me to stay away, I'd be out myself.

Congress passed the Black-McKellar Act on June 12, 1934. The following morning Coastal's Board of Directors voted to change the corporate name to Coastal Airlines, Inc., and elected Barnwell Ernest Burton president.

He was twenty-six, the youngest airline chief executive in the country.

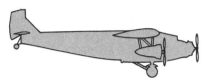

14

The euphoria was tinged with loneliness. For a while he even missed the charade of going to Lindeman for approval of a policy or judgment he already had made himself. After some brief early jitters, he began to enjoy his clear authority. His first and most important task was to bid for a new mail contract under the Air Mail Act, and this time he had competition. A small passenger line operating out of Pittsburgh, Metropolitan Air Service, also bid for Coastal's routes, and Barney knew his airline's fate hung by the thin thread of the Post Office Department's decision. He suspected Metropolitan would bid low deliberately, even if it meant operating at a loss, just to grab the contract; if this worked, it could ask for adjusted pay later. The technique was being employed by more than one new applicant and Barney was scared.

But he didn't panic. He sat down and figured out operating costs to the penny on the Fords and took some educated guesses for the forthcoming DC-2's, deliberately putting them on the high side. Metropolitan had put in its closed bid first, and the minute Barney heard about it he planned his counterstrategy. First, he added a bid for a route not served by anyone—Washington to Minneapolis and

St. Paul, via Pittsburgh, and offered to fly the mail on this segment for thirty-five cents a mile. For part of Coastal's existing system, he bid a low twenty-five cents a mile, figuring this would undercut Metropolitan at the points it sought to serve. The exception was Atlanta–Pittsburgh, for which he entered a bid of thirty cents.

"The DC-2 will make money on that Washington–Pittsburgh–Minneapolis segment," he explained to Aroni, Cal Motts, and others at a staff meeting. "As far as I know, no one else is applying for that route. Potentially, it's a hell of a market—good enough so we can afford to gross less on mail pay over the rest of the system."

"I still don't get it, Boss," Motts questioned. "How come the thirty-cent bid for Atlanta-Pittsburgh? Why not twenty-five cents?"

"Cal, when it comes to showing a profit, the future of this business is in longer-haul routes. We're trying for maximum mail pay over the two segments that will cost us the least to operate because they are longer. That's where we'll concentrate our DC-2 equipment at first."

"I'm just a goddamned mechanic," Aroni put in, "but it makes no sense to me to bid twenty-five cents a mile for flying the mail over about two-thirds of our system. That might not even pay for the gas."

"I want to keep Metropolitan out of it, Larry. I'm gambling they were shortsighted enough not to bid on anything except what we're already operating. And I don't think they can go as low as twenty-five cents and stay in business. When the Post Office opens those bids, we'll be lower than Metropolitan on every segment except Atlanta–Pittsburgh. We'll come in at about a twenty-seven-cent average, and I've got a pretty strong hunch the opposition's figure will come closer to thirty cents."

"You'd better be right," Aroni said softly. "If they undercut us, there goes the ballgame."

"They won't," Barney promised with more confidence than he actually felt.

They didn't.

With the contract secured, Barney went to work on Coastal's internal weaknesses. He knew the airline was pitifully understaffed from top to bottom—too many employees and officers alike had been wearing four or five hats even before the furloughs. Barney winced when he saw Larry Aroni tearing down an engine by himself.

"You're supposed to be supervising," Barney scolded.

"Then go out and hire me a few more mechanics!" Aroni snapped. "Either I do overhauls myself or they don't get done. I don't have enough bodies to keep these Wrights from falling apart."

Coastal wasn't shorthanded only in rank and file, Barney realized. Management was even more undermanned. Cal Motts was in charge of all sales, both passenger traffic and mail/express. Al Davenport not only supervised the pilot force but drew up the flight schedules. But if all his subordinates were wearing four hats, Barney himself was wearing ten, and knew he couldn't keep it up. Coastal still was no United, TWA, American, or Eastern in size, yet it had grown to the point where economizing in manpower, facilities, and service was self-defeating.

Early in August of 1934, Barney flew to Binghamton for a meeting with Frank and Henry McKay.

"We're going to have to steal some money for the DC-2's we've ordered and increase personnel by around thirty percent," he informed the McKays. "That will include about a half-dozen experienced management people, which means I'll have to pay top salaries to get them away from other airlines. We'll be putting the DC-2's into service in October and it's about time we hired some stewardesses. I also want to gradually phase out the Fords, replacing them with DC-2's as soon as possible."

"All of which adds up to money," Henry observed. "How much?"

"I'd like to borrow a million dollars."

"Jesus," exclaimed Henry McKay.

"Part of it from Southern Tier, and the rest from Riggs and maybe one or two other lenders."

Frank McKay lit a dirigible-sized cigar and peered at Barney through the cloud of pungent smoke. "I don't quarrel with any of your reasons for borrowing, son. Each of the moves you've mentioned seems essential and logical, if the airline's going to prosper. But speaking strictly as the president of Southern Tier and not as a personal friend, you're going to have to promise an additional step before we'd even consider joining a group of lenders."

"And that step . . . ?"

"Increase the number of directors. A solid, responsible board made up of men with excellent reputations in varying fields, business and industry in particular. Such a board becomes a definite asset. Particularly when you must go to a lending institution such as a bank or insurance company. Coastal's present board is weak and very inadequate; so much so that I doubt whether you could float a million-dollar loan."

"Dad doesn't mean we should go off the board," Henry McKay added. "We simply think you should add at least three new directors and possibly more. We can suggest a few names. Riggs could provide others, and you yourself may have some ideas."

"You also should remove one name," the elder McKay said.

"Lindeman, I suppose," Barney murmured.

"He's there strictly for sentimental reasons," Frank McKay said bluntly. "And when you go around asking for a million dollars, sentiment had better be left out of your prospectus."

"I'll admit he doesn't do us any good," Barney said, "but I can't see where his being a director would hurt us if the other board members were strong. Hell, you guys are insisting that I field an all-star team, and even Notre Dame has a few weak sisters on the squad."

The bank president shook his head emphatically. "Lindeman's usefulness to Coastal ended the day the Air Mail Act was signed, forcing him to resign as president. And that's a rather theoretical judgment. Actually, he hasn't been worth a thing since you moved to Washington—and you know it, Barney."

Barney was silent.

"I know how you feel," Henry said sympathetically, "but even if you didn't take on a single new director, Lindeman should go. First, he's useless. Second, you've had a four-man board ever since you took Joe McFarland off. An even-numbered board is an impossible situation—sooner or later you'd run into a tie vote on some key policy matter. So even if you won't go along on increasing the board, you'd still have to remove Lindeman."

"Oh, I'll go along," Barney assured him. "I just hate to be the one who breaks the news."

"If it would make it any easier," Frank McKay offered, "I'd be willing to talk to him. He's back in Binghamton, as you probably know."

For the first time in a long while, Barney decided to duck. "I'd appreciate that, Mr. McKay. It was tough enough when he found out he had to resign as president, and I had to be the one to tell him. I don't think I want to go through that again. I have his address if you need it."

"We've got it, too," Henry said. "Well, Barney, getting back to that million dollars. Dad and I will have to work out a few things at this end, of course. We'd be able to handle only a relatively small portion of the loan but we'd be glad to scout around for other lenders. Meanwhile, I'd suggest you talk to Riggs as soon as you get back."

"How about those names of prospective directors? I'll need some help in that area."

"Henry and I will draw up a list," the elder McKay promised. "And you should do likewise in Washington. If I might make a further suggestion . . . ?"

"Sure."

"I believe what we might term a *representative* board would be best. By representative I mean varied interests and occupations, different companies—even different regions. For example, you're moving into the Twin Cities area and it wouldn't hurt to have someone from Minneapolis or St. Paul on the board. The same would be true for another major point on your system, such as Pittsburgh."

"I see what you mean," Barney smiled. "I like that idea."

In the next month, he picked four new directors to give Coastal a seven-man board—a vice-president of Riggs, a top-ranking officer from a Pittsburgh steel firm, the president of a canning company with headquarters in Minneapolis, a retired executive who once headed the life-insurance company that, with Southern Tier and Riggs, underwrote the airline's million-dollar loan.

He could not resist calling Henry after McKay sent him a laconic note reporting that "we officially notified Lindeman that he is no longer a director."

"How'd he take it?" Barney wanted to know.

"Quite well, as a matter of fact. He didn't rant or rave, anyway. Come to think of it, his only comment I didn't understand. He said, 'tell Barney it was worth it.' Do you know what he meant?"

"I'm not sure," Barney admitted. "I suppose he means he had a good time while it lasted."

He was never to find out what Lindeman really meant. Only a week later, McKay phoned to say Bud Lindeman had died.

"Last night—a massive stroke. I thought you'd want to know."

"God, I'm sorry," Barney said—and he meant it. His first reaction was one of guilt. If he hadn't been so quick to boot Lindeman off the board, Bud would have gone to his grave without facing that final humiliation.

"We had no way of knowing," McKay said, as if reading Barney's mind from three hundred miles away. "I realize he had high blood pressure, but I never figured he'd go suddenly. I'm sorry, too, Barney. We should have kept him on the board at least for a while."

"Well. It's over and done with. When's the funeral?"

"Day after tomorrow. Be nice if you could be here. There won't be many mourners. As far as we can tell, he had no family—not even a brother or a sister, and his parents are dead. The American Legion will bury him."

"I'll be there," Barney promised.

He saw Joe McFarland, who seemed actually glad to see him, at the cemetery. Barney wondered if Rosina had ever told him.

"Say," Barney whispered, "how about having dinner with me tonight? Henry McKay and his wife are coming along."

"I think I'd . . ." McFarland began. "We have other plans. Sorry," Joe said, embarrassed. "Give me a rain check for next time you're in town."

"Sure. What are you doing these days?"

"Started a little trucking company. It's been rough but business is picking up. And I fly an occasional charter trip. Friend of mine has a couple of small planes at the airport and he needs a pilot now and then. And, hey, I finally got hitched. Wonderful gal, Rosina."

"That's swell, Joe. Call me if you get to Washington, will you?"

"I'll certainly do that."

They both knew their friendship was over. As dead as the man whose body was lowered into a grave, while the mournful notes of "Taps" poured out of a Legionnaire's bugle. Only two people had tears in their eyes. One was McFarland. The other was the president of Coastal Airlines. For each, the death of a drunken failure was also the demise of the man who had been his benefactor and his friend.

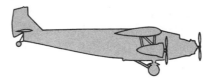

Coastal's three new DC-2's were scheduled for delivery September 15. Barney was ready to put them right into service by September 30 when Al Davenport blew the whistle.

"You're asking for trouble, Barney," he warned. "That bird will be the biggest airplane we'll be flying for a good many years, and size means complexity. Two weeks of training isn't enough for our crews; I need a month. If we bust one of those babies up it'll set the whole industry back five years, not just Coastal."

"We need 'em bad," Barney protested. "How about three weeks?"

"One month, Boss."

"Dammit, Al, it's supposed to be the last word in transports. Fast, easy to fly, reliable, strong. If it's that good, why the hell do our guys need a month to make the transition and qualify?"

"Because while it's a fine airplane, it also has a few faults. Such as a braking system that must have been invented by an undertaker. It's also the toughest airplane to land that I've ever flown. The gear is so stiff we'll have to log the bounces, not the landing.

And whoever says it's easy to handle her must have been comparing it to a steam locomotive. It ain't easy. The DC-2 is a balky bitch. Strong, yes, but temperamental, and with some bad habits that can kill anybody who gets careless. And that, Mr. President, is why we need a month's training."

"You got it." Barney surrendered. The one area in which he was open to argument was flying; in effect, he still was saluting the pilots just as he had done himself that day he first watched Bud Lindeman take off on a trip. In fact, it had become more than a symbolism. He had passed the word to all station managers that ground personnel in charge of boarding flights were to salute the captain just before each aircraft left the ramp area. The first time Larry Aroni watched this ceremony he half-kidded Barney about it.

"This isn't the army, Barney," he said.

"It looks good," Barney insisted. "I'm trying to create an image of respect."

"Respect, my ass. The pilots are lucky nobody's thumbing his nose at 'em. They're getting paid enough without the rest of the airline having to genuflect."

"That I know," Barney conceded. "But most passengers see that salute. I think it makes them look up to the pilots, provides more confidence—and when you do that, you reduce anxiety."

Except for a handful of pilots who secretly relished drawing salutes, the flight crews were far more interested in the growing strength of their union, the Air Line Pilots Association. While it lacked official bargaining power, it had at least emerged from its underground status and become a recognized, respectable organization. The airlines hadn't even known it existed until an ALPA membership card was found on the body of a pilot killed in a crash.

Barney always had gotten along well with the pilots. Unlike the rest of the carriers, he had paid them a flat monthly salary regardless of the actual hours they flew. The other airlines paid a monthly base rate plus a set amount for each mile flown—a formula which encouraged most pilots to fly in marginal weather just to keep up their income. Coastal's pilots felt no such pressure, even though in the balmier months their colleagues had bigger paychecks. Barney's refusal to go along with the majority of carriers wasn't entirely altruistic nor the product of devotion to safety; the more complicated pay formula meant more paperwork and Barney didn't have the manpower to handle it. He had even stuck with the flat montly salary when the industry, early in the New Deal, tried to shift over to a pay scale based solely on hours flown. The dispute almost led to a nationwide pilots' strike that was barely averted.

Four months later, the Wagner Labor Board issued Decision 83, setting maximum flying hours at eighty-five a month and minimum salaries based on hours, miles, and base pay. Barney wanted to stick to the flat pay, but Decision 83 was tacked onto the Air Mail Act of 1934 and Coastal's crews had to be included. For all practical purposes, Coastal's pilots didn't have to wait for the Congressional action; they had, in effect, an informal unwritten agreement with Barney on wages and working conditions, and the lack of contractual status meant little to them. Every pilot knew the president of Coastal was accessible, that he knew every man flying the line on a first-name basis and clearly enjoyed the flight crews more than any other group of employees.

It was true, however, that a few crusty die-hards expressed everything from severe doubts to traumatic shock when Barney announced the hiring of Coastal's first stewardesses. He was behind most airlines in this move, but the advent of the DC-2's made the acquisition of female flight attendants essential. Al Davenport was one of the objectors.

"Rickenbacker is hiring stewards over at Eastern, and Pan American has stewards too," the chief pilot argued. "Why the hell do we have to take on a bunch of silly broads?"

"That's just two airlines," Barney retorted. "Everyone else is hiring girls because that's what the public wants. Hell, United proved that from the day they first hired a stewardess."

Davenport was beginning to irk him on too many occasions. It wasn't so much his persistent defense of his pilots, but his attitude toward areas of airline operations which really weren't his concern. Al had vociferously backed Lindeman when Bud protested the "streetcar" advertisements, had openly scoffed at one of Motts's ill-fated fly-with-your-wife campaigns, and now objected loudly to Barney's decision to sell four of the seven trimotors since the DC-2's had joined the fleet.

"Sell two maybe, but not four," the chief pilot complained. "The DC-2's a relatively untried airplane. It'll probably have a few mechanical bugs which means we're gonna wind up with more than the average delays and cancellations. We'll need a couple of Fords for backup."

"Look," Barney said firmly, "so long as I'm president of this airline, we are not going to have surplus planes sitting idle. Particularly obsolete airplanes. A passenger would rather take a delay or even outright cancellation than be forced into flying inferior equipment. Those Fords belong in a museum and I'm not gonna hang onto them any longer than I have to. We'll keep enough to fly our secondary routes and fulfill our mail obligations, and that's that, Al!"

Davenport had stomped out, but Barney couldn't have cared less. He had a pretty good notion that sooner or later he and the chief pilot would be parting company, but he was not yet ready to make waves. And he had the utmost respect for the little man's technical and administrative competence. Davenport was a disciplinarian without being a martinet; he had excellent rapport with his men, all of whom knew Davenport could fly better than any of them. Barney was willing to tolerate his grouchiness and rather low opinion of anyone who couldn't fly at all, his attitude toward sales-oriented officers like Motts, and his resentment of Barney because of what had happened to Lindeman.

Possibly because of his size, Davenport's personality was essentially negative and belligerent. Like many airmen who had learned to fly Jennies in open cockpits and by seat-of-the-pants instincts, he resisted anything new whether it was a new technique, such as instrument flying, or a new airplane. Once he finished griping and grousing, however, he could accept the inevitable and try his best to make it work. He had denounced instrument training, Barney remembered, yet now there wasn't a better instrument-qualified pilot around, and he insisted that Coastal's crews be just as sharp. This impressed Barney to a far greater degree than Davenport's sour disposition and tendency to interfere with other departments.

If there was one thing Barnwell Burton feared above all else, it was the possibility of a fatal crash. He was only too aware that a bad accident could depress traffic by as much as twenty-five percent during the next day or two, not only on the airline involved but throughout the industry. There were other problems for the affected airline—almost certain lawsuits, the need to juggle schedules to fill the void, not to mention the loss of an expensive airplane, seldom fully covered by the prohibitively expensive "hull insurance." This was why he tolerated the sour-tempered, often obstructive, but most capable chief pilot.

Stewardesses. Barney approached the task in much the same manner as he tackled other areas in which he lacked experience; he was not afraid to seek guidance and accept suggestions from other carriers. In this case, he approached Steve Stimpson of United, who had been the man responsible for establishing the new profession. In 1930, Stimpson had talked Boeing Air Transport into letting eight registered nurses fly as cabin attendants over Boeing's Chicago–San Francisco route for a trial period of three months. The first nurse he hired, Ellen Church, set down the requirements: RN, not more than twenty-five years of age, not over 5′4″ in height and with a maximum weight of 115 pounds. Miss Church herself also designed the first uniforms: a dark green, double-breasted jersey jacket, matching skirt and tam that resembled a shower cap, and a flowing green cape with a gray collar.

By the time Barney got around to deciding it was time for Coastal to hire stewardesses, women flight attendants were commonplace throughout the industry. He called Stimpson, whom he had once met at an airline function.

"We're going to take on some girls, Steve, and before we start hiring I'd like to know if your original requirements are still in effect."

"They are," Stimpson assured him. "We do more training now. Four years ago they learned as they flew; now we give 'em a week's training. Most of the other carriers have followed our guidelines, except for that height requirement. They aren't sticking to the five-four cutoff because the gals don't have to be that short in a DC-2. We'll change ours, too, when we start flying airplanes bigger than the 247."

"What are you paying them?"

"We started them at a hundred and twenty-five a month for a hundred hours' flying. They just now went up to one-fifty for the same hours."

"Why the nurse requirement?"

"Several reasons. Mostly because half the passengers on any flight are guaranteed to get airsick and we figured a nurse could handle this better. Second, nurses are more mature and adaptable to screwy situations; they stay cool and they generally react well to emergencies. And this is important, Barney, when you realize that we put the girls on our planes largely to alleviate the fear factor. The average male passenger might be scared stiff, but when he sees some little gal smiling in the middle of something like turbulence, he figures there's no sense in being frightened himself."

"Or showing fright," Barney chuckled.

"Right. Anyway, they're working out great at United. I think you'll be more than happy if Coastal hires a few."

"Steve, is there any federal regulation or law that requires them to be nurses?"

"Nary a one. We think it's just good policy. For the time being, anyway. I suppose someday the demand for stewardesses will outstrip the supply of nurses. Not many RN's want to fly for a career. We have a rough time finding new applicants. We make 'em quit when they get married, you know."

"Yeah," Barney said. "Well, I guess we'll take the plunge."

"Mind some advice? Hire one girl from another carrier, someone with experience. Make her your chief stew so she can train the others you get."

"I'll take that advice, Steve. How about someone from United?" he asked, and laughed.

Barney checked around and through a friend at American he was given the name of Vickie Doman, one of the first stewardesses American had hired. Time was running out. Barney flew to New York where she was based and took her to lunch at the Astor. Typically, he came right to the point.

"I want to hire a chief stewardess for Coastal," he said. "You've been highly recommended. If you're interested, we'll talk. If not, sit back and enjoy the free meal."

"I'm interested." She was a little taller than he expected, about 5′5″ he guessed, with dark hair, alert, sparkling eyes, a stunning figure, and an air of deceptive nonchalance as if she was trying to hide intelligence behind the trappings of a pretty face.

"Good. I take it you're an RN. Or were."

"Yep."

"Like being a nurse?"

"Not particularly."

"That is a major point in your favor."

She laughed. "You got something about nurses, Mr. Burton?"

"I have great respect for Florence Nightingale and Amelia Earhart, thank you. She was a nurse during the war, you know. Anyway, my personal prejudices are not the point. What I'm getting at is that I can't see any real sense behind this general assumption that a cabin attendant has to be a registered nurse. I'd like your opinion."

Vickie pondered his question. "I'd say that a nursing background would be a point in an applicant's favor but not necessarily the deciding factor. I definitely wouldn't make it a mandatory requirement. That automatically disqualifies a great many women who'd make excellent stewardesses."

"That happens to be exactly the way I feel," said Barney.

"On the other hand," Vickie Doman added with a slight smile, "being a nurse shouldn't disqualify anyone, either. After all, if you can put up with bedpans and unreasonable patients, you can put up with anything or anyone on an airplane."

"Fair enough," Barney allowed. "Vickie, I'd like to have your help in selecting applicants, starting with how the hell we get applicants."

"I take it I'm hired?"

"You are."

"I don't mean to sound crass, but at what salary?"

"Add one hundred dollars a month to whatever you're making as a stewardess. Six months from now, you'll get an automatic increase of another twenty-five. Along with a title go all executive privileges."

Vickie Doman smiled. "Well, I guess I'd better ask—what executive privileges?"

"Unlimited personal passes, and you'll be eligible for something I'm in the process of getting organized. Namely, a bonus system for our officers. If Coastal makes money, so will its executives . . . above and beyond their regular salaries. I'll be honest with you, I haven't established any bonus system yet and I couldn't give you any flat promise as to when we'll be paying our bonuses. It all depends on how this airline does financially. And how it does is largely up to those who run it, including you."

"You have just hired yourself a Director of Cabin Personnel," Miss Doman announced. "I guess I'll have to give American two weeks' notice, though."

"I've already talked to C. R. Smith. You're now employed by Coastal Airlines, as of today. I'll give you two days to get your things packed and moved down to Washington. This is Monday . . . I'll have an office ready for you by Thursday morning. We'll put you up at the Willard Hotel temporarily, until you can find a place of your own. The Willard's right across the street from our downtown executive offices."

"My God, you work fast!"

"In this business," Barney said quietly, "you keep running to stay ahead of the knives aimed at your back. By the way, how much stuff do you have to move?"

"Just my clothes. My apartment here is furnished."

"Good. Here's fifty in cash for incidental expenses. That's an advance, not a gift. I'm glad you're joining us, Vickie. Now let's get to your first assignment. Where do we find applicants?"

"How many girls do you want to hire immediately?"

"Just six to start with. They'll work only our DC-2 trips. We'll add more later."

"When does DC-2 service begin?"

"Hopefully, October fifteenth."

"That doesn't give us much time. I suppose the best thing to do is put an ad in the Washington newspapers, just something to the effect that Coastal is hiring stewardesses and anyone interested can apply in person. Normally, I'd suggest putting ads in papers throughout your system, which would give you a greater variety of applicants, a better cross-section. But there doesn't seem to be much time. We can try Washington first and conduct interviews in other cities when we have to hire more staff. Now, who'll be doing the interviewing?"

"You, me, and probably Calvin Motts; he's vice-president of Sales now. I figure the three of us could arrive at some kind of consensus on each applicant. It doesn't seem fair to have one person pass judgment."

"Next question—uniforms?"

"Christ, we'll have to have them, I guess. Tell you what, Vickie, you work up some kind of attractive ensemble and I'll order up a batch."

She shook her head ruefully. "Mr. Burton, if you think we can design a uniform, get the measurements of six girls, and have it manufactured and ready for fitting in less than one month, you're a hopeless optimist."

"What the hell's so tough about making a uniform?" Barney demanded. "Douglas can build a whole DC-2 in a month. We only need six outfits—no, seven. I guess you should have one."

Vickie rolled her eyes. "Okay. I'll do some sketches and you can look them over after I get down to Washington. Any color preferences?"

"Red." Barney waved for a waiter.

"Red? That'll be pretty loud."

"We have been painting our airplanes silver and red for two years now. We need some red in the uniform. Maybe not an all-red outfit, but something with red in it."

"I'll see what I can come up with. Anything else I should be thinking about in the next two days, other than packing?"

"Yeah. Training. How much time do we need to turn out a good stewardess?"

"Depends on what you'll be asking her to do. Unless your DC-2's are flying hotels serving seven-course dinners, a week should suffice. I'll make up some kind of curriculum which you can approve or modify."

"Hell, I'll okay anything you suggest. That's your department. Let's order another cocktail and celebrate, Vickie."

"Sure . . . Just how many passengers does Coastal handle each day?"

"Three hundred."

She smiled at him. "Not bad, Mr. Burton. Not bad at all."

They were discussing what to offer in the way of in-flight service aboard the new airliners and Vickie offered her own frank appraisal of the galley equipment Barney had ordered. He had gone for the cheapest on the market, against Douglas's advice.

"It's lousy," she said placidly.

"And just what's lousy about it?" Barney demanded.

"Too small, the drawer latches must have been designed by someone who hates women, and the whole thing's so flimsy you'll have nuts and bolts rolling down the aisle every time we land. Anyway, I'll bet American's new DST's won't have such junk."

"American has a lot more dough than—" Barney's mouth stopped in mid-air. "American's *what*?"

"DST."

"What the hell is a DST?"

"I think it stands for Douglas Sleeper Transport."

"Explain."

"Do you know Bill Littlewood?"

"Not personally but I know of him—American's chief engineer. Anytime he says an airplane is good, I'll buy the damned thing sight unseen. Why?"

"I had him on a flight, just before I left American. He was telling me about their ordering a bigger and faster DC-2. One with sleeping accommodations for transcontinental flights, like our old Condors, only a lot better, he said. Bill called it a DST and I asked him what the initials stood for." She made a face. "Maybe I shouldn't have mentioned it. He didn't say anything about its being a big secret."

"There aren't many secrets in this business," Barney observed. "Don't worry, Vickie. If it ever comes up when I'm talking to someone from American, I won't get you involved. I'm pretty curious, though—DST. Of course, we couldn't use a sleeper plane on our routes, but I don't see why it would have to be configured just for sleeping berths. Did Littlewood give you any idea of passenger capacity?"

Vickie shook her head. "No, just that it would be bigger than the

DC-2. I'd rather not talk about it anymore, Mr. Burton. I have the feeling I shouldn't even have mentioned the airplane. Now, about these uniform designs . . ."

Amateur though she was, she had innate taste and talent. Barney liked her sketches, quickly choosing a skirt and simple military jacket with subtly squared shoulders; their only conflict involved color. The chief stewardess suggested a medium gray with red piping, while Barney preferred what would have been her last choice —a white uniform with red piping.

"That's really smart," Barney admired.

"Smart and impractical," Vickie said. "White gets dirty too quickly."

"So what do we have dry-cleaners for? It's a beautiful combination—red and white."

"White and red," she corrected. "Take the darker color. Look at American's dark blue. A stewardess uniform is for work, not high fashion. And white is associated with nurses."

"Also virgins," Barney muttered. "Okay, Vick, gray and red it is, and tomorrow we start interviewing. How many applicants do you figure we'll draw?"

"Well, fifty or sixty wouldn't surprise me. Not after you insisted that the ads specify a nursing degree wasn't required."

The actual number interviewed the next day was two hundred and three. Barney was more of a referee than an interviewer, Cal and Vickie being in constant opposition when judging applicants. They had begun at 9:00 A.M. and still had forty they hadn't seen yet at 5:00 P.M. These were asked to come back the following morning and most said they would.

The three of them collapsed in Barney's office after the first day of interviews and agreed on formal standards, with Vickie laying down the major prerequisites.

"We should look for personality, attitude, maturity, even a sense of humor if we can spot it."

"You forgot looks," Motts put in. "Beauty is important, too."

"Only in a general sense. A good-looking girl is fine provided she has the other attributes. If you judge on beauty alone, you'll wind up with a flock of brainless peacocks."

"Makes sense," Barney said. "However, we wouldn't want to disqualify anyone just because she's a knockout."

"Amen," Motts drooled.

"I'd say we could modify United's original criteria a bit," Barney suggested. "How about a five-foot-seven maximum on height and a hundred twenty pounds in weight?"

"Make it five-eight and one twenty-five," Vickie proposed.

"Five-eight's kinda tall," Motts said.

"Any height standard is rather arbitrary," Vickie pointed out. "All we can do is base it on the physical dimensions of the airplane. Someone who's five-three would have trouble reaching the overhead bin on the DC-2. A girl who's five-nine would have to spend three-fourths of her time stooping on a trimotor or 247."

Barney was startled at the last. "Who the hell told you we might be getting some 247's?"

"Nobody. I was just using that airplane as an example."

"Oh. Well, keep it under your hat. You, too, Cal. I, uh, I haven't said anything to anybody, but I've been talking to United about buying or leasing a couple of their Boeings. Nothing definite yet. Okay, Vickie, go on."

"I'm finished. Five-seven or five-eight—you can decide—and a hundred-twenty-five-pound maximum. Age limit: twenty to twenty-six years."

"Make that height limit five-eight," Barney ruled. "Now you'd better brief us on what questions we're not asking and should ask."

"The same ones I was asked when I applied to American. Why do you want to become a stewardess? Have you ever flown before? What kind of hobbies do you have? Do you like meeting new people? Would you rather read a good book or go out to a lively party?"

Barney was doubtful. "We're supposed to judge personality, maturity, and attitude using innocuous questions like those?"

"They're not innocuous, I keep telling you." Vickie Doman was all business. "For example, suppose like today we have two applicants fairly equal in appearance. You ask if they'd rather read a book or go to a party. One says a book, the other chooses the party. Which one would make the better stewardess?"

The two men looked at each other uncertainly. "Well, I guess I'd take the girl who preferred a good book. More mature, more serious," said Barney.

"That's my choice, too," Motts said.

"You're both wrong. The party-goer's a better applicant. More outgoing, extroverted, receptive to challenge and to passenger needs. See what I mean?"

"I have a hunch," Barney said without rancor, "that you'll be doing most of the final selecting."

She did, largely because Barney tended to follow her instincts and because Motts quickly established his total inability to judge objectively. Barney finally said, "Motts, we might as well have conducted these interviews on a goddamned casting couch."

They had set up a rating scale of one to ten, deciding in advance to reject anyone scoring less than an eight. By the end of the second day of interviewing, they had pruned the hopefuls down to fifteen excellent prospects and from this list they finally picked six girls. Only one was a registered nurse. At Barney's suggestion, Vickie wrote the other nine finalists individual letters informing them that their applications were being kept on file and that they would be contacted if any openings arose.

Vickie Doman trained the first class in four days, working from a manual consisting of five mimeographed pages mostly plagiarized from the American manual she still possessed. There would come a day, she said, when Coastal's training program would last five tough weeks instead of four easy days, working from a manual as thick as a large city telephone directory. Barney was startled at the calmness of her prediction. Presenting somewhat greater difficulties was the matter of uniforms, just as she had also predicted.

He had contracted with a Baltimore clothing manufacturer to make them up from Vickie's sketches, receiving the firm's solemn assurance that they would be completed when the first class graduated. The day before Barney was scheduled to pin on their wings, the manufacturer phoned to confess his inability to deliver on time.

Barney hung up, sighed, and had his secretary phone Vickie Doman to come to his office. Barney told her about the uniform delay, expecting an I-told-you-so and not getting any—which made him feel worse, inasmuch as he was mad and needed someone to fight with.

"It's too bad," she merely said. "We'll have to improvise some kind of makeshift outfit until the uniforms arrive."

"*Makeshift*? What the hell are they supposed to wear on the flights—street clothes?"

"In effect, yes. We'll send all six of them to a reasonably-priced department store or a women's specialty shop. We can buy six skirts, six white blouses, and a half-dozen raincoats all the same color. They'll do for the time being. We'll have to buy some kind of coat anyway for the colder weather, so we might as well do it now. A simple blue or black skirt; the blouses will go with anything."

She was decisive and smart, he thought. Then asked, "How about uniform hats?"

"They'll have to wait. But they should have overnight bags . . . The light-weight Amelia Earhart model would be fine. And they're red."

Barney frowned, then suddenly cheered up. "Red skirts, Vickie? How about six red skirts?"

She smiled. "Okay, Mr. Burton, red skirts it is."

She found the skirts, blouses, and raincoats and the ceremony went off nicely, with Barney springing for champagne and a filet-mignon dinner at the Willard, plus an orchid corsage for each stewardess. He told Vickie he was going to deduct the cost of the emergency outfits from the Baltimore manufacturer's bill—which he knew he'd never get around to doing. As angry as he had been, he was fair enough to admit he hadn't provided sufficient time for the delivery. He also was sharp enough to tell his new director of public relations not to send the graduation photograph to any newspapers.

The PR man was Ned Hoffman, a personable, eager youngster Barney had conned into leaving the Washington *Post*. Hoffman was unhappy; the stewardess graduation was the first real assignment he had handled since Barney had hired him.

"I don't get it, Mr. Burton," he said, looking worried. "They're all good-looking kids. The papers eat up art like that."

Barney snorted. "Ned, I don't want anyone seeing those god-damned off-the-rack outfits. Our stews look like a class from a parochial high school. We'll take another picture when they get their regular uniforms."

The uniforms eventually arrived a week after Coastal inaugurated DC-2 service. Barney assigned the three new planes to his prime route segments: Buffalo–Washington, Washington–Pittsburgh–Minneapolis, and Atlanta–Pittsburgh. But mixed with this undeniable triumph was his now almost paranoid hatred of the dependable but woefully obsolete Tin Goose. At an ever-increasing pace, the airlines were dumping their once-proud fleets of Ford trimotors, Condors, Boeing 80's, Fokkers, and Vegas. The DC-2 was the new queen of the airways, and right behind it was Lockheed's latest transport, the twin-engine Model 10, the Electra. It galled Barney that Coastal was one of the last airlines still flying the Fords.

The Electra—named after a star, like all Lockheed planes—was an ideal choice for the smaller carriers. It carried only ten passengers compared to the DC-2's fourteen, but its higher power-to-weight ratio gave it a cruising speed of 190 miles an hour, which made it faster than the Douglas transport, and its purchasers already were advertising the Electra as "the world's fastest airliner."

It would have been perfect for Coastal's route system but Barney had to face a simple fact: he couldn't afford another brand-new airplane, not even one priced at $50,000—a third less than what Coastal had paid for the DC-2.

The million-dollar loan Barney had floated through three lenders had been spent for the trio of DC-2's, modernized ground facilities, for badly needed maintenance equipment, and to cover the payroll for Coastal's rapidly expanding staff. As of the day DC-2 service started, what once had been a three-man operation was now a company of four hundred employees. Traffic was up and Coastal Airlines was operating in the black, although medium-gray would have been a more accurate metaphor. Yet when in November Barney went before his new board of directors, seeking their approval for the purchase of four Electras, he was confronted by strong resistance.

Henry McKay was his only supporter, while the elder McKay said he would vote for the Lockheed acquisitions only if they were financed through a Reconstruction Finance Corporation loan. The four new directors were solidly against any additional equipment financing from any private source—"for the time being," as one of them put it. "We'd like to see an improved profit picture before the airline spends any more money."

"You aren't likely to improve the picture without spending," Barney said sourly, "but if that's your verdict, I'll have to abide by it."

With no forewarning he suddenly shifted gear and proposed adding two new directors—Larry Aroni and Calvin Motts. He had doubts about Cal, but they were his sole vice-presidents and at least in Motts he had total subservience. Cal would vote the way Barney wanted on an issue. Larry was far more independent but terribly loyal.

"You gentlemen are respected in your own fields," Barney said with ingratiating earnestness, "but I think it is unfair to Coastal that its board includes only one person from within the company itself—namely myself. Mr. Aroni has been with us almost since the airline began operations, while Mr. Motts is generally recognized as one of the best traffic and sales experts in the entire industry. I sincerely believe they could make valuable contributions to the decision-making processes of our board, decisions which on many occasions require considerable technical and industrial knowledge."

The vote in favor of making Aroni and Motts directors was 7–0, the elderly Frank McKay casting his affirmative response with a wry smile. Unlike the four newcomers, he knew precisely what Barney was trying to achieve. Immediately after the vote, Barney called in his two stunned new directors and then asked the board to approve an application to RFC for an equipment loan.

"You told me a long time ago that you'd never ask the government for help," Henry reminded him. "I'm not opposing this, Barney, but I'd like to know why you've changed your mind."

"Because it's apparent that the majority is against raising funds through private financing. However, your father indicated he would favor aid from RFC—a compromise solution. And I'm perfectly willing to compromise. I still don't like going to Uncle Sam with our hat in hand, so to speak, but we badly need replacements for our Fords and if an RFC loan is the only way, I'll have to go along. Reluctantly, I might add."

Frank McKay eyed him suspiciously. "What will you buy if the government grants it? More DC-2's? Or those Electras you're suddenly so enamored of?"

"Neither, if I can help it."

"Neither?"

"I've already talked to United about buying two or three surplus 247's. They're available for thirty thousand dollars apiece—for our purposes, a better buy than new Electras. United's maintenance is superb and Larry is sure those airplanes will be in mint condition. They're available immediately, by the way."

"Well," Henry arched his eyebrows. "You sure won't have much trouble getting only sixty grand from the RFC. They're used to much larger handouts."

Barney had a half-smile on his lips, and Henry sensed he was about to unload a bomb.

"I don't intend to ask for just sixty thousand," he said calmly. "I'm going to ask for a half-million."

"For Christ's sake!" McKay blurted. "What for?"

"Douglas is building a new transport plane. It looks like the DC-2 except it's bigger and faster. It'll carry twenty-one passengers and a total payload of six thousand pounds. It'll cost us less than seventy cents a mile to operate, which is just about what the Ford is running. That's *three times* the payload with identical operating costs. In other words, gentlemen, when this airplane goes into service, the airlines will have a transport that can make money just carrying passengers. And I'm going to make sure that Coastal isn't flying around with inferior equipment while whoever buys *that* airplane is coining dough."

"Why not go along with our present fleet until this new plane is available?" Frank McKay asked.

"Because the DC-3—that's Douglas' non-sleeper version— won't be making even its first flight test until late next year. Then American will put the first one into service in '36. We wouldn't get ours until probably early in '37. That means we need a reasonably modern fleet for the next two years. The DC-2, augmented by a few Boeings, will suffice during that period."

"How much will this DC-3 cost?" asked the vice-president from Riggs.

"If we order now, about a hundred grand apiece. And I'd like to buy five to start with. Okay? If there are no objections, let's adjourn for lunch."

An hour later, the board reconvened and voted unanimously to give Coastal's president authority to file an RFC application for the loan. The two newly elected directors and Barney left the meeting together and stopped by a bar for self-congratulatory toasts. After a quick drink Barney excused himself and went off to meet Henry McKay for dinner.

Aroni was absent-mindedly fingering his glass as Barney made his way out. "You know something, Cal, that Barney has one large set of balls."

"Huh?"

"I mean, he has the guts of a burglar stealing in front of ten cops. He walked into that meeting and committed the airline to those Boeings, and an airplane that hasn't even been off the ground yet, without knowing if the directors would back him. He wasn't sure of any majority—himself, McKay, and us adds up to four on a nine-man board."

"I can't see where that took so much courage," Motts said. "If they had turned him down, we'd just keep operating what we have for a while."

Larry chuckled. "If they had voted against him, we were in the soup, pal. Barney sold our last four trimotors two days ago."

Motts gasped.

"Yeah, a very ballsy guy, our chief. He peddled those Fords to some aircraft broker and guaranteed delivery by March 1. Which is just about the time we'll need to get our hands on United's 247's and train the pilots."

The RFC loan went through without a hitch and Barney promptly flew to the West Coast, met with Donald Douglas, and signed a contract for five DC-3's. He could not help thinking that it wasn't so long ago he would have been in awe of the bluff, outspoken manufacturer. Now he felt himself an equal, called him "Don" without a trace of self-consciousness, and thoroughly enjoyed their conversation on the state of commercial aviation.

"I'll be honest with you, Barney," Douglas told him. "I don't think much of American's trying to make a Pullman-plane out of our bird. Nobody can tell me passengers can do much sleeping while flying. Hell, you gotta wake 'em up before every landing so they won't hurt their eardrums. The only real utilization for an airplane like the DC-3 is to operate it in the configuration you want—twenty-one seats. American's buying twenty DST's, but we'll be lucky if we break even. The damned things cost too much to build, what with all that hardware for the berths. Anyway, who the hell wants to buy a sleeper-plane? Night-flying is about as popular as silent movies."

"But I take it you've got great hopes for the airplane the way we'll be operating it," Barney said.

"Well, let's say I'd rather be concentrating on the DC-2. It's about as big a plane as the airlines need right now and maybe for a good many years. That DC-3 development eats up our profits on the DC-2 as fast as we turn out the planes. I could be wrong, but I think the commercial airliner market is just about at the saturation point. Everyone says the DC-2 is the greatest thing to come along since man invented the wheel, but the public isn't rushing out to buy airline tickets. Between Boeing, Lockheed, and us, we're building too many airplanes."

"I just have a hunch," Barney said soberly, "you could be wrong."

"I hope you're right. But why do you think so?"

"Because the DC-2 isn't the last word in air transportation. By your own specifications, the DC-3 will be miles ahead of anything flying today in every aspect, including safety. That's the magic word—safety. Build an airplane that'll make people feel secure and safe, and you'll build aviation's version of Emerson's mousetrap. If the DC-3 is that kind of an aircraft, you'll sell a couple of hundred —maybe three hundred. And if there *is* going to be a war you'll sell thousands to the military."

Barney arrived back in Washington two days before Christmas. Unaccustomed to the chill after a week in California, he scooped up his mail and hurried into the kitchen for a shot of brandy. A picture postcard caught his eye as he knocked back the brandy. It was from Amelia, sent from dockside. She was by now somewhere in the Pacific aboard an ocean liner headed for Honolulu, her

Lockheed Vega lashed to the deck. Instantly Barney realized what she was up to; the card confirmed it. It was 2,400 miles from Hawaii to the mainland—246 miles farther than her trans-Atlantic flights. But some businessmen had put up prize money for the first successful solo flight and she was going to take a crack at it.

No one who had tried so far—male or female—had made it. *I am confident,* she had printed in bold block letters with a big exclamation mark. *But have painted my Vega a beautiful red just in case it winds up down in all that blue-green.*

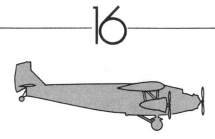

16

The New Year didn't start well.

Barney kept fretting over weaknesses in his managerial corps; Larry Aroni was the only one he thoroughly trusted and honestly respected. For a time, he kept his eyes on Ben Shub for possible promotion, but just as he was about to name him Motts's assistant, Shub informed him he was going over to Eastern as superintendent of stations. Barney offered him the same spot at Coastal—even though there was no such position in the company—but Ben said no.

"Eastern's a bigger carrier," he explained. "It isn't just the salary, Mr. Burton—they're not offering me that much more than I'm already making here. It's the job that's bigger. I figure it's time to move on. I'm sorry, because I'm grateful for the chance you gave me. I've learned a lot working for Coastal, and for you."

"Well, if that's the way you feel, it's a free country," Barney said with a decided effort to sound magnanimous. "I wish you nothing but good luck."

Inwardly he was seething. Shub was his first experience with defection. He was too used to raiding other carriers for talent, and he couldn't stomach such counterpunches. In fact, his immediate and instinctive reaction was to resume his own raiding—and quite deliberately he hit Eastern, hiring their New York station manager and naming him Coastal's superintendent of stations. Then, to replace Shub, he talked American's station manager at Buffalo into moving to Washington.

One area of weakness he wanted to shore up quickly was purchasing. It was one of Barney's ancillary duties, at first not too time-consuming but eventually a job requiring an exorbitant amount of attention. His initial solution was to decentralize it, giving each department head freedom to buy supplies as needed but with Barney's approval required for any amount exceeding a thousand dollars. This worked fine provided his department heads knew what they were doing; Larry Aroni, for example, could be relied on to buy only essentials, look for reasonable prices without compromising quality, and stay within his allotted budget. Cal Motts, on the other hand, operated like an avaricious shopper prowling through mercantile jungles looking for fire sales. He could not resist apparent bargains and on too many occasions he fell flat on his duff.

He came into Barney's office one day to proclaim the greatest coup in airline purchasing.

"I've just bought fifty thousand ice-cream container bags," he announced.

"What the hell do we need with fifty thousand ice-cream bags?"

"Well, Boss, they *were* for ice cream. You know, the lined, insulated bags you put ice-cream containers into so the stuff'll stay hard? But we can use 'em as air-sickness bags. They're perfect, and I got 'em for two cents a bag. We've been paying five cents apiece for our burp bags."

"Yeah," Barney agreed, "but fifty thousand of the damned things? They'll last us for another ten years."

"Right!" Motts said proudly. "But remember we're getting 'em for only five hundred bucks. If the price of burp bags goes up, we're protected."

Barney was dubious, but he told Motts to put his bargain bags on the airplanes as needed and forgot about the incident until Vickie Doman came into his office two days later, wearing an exaggerated smile on her face.

"You look like you were either about to cry or bust out laughing," Barney growled.

"That about describes it. You know those new burp bags Mr. Motts bought?"

"I should. Fifty thousand of the damned things."

"How would you feel about throwing all fifty thousand away? Take a look. One of our stews brought this in to show me—she asked if the guy who bought those bags was crazy." Vickie reached into her handbag and brought out one of Calvin's bargains. Barney examined it and turned red. On the bag, in large black letters, were printed the words: THANK YOU. COME AGAIN.

Motts was penitent but not exactly cured. Three days after the ice-cream-bag fiasco, he decided to order calendars to be sent out as gifts for special customers, travel agents, and the press. This necessitated the purchase of mailing tubes. Motts located a supply at an excellent price in lots of a thousand. Unfortunately they proved too small.

Barney offered cash bonus to any employee coming up with a way to use the thousand mailing tubes. He was unable to award any prize, inasmuch as all seven entries he received were not only identical but also impractical, considering the limited size of the receptacle into which it was unanimously suggested the mailing tubes be inserted.

The phone rang in Barney's apartment, jarring him awake.

"Barney!" It was Ernie Pyle. "She's three hundred miles out."

"Who?" Barney mumbled, half asleep, squinting at the clock. It was 3:00 A.M.

"Amelia, you nit. A passenger liner just spotted her three hundred miles off the California coast."

"Holy cow!" Barney sat bolt upright. "You mean she's in the air?"

"Has been since four P.M. yesterday. Where the hell have you been?"

"In Buffalo on business. Got in late. Ernie, is she all right, do you think? That's the longest flight she's ever tried."

"She'll be fine, just fine. I'll keep you posted," said Pyle, and hung up.

Her flight had been delayed by some sort of political bickering and the Hawaiian sponsors were getting cold feet, according to the note she had sent him. But as it turned out, she had confronted them wearing jodhpurs and her leather jacket and simply informed the gathering she would not hear of calling off the whole thing. "My business is flying," she had proudly told them. "I intend to fly to California this week, with or without your support." And she had, taking off with her customary lack of fanfare.

Barney got back to his office from a late lunch to find a message from Ernie on his phone: *January 12, 1935. Eighteen hours, fifteen minutes.*

Moments later the whole office was excitedly gathered around someone's radio to hear the broadcast of her triumphant reception at Bay Farm Island Airport near Oakland, where a cheering throng of ten thousand had greeted her landing.

Barney stood in the doorway of his office, hands in his pockets, listening and smiling at the news of her success and the repeated descriptions of her red plane.

She had her record.

Of all the people working for Barnwell Burton, only Larry Aroni came close to the category of friendship. It was one of Barney's less desirable traits that he never seemed to have truly close friends; this had been true throughout his school days, when he was something of a loner, and was even more true as an adult. He craved respect rather than affection, personal success instead of genuine relationships. It never occurred to him that he didn't have to give up one for the other. He deliberately kept aloof from his fellow officers, believing that to lower an emotional drawbridge made him too vulnerable, that friendship would become a kind of Trojan Horse permitting infiltration that might trap and destroy him.

He was closer to Aroni than anyone else, largely because he trusted the stocky, candid Italian more than anyone else. Yet he really never let him approach that figurative drawbridge—he merely condescended to cross over the moat himself on occasions and meet Larry on equal footing. And so he was best man at Aroni's wedding when the vice-president of Maintenance took himself a bride—a Nordic beauty named Norma Erickson. She was a model whom Larry had met while she was posing for a DC-2 publicity shot Ned Hoffman had arranged. The introduction was not exactly the type described in spongy love novels—the DC-2 had just gone into the hangar for an engine change which had to be delayed while mechanics towed it back out so a photographer could take his pictures. Aroni was furious and when the cameraman kept insisting "just a few more shots, Miss Erickson," Larry blew up.

"Miss Erickson," he bellowed, "get your goddamned butt away from that airplane or I'll put it back in the hangar while you're still sitting on the wheel!"

She looked at this burly, homely man, a good four inches shorter than she, and turned to the photographer. "He's right. They've got more important things to do with this airplane and you've taken enough shots to paper a centerfield fence."

Hoffman started to protest, intercepted Aroni's look of undiluted anger, and retreated with the photographer in his wake.

"I'm sorry," Miss Erickson said. "They could have finished this crap in five minutes, but every cameraman thinks he's Hurrell."

"Who the hell is Hurrell?"

"A Hollywood glamour photographer. Takes pictures of all the top stars."

"You look like a top Hollywood star," he said bluntly.

"Thank you. I think you meant that."

"I did. I'd consider it an honor if you'd have dinner with me tonight."

"You married?"

"No. But I'm thinking about it."

"Anyone in particular?"

"Yes. You."

They were married a month later; at his request, she converted to Catholicism, and their happiness was in direct contrast to the steady bachelorhood of Barnwell Ernest Burton. Barney left the apartment in Alexandria and built a country house on land he had purchased in Potomac, Maryland, a sleepy crossroads twenty miles northwest of Washington. In 1935, Potomac was rolling farm country sprinkled with a few estates. Barney's house wasn't any estate, but it was located on three wooded acres.

Barney had given an architect carte blanche. His sole insistence was that it be equipped with a newfangled luxury known as air-conditioning. Cooled ventilation had begun to take hold in such places as theaters, restaurants, and office buildings, but it was virtually unknown in private homes. It was typical of Barnwell Burton that he took more interest in such gadgetry than in the overall aesthetics of his home; a technical advancement seemed vastly more important than his personal environment. He had spent more time and effort on the DC-2's interior than on the decor of his own Press Building office, to which he paid mere lip service in decorating.

When it came to buying a new car, he had picked a new Chrysler Airflow, its engineering a decade ahead of its time but a monstrous failure in looks. Barney didn't care; he was interested only in its body construction, streamlining, and rather revolutionary suspension system. Mechanically untalented himself, he translated this deficiency into wholehearted admiration for the mechanically inclined. Barney envied technicians and technology, even though he seldom understood either, and in some cases his envy became avarice—his new house being a good example.

The $42,000 Riggs mortgage on the place didn't bother him. He wasn't affluent by a long shot, having given himself a salary of $15,000 a year, which was slightly less than the industry average for airline presidents; but he spent little money on himself except for a new suit about every six months. His excitement over the new house lasted only as long as its construction. Once he moved in, the challenge was over.

He was the same when it came to the infrequent women in his life. He already had a mistress: the airline.

That spring Barney was invited to attend a U.S. Chamber of Commerce reception for airline presidents. Coastal, being one of the Washington-based carriers, was asked to have some stewardesses on hand. Vickie by now had twenty-three girls flying the line, but schedule conflicts and illnesses depleted the numbers available for the function.

"I can send Mary Ruth Webster," she told Barney, "but that's it unless you think this affair warrants canceling a flight."

"Nothing is *that* important," Barney said. "How about yourself? Can you make it?"

"I hate these affairs, Barney. But I guess you've reached the bottom of the barrel."

Barney drove them out to the party, was highly pleased with their poise, and noted with smug satisfaction that Vickie herself was the prettiest stewardess there. Even the severe cut of her military jacket couldn't hide her figure, and she had a deftness about her that Barney had to admire. She was informal without being flip, friendly with no trace of forwardness. While he spent most of the evening talking shop, he kept watching her, feeling not a little gratitude toward her. When the reception was over, he thanked her and offered to drive her home.

"Your offer is accepted," she said, smiling.

They set out to her apartment in Georgetown, talking quietly on the way about some of the people at the party. Barney was especially voluble on the subject of American's C. R. Smith.

"He's quite a guy. A real giant. And to tell you the truth, I was surprised when he came right up to you and called you by name."

"That's typical of C. R. I think he knows the names of nearly all the flight crews. The one I loved was Patterson of United. He's cute. Like a little pixie, yet you could sense the toughness under that smile of his."

"Yeah. Fair but tough. That's the impression I got of Al Adams, too."

"Adams?"

"Western Air Express. The short, young-looking guy with the black hair. Matter of fact, he *is* young. Let's see, he took over at Western two years ago and he was only twenty-nine. That makes him thirty-one now, and I'm twenty-eight."

Vickie reached over and brushed something from his dinner jacket. "The baby of the industry. Barney, you're an amazing person. To come as far as you have in so short a time."

"I'd say about half of it was luck, or maybe opportunism."

"I've heard it said that a lucky man just hears opportunity knock. It's the genius who knows when to open the door."

He frowned. "I've also heard an opportunist defined as one who knows how to take advantage of people as well as situations."

"You mean stepping on people to get ahead?" she asked.

"Partially."

"Isn't that something no one with an ounce of ambition can really avoid? If you go up, you usually have to pass somebody who's on the way down."

He had to chuckle. "You make it sound inevitable."

"So don't lose sleep over it."

"I don't lose sleep, Vickie," he said with a touch of grimness, "but sometimes I wonder if I'm not losing some self-respect. When I have to hurt somebody, for example."

"Such as firing someone?"

"Yes, or someone I've stepped on trying to climb up the ladder."

Vickie shrugged. "Some people you have to climb over." She looked out of the corner of her eye, trying to gauge the effect of that last remark. All he did was lick his lips. He said nothing.

They drove the rest of the way in silence. Vickie invited him in for a nightcap. Barney accepted. Her apartment was simply but tastefully furnished, and Barney, his coat off, sank into the welcome softness of her oversized couch.

"I'll get out of this uniform," Vickie said. "Mix yourself a drink . . . the scotch is in the cabinet under the sink," she called back over her shoulder as she disappeared into her bedroom.

"I think I'll just sit here for a minute and relax," Barney sighed.

He was half-asleep when she returned from the bedroom. He had indulged in a brief fantasy which had her coming back wearing a thin negligee and was mildly disappointed when he saw her slacks and a dark-blue peasant blouse. So much for getting laid, he thought. Yet he was not unhappy; she was easy to talk to, a thoroughly relaxing woman with the gift of quick banter and the ability to shift easily to more serious subjects. Between several drinks and their animated conversation, the time passed faster than either supposed. Barney looked at his watch and found it was almost 2:00 A.M.

"Well, I've got a long drive home," he said regretfully. "I'd better get going. Vickie, I haven't had a nicer evening for a long time. I'm grateful. Not just for the way you handled yourself at the reception, but for your company."

He started to rise but her hand stopped him. "Barney, it's pretty late to be driving all the way out to Potomac. You can stay here if you want."

He stared at her. "Just sleep, Vickie . . . or sex?"

"Both, if you want."

She was so matter-of-fact, so devoid of coyness, that he felt something surge in him. He settled back on the couch, put his arms around her and kissed her, softly at first and then hard. He touched her and discovered she was not wearing a bra.

"Were you planning to seduce me, young lady?" he murmured in her ear.

"Frankly, no. I just happen to hate bras. If I wanted to be blatant about it, I wouldn't have worn a blouse you can't see through."

She pushed his hand away but held it. "Barney, before we go into that bedroom, I think we should discuss motives—mine. I'm not going to bed with you because I want more job security, because you're my boss, or because I enjoy screwing any guy that happens along. You're attractive, exciting. You're also having problems—you seem restless and frustrated. When we came back here from the reception, I actually worried whether you'd make a pass. I didn't want you to and I didn't want to hurt your feelings. The longer we talked, the better I liked you, and then I started to want you. And there's one more thing you should know."

His eyes asked the question.

"There's a guy in my life. An Army Air Corps lieutenant. He's down in Texas and I suppose someday we'll get married. Meanwhile, I'm horny as hell. I'm telling you straight so you won't get any ideas of making this a more or less permanent arrangement. You read me loud and clear?"

"Very loud and very clear."

"Good." She shifted, turning her back to him. "Now unbutton the back of this blouse so I can take the damned thing off . . ."

Their relationship was clandestine—a decision of his own making.

He had reservations about getting involved with anyone in the company. He was sure she would never take advantage of their friendship—and she never did—but he feared it would create problems for her as well as him.

In public he went so out of his way that she could never be assured of his support. He imagined that anything less might give away their being more than boss and employee. For a while, at least, she put up with it—always aware that when they were alone, he would be different. Victoria Doman understood his fears even though she didn't really agree with them.

"You know, Barney," she told him one night, "this game of secrecy we're playing is silly. I don't think there's a person on this airline who doesn't know we're dating, and probably sleeping together."

"That couldn't be true," he protested. "We've both made every possible effort to keep this . . . this, uh, relationship private."

She laughed. "Don't sound so damned formal, Barney. We're screwing almost every night. *That* part I would like to keep between ourselves. But I can't honestly think there's much sense in hiding away like a couple of spies. You'd think one of us was married and we had private eyes following us."

"Well, one of us is *almost* married," he added rather lamely.

"That bother you, Barney?"

"A little."

"Why?"

He couldn't answer her with complete honesty; he was afraid to. "Well, your being engaged gives me the feeling that this might end someday."

"And does *that* bother you?"

He was a little angry. She was backing him against a wall and she knew it.

"Of course it bothers me," he growled. "I don't want it to end. You're . . . very special."

"How special?"

"Dammit, Vickie, what the hell do you want me to do—propose?"

"For God's sake, no! I don't feel like playing second-string to Coastal."

"So what are you bugging me for?"

She softened. "Slow down, Barney. I guess I'd just like to be seen with you in public a few times."

"I'll ask you what you asked me. Why?"

"Now you're fishing for a compliment."

"So were you—maybe for commitment?"

"*Touché*. All right, I want this little romance of ours to emerge from behind closed doors, out-of-the-way restaurants, and assignations in cities all over our route system. I'm rather proud of our friendship. I'm very proud of you as a person. I'm even proud that you want to make love to me with surprising frequency. And as I said before, I see no use in hiding something that nearly everyone knows about already."

"Well," he said grudgingly, "I just don't want to be too blatant about it. It's not good for discipline."

"Barney, let me ask you something. When you make love to me, do you ever think about the airline? Some business problem?"

"Yeah." He was so startled, he blurted out the truth. "Yeah . . . a few times."

She didn't get mad; she laughed. "That's what I meant . . . about not marrying you. I'd be getting into bed, figuratively speaking, with DC-2's, a couple of vice-presidents, and Calvin Motts's latest boo-boo."

He grinned ruefully. "You have a point. Tell you what—we'll call off this little charade of ours and start going out in the open. But don't expect any favors from me during business hours. That'll be far worse than being seen together."

"Deal."

Contrary to his worst fears, nothing happened when he ceased hiding his relationship. People accepted it easily, the few who were not already aware of it. Nor were there any problems at work; she was simply too respected for anyone to think she might take advantage of the situation. Besides, no one who knew him could think it possible. Barney Burton relaxed, pleased with how comfortable life could be. Vickie had tapped in him a long-dormant vein of thoughtfulness. He was not affectionate but she was, in such a totally natural way that he responded in spite of himself. She wore a delicate cologne that had the subtle, spicy odor of flowers. He was constantly complimenting her on it and finally confessed that carnations were his favorite.

"I would never have guessed it," she said. "I never see any flowers around your office."

"Flowers don't belong in business offices," he growled.

"Balderdash. They're a ray of sunlight in a gloomy prison, which is what your office reminds me of, come to think of it. I believe I'll do the inmates a favor one of these days."

"Vick, don't meddle. If you're so crazy about flowers, go sleep with a florist."

"You like my cologne. Just have a few carnations around—they'll remind you of me."

"They'll remind me of a dozen Vickie Domans, and I've got enough trouble with one."

"You have a point. And I have a solution."

"So what the hell do you want me to do, start shaving with your cologne?"

"Nope. Start wearing a carnation in your lapel. It'll look nice."

"Go to hell."

The next morning she walked into his office carrying a small florist's box, opened it, and took out a white carnation.

"Mr. Burton, you will wear this for the rest of the day or you are going to have a very frustrating evening, devoid of sex and possibly even conversation."

"If there's one thing in this world I hate, it's blackmail."

"Wear it and shut up."

He placed it in his lapel. "I don't mind missing the sex, but the lack of conversation would kill me," he said. "Now get out of here before my secretary starts broadcasting the news that I've gone soft."

As soon as she left, however, he phoned a florist and left a standing order for daily delivery of some flowers. A single white carnation sent to his office each morning and a dozen red roses to Miss Vickie Doman, Director, Flight Service Department.

Being seen together advertised their friendship; the roses confirmed that it was more than friendship, and eventually Barney stopped really caring what anyone around the airline thought. In Vickie, he had found a security and warmth he never had missed because he did not even know it existed. Unfortunately, the reverse was not true. He did not give her the same sense of security. He kept breaking dates because of some crisis or other, and he was inevitably late for what dates he kept.

"If my stews reported for flights with the same punctuality," she remarked once, "I'd fire the whole lot."

But she put up with him. His generosity was spontaneous, at times a bit clumsy because of its magnitude, and she recognized it for what it really was—the gratitude of a man who by his very nature tried to make up in a materialistic way for what he could never give of himself. But she knew that in his own groping way, he was trying to compensate for failing her.

His gratitude did not extend to the office, however. She had had enough of Cal Motts's fumblings and pressed her boss to put Flight Services under the jurisdiction of Operations instead of Sales. She argued that a flight attendant actually was a member of the flight crew. This stand brought her into bitter conflict with Motts, who said that inasmuch as the chief duty of a stewardess was to serve passengers, she had to be directly responsible to Sales.

"You might as well have an automobile salesman reporting to the service department," Motts told her in Barney's office.

"Hold it," Barney interrupted. "It's Friday afternoon and I don't intend to sit here all weekend. Let's get back to the airline business. Calvin may have a point, Vickie. Now I'd like to hear your side."

"It's very simple. If the girls have to answer to Sales, they're sitting ducks for every screwball idea on new cabin service. Ideas that never take into account whether the stewardess can handle it, whether there's time for it, or whether it's practical. Furthermore, I don't like the way you jokers in Sales treat the girls. Every time you get a passenger complaint, it's the stew who gets the blame—the customer is always right. Everything that goes wrong on an airplane you blame on the stewardess. She's in the front lines taking all the guff, and you rear-echelon types won't listen to her or stand up for her even when she's right and it's the passenger who's wrong."

"I think I've been very fair in all cases," Motts said pompously. "Name just one instance where—"

"I'll give you more than one, Calvin. You put into their personnel file every complaint letter that comes in, regardless of whether the complaint is justified. It means an automatic black mark on a record no matter what the circumstances. You never bother to investigate a complaint; you just write the sonofabitch a soothing letter and send me a nasty note ordering me to tell Miss So-and-So to behave herself in the future."

Motts bristled. "Now just a minute. Don't tell *me* that stewardesses never goof, insult passengers, provide poor service, or show a lackadaisical attitude toward their job. I can show you case after—"

Vickie thumped the arm of her chair. "I never said there's no such animal as a poor stewardess. All I'm asking for is fair play, some tolerance on your part. I can ream out a bad stew just as fast as you can, Mr. Motts, and I've fired seven since I took this job. But if you had your way, you would have fired a hell of a lot more. And they would have included some fine kids, assets to any airline."

"I've never ordered you to fire any girl in particular."

"The hell you haven't. You've suggested it a few times. And in my book a suggestion from a vice-president is tantamount to an order."

"But you didn't fire them. I fail to see why you're getting so upset."

Vickie's eyes were shimmering. "I didn't fire them because I wasn't about to take any guff off you, that's why. The point is that someone in my job who's afraid of bucking a vice-president would have knuckled under. I won't be here forever. I'm trying to establish a principle for the future, and it's a pretty bleak one if Sales is allowed to keep running the stewardess department. One of these days you'll have a weak sister sitting behind my desk and Calvin, here, will have himself a field day."

Motts, unperturbed, shrugged and turned to Barney. "I'd like your views, Chief."

"So would I," Vickie said.

Barney felt like Solomon. He was impressed by Vickie's arguments and the vehement manner in which she expressed them, but he also felt she was crying foul a little too vigorously. Cal Motts *was* prone to finding a stewardess guilty without investigating a situation thoroughly. Yet he could not see any overriding advantage to having them in Operations, other than self-protection.

He made his decision reluctantly. "I think there's much to be said for both sides, but let's leave things the way they are, with one exception. Vickie, anytime you feel Sales has been unfair to one of your people, you bring the facts to me and let me be the judge. You can be damned sure I'll stick up for an employee if he or she is right and the passenger is wrong. Is that okay with you?"

"I guess so," she said in a doubtful tone.

"And, Cal, I suggest you do some checking before you take sides. I don't want any passenger complaint to appear in a stewardess's personal folder until the complaint has been investigated. That clear?"

"Righto, Chief." Motts left with gusto as if he had won a great victory. Vickie waited until he was out of the room before she voiced her real opinion. "It'll work fine, Barney, while I'm chief stew. But one of these days, you're going to have a stewardess morale problem that'll wind up exactly where Mr. Motts doesn't want it—in the cabin."

"Yeah, yeah," he said grumpily. "Look, Vickie, I've got more things on my mind than your platoon of prima donnas. Cal Motts is a shithead at times but I promise I'll keep my eye on him and that's all you're gonna get out of me today."

She was on the verge of continuing but checked herself. Barney looked tired and harassed, and she knew he was in no mood to argue further. Obviously he was worried about something a lot bigger than her feud with Motts.

"You're the boss." She smiled. "I'll try not to bother you unless the bastard gets out of hand," she said and left.

Barney *was* worried. The first of Coastal's DC-3's were scheduled for delivery by February 1, 1937, and he was facing up to the fact that the airline's route system had stagnated. He was close to having too good a fleet for the system it served. Washington–Pittsburgh–Twin Cities had been his last expansion move, and there could be no new route awards without an accompanying mail contract. The latter seemed impossible; the cities where Coastal operated were too far away from areas still needing new or additional airline services. Barney spent hours examining and dissecting maps trying to figure out in what direction he could advance, and was resigned to the status quo indefinitely.

He had to do something about what seemed to be the over-balanced composition of the fleet. Meanwhile, he was booked on a night flight to L.A. for a progress meeting with Donald Douglas. Then he was due in Chicago for a meeting with other company heads, to establish the Air Transport Association of America, the industry's first real trade organization.

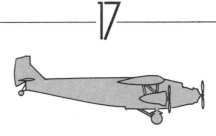

17

Production on the new DC-3's was proceeding on schedule, Barney was happy to hear. Donald Douglas even gave him a guided tour of the plant and introduced him to their top designers, then escorted Barney back to his office, where they chatted for half an hour about all the new innovations being introduced to improve aircraft.

For the first time in weeks, Barney had slept well, thanks to the balmy California weather. Relaxed and feeling good, he was thoroughly enjoying the conversation when Douglas suddenly rose from his chair.

"Hey, I nearly forgot!" exclaimed Douglas, looking at his watch.

"You have an appointment?"

"No," said Douglas, "but you do." He ushered Barney out of his office and into the capable hands of a Japanese gentleman who spoke little English but managed to convey his wishes nonetheless. The little man deposited Barney in the back of a station wagon and shot off into the late afternoon with total abandon and apparent disregard for the polite California drivers he mesmerized with his technique.

It seemed to Barney a lifetime later that the station wagon approached Union Air Terminal in Burbank, blithely shot past warning signs and onto the runway apron, and suddenly came to a screeching halt in front of a closed hangar. Motioned out of the vehicle, Barney hardly needed encouragement. Straightening his tie and jacket, he backed away from the car and made his way cautiously toward the lighted side office of the hangar, certain that all this was some horrible practical jokc.

He went inside. The place was deserted. Through the interior window, looking into the hangar area, he could make out the dark silhouette of a plane, but that was all. Then he heard someone in the back room and the door opened.

She had oil smudged across her cheek and in her hair, and grease smeared across her coveralls, and she looked beautiful.

"Amelia!"

"Barnwell Ernest Burton! You finally got here. Don was supposed to have sent you out an hour ago. I was beginning to think you might not make it!"

"Good Lord, if I had known, I would've come straight here without even stopping for business."

"Great to see you," she smiled, all freckles and dirt and having to hug him with her elbows, her filthy hands held askew like a surgeon's.

"This is wonderful," he said. "But what'n the heck are you doing out here? I thought you were in Indiana."

"Was, for a while. Oh, mercy. Look at the time. Here, come on back. I've got to get this stuff off me first, but then I'll treat you to a first-class meal."

He followed her through the swinging door, then on through a workroom, down a short, narrow corridor and through another door marked *Showers*, and on into a locker room.

"How long are you going to be out here?" she asked, ducking around a corner.

"Just until tomorrow, I'm afraid."

Boots and coveralls thumped to the ground in a pile, with shirt and slacks quickly following.

"Can't you stay longer, Barney? That's hardly enough time to catch up on anything."

The steamy hiss of a shower interrupted momentarily.

"Can't!" he half-shouted.

"What?"

"Can't!"

"Oh!"

A wet face poked around the corner, still very much blackened.

"Barney, do me a favor. The broken locker there, behind you. Right. Would you get me the can of solvent and the shampoo on the top shelf?" She shivered. "Bring it on back. I've got to get into the water before I catch pneumonia," she said, and disappeared.

Barney did as asked and walked around the corner into the tiled shower area. A sign with *Theirs* printed on it pointed back toward him, while on the back wall an arrow sign with *Hers* on it pointed at the last stall.

Taking a stool, he walked to the end.

"Here," he said, handing the can of solvent and the shampoo over the half-door.

"Oh, great."

"Don't mention it," he said, smiling and sitting down on the stool, his back propped against the tiled wall. "So tell me what's been happening."

"Oh, where to begin?"

"Where you left off—"

"Well, let's see. I made the Honolulu flight—thank you for the beautiful cable, by the way—then the Mexican government invited me to try a long distance flight to Mexico City."

"How was it?"

"Sissy stuff, it was so smooth. Started here, landed there. Same thing coming back—simple. Mexico City to Tampico, northeast over the Gulf of Mexico—that was pretty—then New Orleans, right up through Mobile, Atlanta, Charlotte, Richmond, Washington, Newark. I almost landed at Hoover but there were too many people waiting for me in New York."

"You make it sound easy."

"To tell you the truth, it was. Just one of those times everything stays perfect and lucky all the way. The most dangerous part of it was the crowd in Newark. I barely got through it in one piece."

The shower stopped. A moment later Amelia appeared, wrapped in a towel, a smaller one over her head. She rubbed her hair with it.

"Now I know why you wear your hair short," he said.

"Huh? Oh, yes, of course. Long hair and skirts just weren't meant for the likes of me. Come on," she said, leading him back to her locker, where she laid out a pair of slacks, brown loafers, and a tan cashmere turtleneck.

Barney turned away to let her dress, though she seemed oblivious to such concerns.

"So what happened after the Mexico flight? I heard you and Paul Muntz teamed up for the National Air Races."

"Right. It was pretty much a lark, though. We didn't stand any chance at all against Roscoe Turner's machine and Benny Howard's *Mister Mulligan*. But it was fun."

"And then?"

"Well, the race was Labor Day . . . right . . . after which I headed for my new job at Purdue. You see, the esteemed Dr. Edward C. Elliott, president of the University, had asked me to come and teach at his school."

"Teach?"

"Yes. Sort of aviatrix in residence. Encourage the girls, talk to them about their careers. Purdue has its own airport, too, you see. A progressive place. And students could take instruction in flying."

"Sounds like you enjoyed it."

"Oh, I did, for a couple of semesters. It was interesting to see what young women think of themselves and their future. The world is in for some changes."

"And another war," said Barney.

"Not us," she said firmly. "I just can't see us joining in again. No."

"Yes, I heard about your address to the DAR."

"I warned them."

"So what happened after Purdue?"

"Well, I got involved with the Amelia Earhart Fund."

"The what?"

"Okay. You can turn around." She was again rubbing her hair with the towel. "A fund established to promote research."

"What sort?"

"The kind that could produce practical results for commercial aviation. I mean, the manufacturers are concentrating on solving mechanical problems, and you airline people are naturally concerned with the economics of air transportation."

"Leaving you with—?"

"The effect on people. What does air density do to people? How does it affect a person's metabolism during long-distance flight? Do women react to flying differently from men?"

"I see. And where are you conducting these tests?"

"Just preparing. Come on, I'll show you," she said, glancing at herself in the wall mirror and then taking him by the arm. "This way."

She led Barney back the way he had come, except this time she took him into the hangar, a mischievous bounce to her step.

"The laboratory," she said, switching on the lights.

Barney whistled at the sight of the plane. "Quite a test tube."

"Yes," she said, touching a propeller. "It arrived on my thirty-eighth birthday. Twin engines, dual controls, pressurization, and we're putting in a Sperry Robot Pilot."

"Gyroscopic automatic pilot?"

"The same."

"A flying laboratory, supported by Purdue and the Amelia Earhart Foundation," he said in a suspicious tone.

"Right. A Lockheed 10-E Electra." She was beaming up at the ship, her arms across her chest.

"And just where is this so-called flying lab going to fly?"

"The equator."

"What?"

"It's going to the equator in about a year. Then it's going to follow the equator, around the world."

"That's a long way, Amelia."

"Only twenty-seven thousand miles," she said.

She drove him along the coast in her red roadster. She drove, Barney observed, the same way that she flew—throttle wide open. She'd have to change that for an around-the-world flight.

The car zoomed smoothly along the road, its excellent and sturdy construction belying their inordinate speed.

"*Wonderful, isn't it?*" she yelled. The top was down, so as to finish drying her hair, and the wind swept by with a great rush.

"*Yes*," he yelled back, nodding exaggeratedly, when she suddenly down shifted.

"Here we are—the Pier."

It was a lovely place, jutting right into the water, "and full of movie stars," she whispered to Barney as they made their way to a window table. It was, too, except that all those famous faces turned around to see her, but she was too excited by who was staring to realize that they were doing the looking. Barney shook his head as she discreetly glanced around, reciting names. She had been dined and decorated by royalty, had danced all night in a London club with the heir to the British throne, and had been hailed by thousands of adoring fans the world over, and still somehow remained herself. Always, thought Barney, always. Like that evening at the White House when she had described the appeal of night flying to Eleanor Roosevelt and then the two of them had slipped off to National Airport. They had soared over Washington and Baltimore, both still in evening dress, Amelia at the controls in her white gown and long, formal gloves.

The waiter appeared and they quickly ordered. Amelia suddenly looked serious.

"I heard about Bud."

Barney only nodded, not knowing quite what to say, puzzled that she was bringing it up so long after the fact of his death.

"Why do fliers drink so much?" She shook her head sadly. "They must think it's the Wild West or something. Well, it's another thing we have in common."

"Drunks?"

"I'm afraid so. My father drank, a lot. Alcoholics have been dogging me since I was a child."

"Really?" Barney was surprised.

"Yep. My father, then Wilmur Stultz. He was twenty-seven that first time I crossed the Atlantic. I was only along for the ride, actually; he did every bit of navigating and flying. The next time I went alone. Marvelous pilot, Stultz. By twenty-eight he was dead: crashed." She sighed and looked at Barney. "Now I'm paired with another one—the best navigator in the world, and an alcoholic. I don't know why pilots are such hard drinkers, but they are. Maybe it goes with their fatalistic, romantic self-image as pioneering vagabonds. Or maybe they had horrible experiences in the war. Whatever, Barney, you and I aren't responsible for that. Our job is to fly, and to put planes back on the ground in the same shape that we found them. And *everything* else has to come second—alcohol, food, sex, marriage, friends, family, fame."

"Are you trying to make me feel better?" said Barney.

"Yes."

"You have," he smiled, as dinner arrived.

After the initial session of the Air Transport Association in Chicago, Pat Patterson asked him out for a drink. The head of United was one of Barney's favorites. Pat's handshake, Jack Frye had once told Barney, was better than anyone else's signature on a binding contract.

"I won't beat around the bush," Patterson told him after they ordered drinks in a small bar on Michigan Avenue. "We're ordering a flock of DC-3's and we're phasing out our Boeing 247's as fast as we can. Are you happy with the three we sold you?"

"Very. They're a fine little airplane. Low operating costs and the pilots like 'em, better than the 2's in some ways."

"You paid us thirty thousand apiece for the 247's you bought. How would you like three more for sixty thousand, including spares?"

Barney's face showed his surprise. "That's quite a bargain. But what am I gonna do with three more? Frankly, I'm putting the ones we've got up for sale as soon as we get the first of the five DC-3's we've ordered."

Patterson grinned. "Barney, I can't tell you how to run your airline, but think a minute. I take it you'll put your DC-2's on the trips now operated by the Boeings. That right?"

"Sure, but—"

"Isn't the 2 a pretty big airplane for those schedules?"

Barney frowned. "Yeah. The way traffic is now, anyway. We're averaging a fifty-five percent load factor on the Boeings."

"And if you put in the DC-2, your load factor'll drop below fifty percent."

"I'm afraid so." He looked quizzically at Patterson. "I'm getting the notion you think I'm peddling the wrong airplane."

"Exactly. You could sell those DC-2's for a lot more than three more 247's would cost you; you'll get a lot less for the Boeings you want to put up for sale."

"In other words," Barney said slowly, "I could tailor our equipment for the routes—phase out the DC-2 instead of the 247. Pat, you may have something. How long will you hold that sixty-grand price?"

"Two weeks. That sufficient?"

"I should be able to get back to you in two days. I'd like to talk it over with some of our people. I know one of 'em will scream like a panther."

Calvin Motts did.

"You can't be serious," he protested when Barney outlined the Patterson offer to him and Larry Aroni. "We've spent thousands publicizing how great the DC-2 is, and now you want to get rid of them. I just can't understand it, Boss."

"I can," Aroni said quietly. "The Boeing's a better airplane for our secondary routes: cheaper to operate and in some ways safer. The 2 would need a shoehorn squeezing into some of those airports where we're using 247's."

"Then you're in favor of this?" Barney asked, pleased.

"I'll go along."

"Cal?"

Motts hovered, then stepped back in retreat. "Well, I'm already outvoted. I'll have to say yes."

It turned out to be a wise decision. The three DC-2's were sold a few days after the fifth DC-3 was delivered—for a total of $190,000. This was only $35,000 less than what they had cost new, and considering the use Coastal had gotten out of them, the transaction was something Barney could report to the directors with pride.

And, in fact, the DC-3 proved to be a far superior airplane. Far more stable than the 2, with lower seat-mile costs and such rugged reliability that even the rather cynical Aroni fell in love with it. the DC-3 would be just what C. R. Smith had said—"the first airliner ever built that can make money carrying just passengers."

It rapidly achieved such a reputation for safety that air-travel insurance became available to the public for the first time—twenty-five cents for a $5,000 policy. The DC-3 literally had taken the airlines out of knickers and put them into long pants but Al Davenport looked unhappy as Barney and he paced around one of the ships in the main hangar.

"The damned cockpit windshield leaks even in a light rain," Davenport grumbled. "Our guys are having to wear raincoats when they fly. Imagine that, in a hundred-thousand-dollar airplane! An American captain was telling me the other day a station asked him what the weather was like at seven thousand feet. He radioed 'light rain outside, heavy rain inside.' "

"Aside from that idiosyncracy," Barney said, "how do you like the plane?"

"Well, it's immensely strong. Not as fast as I expected. It climbs like it had an anchor tied onto the tailwheel. It's a forgiving airplane, but you can't really take liberties with it. It has one thing in common with our DC-2's—you can't land it with consistent smoothness. Anytime you feel like patting yourself on the back for a runway 'paint-job,' you'd better realize the next landing will probably jar your fillings loose."

"Al," Barney said eagerly, "how about taking me up for a test hop? Just the two of us. Then maybe I could handle the controls for a couple of minutes."

Davenport eyed him sympathetically. "Bud Lindeman told me once he had to wash you out. No coordination, I think he said. Barney, I'm sorry, but nobody touches a yoke on an airplane I'm commanding unless he's a qualified, certificated pilot. I know you're president of the airline but I won't make an exception even in your case, and I shouldn't. I know how you feel about flying the bird once, but you're also playing with a toy that cost a hundred grand."

"Then just let me taxi it, Al. About fifty yards—that's all I want."

Davenport started to say no again and then relented. "Oh, shit, I don't suppose you can do any harm while you're on the ground. Okay, I'll check you out. Get aboard. *Sid*," he shouted to the mechanic on duty. "We're taking this lady out but not up."

Davenport warned Barney, just before he started the engines,

"Taxiing this baby is harder than flying it—it's the only airplane that has to be flown while it's still on the ground."

"Don't worry," Barney said confidently. "Just tell me what to do."

"Okay. You steer with rudder pedals and the engines. If you want to turn left, hit left rudder and advance your right throttle. Vice versa with a right turn. Add power to your left engine and kick right rudder. The engine torque pulls you in the opposite direction. Get it?"

"Roger," Barney said.

"I hope so. Lemme take it out of this ramp area and then you can try it."

It looked easy, watching Davenport. But when he motioned to Barney to grab his yoke and ordered him to turn left, Barney instinctively reached for the left throttle as his left foot pressed the rudder pedal.

"*Right throttle!*" Davenport yelled.

Barney obeyed instantly, but with such alacrity that he applied too much power. The DC-3 almost ground-looped and just missed ramming a Piper Cub waddling by toward a runway.

"That did it!" Davenport said. "No more, Barney."

Barney felt humiliated, but the chief pilot made light of his failure. "A monkey could fly this damned thing, but only a pilot can taxi it."

Barney was crestfallen but managed a weak smile.

Like all new airliners, the DC-3 had its share of teething troubles. In the development stages, the plane caused some concern over its habit of fishtailing at certain speeds and altitudes. This was cured by increasing the movable rudder surface and altering the shape of the airfoil on the horizontal tail. Generally the bugs didn't seem serious and were all correctable. Then in February a brand-new United DC-3 crashed into San Francisco Bay while making what appeared to be a routine night landing at Mills Field. The weather was clear and there was no explanation for the accident. The aircraft had gone into a sudden 45-degree dive as it lined up with the runway.

Barney went into an immediate huddle with Davenport and Aroni the moment he heard about the accident.

"It's a complete mystery," Davenport confessed. "It was as if he flew it right into the water. Visibility was perfect. They've fished out the wreckage and there's no sign of engine trouble or structural failure of any kind."

"Keep me posted on anything you hear," Barney ordered. "If there's any kind of major flaw in that airplane, the whole industry's in trouble."

Five weeks later, with the San Francisco crash still unsolved, Captain Andy Vaughn came into the chief pilot's office.

"Al, something happened when I was taking off on Flight 20 to Minneapolis yesterday, and I just wonder if it might have something to do with that United accident."

"Spill it."

"Well, I was testing the ailerons, elevators, and rudder for movement before I started my roll. Al, they wouldn't budge. They were frozen stiff. I didn't know what the hell was wrong. Then I happened to look down. You won't believe this—the radio mike had fallen off its hook and was jammed into the V-shaped well, a little opening between the control column and the cockpit wall. So I pried the mike loose and the controls worked fine. Well, do you suppose that poor United guy—?"

"I don't suppose," said Davenport. "I'm gonna call Barney right now."

He told the president what Vaughan had reported and Barney immediately phoned Patterson and briefed him on the Coastal incident.

"That seems to wrap it up," Patterson said. "C. R. called me just two hours ago. The same thing happened on an American DC-3 at Newark this morning. I've already notified our people in San Francisco to take another look at the cockpit wreckage. I'll call you back, Barney, and thanks."

A fresh examination of the UAL wreckage confirmed it. The mike was found jammed into the control well. The United captain, committed to a landing, had had no time in which to determine the cause of the frozen controls.

Larry Aroni quickly designed a crude boot to go over the control well, while Douglas designed a permanent leather boot for complete protection against the freak mishap.

To Barney, it was a there-but-for-the-grace-of-God-went-Coastal tragedy. He was inordinately proud of his airline's perfect safety record, but he was acutely and uncomfortably aware of how sliver-thin an opening disaster needed. He would fight with Motts, Vickie, and anyone else over a five-dollar expenditure, but if either Davenport or Aroni told him something was needed for safety, they had little trouble convincing Barney.

He had long admired the growing practice of most airlines in using dispatchers—men trained to judge the conditions under which flights should and should not operate, taking into account such factors as weather, loads, fuel requirements, alternate fields. He put the dispatcher system into practice at Coastal, hiring as chief dispatcher a tall, sandy-haired young man named John Myler who had been trained at TWA. As usual, Davenport objected to the whole idea. "I don't want any desk jockeys telling my pilots how and when to fly," he stormed.

"I'll have to overrule you on this one," Barney said calmly. "Every carrier that has dispatchers swears by them. And from what I hear, even the pilots have come around. Your aces won't lose any authority. Anytime a captain says it's unsafe to fly, the plane stays on the ground."

"Yeah, but by the same token a dispatcher can ground the flight, too."

"Al, I'll give you five bucks every time you find a captain disagreeing with a dispatcher on whether to take off or land. Believe me, they'll be working together, not in opposition. Tell you what, you grouchy old goat, let's try the dispatch system for six months, and if there's too much friction, we'll both take another look. I'll keep an open mind if you will."

In a month Davenport was completely converted. Particularly when most of his pilots were telling him the dispatchers were relieving them of not a few ground chores. The belligerent little chief pilot even got to like Dispatcher Myler, who did his job in a quiet, competent way, making a lot of friends and virtually no waves in the pressure cooker that was Operations.

The advent of dispatchers was one more sign that the industry was maturing and achieving respectability. The airlines had also voluntarily relinquished all responsibility for controlling air traffic, turning this over to the Federal government, which was operating eight traffic centers throughout the country, including the three original installations at Newark, Chicago, and Cleveland. Accompanying the government's assumption of traffic control was a $7 million appropriation for airways modernization.

The Congress would pass and President Roosevelt would certainly sign the legislation which would become the industry's Magna Carta, the Civil Aeronautics Act. It would create a five-man Civil Aeronautics Authority, ending the unwieldy, bickering system of having aviation regulatory power spread among three different agencies. Under the new law, the CAA alone would have the Post Office Department's authority to hand out mail contracts and routes, the Interstate Commerce Commission's control over fares, and the jurisdiction of Air Commerce over safety, pilot and aircraft licensing, and the airways themselves.

Within the CAA a new three-man Safety Board would investigate air accidents with complete independence. Of major importance to Barney was the Act's most radical provision: all route authorizations were to be made permanent but not exclusive. With that, the CAA would have the power to grant competition in markets where the traffic justified more than one carrier.

It was going to be a whole new ballgame, and Barney didn't waste any time getting into it. One of his directors tipped him that Air Central, a small carrier operating between Minneapolis and Wichita with several interim points, was in deep financial trouble.

"They'll sell out for a song," he told Barney. "If you can swing it, I promise you our other directors will approve an acquisition or merger."

Barney made a fast trip to Minneapolis and met with the president of the failing airline. He worked out a deal in three hours—assumption of about $82,000 in debts and payment of $50,000 in cash, in return for Air Central's routes and equipment. The latter was nothing Barney wanted—three single-engine Lockheed Orions in reasonably good condition—but he already knew of a Mexican airline that was scrounging around for surplus small transports and he was sure he could dispose of them. Air Central had only forty-three employees and Barney promised to retain all but its six pilots for at least another year. The employment guarantee, however, was not extended to Air Central's three officers; Barney wasn't impressed when he met them, albeit briefly, and the company's record didn't indicate any great supply of latent talent. He did agree to give the four most senior pilots interviews with Davenport, who would determine whether they could fly for Coastal.

The new company counsel, Bill Sloan, accompanied him to Minneapolis for the negotiations, and as soon as they returned home, Barney had Sloan file an application with the CAA for approval to merge Coastal and Air Central. Simultaneously, Sloan drew up another application seeking authority to operate between Wichita and Phoenix via Amarillo and Albuquerque. Barney knew he was butting heads against Jack Frye and TWA, which already had a Kansas City–Wichita–Albuquerque–Phoenix route, but he figured TWA wouldn't fight too hard against a proposed route that would compete only between Wichita and Phoenix. He phoned Frye at TWA, as a matter of courtesy, and told him about the application before it actually was filed.

"It's Minneapolis–Phoenix we're really after," he explained. "And right now the only way we can get there is via Air Central's route to Wichita. If you feel strongly enough about it, I'd be willing to overfly Albuquerque. I think our DC-3's could make it nonstop Wichita–Phoenix. It's only about an eight-hundred-mile leg."

Frye wasn't happy, but he took it rather philosophically. "Well, I dunno, Barney. If you guys go all the way to Phoenix, next thing I know you'll be wanting an extension into Los Angeles."

"I don't think so. The Los Angeles market seems a bit overcrowded. You and American already are in there, and United's interchange with Western at Salt Lake City makes it three transcontinental carriers. I don't feel like taking on a trio of Notre Dames at one city."

"Okay," Frye said, "it's a free country. We'll probably have to put up some kind of fight, Barney, but off the record I wish you luck. If we can't lick Coastal's competition, we might as well get the hell out of this business."

TWA's opposition was token. Coastal's application for a merger and a route from Wichita to Phoenix went through.

Barney celebrated by taking Vickie to dinner, stopping first at his new country house for drinks. She had been there before and loved its rusticity. This time, while they were on the patio sipping a pair of Tom Collinses, she was looking at the large meadow adjoining his property.

"Who owns that land over there?"

"I just heard some real-estate firm bought it from a farmer. I suppose eventually it'll be subdivided—and when that day comes, I think I'll move."

"Why do you have to move? Why don't you buy it?"

"What the hell for? That land must cover about five acres. I could get two hangars and an office building on it."

"Buy it for protection. Then nobody could move next door. And on your other side you already have about a one-acre buffer zone between your property and your nearest neighbor."

"That would be pretty expensive protection—five acres just sitting idle. I sure as hell couldn't plant it; I have a black thumb."

"It would be a great place to keep a couple of horses," she said wistfully.

He chuckled. "Sure, if I rode horses."

"I do," she said, looking over the field studded with flowers.

Something in her tone made him look at her sharply. Her pretty face, framed and crowned by that black hair, was serious—almost sad.

"Got something on your mind, Vick?"

"Uh-huh."

Without realizing it, he took a deep breath. "Would it be marriage, by chance?"

"Yep." She pushed back the hair from her eyes.

"To an old-fashioned type like myself, marriage implies love," he said.

"Exactly. Or could I be wrong in thinking it's mutual?"

"You're not wrong. I do love you. I have from the first," said Barney.

"You took a long time to say it."

"So did you."

She smiled and reached over for his hand. "I was following protocol and waiting for you."

"How about the guy in Texas?"

"Wrote him last week. Told him I had met someone else. Namely you, Mr. President. I do love you, but I'm not sure I'd want to marry you."

"Because of the airline?"

She nodded.

"I'll admit to my preoccupation, but what makes you think I can't be a good husband as well as a good airline president?"

"Because your name is Barney Burton and that's the way you are. I told you once I can't play second fiddle to an airline and I haven't changed my mind."

"Why can't a man love his job as he does his wife?"

"How about loving his wife a little more than his job?"

"You're assuming there has to be some conflict between the two. A job requires a different kind of love."

"You're right, it's different. That's what scares me. I remember you telling me that first night in my apartment that anybody you married would have to compete with Coastal and it would be a very one-sided contest. Have you changed your mind?"

"In a way, yes. I said it and I meant it. But that was before I fell in love with you. That's the difference."

"What's different about me, Barney?"

"You love this racket, too. Not as much as I do, but enough to let you understand what would make me be a good husband at times and a bad one at other times."

She smiled a little. "I'd like some kind of guarantee that the former would slightly outnumber the latter."

"I couldn't give you any. I'd be a liar if I said I could and a hypocrite if I actually handed you one. The only guarantee would be the fact that I love you and would try never to hurt you."

She studied his sober face. "Well, you're honest, anyway. That's one of the reasons I love you. More than you realize, by the way. So much that I'm almost willing to take the chance. Do you want kids, Barney?" she suddenly asked, then continued without waiting for him to answer. "I do. No more than two, though."

"Someday, of course," he hedged, but her own emotions out-paced her awareness that his answer was evasive. "Not right away. We've got to get used to each other first. Have some fun, just the two of us, for a couple of years. Then we can start thinking about a family."

"I'd settle for that, Barney. Okay, Mr. Burton, you may go ahead and make a formal proposal. I'll waive the on-bended-knee bit. This patio hasn't been swept since Orville and Wilbur left the bicycle shop."

"I'll do more than ask you to marry me, Vickie. I promise I'll try to make you happy."

"The heck with dinner," she said gleefully. "Let's celebrate in bed!"

They were married in a Methodist church near Barney's home. Vickie's parents flew in from Los Angeles for the ceremony. And Larry Aroni was the best man. The only person missing was Amelia, who was in Miami, making final preparations once again for a record flight—this time around the world. Somewhat to Vickie's surprise, Barney actually took two weeks off for a honeymoon on Martha's Vineyard—the fact that he would accept the solitude of an island impressed her as much as the two weeks. And at the end of the first week, it was Vickie who suggested he call Washington and check on the airline—a gesture which he appreciated, inasmuch as he *had* been worrying about it. "Privately, of course," he confessed.

"About as private as our premarital dating," she laughed. "Barney, you can't fool me. You started thinking about Coastal when we got on the plane to Boston."

"Thinking about it, yes. But remember, I didn't turn around and go back. *That* was an achievement."

When they returned home to what was now their house, he handed her a wedding present—a formal-looking document.

"What is it, Barney? It's all legal gobbledygook."

"A deed to those five acres next door. Now come see your other wedding present."

He marched her outside and steered her toward the new property. She couldn't believe what she saw. It had been fenced in, and about fifty yards from the nearest fence was a small barn, spanking new.

"Climb over, Vickie. Figured you might want to check out that barn in case we decided to buy a mule one of these days."

She ran to the barn like an excited schoolgirl, Barney panting to keep up with her. She was no sooner inside than she gave a small squeal of delight. "Oh, my God! What have you done?"

Facing her from a hay-cluttered stall was a black filly, a three-year-old with a white star on her forehead. The filly eyed Vickie curiously, whinnying softly as if she sensed that she had found a friend. Vickie first hugged the horse and then threw her arms around Barney. "What can I say, honey? She's absolutely beautiful. She must be sixteen hands high. Does she have a name?"

"Queenie, I think. But you can call her anything you like."

"I'll name her . . . Raven."

Barney was pleased at her glee. "Had the whole thing done while we were away," he informed her with obvious pride. "Had to pay through my nose to get the fence installed and the barn built in two weeks."

"Where did you buy Raven?"

"Billy Raymond, our communications superintendent, is a horse fancier. He went with me to some Potomac horse dealer to pick her out. Hell, I wouldn't have known if I was looking at Man o' War or some candidate for a glue factory. I figured you could buy the saddle and all that stuff yourself. Matter of fact, you can do it this afternoon if you'd like. Then you can ride her before dinner tonight."

"Who needs a saddle?" she said, and she led the horse out into the enclosure and easily threw herself up. Hanging onto the mount's withers, she slapped her legs against its sides and off they went, flying around the pasture like overgrown kids, but seemingly pleased with one another.

She looked beautiful, and so terribly happy, and what a good rider, Barney observed as they came trotting back.

She pulled up next to Barney and slid down into his arms, breathless and smiling.

"Wow, Barnwell. She's *wonderful*."

"Glad you like each other."

"Okay, Raven," she said, turning to the horse, "time for bed." And gently led the filly back toward the barn, Barney walking alongside.

"A little early isn't it?" he said.

"Keep your opinions to yourself, buster," she said with mock menace, then leaned in toward Barney as they walked and whispered in a secretive voice, "Do you know that the Arabs used to make love on horseback?"

"No!" said Barney, leaning away in feigned shock.

"Yes," she said loudly, punctuating her exclamation with her index finger. She patted her husband's arm. "Don't worry, Barnwell, you'll soon get the hang of it."

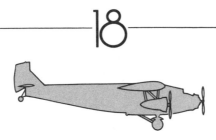

18

It was the worst moment of his life and he didn't quite know what to do with himself. So he put on his jacket and walked out of the little office at Hoover Airport and wandered aimlessly until somehow he found himself at the Coastal dispatcher's desk and booked aboard the evening flight to Binghamton.

He slumped into an empty starboard seat by a window, not bothering to fasten his seatbelt, and the plane took off, climbing, banking sharply over the Potomac and then turning north. It was a cloudless night, like the ones she so much liked, filled with stars and darkness, hot soup in the thermos beside her, a punctured can of tomato juice with a straw inserted. Always she started out in late afternoon, much preferring night flying to daylight, unfolding the precise map of her route, one section each hour, like an accordion, until the last fold brought her in sight of her destination.

Gruff Al Davenport had come to his office with the news, somehow knowing. She was down in the Pacific, she and Fred Noonan, her navigator, for the round-the-world flight. Noonan, once chief navigator for Pan Am; no one more expert.

The plane was down somewhere in the ocean on the 2,556-mile

flight from New Guinea to Howland Island, a speck two and a half miles long, one-half mile wide.

She had come so close really, right down to the home stretch, and now this. Davenport had exuded unconvincing confidence like sweat. A veritable armada had been committed to the search—an aircraft carrier, a battleship, four destroyers, countless planes—all trying to spot the Electra 10-E, a dot in the Pacific.

Except they wouldn't find her. Barney knew it in his bones, in his lungs. She was gone. Amelia Earhart, thirty-eight years of age, out of Kansas City, Kansas. Recipient of the Distinguished Flying Cross. Lady Lindy. Joan of Arc.

He could feel Ernie Pyle hunched somewhere over his typewriter, staring at the keys as his fingers reluctantly hammered out the story.

Was it worth it? Sandwiches in waxed paper, smiling stewardesses in fetching outfits serving hot cocoa on a tray, expertly bobbing with the turbulence as if it weren't there. Was it worth her?

The flight landed in Binghamton and taxied up to the Coastal hangar. The original office looked like a shed next to the two new structures housing the waiting room and the maintenance shop next door.

Barney got off in a daze and wandered away from the line of eight other passengers trekking single file toward the terminal. Car horns beeped to attract attention, relatives waiting for their loved ones' safe return. He walked into the darkened old hangar, back toward the corner Aroni had once filled with his tools and dissected engines. The bench was still there, covered with a tarpaulin.

A vague shadow loomed against the far wall. Not an airplane shape of any sort; something else. He walked toward it, further back into the empty hull of the building. It was a car—the old Jordan, its Red Hawk ensignia a blurry motif on its door and the words *Courtesy Car* just above the crest. He wondered who had mothballed it here. Probably Henry McKay.

He sat down on the running board and looked back over his shoulder at the Red Hawk symbol and remembered the red Lockheed Vega she had flown from Hawaii.

Amelia Earhart. Why did it have to close now? There was so much more for her to do, for all of them. He remembered the look on her face the day she presented the wristwatch to Ernie. Smiling, freckled, so alive.

He reached up to wipe the July sweat from his face and found tears.

THREE

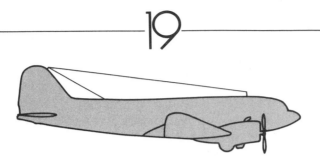

19

Barney had joined the America First movement not so much out of the solid convictions of an isolationist, but from his admiration for Charles Lindbergh. It was Jim Farley who had introduced him to the Lone Eagle at a private stag dinner party in Washington the day after France fell in June of 1940.

The one-time Postmaster General—out of the Roosevelt cabinet since he broke with FDR over the third-term issue—had invited Barney plus a few other airline officials to meet Lindbergh.

Vickie took a dim view of the stag aspects, bluntly pointing out it was the fourth such affair he had attended in the last six weeks.

"I don't want to sound like Susan B. Anthony, Barney, but doesn't this town ever have anything but all-male dinners?"

It had been a bad day and what he normally would have considered a justifiable complaint assumed the proportions of ugly nagging. "I don't make the rules or send out the invitations," he said, more brusquely than was necessary.

Stung, she was tart herself. "Maybe if you'd refuse a few of those invitations, they'd start asking wives."

"Oh, for Christ's sake, be reasonable. Would you want me to turn down a chance to meet Lindbergh?"

She was angry enough to continue the exchange but didn't. There had been an increasing number of occasions recently when Barney had come home in an arbitrary, unreasonable mood ready to start a fight over some petty matter. She knew him well enough to realize that fatigue and worry were responsible, and so once again she tried hard to be tolerant. Even now, disappointed that he was going out again, and to an affair she would have loved attending, she suddenly relented.

"I'm sorry, Barney," she apologized. "I know you've been looking forward to tonight. You go have a good time, and don't drink too much. I just bought a new nightgown that would turn a monk into Jack the Ripper."

She sent him off, mollified and pleased that she was so understanding. And she was, but she also was lonely. The trouble with living out in the Potomac horse-country was its isolation. She hadn't made many friends in the area. A neighbor, in fact, had snubbed her when she found out that Vickie was an ex-stewardess, an incident she had never confided to Barney. And she discovered she had pitifully little in common with most of the women in the sprawling, affluent area. The few social affairs she had attended seemed to consist largely of gossiping, comparing bank accounts, discussing clothes, and agreeing that Franklin Roosevelt was a dangerous radical who wanted to be a dictator.

Vickie had a few casual acquaintances but no real friends; mostly these were women who simply shared her love of horses. Some of these dropped her when they invited her to go fox-hunting and Vickie refused, on the grounds that she'd be rooting for the fox. Nobody had thought it funny. Riding to the hounds around Potomac was taken seriously. For a few it was the major reason for owning horses.

In truth, Victoria Doman Burton found herself existing solely for her husband and hated herself for falling into this deadly feminine trap. She had always been fiercely independent; she had gone to work at seventeen and enjoyed being active and being her own person. She could relish solitude but strictly on her own terms and her own time; as a steady diet, she found it depressing. Nor could she sublimate her restlessness in working for some charity. To Vickie Burton, it was like penitence for one's wealth. She could dredge up respect for such activities but hated the idea of doing it herself, and she was no hypocrite.

A week earlier, at an airline party, she had bumped into C. R. Smith, who still remembered her, much to her amazement, and in the course of a lengthy conversation, he offered her a job.

"When National Airport opens next year we'll have a VIP room —Admirals' Clubs, we call them—and our plan is to staff them with former stewardesses. That qualifies you, Vickie, if you're interested."

She was, enough to ask Barney about it on the way home. First he laughed and then he got angry when he realized she was serious.

"Let you work for American? You must think I'm crazy. That damned C. R. would go around bragging he hired my wife, that's what he'd do."

"Okay, then," she said stubbornly, "how about letting me go back to work for Coastal? Not as chief stew, of course, but any kind of a job that would keep me busy."

"The answer's no, Vickie. I won't have my wife on Coastal's payroll. That's pure nepotism and there's enough of that crap in this town already. Why this sudden desire to become a wage slave again?"

"I'm bored, that's why. There isn't enough to do at home. I can't spend all day currying Raven. We have an extremely competent housekeeper, and besides I hate housework anyway. What's more important, I miss you . . . with increasing frequency. You worked late three nights last week and came home so tired I felt like walking you around until you cooled off."

"You complaining?" His tone was ominous, she thought.

"No, but it's an awfully long layover between kissing you good-bye in the morning and kissing you hello at night."

"Well," he said with a sudden surge of sympathy, "I'll try to do better. Tell you what, let's go away next weekend—drive somewhere. Get us a good hotel room, and have some fun."

She hugged him. "I'd love that, Barney. You pick the place and I'll be all packed for both of us by the time you get home Friday night."

He got home close to midnight that Friday and announced he had called a staff meeting for the next morning. "We've had to revise our route application for Washington–Chicago. Has to be filed first thing Monday. I'm sorry, honey. Maybe next week."

She said she understood, and didn't bother planning the rain-check weekend. Her life with Barnwell Burton was becoming a succession of disrupted plans. Yet she still thought she loved him and she even managed to feel a little sorry for him. So she sent him off to the Farley dinner with a false smile on her face and a voice that kept saying, your heart made a mistake.

For Barney it was a memorable evening. Normally, he had the poise to meet celebrities on an equal footing. After all, he *was* president of a major airline. But when he shook hands with Charles Lindbergh, he felt more like that twelve-year-old who had been introduced to Bud Lindeman before his birthday plane ride, yet the initial awe was quickly displaced. Lindy was easy to talk to and with; Barney eventually found himself calling him "Slim" as did those who had known him before, and while Barney stayed on the fringe of the table conversation he still did not feel like any awe-struck outsider. The two airline executives present who were best acquainted with Lindbergh were Jack Frye and Juan Trippe of Pan American; Lindy had been a valued consultant to both carriers in the past and TWA, in fact, had been called "the Lindbergh Line."

Frye sat on Barney's right during dinner, while a quiet Army Air Corps colonel was on his left. The colonel was a close friend of Lindbergh's, introduced to Barney as Truman Smith. The name meant nothing to him until Frye confided in a whisper that "Smith was the guy who served as our military attaché in Berlin. He and Lindbergh drew up that report on Germany's growing airpower."

Barney nodded in feigned recognition; all he really remembered was that two years ago Lindbergh had been called pro-Nazi for accepting a medal from Herman Goering and later publicly declaring that Germany's progress in military aviation was far greater than France, England, and Russia were willing to admit. He had had no idea that this Colonel Smith was co-author of the first real assessment of Nazi strength. He was impressed enough to engage Smith in conversation.

"Is Lindy really anti-Semitic?" Barney asked.

"No," the colonel replied, mildly taken aback. "He abhors Hitler's policies against the Jews. But Slim does admire German scientists and pilots and their industrialists. He thought a European war would be a catastrophe because it would result either in a German victory or total Russian domination of Europe. The situation's different now, of course. France is whipped and Slim doesn't think Britain can hold out. Anyway, Hitler will move against the Soviet Union one of these days and Lindbergh is against our getting involved. He figures it's too late to save England and that a German-Russo war would just be none of our business."

"Do you agree?"

Smith grinned wryly. "No comment. I'm an Army officer. If war comes, I'll follow orders. But, yes, I think it will be close for England."

Barney listened intently when Farley asked Lindbergh to say a few words. This man who had become an American legend spoke in a high-pitched voice, expostulating his isolationist views in a manner that impressed Barney with its earnestness. By the end of the evening, Barney had been nearly convinced, hero worship superseding his misgivings that Lindbergh might be wrong. Some of his fellow airline chiefs remain unconvinced.

He stopped at the Monocle for a drink with Jack Frye after the dinner, and the TWA president shook his head when Barney asked him if Lindbergh's views made sense.

"I don't think anybody really wants to go to war, Barney," Frye said soberly. "But there's an excellent chance it'll be forced upon us. I don't know under what circumstances or exactly by whom, but it's my personal feeling that we'll be at war within two years."

"I hope not," Barney said. "This industry is going places, what with the Civil Aeronautics Board governing the routes, fares, and even accident investigations. And now with the Civil Aeronautics Administration cleaning up air traffic problems—though I wish FDR had made it independent instead of putting it under Commerce like an unwanted stepchild. The last thing we need is a war."

"If war comes, the whole industry will be involved up to the top of its collective rudder—those five new pressurized Boeing Stratocruisers we've ordered will be going over to the Army along with God knows how many other aircraft."

"Well," Barney allowed cautiously, "maybe if we take Lindbergh's advice we can stay out of the actual shooting."

"Maybe. But I doubt it. The military is already talking to us about leasing some DC-3's. And Gorrell's plan has been in the oven since '36."

"The what?"

"You haven't heard about it yet?"

"I know Edgar Gorrell, President of the Air Transport Association. I don't know anything about a plan."

"Well, Ed first proposed it four years ago. It was a blueprint for mobilizing the industry in the event of war."

"I've seen some references to airline mobilization somewhere," Barney said, "but frankly I gave it little attention."

"The plan is being revised again right now. C. R. has one of his top guys working on a specific program."

"I'll look into it," Barney promised, and called it a night. He telephoned the very next day, and for the first time realized what war would mean to Coastal and all the carriers. There were no definite commitments or promises, but as Gorrell told Barney that afternoon, "You'd better be prepared to turn at least half your fleet over to the military."

In 1941, United began contract training of military personnel at Oakland, and Pan Am undertook the construction of airfields throughout the Caribbean. Barney felt Coastal still was too small to commit itself to such projects, but he had a few ideas of his own by then. One development he noted with interest was Western's application to the Civil Aeronautics Board to serve several points in Alaska via Calgary and Edmonton. He called in Bill Sloan and asked him to bird-dog the proceeding.

"Just keep me advised if there are any developments on it," he told the young lawyer.

"Sure, but I can't for the life of me see why you'd be interested."

"Let's say it's one of my hunches," said Barney and smiled.

On June 16, the first plane landed at Washington National Airport on the Potomac River, the brand-new 750-acre facility less than four miles from downtown. Years earlier Barney had laid plans to shift the company's entire Washington organization to the new field. He had leased two hangars with office space above each. Three weeks before the airport finally opened, Barney moved reservations, the general offices and flight operations into Washington National. In six months, Coastal and the other carriers serving the capital were operating more than two hundred daily flights in and out of the model airport. All Barney retained of the old downtown facilities was a single ticket office on the ground floor of the Willard Hotel. Coastal's share of constructing offices above the hangars, plus the cost of moving, ran to more than a half-million dollars, but to Barney it was worth every penny. "Now we've got everything under one roof," he told an executive staff meeting exuberantly. "In the long run, the consolidation will pay for itself in greater efficiency."

He didn't have much time to enjoy the new quarters or his first really swank office. The war was coming closer, and Barney was made acutely aware of it when suddenly one winter morning Gorrell summoned all company presidents to an emergency meeting in downtown Washington. Tiny and stern, Gorrell pulled no punches.

"Gentlemen, we don't need any crystal ball to realize this country is going to be at war soon. When it happens—and I won't even say *if* it happens—this industry has to pool its experience and knowhow and contribute enormously. We've already had clues as to the effect of a global conflict on our normal operations. The War Department, for example, has taken over the entire output of DC-4 production. Many of you in this room have been, or are in the process of, leasing aircraft to the military. So let's get one thing straight. If you don't want your airlines taken over completely, you'd better agree on a way to fit them into the war effort. We have a tentative mobilization scheme ready for consideration. It's not perfect. Some of you may think it's too stiff and others might think it doesn't go far enough. That's why you're here today: to have an exact blueprint ready. If we don't, the government is going to shove one down your respective throats. Now, let's get to work."

Out of the marathon meeting evolved a plan to put all airline technicians and operations specialists at the disposal of the armed forces overnight. The industry would literally hand the government a ready-to-fly global transport system. Barney emerged worn out but feeling slightly patriotic, his America First membership notwithstanding. It was very late, but he knew he was too wound up to sleep. He only hoped Vickie would not be waiting up.

"I need a drink," he muttered to Jack Frye.

"An eminently practical suggestion, Barney. Want to join us, Bob?" The last question was addressed to a tall, burly man whose massive head and battleship-prow jaw matched his husky frame.

"Hell, yes!" he growled.

"Have you met Barney Burton of Coastal? Barney, this is Bob Six of Continental."

Barney shook hands with the towering Westerner, who was reputed to be the toughest, most fiercely independent airline man in the U.S. "We haven't met formally," Barney said, "but I've heard a lot about Bob Six."

"Most of what you hear is libelous, vicious slander—and generally true," Six chuckled. "Barney, how the hell are you? It's about time we get to talking. I liked what you said about setting up some kind of air-travel priority system. We're gonna have fifty people fighting for each available seat. Frankly, I wish the others had bought your idea."

"A lousy way to achieve a hundred percent load factor," said Frye. "A war will be a lot tougher on the smaller airlines like Continental and Coastal. Barney, you'll be lucky if you wind up with three airplanes for your entire route system."

"That's why I need a drink," Barney sighed. "Let's find a quiet bar."

They were heading outside when Pat Patterson of United joined them. The four strolled in silence through the chilly night until they came upon a hotel bar. The conversation continued once they settled down behind some drinks in the half-empty lounge.

"It's going to be rough on all of us," Patterson was saying. "The airlines are operating three hundred sixty-three planes, and if war breaks out we'll be lucky to retain two hundred of them. That's not much more than half the present fleet. United has sixty-nine aircraft. If the mobilization plan is followed, we'll have only about thirty aircraft left to operate a system that kept all sixty-nine busy."

"Which is why Barney's priority suggestion has merit," Six grumbled. "We'll be forced to go with something like it sooner or later."

"You don't think the compromise we agreed on will work?" Frye asked.

"Selling tickets to regular customers, subject to cancellation if military or government people need the space? Hell, no. Barney's right—establish some priority categories and stick to 'em. That'll discourage nonessential travel right from the start. If a guy knows he stands a ninety-nine-percent chance of getting bumped off a flight, he won't even bother to go to the airport."

The quartet argued on into the night. By the time Barney drove up to the house, the birds were chirping in anticipation of dawn.

Prepared as he was to expect war, Barney still was shocked as he listened to the reports on Pearl Harbor. On Monday morning Edgar Gorrell phoned him.

"Barney, I've been called to the White House one hour from now. You're the only airline president based here. Would you go with me?"

"Sure. Where should I meet you?"

"Pick me up at the Carlton Hotel. I'll be waiting in front, say, forty-five minutes from now."

"I'll be there. What's it all about?"

"I'm not sure, but I think we're in for a complete takeover of the whole industry. General Arnold will be there."

"Hap Arnold? The Chief of the Air Corps?"

"None other. This could be trouble."

Barney and Gorrell were ushered in exactly at the appointed hour; General H. H. Arnold was already there, seated across from the President's surprisingly cluttered desk. The General rose as they entered, a warm smile accentuating his rather jolly features. The appearance was deceptive; Hap Arnold was harder than cast iron.

"Mr. President," the Air Corps chief said, "may I present Edgar Gorrell of the Air Transport Association. Sir, I haven't had the pleasure of meeting your colleague."

"Mr. President, General Arnold, this is Mr. Barney Burton, president of Coastal Airlines. I took the liberty of asking that he be present. His carrier has its headquarters in Washington and as an

ATA member, I felt it would be appropriate for its chief executive to be here as a delegate for all the other airline officials."

"Delighted you could be present, Barney," Roosevelt boomed.

He had never met FDR in person, despite his long friendship with Jim Farley, and the first thought that sprinted through his mind was that Roosevelt simply could not be a hopeless cripple. He was too vibrant, too much alive. The great leonine head, the inevitable cigarette holder jutting from the corner of his handsome mouth like a stiff flagpole, his massive shoulders. Barney actually expected the President to get out of his chair and walk toward him. FDR's voice knifed into his reveries. "Gentlemen, if you'll pull over those chairs and sit down, I'm afraid we've some grave business to discuss. Hap, here, already knows why I've summoned you. I think you'd better take a look at this."

He handed Gorrell a piece of White House stationery, which the ATA chief held so Barney could read it, too. Barney felt his mouth go dry. At the top were the foreboding words: *Executive Order.* Gorrell read aloud the typewritten words underneath:

" 'An executive order authorizing seizure of the airlines for the duration of the war,' and turning them over to General Arnold's command," Gorrell muttered. "Mr. President, I can't believe this."

"You'd better," Roosevelt said grimly. "If you'll look at the bottom, you'll see I've already signed it."

"If it's not too late, Mr. President," said Gorrell, "I'd like to offer some comments on the wisdom of this course."

"I'm no dictator," FDR said amiably, "regardless of what my Republican friends like to claim. If you have some legitimate arguments against this course of action, I'm perfectly willing to listen. And so will Hap."

Gorrell took a deep breath. "Mr. President, before we leave this room, I'm going to reach into my briefcase and turn over to you a document agreed to by every airline operating in the United States. Briefly, it is a detailed plan which as of this very day will have the airlines flying for the Army, Navy, or any other war agency. We have the operational experience, technical background, skilled personnel, and—equally important—the will and desire to do whatever this industry can to win this war. In other words, the global air transport system you're trying to achieve through this executive order already exists. There isn't an airline in the country which isn't willing and eager to give military requirements the highest priority. If your order stands, it would take weeks or even months to organize a government-operated system. We could do the same job, under a contract arrangement, and we can do it faster, better, and immediately. I implore you, sir, to leave the airlines in the hands of civilian operators and they'll come through. I promise you they will. I pledge my word on it."

Roosevelt looked over at General Arnold, who was grinning. "As an airline president, Barney, do you concur?" the President asked.

"Completely, Mr. President. You already have a historical precedent showing that nationalization in wartime can hurt more than it helps. When the government took over the railroads in 1917, there was utter chaos." Gorrell looked both surprised and pleased at this tack.

Roosevelt tossed back his big head and laughed. "Neat point, my friend. I was afraid for a moment you were going to bring up what happened when the Army tried to fly the mail."

Barney smiled ruefully. "No, sir, but I'll admit I thought about it when I saw this executive order. With due respect to General Arnold, I think the airlines would have to spend an exorbitant amount of time teaching military personnel how to operate. May I tell both of you a true story?"

"If it doesn't take longer than five minutes," FDR said.

"A few months ago we leased one of our Boeing 247's to the Army. They sent a rather pompous young second lieutenant to our hangar so he could inspect the plane. I'm sure General Arnold knows how a 247 is built, but for your information, Mr. President, the main wing spar runs through the center of the cabin. There's a small step on either side of the spar so passengers won't trip over it. Well, the lieutenant boarded the Boeing and was walking from the rear toward the cockpit when he failed to notice the hump and stumbled. He picked himself up, glared at our maintenance chief and said bitterly, 'The first thing we'll do is get rid of that goddamned step!' "

FDR laughed while Arnold managed a wry smile. Ed Gorrell, sensing their good mood, knifed into the breach. "Mr. President, I know you're busy but I don't want to leave here knowing that order still exists."

Roosevelt turned to Arnold. "Hap, I'd like your views on it."

The general glanced shrewdly at the two airline officials. "I have to admit these gentlemen here made an excellent case. Frankly, I think the Air Corps has enough problems without trying to run a transport operation. I'd buy their arguments, with certain understandings."

"We'll do everything within reason, Hap," Gorrell said quickly.

Arnold's normally pleasant expression hardened suddenly. "You may have to do quite a few things, Edgar, that are completely unreasonable. You're going to wind up modifying bombers at your maintenance bases. You'll be ferrying combat planes to the war zones. You'll be training everything from pilots to greaseballs. You'll be handing over to us your top meteorology experts. And God help the first airline I catch hauling somebody's vacationing grandmother around in a seat that should be occupied by a man in uniform on a military mission. In other words, Colonel, I'm willing to let you try your own plan. I've spent a career getting private industry to do the impossible for the Air Corps. I've stuck my neck out more than once convincing aircraft manufacturers to design new military planes before Congress voted the appropriation. Yes, I think the airlines can do the job. I just hope they realize how big it'll be."

"I think we do," Gorrell said quietly, and Barney nodded.

Franklin Roosevelt reached across the desk. "Give me that order." Gorrell handed it over. The President tore it up. "I think you people can do the job, too," he added. "I want to thank both of you for coming to see me."

Barney was following Gorrell out of the Oval Room when FDR's voice intercepted his departure. "Barney, one last word of advice . . ."

"Yes, Mr. President?"

"For God's sake, don't get any foolish ideas about enlisting just because you're of age. You can do more for the war effort running your airline than being an officer somewhere."

Startled, all Barney could do was grin foolishly and leave, although he suddenly understood firsthand the uncanny intuitive powers of the man. As he and Gorrell walked the two short blocks back to the Carlton he could not help asking, "Was he right, about staying at Coastal instead of putting on a uniform?"

"I think he was, yes. There will be a few exceptions. I happen to know Arnold's tapping C. R. Smith to run the Air Ferry Command, and there'll be some airline officials who'll go into the military because they have special training or knowledge that Air Corps men lack. But generally speaking, you'll do more good by staying just where you are. So will most of us. Just hope your grandchildren don't ask too many questions."

So Barnwell Burton took this advice and joined World War II in mufti—a decision cinched largely because Vickie bluntly told him that enlisting would be cowardly.

"Cowardly? What's cowardly about joining up? I don't feel exactly brave parked behind a desk while other guys my age are—"

"Barney, use your head. If you enlist, you'll just be parked behind some other desk. With your background, they'd simply give you the same kind of job you're already doing, only maybe with less importance. If you insist on indulging yourself by getting shot at, you can go in as an infantry buck private—and I don't think you're selfish enough to do that."

"Nuts," he said doubtfully, "I suppose you're making sense."

"More than you would make as a nearsighted Sgt. York."

He laughed, but it took very little time for Vickie to realize Barney might as well have gone overseas. Under the pressure of wartime operations, he spent so many nights at his office that a crude shower and toilet had to be installed in a small anteroom. His workload was brutal as he fought to keep the airline operating its schedules with a fleet that had been decimated and on May 15, 1942, things got worse. He attended a War Department meeting at which the airlines were told exactly how many planes each would have to turn over to the government. He blanched when an Air Corps major read off Coastal's contribution.

"Coastal," he droned blandly as if reciting a shopping list, "will provide four DC-3's and three Boeing 247's."

The military was commandeering seven of its twelve planes. "That's rough," Jack Frye murmured sympathetically.

"I feel like Pearl Harbor was a Japanese attack on Coastal," Barney whispered back.

"Christ, I don't blame you," said Bob Six. "We got away with a fifty-percent cut. We're flying six Lockheed Lodestars and they're buying three of them. But Western's losing two-thirds of its fleet, same as you."

"I don't know," Barney said, "how we can fly our routes with only five aircraft."

"Do what I'm doing," Six said cheerfully.

"What's that?"

"I'm going into the service in September, as an Air Corps captain. Terry Drinkwater will run Continental while I'm gone."

Barney shook his head. "I wouldn't mind enlisting, but I'm not sure I'd have an airline to come home to. There's nobody around my shop to run things."

Six nudged him. "What do you say? You're young enough, unlike most of these poor old guys at this meeting. And you have no children to worry about."

"Unless you could count the airline as a kind of collective child." They're all dependent on me, he thought. "If I left, who could take over for the duration? When this war is over, I'll do something about it. Find a savvy guy about my own age . . . make him executive vice-president or something and train him as my replacement . . . then maybe I can make things up to Vickie."

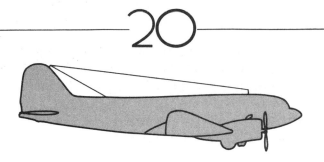

Inevitably, the ranks of experienced employees began to thin as they were called into service or enlisted voluntarily. The biggest loss was Al Davenport, who walked into Barney's office one day and announced he was going into the Air Corps Training Command.

"I'm too old for combat," he told Barney, "but I sure can teach a few things to these grocery clerks who think they're gonna be Rickenbackers and Doolittles overnight."

"Jesus," Barney groaned, "you can't do this to me. I need you more than the Army does. Who the hell will ride herd on those prima-donna pilots of ours?"

"You've got plenty of experienced line pilots, Boss. There are four or five who'd make good chief pilots: Bert Costin, Mark Culbertson, and there's a youngster I think a lot of—Andy Vaughn. He'd be my choice."

"A junior captain promoted to chief pilot? Are you—? Guys like Costin and Culbertson won't take orders from a pilot who's fifty notches below them on the seniority list."

"They'll take orders, mostly because they make more dough flying line than they would sitting behind a desk. As for young Mr.

Vaughn, he's more than just an airplane jockey. He's got a degree in aeronautical engineering from MIT, and he flies by the book. Believes in cockpit discipline and that's the kind of man you want for a chief pilot. Screw seniority. Andy Vaughn lives, breathes, and eats by the book. I think he's got the guts to crack down on any black sheep who thinks he's still barnstorming."

"How old is he?"

"Twenty-six, maybe twenty-seven."

"That's too young, Al. Christ, we'd name him chief pilot and he'd be called up a week after we promoted him."

"He's married and has two kids. He also happens to be a Quaker. Take my word for it, he'll do you a job."

Barney sighed. "Okay, you talked me into it. When are you leaving?"

"A week from tomorrow."

"That doesn't give you any time to break in Vaughn. Can't you make it two weeks?"

"I could but the Army won't," laughed Davenport.

The last was Calvin Motts, who somehow had wangled a captain's commission and was going into the Quartermasters Corps. He had three full weeks before reporting to Fort Meade, Maryland, and insisted on wearing his new uniform to work every day during the interim, strutting around the general offices much to everyone's annoyance. It came as something of a shock to Motts that Al Davenport was going in as a major. Barney threw them both a hastily organized farewell party and talked Davenport into showing up in uniform. On the undersized vice-president of Operations, it looked as if it had been tailored by a welder, but all Motts saw were those gold leaves on his epaulets.

With their departure, Barney's own workload doubled. Motts's responsibilities were the easiest to assume. No airline really worried any longer about such luxuries as marketing and advertising. There was no point in promoting air travel; virtually every flight ran full. There was only one way to come close to meeting the insatiable demand. Barney sat down with John Myler, freshly promoted from chief dispatcher to traffic manager, and worked out revised schedules that had each plane in service twelve hours a day. With less than half the number of planes to fly, the airline was carrying twice as many passengers as in 1941, and the mileage flown almost doubled. Barney hardly ever got home.

A priority system was put into effect with five classifications. Those ineligible for any one of the five were advised to go by train or bus. It was an incongruous situation for Barney, who had spent the last thirteen years scrounging for passengers, but he wasn't complaining, what with record traffic. Higher taxes notwithstanding, Coastal's bank account swelled steadily. It became even healthier when Barney signed a contract to fly military cargo and personnel from the East Coast to Great Falls, Montana, where shipments were turned over to Western and flown north through Canada to Alaska.

He actually had hoped to win a contract that would have hooked up with Western's proposed route expansion to Calgary and Edmonton, but that had been pigeonholed for the duration by an unofficial Civil Aeronautics Board moratorium on new route applications. Barney had envisioned expanding west beyond Minneapolis all the way to Calgary; in the back of his mind was a possible merger with Western, with this link making their mutual route systems not only compatible but transcontinental.

"Trans-Western," he said, unveiling the idea to Larry Aroni over a fast dinner before returning to the office. "When this war's over, commercial aviation will be in for the biggest boom in history. Just look at what's happening. Thousands of GI's who might never have flown in their whole lives are climbing into airplanes every day. They're getting used to air travel. They're becoming accustomed to it, even taking it for granted. Guys like that—and their families, too—they're our future market. Every time they board an airplane, they become future passengers."

"*That* I have to question," said Aroni. "A hell of a lot of them won't even want to see an airplane again."

"Not as many as you think. They may hate flying because in wartime it's dangerous, but they also know it's fast. They'll realize that peacetime flying will be entirely different. Nobody'll be shooting at 'em. They'll get over their fears. They'll accept air-travel as commonplace and completely natural. And that's what we want, Larry—just one huge potential market waiting to be tapped. We'll build bigger and faster planes."

"Like the DC-4," Aroni said smiling. "I figured you'd be lusting for some of that four-engined stuff one of these days."

"You're damned right. Not just the DC-4, but maybe also that new Lockheed Transport—the Constellation, four engines and pressurized. That's the future! Fly above the weather. No more grinding through thunderstorms because you can't get out of the way."

"Come down to earth. Those Connies will run three-quarters of a million apiece. They're strictly for long-haul routes, which we ain't got."

"But we will have. We will. I've got Bill Sloan drawing up tentative route expansion plans right now, including Minneapolis to the West Coast finally. Plus a couple of other markets I've got up my sleeve—markets nobody has thought of developing. Hell, I don't even want to confide them to you. For all I know, you might leave me to go with some other carrier, and you'd take a few of the dreams of mine with you."

Aroni laughed. "You're a trusting sonofabitch, aren't you?" His smile suddenly faded. "I doubt if I'd leave Coastal for another airline, my friend, but I might as well tell you I'm figuring on leaving for another employer."

"You're kidding me. You gotta be kidding!"

"I've talked it over with Norma. She hates the idea worse than you do, but she knows how I feel."

"And how *do* you feel? So goddamned patriotic all of a sudden that you'd leave your wife and a two-year-old daughter, not to mention your airline, just to go running off to some godforsaken jungle and get your balls shot off?"

"Don't go dramatic on me. I won't be in combat. I'll be doing what I've always been doing for you—keeping a large collection of spare parts flying in close formation."

"You picked a lousy time to leave. I was just going to name you executive vice-president."

Aroni sighed. He had a strong notion that the offer was being made on impulse. "No, thanks, Barney. I have no crown-prince ambitions, and you know I'd be lost outside of Maintenance and Engineering."

"Yeah," Barney agreed sullenly. "Look. How close are you to signing up?"

"I've got an application in. With C. R. Smith's endorsement. If Hap Arnold's office okays it, I'll go in as a bird colonel in charge of Air Transport Command maintenance—what used to be Air Ferry Command."

"If I lose any more guys, I'll be running this company by myself. If I lose you, we're in deep trouble. I have no competent replacement—nobody who comes close in ability. You know what good maintenance means to an airline. I don't have to draw you a diagram. We're not like American, with a reserve of supervisory manpower." Barney sighed. "Look. The War Department has just agreed to keep its hands off key airline executives unless they get the permission of their respective companies to enlist. Of course, you could go into the service if you wanted to, but not with an automatic commission."

Aroni shook his head. "I wish you'd release me, Barney, but I don't suppose I could talk you into it."

"No, you can't. I need you too badly." He filled Aroni's wine glass. "Tell you what I'm going to do, though. As of right now, I'm giving you a fifteen percent salary increase along with a ten-year contract that boosts your pay two percent annually over that period. Just to show you how much I appreciate your staying with me."

Aroni eyed him, a look that vacillated between affection and a kind of cynicism. "You can't buy me."

"What I'm handing you is sort of a bonus. I don't have to buy you off."

Aroni shrugged and resumed eating. "Well, I will say you're being suspiciously generous, and I'd be a fool if I told you to stick that raise and the contract up your butt. Only thing is . . ."

"Only thing is what?" Barney suddenly looked happy.

"A few years from now, when that kid of mine gets to be seven or eight and asks me what I did in the war, what the hell do I say? That Barney Burton kept me out of it?"

"Sure. Blame it all on his uncle. How's the family doing, anyway? We don't see as much of you these days as we'd like. Vickie was telling me the other day she'd like to have you and Norma over for dinner."

"All you gotta do is ask. Norma's awfully fond of Vickie, and so am I. Marrying her was the smartest thing you ever did."

"Yeah. But sometimes I wonder if marrying me was the smartest thing *she* ever did."

Aroni looked up from his plate. "I don't mean to pry, but are you two having trouble?"

"Not really. At least I'm not. But Vickie's pretty lonely out where we live. Hasn't made many friends. And as usual, I'm spending too much time here."

"More time than you have to. Marriage, Barney, is something you have to apply yourself to."

"You think I enjoy being away from her?"

"Apparently," Aroni said softly.

"That's not true."

"Isn't it? I'll admit I don't have your responsibilities and headaches. But I have my share. Only I'll never let them louse up my life with Norma. Your trouble, pal, is that you're manufacturing your own overwork. Every man has to establish certain priorities. You're putting the company at the top of the list and it's a hell of a long way down before you get to Vickie. Okay, keep the company first if you insist, but move her up a few notches. It still wouldn't be fair to her but it would help."

Barney stared past Aroni. "I wish I could. I wish to God I could. I take the office home with me and I think about it even when I'm asleep. Dream about it. I'm like a man hooked on alcohol."

Aroni was somber. "The divorce rate among alcoholics is extremely high."

Barney seemed startled. "It's not that serious. Vickie wouldn't divorce me. She loves me. And in my way, I love her."

Aroni shrugged—a helpless, half apologetic gesture—and said nothing.

"Has she said anything to you or Norma about us?"

"No, she hasn't. Vickie isn't the kind. She wouldn't have to. I'm no marriage counselor, but I know you. You'll keep slapping her face with this love affair you've got with your airline and she'll pull the cork, just as sure as if you were having an affair with some broad."

"She knew what she was getting into when she married me," Barney said without much conviction.

"She didn't know she was marrying a damned fool. Most guys

would do a lot to have a woman like Vickie. You prefer a collection of airplanes, a few pages of flight schedules, and a daily diet of crisis."

"You're probably right," Barney said. "Maybe when the war's over, I'll make amends."

"Barney, if the war ended tomorrow, you'd be working just as hard. Harder. Airline problems are simple in wartime. All we gotta do is keep the fleet in the air. We've got more customers than we know what to do with. But when it's all over, then we'll face problems we can't even imagine right now."

"I can," Barney said. "That's why I'm hurting her."

"Then how can you say that when the shooting stops, you'll live any different? You'd better start reforming right now if you want to keep her in your life. It just won't last this way."

"I'll try, Larry. I'll try."

He did try. Or at least his intentions were good. He took Vickie out to dinner at least twice a week, reduced his sleeping at the office to once every four days, and even proposed that they rent the house and get an apartment downtown for a few months. Touched and pleased, she refused.

"I still have to take care of Raven," she pointed out. "And finding an apartment in Washington these days would be like searching for gold."

"I could at least try," he argued. "It would give us more time together—that drive out to Potomac takes an hour with a good tail wind. You could have lunch with me occasionally, too . . ."

"I appreciate the offer, honey, and you're being very sweet. But I'll stick it out. The war can't last forever."

Reprieved, he didn't mention it again and soon lapsed back into his old work habits. There were specific times when he was considerate and generous. For Christmas, he gave her a two-month-old German shepherd puppy whom she named Noel, and although she wryly admitted to herself that the dog usually was better company than her husband, she was grateful.

For their anniversary he gave her a mink coat. On the morning of her birthday he promised to come home reasonably early so they could celebrate.

Arriving at work, he went into a conference with Aroni and Andy Vaughn who had just returned from inspecting two DC-3's that the Air Corps was ready to sell to Coastal.

"They're a bit beat up," Aroni reported, "but we can put them in mint condition inside of a month after we take delivery. And the price is good—forty grand per."

Barney nodded. He looked at Vaughn. "Andy, you agree with him?"

"Yes, sir. The Air Corps took good care of those Gooney Birds. Control systems are like new. Engines need overhaul but the airframes are in good shape. Strip the interior, put in new or refurbished seats, and they're ready for service. I'd say they look like a good buy."

"How soon can we get our hands on them, Larry?"

"I brought the papers back with me. All you have to do is sign, write out a check for eighty thousand bucks, and dredge me up a couple of pilots to ferry them back here."

"Will you guarantee we can put them into our schedules thirty days after we take delivery?"

"Absolutely. The only bottleneck might be the seats. Both airplanes carried cargo and passengers. One has six seats and the other eight—and they're pretty worn, right down to the floor attachments. They have to be replaced."

"I doubt if I can get new ones," Barney said, "but I think I know where I can buy some pretty good used hardware. The frames are good, anyway, and our upholstering shop can do some beautifying. Okay, guys, I'll get the paperwork done tonight. Andy, find me a couple of crews who wouldn't mind spending a night or two in Miami."

"You only need one and a half crews, boss," Vaughn said. "I'd like to fly the left seat on one of them if there are no objections. Things are fairly quiet around my shop and I haven't had a day off for almost a month."

"Go right ahead, Andy," Barney said grandly. He was getting fond of Vaughn. A real sharp youngster, just as Davenport had said. There had been resentment among the crews when he was first named chief pilot, but even the most hard-nosed captains had come around to respecting him. He certainly had a no-nonsense attitude toward pilots. "By the way, Andy, the union rep came to see about Duane. They think you're being too hard."

Andy Vaughn had caught a senior captain with liquor on his breath before a flight and had fired him on the spot—standing up against ALPA's efforts to soften the punishment with a ninety-day demotion to copilot and a year's probation. Rebuffed, the union had approached Barney, who agreed to intercede. But Vaughn wouldn't budge.

"I'm a chief pilot, not a social worker. We don't have time to reform alcholics."

"Well, calling Duane an alcholic seems a bit harsh," Barney said mildly. "The union says he promises to be good if we give him another chance."

"Did ALPA tell you I've already talked to him on two other occasions about his drinking? Did they tell you one of those occasions involved his being seen in a bar while in uniform? The man is an accident looking for someplace to happen. The only concession I'll make is to suspend him without pay for six months on the condition that he joins AA. If he keeps his nose clean during that time, I'd take him back, but only as a first officer and then on another six months' probation."

"That's pretty strong medicine," said Barney.

"Granted. But that's how I feel, and if you override me, you can go get yourself another chief pilot. I'd just as soon go back to the line anyway."

Barney smiled. "I'll pass your decision on to the union. And it'll be my verdict, too, Andy."

It was only after Aroni and Vaughn left that he remembered his promise to Vickie, yet he decided it wouldn't hurt to be a little late. He intended only to glance through the papers Larry had left with him so he could be ready for a meeting with John Myler the next morning. But he made the mistake of studying them too closely and decided to summon Myler to his office. For the next three hours, they grappled with the complexities of fitting the two additional DC'3s into the schedules—a task involving rejiggering flight-crew assignments, aircraft availability, maintenance requirements, timetable revisions, and interline connections. Aroni and Vaughn were called back in to help; they were still working at midnight when Aroni slumped onto the couch.

"We won't be putting those damned planes into service for another month. Why the hell are we doing the whole fleet integration job in one night? And I thought this was Vickie's birthday."

"Jesus."

He phoned Vickie, oozing with futile apologies and empty explanations. She sounded curt; he didn't blame her. But hopes for making up for his tardiness with the expensive gift expired when he got home and discovered she had already gone to bed. Her thanks the next morning, when he gave her the diamond pendant at breakfast, were perfunctory. Perversely, as if the cool reception was her fault, he left in a huff. In an impulsive burst of self-recrimination, he took the following weekend off, but Vickie was moody, spiritless, and, worst of all, indifferent.

In desperation she finally confided her troubles to the Aronis. Larry Aroni became cool and distant toward Barney, even abrupt at times. The result of this chain of resentment toward him was Barney's turning increasingly to Jack Myler. He enlarged Myler's responsibilities, although not with proportionate authority. Just before the war ended, he named Myler vice-president of Traffic and Assistant to the President, justifying the second title on the grounds that he needed someone to relieve him of routine chores, nonessential paperwork and day-to-day problems so he could concentrate on major decisions and long-range policy.

Jack was no sycophant but admired Barney so much that his loyalty had the same effect. His was more than devotion based on respect; it also was sheer ambition. His dream was to be president, and he had long ago determined that blind allegiance to Barney was the only way to its fulfillment.

Barnwell Burton prepared Coastal Airlines to enter the postwar era with new route applications of 15,000 miles stuck in a bureaucratic logjam of the Civil Aeronautics Board, and with a chief executive who was subconsciously molding what past pressures and circumstances had dictated: an airline guided and governed by a single dominant force. The image of the corporation imperceptibly blended into the image of the man and became a single identity.

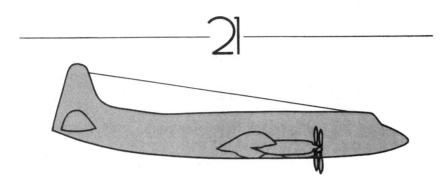

21

Al Davenport did not come back from the war, and Ernie Pyle died in action in the Pacific, still wearing the watch Amelia had presented to him that day at old Hoover Airport. But there was little time for Barney or anyone to reflect upon the preceding years and their losses. Such reveries and private considerations were swept aside by the postwar boom.

When World War II ended, the public was ready to embrace air travel, as many had hoped. Unfortunately the airlines weren't ready for the public. But then the growth was more like an explosion than an expansion, leaving the air carriers in disarray. Schedules were inadequate, airports overcrowded, equipment overtaxed. Yet Coastal, like all the rest, poured all its energy into acquisition of new routes even though it lacked the trained employees and equipment to properly service the routes doled out by the Civil Aeronautics Board. The new war was on—routes and traffic.

Personnel was Barney's greatest headache. Coastal, with just under six hundred employees at the start of the war, had nearly three thousand by V-J Day. Most had been frantically recruited, hastily trained, and inadequately motivated, creating an impossible situation for the supervisory staff. But then Coastal lacked not only top management people but was weak in middle management as well, right on down to the rank and file. All this Barney Burton realized as the postwar era began in earnest, but the top priorities had to be route expansion and rebuilding of the fleet.

Thanks to the availability of surplus transports, Coastal wound up with ten DC-3's. However, Barney had long coveted the DC-4, originally a huge triple-tailed ship with large windows, above which were smaller ones where night berths were to be located. "Grand Hotel with Wings" had been the manufacturer's pitch, and it was— forty-two passengers by day, thirty at night, air-conditioned and with a ladies' lounge, men's dressing room, enormous galleys, and the revolutionary tricycle landing gear. Yet only one had been built, which United had operated briefly before candidly advising Douglas that the big plane was something of a turkey. Douglas had modified the design, substituting a single tail for the triple version and eliminating the sleeping facilities. The results had been splendid. However, the Army had taken the entire production output, operating them as transports, C-54's. More than eleven hundred had been built for the military by Douglas, and at war's end, half of them were made available to the airlines at bargain-basement prices.

Barney had quickly petitioned the board of directors to acquire four brand-new planes, especially as he envisioned expanding air service to Los Angeles and Miami. The board stalled, denying his petition for new planes such as the DC-6 and the Convair 240, but approved purchasing DC-4's from the military and refitting them for civilian use. President Burton was not very perturbed, being confident that traffic would develop rapidly, and that they would need every airplane they could get. And traffic did develop, so fast that the newly returned sales and marketing director, Cal Motts, was barely able to keep his people from collapsing under the barrage of passengers.

The crush was awesome, Barney noted on his customary Thursday-afternoon tour of National Airport. The place was a shambles; the main floor of the terminal looked as if a garbage truck had emptied itself into the lobby. The unintelligible metallic squawks of the loudspeaker, the crying babies, the almost degrading patience of the passengers looking like a tribe of airport nomads, the airline employees—harassed, overworked, arguing instead of helping. It was a madhouse, he thought, passing the little coffee shop that bulged with customers. Air travel, 1946. Well, it was just as bad on most of the rail lines.

The flights themselves were not much better. Instrument landing systems, routinely used by the Army and Navy, had been installed at less than ten U.S. airports. The result was constant delays in takeoffs and landings, stacking over airports, and often diversion to alternate fields—an expensive proposition. By the time an airline got through paying for hotel accommodations and rail tickets, revenue was lost along with goodwill.

"Here you are."

Barney turned at the sound of Cal Motts's voice. Jack Myler and Andy Vaughn were with him.

"Hello, boys," said Barney, sighing. "Cal, dump that 'It's fun to fly Coastal' campaign. It's a bunch of crap. If this is fun, the Spanish Inquisition was a church picnic."

Motts's feelings were hurt. "Well, if you can come up with something better, Barney, I'll be glad to listen." It was not lost on Barnwell Burton that his vice-president of Sales and Marketing no longer referred to him as "Chief"; Barney didn't really mind—in some ways, Calvin's new lack of obsequiousness was an improvement, but it also hinted at independence and potential disloyalty. He decided not to risk any loss of support.

"Actually, it's not a bad slogan," he said soothingly, "but it doesn't seem quite right at this particular time. Not when we're getting so many complaints. Let's put it in abeyance for a while. Seems to me we might do something about our service before we start bragging about it."

"Amen," said Jack Myler, glancing around the air terminal.

Mollified, Cal Motts crossed his arms and nodded wisely. "I think the first thing we might consider is pruning away some of this civilian deadwood we've got around the system."

Andy Vaughn frowned. "If you're suggesting that we can anyone who didn't fight in the war, you'll put us out of business."

"Oh, I didn't mean civilians per se," Motts said hastily. "I used the word 'deadwood' quite literally. I'm referring to the people we hired during the war who aren't really qualified for the airline business. We should be replacing them with returning servicemen."

"We're taking back every man and woman who went into service," Barney pointed out. "They've been guaranteed their old jobs or even better positions. But that doesn't mean we should fire the people who replaced them. We still need plenty of bodies around here. Good Lord, Jack here told me just the other day that a customer has to make seven or eight phone calls before he can get our reservation people to answer."

"That's not lack of manpower, though," Myler said. "We just can't get the extra lines from the telephone company."

"We'll get 'em sooner or later," Barney said. "The trouble isn't with having too many people: we just don't have enough good ones. We haven't really trained the ones we've got. I want to beef up supervisory personnel—that's the way to get productivity out of the rank and file."

"And that's exactly what I meant by deadwood," Motts said. "Precisely why I told our station manager in Nashville to start looking for another job."

"You *fired* a station manager on your own?" Barney demanded.

Motts was flustered. "Well, I didn't actually fire him. I suggested he wasn't cut out for airline work and that he should, ah, be prepared for dismissal."

"Cal, you know that nobody with supervisory status can be fired without my approval."

"I didn't really fire him. Anyway, I've been meaning to talk to you about this man, Charlie Cogswell. He's a positive menace. An absolute flake, believe me. Every time he opens his mouth he sets air transportation back twenty years."

"Charlie Cogswell." Barney paused. "Isn't that the old geezer we hired away from American? Had one eye?"

"The same."

Barney frowned. "Nashville's always had a good record. What's your beef against old Cyclops?"

Motts pursed his lips in the expectant manner of a gossip about to unload a few tantalizing tidbits. "Well, you guys won't believe this, but I personally observed Mr. Cogswell's method of operation when I was in Nashville six days ago. I heard one passenger ask him if his trip to Pittsburgh would be smooth. Cogswell told him the inbound flight from Atlanta was so rough, the captain's martini had whitecaps! Would you believe *that*?"

Vaughn and Myler laughed. Barney, also grinning, shook his head. "From what I've heard about Charlie, I can believe it. But I doubt if the passenger did. He knew Cogswell had to be kidding."

"The passenger took him seriously," Motts insisted. "And that's not all. While I was standing there, some woman came in with nine suitcases—nine. I counted them myself. So she asks Cogswell if Flight 23 was on time. He looked at her baggage, glared at her— *glared*, mind you—and says, 'It was until now.' "

Motts glanced around, anticipating frowns of disapproval. All he saw were teeth. "Apparently you don't think this is serious," he said indignantly. "Well, I'm not finished. You know that arrangement we made with some of the smaller stations to sell flight insurance at our ticket counters?"

Barney nodded. "Yeah, for a commission."

"Well, *your* Mr. Cogswell has pictures of crashed planes all over the wall in back of the counter."

There were more smiles, but also rueful shaking of heads. Vaughn turned away and pretended to cough.

"That explains why Nashville has been near the top of insurance sales," Barney said sadly. "Anything else, Cal?"

"My God, do you need anything else? The man's a total incompetent."

"I'll think it over," Barney promised. "Andy, what the hell are you grinning at?"

"I was just remembering something a captain told me about Charlie Cogswell. Charlie came out to unload a flight and the copilot was an arrogant young pup. He told Charlie to keep an eye on the airplane while he went inside to check the weather. Charlie says, 'Sure.' Then he took out his glass eye and put it on the wing. The copilot damned near fainted."

Barney looked at the young chief pilot. "The crews like the old goat, don't they?"

Vaughn nodded. "From what I've heard, so do the passengers. Sure he insults people, but it's a rare one who takes offense. He has been a fixture around that Nashville airport so long, it's like he was part of the scenery. You may be right about his being flaky, Cal, but guys like Cogswell are a breed unto themselves. They grew up with this crazy business and maybe you have to be nuts to keep your sanity. Let me ask you something, have you ever gotten a passenger letter of complaint about Charlie Cogswell?"

Motts hesitated. "I can't remember," he hedged. "I think there may have been a few but—"

"I'll call him later today," Barney finished up for him. "Meanwhile, I want all of you to keep your eyes open for young blood—even if it means stealing a few people away from other carriers. Jack, beginning next week I want you to start touring the system. Talk to as many employees as you can. Listen to their gripes, complaints, suggestions, ideas, worries—even if you have to discuss their sex lives, that's okay, too, if it'll open 'em up so they'll talk about this airline. Above all, about their bosses, from immediate supervisors to station managers."

"You may have a little trouble getting somebody to call his boss a prick," Vaughn observed. "Jack's liable to come back with what a few malcontents and whiners are saying. I'm sure as hell not gonna crucify somebody because some goof-off says he's a Simon Legree."

"There won't be any crucifying," Barney promised. "I'm looking for a consensus—good or bad—about individuals. People we may want to promote, demote, or even fire."

When he got back to his office, Barney phoned Charlie Cogswell in Nashville.

"Charlie, Barney Burton, here."

"Hi, Mr. President, sir. I assume that jerk Motts must have been talkin' to you or you wouldn't have called."

"Charlie, take those goddamned crash pictures off the wall or I'll have your ass."

"Sure. That all?"

"That's all."

"I figured ol' Calvin would have a list of complaints the length of King Kong's prick."

"He did. Look, Charlie, I don't mind your being flippant but for God's sake, don't insult anybody. Okay?"

"Read you loud and clear. 'Bye, Barney."

Barnwell Burton already had taken notice of the quietly efficient, somewhat iconoclastic young man out in Phoenix. He had made it his business to find out something of Don Littlefield's background even before Jack Myler's scouring of Coastal turned up the name again—a lieutenant on a cruiser in World War II with a Navy Cross for bravery in combat; single but with no reputation for being a carouser and swinger; enormously competent and well liked in Phoenix although he had never been there before his Navy discharge. Littlefield had majored in business administration at Stanford, graduating six months before Pearl Harbor and enlisting with the outbreak of war. At the time he had been with a small advertising agency in Los Angeles.

"You like working for an airline?" Barney asked the young man sitting across from him in the Phoenix House bar.

"Yes. It's challenging, exciting, and most of the time pure fun. Even when things get rough, it's not like any other industry. I think it's the only business in the world where a sense of humor has to be one of your major assets."

"I never thought of it that way. Your reasoning somehow escapes me."

"Well, it's just that airline humor is like military humor—it's based on adversity. The things airline people laugh at the hardest are their own mistakes, their own goofs."

"Which usually aren't anything to laugh at," Barney said sternly.

"Admitted. But most of them are made under pressure and strain. We can learn from errors, but if we brooded over them, we'd go mad. The average airline job, Mr. Burton—especially if it involves dealing with the public—could give a statue ulcers."

"Yeah," Barney said with a kind of vague understanding. "Cal tells me you're not married."

"No, sir."

"Then you wouldn't be averse to pulling up stakes on a moment's notice."

"Depends on the job. I don't particularly like change just for the hell of it—or on somebody else's whim."

"I had in mind Washington."

Littlefield's lips pursed in a soundless whistle. "When? And what would I be doing?"

"As soon as Motts can get a replacement for you here, I'd like to have you at GO, in sales and marketing."

"So I'd still be under Mr. Motts."

"Any objections?"

The younger man shrugged. "Not really. I'm working for him here. The difference is that there's about twenty-five hundred miles between us."

"Exactly what do you have against our vice-president?"

Littlefield grinned. "You want an honest answer or should I be dutifully diplomatic?"

"If I ever catch you being dishonest, I'll fire you. Save the diplomacy for passengers."

Littlefield looked toward the crowded bar. "Okay, Mr. Burton. I consider Calvin Motts a pompous ass whose exalted vice-presidential title has gone to his rather empty head. He may have been a good marketing man, but right now he's too afraid of you to do anything on his own. For every good idea he has, he comes up with five that are half-assed. His marketing philosophy consists of clichés and platitudes right out of *Babbitt*. I haven't heard him present one original marketing idea since I've been with Coastal. Our advertising is, to put it charitably, uninspired. We could put the money to better use if we improved food service and just advertised by word of mouth. Right now it's a waste of time and effort, not to mention money, because it isn't doing the job. It doesn't make people want to fly with us."

Barnwell Burton's eyes narrowed. "And what would you propose to do about it?"

"I'd be a fool if I laid out a specific advertising campaign on the spur of the moment. It would be superficial and you'd probably shoot it down before I had a chance to work out details."

"But you've obviously thought about it, or you wouldn't be so blunt about Cal."

"Certainly I've thought about it. But I don't think this is the time or place for an unveiling. I need more facts, figures—and some assurance that you guys in GO won't be wearing earplugs just because it came from a greenhorn in Phoenix who's been with Coastal less than two years. I can just hear the esteemed Mr. Motts —'Why, gentlemen, that young squirt Littlefield is a high-school freshman trying to tell the Chicago Bears how to play football.'" He had imitated Calvin's voice so accurately that Barney had to chuckle.

"If you come to Washington," Barney said, "I promise you I, for one, won't be wearing earplugs. I'm only surprised you didn't ask me if you were getting a raise along with the transfer."

"I'll stick you for a raise when I can show you I deserve one."

"You'll get the chance, Don." Barney looked at his wristwatch. "You'll have to excuse me right now, though. I have to meet Larry Aroni in a few minutes. We're on the afternoon flight to L.A."

Barney pushed back his chair and rose to his feet, as did Don Littlefield, and the two men shook hands.

"By the way, Don."

"Yes, sir?"

"How big will Phoenix and Las Vegas be as vacation spots?"

"Big. Especially Vegas. And year round, too."

"Excellent," said Barney. "Excellent."

"Why?"

"We just added it to the system."

L-049 was the Constellation's official designation. It was thought to be something of a glamour girl, with a sharklike fuselage and graceful triple tail. The plane, first flown January 9, 1943, had reportedly been designed in part by Howard Hughes, but Barney knew this wasn't really true. When he first considered taking the Constellation over the DC-6, he had consulted Jack Frye, since TWA had already ordered forty of the big ships.

"We think it's gonna be one hell of a fine airplane," Frye had told him. "Top cruising speed of three hundred, capable of doing New York to Los Angeles with just one stop, in eight hours and forty-five minutes."

"What's this about Howard Hughes having a big hand in the design? I hear he dreamed up the wing, for example."

"Off the record, pal, it's a bunch of bull. Basically, the Connie's wing is nothing but a bigger P-38 wing. Howard did give Lockheed some good ideas on cockpit configuration and cabin layout. A lot of his stuff was sheer nitpicking—like insisting on large buttons for the curtains on the berths of the sleeper planes. I remember him telling me, 'Who the hell wants to get it caught in a zipper?' I will say this, though—he drew up most of the specs for the plane even before we broached the idea of a four-engine transport to Lockheed or anyone else. Last time I was in New York, he called me from Los Angeles. So help me, he kept me on the phone for eight hours talking about the specs."

Despite Frye's obvious love affair with the Connie, Barney still had made no definite decision on buying it. The subsequent visit to the Lockheed plant in Burbank just about convinced him, although Aroni was not as enamored. Barney and Larry Aroni genuinely liked the three Lockheed executives they met—sales manager Carl Squier, chief engineer Kelly Johnson, and Bob Gross, the president. Squier, kindly and rather soft-spoken but with the disarming persuasiveness of a born pitchman, was their guide.

Larry liked the L-049 but with a few reservations.

"It has the worst cockpit visibility I've ever seen in a transport," he told Kelly after a brisk inspection. "I'm no pilot, but I'll give you ten to one that our guys sound off about that item."

"It's no flying greenhouse," Johnson conceded, "but weigh that one drawback against performance. The Connie's the fastest thing in the air. A pressurization system you won't believe. At twenty thousand feet your atmospheric pressure in the cabin is less than at eight thousand. She'll climb to twenty-five thousand if you have to. Top cruising speed of three hundred at sixty-five percent of rated power and you can maintain altitude up to nearly seven thousand feet on two engines."

"It's the ideal plane for you," Squier said. "The landing speed's only eighty miles an hour, so you can put the bird down at almost any airport. I really think you're being overly cautious in buying only four. Nobody'll want to fly in a DC-4 once they've ridden in a Connie."

"It's still primarily a long-range aircraft, Carl. We've tied up a lot of dough in our DC-4 fleet, and I'd like to amortize them before I replace 'em with Constellations. And about those four—I'd like to sign a letter of intent instead of making it a definite order."

Squier looked unhappy. "Well, I don't know. Bob Gross would have to approve a deal like that. Why all the doubts? You figure you might get a better deal with Douglas later on? Let me tell you something—we've just got a better bird. You know about the speed record Hughes and Frye set—seven hours, Burbank to Washington! Why, the Connie's a—"

"Save the sales talk," Barney grinned. "I'm sold on the airplane.

I just wish I could be as sold on the prospects ahead for this industry. We're all going overboard on equipment investment, new
routes, bigger payrolls. If there's any kind of a major postwar
economic slump, the airlines will be sitting ducks. Those four
Constellations will cost us more than two million, and I haven't
even started arranging for financing. I'd like to wait three or four
months before a definite commitment. Even that delay won't hurt
us competitively. From what I hear, the DC-6 is about a year away
from going into actual service."

They left Burbank tentatively committed to buying four Model
L-049's, the letter of intent giving Coastal six months in which it
could exercise the options.

"I think we made a good deal," Barney said happily to Aroni as
they drove back to their hotel. Aroni merely grunted and stared
out at the palm lined-streets.

"Your enthusiasm is absolutely inspiring, Larry. What the hell's
eating you?"

"I think it may be too big an airplane for us."

"Look, old gloomy-puss, the game in this business is modern
equipment, and we're getting the most modern plane in existence.
Suppose we get L.A. and San Francisco?"

"And when the DC-6 comes out, you'll want that one, too. I
know you, Barney. You'd hock our underwear just to buy a new
transport. Why not wait till we get a closer look at the DC-6? It
might just be a better airplane."

"If it's better than the Constellation, we may buy a few of those,
too. And we *are* waiting. For six months."

They could have ridden out the postwar adjustments in the
economy, tortuous as they were, but it was impossible to overcome
the wave of crashes that just began happening during 1946—nine
of them. It started with an American Overseas DC-4 hitting a
Newfoundland mountain, and before the year was up, not many
airlines were exempt from the deadly rollcall. Western lost two DC-
3's on scheduled flights and a third on a test flight. American and
United both suffered fatal DC-3 accidents and two TWA Connies
went down—one in Egypt and the other on a training flight near
Reading, Pennsylvania. Foreign carriers such as Sabena, KLM,

and Air France all drew black headlines following air disasters, and a public suddenly surfeited on the terrors of air travel simply stopped buying tickets.

The two proudest planes in the skies went through the ignominious experience of mandatory grounding by order of the Civil Aeronautics Administration. First it was the Constellation, grounded in July after the training accident in Pennsylvania disclosed defects in the 049's electrical system. In June of 1947, four DC-4's went down in three weeks' time, killing 146 people. In October a new United DC-6 caught fire over Bryce Canyon, Utah, and crashed, killing all 52 aboard. Investigators were still trying to put this jigsaw puzzle of death together when an American DC-6 also caught fire in mid-air over New Mexico but managed to limp down to a safe landing. Both aircraft had been engaged in transferring fuel from one tank to another—ostensibly a routine procedure which turned out to be the cause of both accidents. The damaged but still-intact American DC-6 disclosed that during the transfer, gasoline vapors had been sucked into the heating ducts through a belly air-intake system and were ignited by the cabin heat. Subsequently the DC-6 was also grounded while the location of the intake was changed. Coming on the heels of the Constellation's troubles, it was one more blow to passenger confidence.

When the spate of crashes continued, Barnwell Burton could only watch miserably as load factors tumbled. He had exercised his options on the four Connies before the six months were up, mostly because the CAB had granted Coastal authority to operate one-stop Washington–Phoenix service via Minneapolis, and two-stop service between Washington and Las Vegas via Nashville and Wichita. He badgered Calvin Motts unmercifully on market development plans for the two new routes, but not even the resourceful if overimpulsive vice-president of Sales could do much about soft demand for two cities that had not yet become tourist meccas.

Under the pressures of adversity, Barnwell Burton's one-man rule became a kind of patriarchal despotism. No problem was too small for him to handle personally, no responsibility minor enough to delegate, no dispute too petty. Nor was it coincidence that his dominance hardened as his marriage deteriorated. He was caught in a vicious cycle largely of his own making; he was miserably aware that he could not blame Vickie, yet with that admission came the impulse to escape her growing coolness by retreating further into the world in which he answered to no one.

He began making surprise inspection tours around the system, and employees began to dread his unexpected invasions, for he could be brutal in his criticism, ruthless in his punishment, and—when a station manager or supervisor was involved—bitterly sarcastic in front of the man's own subordinates. Catching the Atlanta station manager with a large grease spot on his trousers, Barney shoved a five-dollar bill into his hand and, with two agents and several passengers watching wide-eyed, he snarled, "Get your ass to a dry cleaner and don't ever let me catch you looking like some gas-station attendant."

He popped unannounced into Operations at the Minneapolis station, where several pilots were relaxing between flights. Barney, without saying a word, strode over to the hat rack and removed one. He carried it back to the cluster of startled pilots.

"Whose hat is this?"

"Mine, Mr. Burton," a thin-faced first officer admitted.

Barney held the cap where his foot could reach it, kicked clear through its lining, and threw it at the pilot. "I'm paying you jokers enough dough to keep your clothes neat. Where are you based?"

"Washington, Mr. Burton."

"Okay. When you get back home, you go right out and buy yourself a new cap. And I'm telling Andy Vaughn you're grounded until you do."

No one knew when and how his wrath would strike. Vaughn had to call one senior captain in and inform him he was suspended for a week without pay because Barney Burton had seen him walking through the terminal building with his uniform coat unbuttoned.

In sheer self-defense, the troops tried to cope with their rampaging general's appearances. There was one thing he could not hide—his presence on a Coastal flight. Before reaching any station which Barney was about to invade without warning, the crew would radio the station manager: "We have Daisy with us today." This was only partially effective, however. Even if they knew he was coming, nobody could be sure what transgression, omission, or mistake those icy-blue eyes might spot.

And yet, thanks to the resilience of airline people, they could also find enjoyment in his visits. He was, finally, refreshingly informal and frank in answering questions, and even the most lowly employees sensed his genuine concern for anyone who worked for him.

When he wasn't raising hell about something, he was seeking suggestions and telling jokes. He had the ability to draw out the shyest and to establish a rapport even with the most dissident and cynical. There was nothing phony about his interest in people, either; he never gave the impression that he was royalty condescending to the commoners. Somehow, he made them feel he was as much an employee as anyone, that every man and woman in Coastal had something in common—the welfare of their airline, regardless of salary, title, or position.

"Call me Barney," he'd tell them, and he meant it.

Yet, sadly, the pride and affection and respect he craved from the people of his company was no less important, no more satisfying, than what he could have received from Vickie but kept rejecting. When she suggested accompanying him on one of his inspection trips, he turned her down.

"People might feel a little uneasy if you were with me," he said. "They might tighten up, not talk freely—things like that."

She accepted this excuse as sounding logical. It sounded logical to Barney, too—except he knew there was another reason. Her presence would be an intrusion of his domain and a restraining influence on his thunderbolt discipline, almost like introducing your wife to your mistress, he thought sardonically, aware that he was being unfair to Vickie, with her airline background.

It wasn't that he didn't enjoy her company. He liked to take her to various functions, proud of her beauty and saucy poise. But to him, she was more of a corporate asset than a wife, a presidential possession instead of a partner.

In the early days of their marriage, he would discuss airline business with her, seek out her opinions, and sometimes even rely on her reaction to a given problem. As her own bitterness increased and her love for Barney degenerated into a dull indifference, he struck back at her by totally separating his two worlds. That alone did not doom their marriage, for it was Vickie herself who still thought there was a chance to save it.

"I figure it's time we had a baby," she told him one morning over breakfast. "It would help our marriage. I think so, anyway."

"I thought we agreed not to have kids for a while."

"'A while' passed us by a long time ago. You told me you wanted children someday. Someday is right now."

"I'd make a lousy father," he muttered.

"No lousier a father than a husband. As a matter of fact, a son or daughter might make you a better husband. You haven't given me much of your life. Maybe you'd feel more responsible toward a child."

"I don't really like kids, Vickie. They make me nervous. I don't know anything about raising one. You'd wind up doing everything."

She stood up. "That in itself is one reason for having a baby. I need some responsibility, too. I need a reason for being out here in the middle of merry Maryland. Someone to worry about other than myself. I'll readily concede you won't be a model father. I won't expect you to come home earlier, to spend every weekend with us, or to really help me raise a child. On the other hand, I can't believe you could ignore a baby or resent one. Most men are afraid of parenthood. I'm afraid too, Barney. Afraid of nine months of looking dowdy, of whether I can hack it as a mother—a role for which I probably am constitutionally and emotionally unsuited, not to mention unprepared. But I'm willing to take a chance and if you have one ounce of love for me still lurking in that corporation-enslaved brain of yours, you'll take a chance, too."

He gave her a look not of anger, but of pity. "I'm sorry, Vick. You think a baby will help our marriage. I think it would make it worse. It would be impossible for me to be a good father to a child I didn't want in the first place. I can't defend myself. I know I've disappointed and hurt you. I wouldn't blame you for hating me. But if I gave you a baby, I'd wind up disappointing and hurting the child, too. I couldn't share enough with a kid, any more than I've been able to share my life with you."

"Well," she said slowly, fighting to keep the tears from her eyes. "You're honest, anyway. I'm afraid that's it, Barney."

He had to force the words from his mouth: "You want a divorce?"

"I don't know. I don't know." She turned away. "I suppose the conventional thing to do is to go away for a few weeks and think things over. But that's my trouble—all I've been doing is sitting here alone, thinking."

He stared down at his coffee. "If it means anything to you, I don't want a divorce. You may not believe this, but I still love you," he said, feeling strangely detached from the situation and even his own words. He wondered if he really meant what he had said or if he had said them because they seemed called for under the circumstances.

Now it was Vickie who looked at him with pity. "That I *can* believe. Unfortunately, you love your airline even more. What it boils down to is choosing between us—and like you once told me, it's no contest."

He didn't reply. It's over, he thought.

"Barney, I think I will go away . . . spend a few weeks with my folks in California. We can talk when I get back. Just make sure someone takes care of Raven while I'm gone. And my dog."

He nodded. "We should talk again, Vick. Somehow it seems impossible that what we had is gone," he said, thinking how ridiculously melodramatic that sounded.

There was no second talk.

Six weeks later, she sued for divorce.

Barney did not contest it. He sold the horse at her request and offered her either alimony or a large settlement, both of which she refused.

"I cannot find it in my heart to accept compensation for a mistake both of us made," she wrote shortly before the divorce became final. "I guess down deep I thought I could affect you more, if that's the right word. I was wrong and I am deeply sorry, just as sorry as I know you are. You are a decent man, Barney, with indecent drives and a tragic inability to divide your loyalties. I should have known better."

He read it as if it was a junk-mail brochure—feeling nothing. He took the letter with him the next day. That evening, still in his office, alone, he reread it and wondered why he was so immune to feeling very much about it. Was it like the death of someone close, the reality of which you first block out in order to survive the initial shock? Or did he really not care all that much?

His eyes fell on a copy of the latest issue of *Aviation Week*. His picture, with a Coastal DC-4 in the background, was on the magazine's cover. The caption described him as "one of the industry's new breed—proud of the past but unafraid to face up to the problems of the present and future."

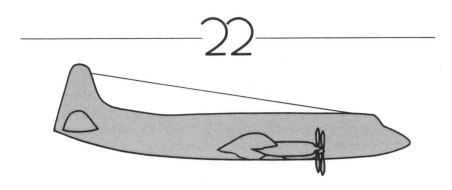

22

"I still think 'VIP Club' lacks color and originality, plus the fact that it has absolutely no relationship to aviation," Barney fretted.

"Neither does 'Admirals Club' or 'Red Carpet Room,' " Aroni observed, biting off the stub of a fresh cigar. He was bored by any proceeding that took him away from his beloved shops, and staff meetings to him were a waste of time. He tolerated them because he knew Norma Aroni was proud of his vice-presidential status, and he tried to contribute because he was grateful for it. Yet there were times, both at directors' meetings and in sessions with his fellow executives, when he felt like a burr among petals. It was more of a feeling of frustration than inferiority; if anything, he felt superior to men of Calvin Motts's ilk.

"Agreed," Barney conceded. "Anyone have a name with some connotation, something to do with Coastal itself?"

Aroni studied the end of the cigar as if he could see ideas emerging from the smoke. "Well, seems to me we've got a pretty damned good symbol we've never made real use of. It's been 'Route of the Red Hawks' ever since I started working for this company. How about a name with hawk in it?"

"Hawk's Nest!" Motts said excitedly.

"Not bad," Barney grunted, "but maybe a little too tame."

"Aerie," Myler suggested.

"I think aeries are where eagles live," Bill Sloan said learnedly.

"Hawks' Aerie," Barney repeated, testing the sound. "Nope, that's not it."

"Hawks' Den?" Motts offered hopefully.

Barney shook his head. "Wolves live in dens. Where the hell do hawks live—in trees?"

"We need an officer who's also an ornithologist," Sloan chuckled.

"What's wrong with lair?" Barney demanded. "Hawks' Lair. By God, that sounds good. We call the lounges 'Hawks' Lairs.' "

"I like it," Jack Myler said promptly, as if programmed.

"How about the rest of you guys?" Barney asked. "Anyone got a better idea?" The last question was delivered in a tone implying that they'd better not, so all he got was a nod from each officer, with the exception of Aroni, who smiled enigmatically, which Barney duly noted.

"You don't seem very happy about it, Larry. Hell, using 'Hawk' was your idea to begin with. What's your objection?"

" 'Hawks' Lair' is fine, Barney. If I don't seem too enthusiastic, it's not the name of these bloody VIP lounges that bothers me. We've spent too much fucking time on the subject and we'll spend a lot more—not to mention money—setting them up."

"They're proven traffic generators, they assure customer loyalty, and they promote goodwill," Barney said. "For Christ's sake, Larry, you've sat in Admirals Clubs with me and told me you enjoyed a nice place to relax and talk. Now all of a sudden you're crabbing about the cost."

Aroni shrugged. He knew he was going to lose the argument, anyway. "I just happen to think we could spend some dough in other areas and get more out of it."

"Such as?"

"Such as cleaning up a few of our terminal facilities for the bulk of our passengers, instead of providing special luxuries for a handful of the better-heeled. There's nothing wrong with VIP lounges. I agree, they're a damned good idea and I think we should have them. But not right away. Not when traffic's depressed and we're losing our shirts. Anything we spend these days should be according to a list of priorities, and I'd put immediate establishment of VIP clubs pretty far down on that list. For example, we've assigned the only four pressurized aircraft in our fleet to the Vegas and Phoenix routes, and we're getting beaten in every other market where we're competing with carriers operating pressurized aircraft. You're talking about lounges when we should be discussing better fleet utilization and maybe modernization."

"It wasn't too long ago that you were reaming me out for ordering those four Connies," Barney observed sarcastically. "Now you're telling me we need more new airplanes."

"It's a matter of realistic priorities. If you and Cal Motts insist on assigning our Connies to two undeveloped markets, we need at least a couple of more competitive aircraft elsewhere on our system. Either that, or use what we do have more realistically. If you wanna know how we should be spending dough, take a look at United. They just shelled out one million bucks equipping their DC-6 fleet to take advantage of the CAA's new Omni-beacons. There are ninety of them on the airways and not one of our planes is equipped to utilize a navigation aid that makes flying safer. And here we sit yakking about VIP lounges! Do you have any idea what furnishing one of those places will cost, not to mention the rental fees?"

Barney was stung. His first instinct was to lash out at the vice-president of Maintenance and Engineering. While the others waited for the expected outburst, Barney suddenly grinned.

"You may be right about priorities," he said without rancor. "How come you didn't bring those Omni-beacons to my attention earlier, Larry?"

"I did. I gave you a memo on it three weeks ago. Apparently you haven't gotten around to reading it yet," Aroni said quietly and seriously.

"Apparently not," Barney murmured. "Okay, Calvin, I suggest you spend a week getting estimates on how much it would cost to set up our Hawks' Lairs. Right down to the penny, buster. Furniture, salaries for the hostesses, the cost of those members' plaques, leasing figures, and anything else you can think of. If I decide to go ahead with the clubs, I think it's best if we start with just one right here at National Airport, where we can keep a close eye on it and work out any bugs. But for your cost estimates, I want to know how much we'd have to spend setting up similar clubs at other locations—say Minneapolis, Vegas, and Phoenix, to start with. Now you can all go back to work. Larry, you mind staying a few minutes?"

The officers filed out, Motts whispering to Sloan, "I'll bet Larry gets his ass chewed out."

Barney waited until the room emptied, and turned to Aroni. "Something on your mind, Larry?"

"No. I just think you're driving yourself and the rest of us too fast. You always gave it ninety percent. Ever since you and Vickie split up, you've been at it around the clock. You're getting hard. Not just stubborn. Hard."

"Don't push me, Larry."

"I don't have to. You're pushing yourself. Ease up before it's too late."

With that Aroni relit his cigar and walked out.

Over eighty percent of the system, Coastal was pitting DC-3's and DC-4's against a growing number of Constellations, Corvairs, and DC-6's. The DC-6's in particular were giving Motts competitive fits—American, United, and Northwest all were operating the new Douglas transport, which was even faster than the Constellations Coastal had.

"I can't sell tickets without the ammunition," he complained. "Nobody in his right mind would take a DC-4 when he could fly a DC-6 to the same place at the same price."

"I realize you're operating under a handicap," Barney said soothingly, "but we can't afford new airplanes right now, Calvin, and you might as well make up your mind to do the best you can. I promise you that when the time is ripe, I'll give you something that'll be easier to sell than rye bread in a kosher delicatessen."

"Chief, I hope it's soon. Every passenger poll we've taken shows that customers regard the DC-4 as obsolete and inferior. Especially when they compare it to the DC-6."

"Bullshit," Barney scoffed. "The average passenger couldn't tell a DC-4 from a DC-6 if they were standing side by side."

"I think most people could," Motts said with rare argumentativeness. "All they have to do is compare the windows—the DC-4's are round and the DC-6's are square-shaped."

"Externally, though, that's the only major difference," Barney persisted.

"Well, yes, but . . ."

"So that gives me an idea. We'll paint squares around the windows of our DC-4's so they'll look like DC-6's."

Motts stared at him, not quite sure whether the president was being serious. "I, uh, don't you think that would be misleading?"

"What's misleading about it? We aren't claiming we fly DC-6's. We're just doing a little cosmetic job to improve appearance—you might even say we're using makeup to hide the old gal's age. And all you have to put in your ads and the timetables, too, Calvin, is that 'Coastal operates modern Douglas four-engine equipment.' Which is absolutely true. Right?"

"Right, Chief," Motts said weakly.

"I'm glad you agree. I'll get Larry over here and tell him what we want."

Larry Aroni's reaction was decidedly negative but he didn't put up much of an argument. Barney could sense that he wanted something.

"I'll falsify those goddamned windows for you," he agreed, "but while we've got the paint buckets out, I'd like to try something."

"I think 'falsify' is a bit strong. What I'm really trying to . . . oh, what the hell, you old Dago—you're right. It's falsifying. What else do you have in mind?"

Aroni lit his inevitable cigar. "I've been corresponding with a guy named Karl Brocken—he's an industrial designer in Milwaukee, and he has a hell of an idea about aircraft paint. He claims if the top of the fuselage is painted white, it'll be fifteen degrees cooler inside the airplane. That's in hot weather, naturally."

"Fifteen degrees—that much?"

"He sent me test results. It has to do with the ways different colors reflect sunlight. Black, for example, absorbs it, while white is the best reflector. How about letting me try it out on the first DC-4 we bring in for a window job?"

"Well, okay," Barney said slowly, "but if we're gonna screw

around with windows and this fuselage stuff, maybe we should consider a whole new paint scheme. Our airplanes have looked the same since we got our first DC-2."

"This Brocken seems competent. He's dolled up North Central's fleet and he's worked with other carriers. I can ask him how much he'd charge for a new exterior design."

Three weeks later, Brocken appeared before an executive staff meeting in Barney's office and presented a proposed new exterior paint scheme along with sketches for revised interiors. The former depicted a Coastal Constellation and DC-4—the fuselages were white down to the window lines, which were painted a dark red. On the white tail was the traditional hawk but done in a side view instead of the original head-on version with the fierce eyes and outstretched talons.

There was no immediate comment, everyone waiting for Barnwell Burton, who hmmmed, grunted, and finally cleared his throat. "Except for the hawk on the tail, I like it."

"What's wrong with the tail?" Aroni asked.

"It looks too much like American's eagle, that's what's wrong. I think we should go back to the bird coming right at you."

"I like the side view," Larry said, looking around for support and discovering, as usual, that he was leading the charge solo.

Brocken, a patient but firm man who had worked with recalcitrant airline presidents before, diplomatically explained. "The trouble with the old design, Mr. Burton, is that it was too fierce-looking. It seemed to be springing at you right off the tail. The side view softens the image without changing it too drastically."

"That's what I liked about our old version," Barney insisted. "It was coming at you. Very effective. Very dramatic."

"And that's what I felt was wrong with it, Mr. Burton. Too effective and too dramatic. Frankly, it scares the hell out of you. And fright doesn't enhance an airline's image."

Bill Sloan chuckled and Barney glared at him. "You undoubtedly know your business, Mr. Brocken, but for the ten grand I'm paying you, I want our airplanes to look like *I* want them to look."

"You're the president," Brocken said easily. There was silence and he sensed that no one in the room, not even Aroni, had the nerve to challenge Barnwell Burton on a matter of deep personal taste. But Karl Brocken was not going to let him get away with what was an abysmal decision.

"If you don't mind a suggestion, Mr. Burton, let's stick to your head-on view but tone it down a bit. Here, let me show you what I mean."

He took a sketch pad out of his briefcase and began drawing.

"How . . . how does this strike you, Mr. Burton?"

Barney looked, looked again, and whistled, his hostility evaporating.

The hawk still was in a front view. But instead of diving down, Brocken had drawn it in a climbing stance—the taloned legs tucked back and the great wings outstretched. The instant image it gave was of looking up at a plane that had just taken off, the wheels about to disappear into the main gear well.

"That's beautiful," said Barney and drew murmurs of approval from all. "Just color it red, please. This is it. Do us up some final drawings—the whole design concept depicted on each aircraft we operate. DC-3's, DC-4's, and our Connies. That's it, gentlemen. We've given Coastal a new image."

Don Littlefield, freshly arrived from Phoenix, picked up the sketch. "Like a plane taking off," he murmured. "Take off with a new Coastal."

"Say that again," Barney snapped.

"Take off with a new Coastal," Littlefield repeated. "We could peg a new ad campaign to the revised logo."

"Keep talking."

"When you change a logo, you really change an airline's entire image, like you said. There's only one thing wrong, though."

"What's that?"

"For a new ad campaign, we need something to brag about besides a new paint job on our planes."

Motts's face was florid. "This is a subject you might better discuss with me privately, instead of taking up Mr. Burton's valuable time and that of the other officers," he said coldly.

Littlefield merely looked over at Barney, who grinned. "Well, suppose you give some thought to what Don's brought up, Cal. I guess we'd all better get back to work." But as Littlefield turned to leave, he added, "Not you, Don. I wanna talk to you for a few minutes."

Motts hesitated as if to protest, then changed his mind and left the room with the others. Aroni, just behind him, looked back at Barney.

"I think you hurt his feelings," he said in an exaggerated whisper.

"Fuck him. See you later." He motioned Littlefield into a chair opposite his desk, and looked searchingly at the younger man. "This new ad campaign . . . I have a hunch you didn't spring it on the spur of the moment."

"No, sir. I've been thinking about it. That logo business just triggered it, like a final ingredient."

"Okay, what's on your mind?"

Littlefield took a deep breath. "Special coach fares—about thirty percent lower than the regular tariffs. Applicable to off-peak hours, especially night flights. With a minimum of amenities in cabin service. And using high-density seating. We can get sixty passengers into a DC-4 by sacrificing some leg room, installing smaller galleys, and a few other minor modifications."

"Where did you get that data?"

"I asked Mr. Aroni how many seats we could put into a DC-4 without making it look like a rush-hour subway. He did some checking and came back with that figure of sixty."

"Larry know about this coach-fare idea of yours?"

"No, sir, I . . . uh . . . I asked him not to say anything to anybody. I said it was just an idea I was playing around with."

Barney rocked in his chair for a moment. "Coach fares aren't anything new, of course. United tried it back in 1940 between L.A. and San Francisco. They justified it to the CAB on the grounds that they were using 247's that were fully depreciated, cheaper to operate, and what amounted to second-class equipment. The project was dropped when the war broke out."

"I'm aware of United's experiment," Littlefield said. "It didn't last long enough to determine its worth, but the early results were promising. After the war, we had a seller's market and nobody apparently thought of lowering fares as a traffic inducement."

"How much of a cut would you make?" Barney leaned back and propped his feet up on the desk.

"We're charging six cents a mile now for first-class travel. I think we could make money going down to four cents a mile. Remember, we're also achieving better utilization of aircraft, we're increasing capacity, and we're reducing in-flight service costs. For example, we could offer sandwiches instead of hot meals and sell liquor instead of giving it away. The point is, Mr. Burton, what we lose in revenue per passenger we'd get back through higher load factors. We're averaging only a forty-nine percent factor system-wide. I'm convinced our load factor could jump to sixty or even seventy percent with coach fares."

"That's one hell of a fare cut, though—one-third. It'll take a lot of passengers to make up the revenue difference."

"I've already figured it out. A coach flight would break even at fifty-two percent. That's taking into consideration lower operating costs, naturally."

"It's still a gamble," Barney said cautiously. "I wouldn't want to convert all our DC-4's to coach configuration."

"We're operating ten right now. I'd recommend converting five of them, assign 'em to our highest-density routes—Washington–Atlanta and Washington–Minneapolis—and then add coach service to Cleveland and Detroit."

"You're being pretty damned optimistic," Barney said. "We haven't even got Cleveland and Detroit authority yet."

"We will. Probably in another two weeks."

Barney was incredulous. "How come you're so certain?"

"I've been dating the secretary of a CAB member—no names, please. She tipped me off just the other night."

"Well I'll be—" Barney chuckled. "I think I'll buy this brainstorm of yours. I want you to spend the rest of the day putting all this down on paper. Projected traffic data, reconfiguration costs, aircraft-utilization figures, cabin-service savings per flight, suggested schedules—the works. I'll call an executive staff meeting for tomorrow morning, nine o'clock sharp."

"I don't need the rest of the day," Littlefield said calmly. "I've got the whole project outlined down to the last penny. It's sitting in my desk, locked up, I might add. I've been waiting for the right time to unveil it. I've even got a name for it, assuming we'll start out with night service to see how it goes."

"Okay, what would you call it?"

"Nighthawk Service."

Barney said nothing. He rose, walked over to the window over-looking Coastal's maintenance area, and stared out. A tractor was towing a DC-4 into the hangar and Barney suddenly began pictur-ing what the new paint job and logo would look like. He was still gazing at the airplane when Littlefield, worried, spoke. "I'd like to know what you think of it, Mr. Burton. Nighthawk Service, I mean."

The president turned around. "Nighthawk Service it is. And Don, for Christ's sake, I think our new assistant vice-president of Sales and Marketing should start calling me Barney."

He had no intention of giving Littlefield any delusions of power or favored status. He liked and respected the boy for his intelli-gence and spirit but he was not about to create a potential rival or threat to his own authority. Even though he recognized Littlefield as a decided asset to Coastal, he did not wish to create a crown prince. Thus, there were times when he fought the younger man bitterly, stubbornly, and even arbitrarily, yet taking care not to alienate him or discourage him.

It was a tightrope act Barnwell Burton performed with skill, so much so that he retained Littlefield's respect and still managed to keep Calvin Motts happy and off his assistant's back. Occasionally, Barney felt an irresistible urge to either strangle Motts or at least fire him. The vice-president of Sales and Marketing avoided both fates by alternating between brilliant sales coups and momentous boners.

Barney was still trying to build up his executive echelons. He finally made Bill Sloan vice-president of Legal, and two months later he did something Henry McKay had been urging for more than a year—he hired a specialist in finance.

He was not overly enraptured when he met Roger Campbell, a short, portly man in his mid-thirties. Rather jolly in appearance with a beatific smile, his eyes were cold and hard and seemed to belong to another person residing inside the man who looked for all the world like Santa Claus without the beard. Yet Campbell obviously was knowledgeable without flaunting his acumen and he was deferential without fawning. Barney offered him only slightly more than he had been getting at United, but accompanying the modest raise was the title of vice-president. Campbell accepted and spent the first two weeks ascertaining which of his fellow officers might be classified as Barnwell Burton's fair-haired boys. His discreet but diligent research led him to zero in on Jack Myler, with whom he made a point of becoming friendly. Roger Campbell was an opportunist, but also happened to be an able financial man.

There had been more than one instance when Barney had gone into a bank loan conference armed with a few figures scribbled on a piece of scrap paper. Campbell, who had been a bank officer once, was a very organized, orderly person and wondered privately at times how Coastal could have made money under its rather haphazard president.

"I'd have said the company's cost-accounting system was weak," he confided to Myler, "but after taking a look at the books I'd have to say there *is* no cost-accounting system. Barney just takes money in, pays money out, and at the end of the year he must go to church and pray that the influx amounts to more than the expenditures."

"You have to know him," Jack Myler explained loyally. "Barney's philosophy is to make profitable policy decisions, and he depends on the rest of us to fill in the details."

Roger merely shrugged, but two months after he arrived at Coastal he got the president's permission to revise the airline's budgeting procedures. In the past, Barney alone had decided who was to spend how much.

"From now on," Campbell informed a staff meeting, "each department will submit to me an individual budget for the following fiscal year, and I want them in my hands by November first. In other words, the input will be upward instead of downward. Barney and I will go over your requests and decide on their validity. You'll be given a tentative decision by November fifteenth, and you'll have exactly one week in which you can defend your respective cases."

Calvin Motts looked at Barney, apparently unwilling to believe that the president had abrogated his authority on spending.

"I'll have final word," Barney said as if he had read Motts's mind. "Any questions?"

"Yeah," Aroni drawled. "Meaning no offense, Roger, but I'd like to know what kind of technical knowledge you have that would qualify you to pass judgment on a piece of complex hardware I think is essential to this airline."

"None whatsoever," Campbell replied affably. "I'll take into account every department head's expertise in his own field. In your case, Larry, I'd certainly have the utmost respect for your opinion on whether a large capital expenditure would be warranted from a purely technical standpoint. But you—all of you, in fact—must realize that just because a request is worthwhile does not mean it will be approved. Let's use Mr. Aroni, here, as an example. Suppose his budget includes spending some fifty thousand dollars for new tools. Now to our vice-president of Maintenance and Engineering, those new tools may be highly desirable, more efficient, and easier to work with. But I won't be . . . or, rather, Barney and I won't be judging that item purely on a technical basis. We're going to be asking if those tools will increase maintenance efficiency and thus save us money in the long run. Can we get along with the old tools for a while? Would it be better to wait for even better new tools?"

"Balls," Aroni growled. "If you think I'm going to the mat with you white-collar bastards over every little item I think our mechanics need, you can shove this budget bullshit right up your ass. Calvin might be able to predict the profitability of a capital expenditure, but I don't have the time to fool around with that crap."

"You're going to have to take the time to 'fool around with that crap,' as you so delicately phrase it," Campbell said softly.

"Look, Roger, you can write this one fact down on those neat little arithmetic columns of yours: I've got one job on this airline and that's to give our crews flight equipment that'll fly reliably and safely, without which there ain't no profits. Every cent Maintenance spends goes toward reliability and safety. And I won't have you or any other pencil-pushing bastard tell me I'm wasting dough."

"Ease back," said Barney. "Have I ever turned you down on anything you really needed?"

"No, but that's when *you* were running this goddamned army."

Barney's eyes flashed. "And I'm still running it, pal! Don't you or anyone else ever forget *that* little fact." His anger was spent as quickly as it had erupted. He grinned at the burly Aroni. "Aw hell,

Larry. Relax. I'm not gonna be unreasonable about any of your budgets, and neither will Roger. Right, Rog?" Campbell said nothing and nodded so slightly that it was almost imperceptible. "The fact is," Barney continued, "it's my own fault that we're going to have to do better with our cost control. I've been paying too little attention to what's going out because I've been concerned mainly with what's coming in. And that's why I hired Roger two months ago. There's no reason for anyone in this room to get in an uproar because we might question a few items in your budget. Christ knows, I haven't been afraid to spend dough. But from now on, I'm gonna make sure we're spending wisely. Every penny we shell out is a kind of investment, and when we invest, we expect a return. One last word: my door is always open to anyone with a beef about anything, and that includes listening to a legitimate argument when you think we're being unfair or outright stupid. Is that understood?"

They understood, or at least implied it with a collection of subservient nods.

Campbell cleared his throat.

"I suspect what some of you may not have grasped is the necessity for some kind of centralized cost control. If I may paraphrase, we need the ability to see the whole forest in spite of the trees. It does Coastal little good for Maintenance to get every penny it asks for, if automatic approval of its budget means hurting that of another department. For example, we might give Larry X number of dollars and then discover that by doing so, we have to take X number of dollars away from Cal Motts. I'd like our budget to be cooperative, if that's the right word. Some departments might have to go without, temporarily, so as not to hurt our overall collective efforts toward greater profitability. And to echo Barney, is *that* understood?"

There were more nods, the general effect being that of children who had just been dressed down by a teacher with the full approval of the principal. But when the meeting ended, Larry Aroni hung back to talk to Barney alone.

"I said I understood, and I do, Barney. But there's something about that Campbell creep I don't like. He'll give us trouble one of these days."

"He might give *you* trouble," Barney corrected. "Get it straight, he has my full support with this budget program of his. Why the hell can't you admit what I've admitted—that Coastal is ten years behind the industry in cost control? Every other airline has roughly the same kind of budget system Campbell's setting up, so just accept it and live with it."

"I'll live with it and I'll accept it, up to a point. But the first time that sonofabitch axes one of my budget items for no good reason, I'll cut his calculating heart out."

"And I'll hand you the scalpel," Barney promised.

As it turned out, the first revolt against Campbell came not from Aroni but from Andy Vaughn. The chief pilot hadn't even reached vice-presidential status—an omission due to Barney's procrastination. The lack of titular clout, however, didn't deter Vaughn.

His flight department had somehow wound up under the jurisdiction of John Myler as vice-president of Traffic. The fuse was lit when the chief pilot convinced Myler he should put a million-dollar Constellation Flight Simulator into Flight Operations budget for calendar 1950. Myler was a very decisive person—decisive in the sense that he bought whatever argument had been poured into his ears most recently. When Barney and Roger Campbell called him in and decreed that the funds for the training simulator had to be removed from the budget, he reversed himself and so advised Vaughn—to whom he had previously pledged his unyielding support.

"You agreed that every reason I gave you for buying a flight simulator was logical, justifiable, and important," Andy reminded him.

"I haven't changed my mind," Myler said stoutly. "I still agree with you that a simulator would be very worthwhile. Unfortunately, it's not absolutely essential."

When Myler declined to press the matter further, Vaughn went straight to Barnwell Burton. "I want to know why you turned down Operations's training simulator," he said without preamble, standing in front of the cluttered desk.

"Because it's worthwhile but not absolutely essential," Barney said, rubbing his eyes.

"Is that your verdict or Campbell's?"

"You sound like Aroni. No, it's my verdict. Rog happens to agree with me. Sit down."

"Did Jack explain why we need a simulator?"

"Oh, he gave us what you probably put into his head—exact replica of a Connie cockpit, recreates any in-flight emergency from an engine fire to electrical failure. Control forces identical to the real airplane. Realistic even to the motion and pitch of an actual Constellation. Pays for itself in the long run. Hell, all you guys try to justify expensive hardware with the claim that it'll be more economical 'in the long run.' I've heard that phrase so often I've stopped believing it."

"You can believe it with a simulator," Vaughn said heatedly. "Didn't Jack give you my figures?"

Barney had the grace to look embarrassed. "Well, he started to, Andy, but I didn't give him much of a chance. By the time he got through explaining to me what a simulator can do—which I already knew—I told him we had heard enough and the answer was no."

The chief pilot shook his head. "Will you listen to *me*?"

"Sure. But make it brief." Barney leaned back, tossing his glasses onto his desk.

"It costs us twelve hundred bucks an hour to train pilots on the Connie. We can do the same thing, only better, in a simulator at a hundred and twenty-five bucks an hour. Furthermore, we can give the crews more training time, we don't have to risk valuable men and aircraft on risky training maneuvers, and we wind up with superior pilots. If that doesn't make sense, you're not as smart as I think you are."

"Twelve hundred versus a hundred and twenty-five? You kidding me?"

"Nope. Those are actual figures. I got 'em from United, and American's had the same experience. Barney, I know a million bucks is a lot of moola, but those damned humbilizers will pay for themselves in two years."

"Humbilizers?"

"That's what the pilots call the simulators. It's so damned real, guys'll come out of the cockpit dripping, and I wouldn't be surprised if there were a few cases of soggy underwear, too."

"You make quite a case," Barney admitted. "Let me think it over for a day or so. I'll talk to Roger about it."

He did talk to Campbell, who made the mistake of laughing when Barney asked his opinion.

"I'm surprised you let one of those pilots talk you into even considering spending a million dollars for an electronic toy," Campbell scoffed.

"Vaughn's a part of management," Barney said tartly. "He's no prima donna. Now, are you in a position to deny those training cost figures of his?"

"No, but—"

"Then don't reject an idea you know nothing about. I'm ordering a simulator."

For the next few days, Campbell was a model of meekness and made a point of apologizing to both Myler and Vaughn for his original attitude toward such training devices. By the time he reverted to his old arrogance, not only had Barney contracted for a simulator, but he had finally named Vaughn vice-president of Operations and gave the department independent status by removing it from Traffic.

Larry Aroni said it was about time. Jack Myler publicly praised Barney for enlightened corporate organization and privately worried that his own status might have been weakened. Calvin Motts also praised Barney and privately thought Vaughn should have been made only an assistant vice-president. Don Littlefield guessed quite accurately at what Motts was thinking and made no comment. Roger Campbell was invited to make a speech to the American Bankers Association and included in his remarks fulsome praise of flight simulators as an example of "judicious airline-industry spending with an eye not to present costs but to future profits."

FOUR

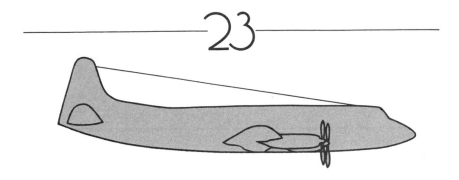

23

The outbreak of the Korean War ironically brought new heights of prosperity in which Coastal shared despite its still-limited route structure. Barney ordered four more Constellations, the latest version known as the L-1049—the Super Constellation.

He ran Coastal like a Mafia don, ruling with terror, benevolence, and inconsistency. He was more respected than liked, more feared than hated. And it was in the halcyon fifties that officers and employees alike began referring to him as "the old man." It was a title of fealty, homage, and sporadic affection, but most of all it represented a kind of dependency upon the forty-two-year-old president.

This was particularly evident when it came to capital investments. He hadn't meant to keep Larry Aroni and the other officers mystified as to his equipment plans, but it became sort of a game that he hated to stop playing. It also happened to be a game with large stakes, so large that Barney feared that once he let the secret out, the opposition might be overwhelming. Almost daily, he studied confidential technical reports, correspondence, and test-flight data. Only his secretary ever saw the return addresses on the envelopes in which this information came. Seldom did his colleagues see him socially; he had dinner occasionally with Larry and Norma

Aroni and went to Washington Redskins games with Jack Myler. Barney loved football. He became acquainted with George Preston Marshall, the volatile, controversial owner of the Redskins, and wangled a contract to fly the team to several out-of-town games during the 1952 season. Marshall was a big hawk-nosed man with an explosive temper and political opinions that were miles to the right. He refused to fly and regarded the train as man's noblest technological achievement, but with the NFL's expansion to the West Coast, he was forced into team charters.

Charters became a Coastal specialty, a lucrative sideline at which both Motts and Littlefield excelled. That year charters represented only five percent of the airline's revenue but generated twelve percent of the profits. They did create equipment-scheduling problems, however, yet Barney continued to resist mounting pressure for additional aircraft. Instead, he poured every available penny into a swelling "Capital Investment Reserve Fund" and just laughed when Aroni sarcastically asked, "What the hell are you saving up for—a party at Yankee Stadium?"

There was a party of sorts in 1952, early in the year, when the new director of public relations, Mike Ashlock, came into Barney's office and tossed a yellowed newspaper clipping on the president's desk.

"What is this?"

"Found it going through some old files that used to belong to a guy named Lindeman. It's a clip from the Binghamton *Press*."

Barney read aloud: " 'Local War Ace Announces Start of Airline Here. Rodney 'Bud' Lindeman, Binghamton's famed pursuit ace, announced today he is starting an airline that will fly between the Triple Cities and the New York area.' " Barney put down the clipping. "Am I supposed to turn handsprings or something, Mike? I know all about this. I don't even have to—"

"Look at the date, Boss."

Barney glanced at some numbers inked above the headline.

"For Christ's sake. Twenty-five years . . . This is March third . . . in twenty more days we'll celebrate our silver anniversary."

"Exactly," Mike Ashlock beamed. "I thought I'd better call your attention to it in case you wanted to have some kind of a special observance. It's a great publicity handle." He was disappointed to see Barney frown. "Or don't you think it warrants any celebration?" he asked somewhat plaintively.

"That's not it," Barney said. "I just wish the anniversary was a little later in the year—like April or May. Then I'd really give you something to publicize along with the birthday."

"Huh?"

"No matter. Tell you what, Mike, I'll set up a meeting with you, Cal Motts, and Don Littlefield. We'll have to do something to commemorate the occasion, but I don't want to make too big a splash right now. I've got something coming up later that we can tie into the anniversary. After all, this isn't just one day, it's an anniversary year."

On March 23, 1952, Barnwell Burton unveiled a bronze marker at the Triple Cities Airport.

> PRESENTED TO THE PEOPLE OF THE TRIPLE
> CITIES WHERE, ON THE 23RD OF MARCH, 1927,
> AN AIRLINE CALLED TRI-CITIES WAS BORN.
> THIS PLAQUE HONORS NOT ONLY THE FOUN-
> DER, RODNEY LINDEMAN, BUT ALSO THE COM-
> MUNITIES WHOSE SUPPORT AND FAITH IN AIR
> TRANSPORTATION FORMED THE NUCLEUS OF
> A GREAT AIR CARRIER NOW KNOWN AS
> COASTAL AIRLINES.

Henry McKay also had a presentation of his own. After Barney had shaken hands with the mayor of Binghamton, McKay stepped to the microphone.

"Ladies and gentlemen, if President Burton will give me his attention, please . . . thank you, Barney. Ladies and gentlemen, not quite twenty-five years ago, the man who now heads Coastal Airlines, and who has given the Triple Cities this handsome symbol of his company's proud origins, turned over to the airline—" Henry paused, milking the moment of all possible drama. "—turned over none other than his family's automobile. Some time ago, Barney told me I could have the car if I wanted it. So I took it . . . but not for myself. I was saving it for an occasion like today. So, President Burton, I'd like to give you back your car, as a token of our pride in you personally and in your fine airline."

McKay gestured toward a nearby hangar, and on his signal a car came from in back of the building and wheezed up to the small ceremonial platform. Barney's old Jordan, freshly painted, the refurbished red hawks on the door panels gleaming in the spring sunlight. There, also redone, was the original lettering.

COURTESY CAR
Tri-Cities Airline
"Route of the Red Hawks"

"Well I'll be damned," Barney said after muttering a few appropriate words to the crowd.

McKay thought Barney hadn't been touched until he saw the president's eyes were moist. He leaned closer.

"I had enough trouble getting it from the paint shop to the airport under its own power. Come to think of it, what will you do with the thing now that you've got it back?"

"Keep it around at National. Maybe I'll start a museum one of these days. Anyway, I'm really grateful, Henry. It was a very nice gesture. I had no idea."

"There have been times," the banker observed, "when I had my doubts this airline would be around to accept the gift."

Barney laughed. "Well, now you can start planning something for our fiftieth anniversary. Maybe we could locate one of our old Stinsons." Smiling, he leaned toward Aroni. "Larry, do you think Norma would let you go on a little trip with me for about ten days?"

"I guess. I assume it's important."

"It is."

"Where're we going?"

"England."

Aroni's jaw went slack. "England? What for?"

"To buy a few million bucks' worth of new airplanes. Equipment that'll put us five to ten years ahead of every other airline in the U.S."

Aroni could only gape.

"Yeah, Larry, this is it. We're rolling the dice, pal. Only we're spelling craps j-e-t."

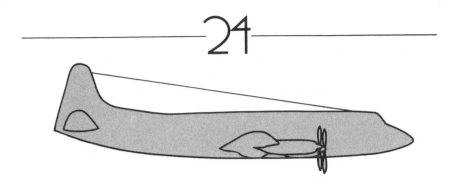

24

They took a TWA Constellation from Washington to London and talked heatedly most of the way across the Atlantic.

It was a nonstop conversation that was largely a continuation of what they had discussed in Barney's office a week before. Then, Larry had been stunned at what the president was proposing, and he still wasn't sure whether Barney was being a genius or a madman, whether he was about to pull off one of the great equipment coups or wreck the company.

Barney had explained it carefully and calmly.

Twenty new Vickers Viscounts—each with four Rolls-Royce turbine engines hitched to propellers, at a million dollars per airplane. And four de Havilland Comets, Britain's vaunted new jetliners and the world's first passenger jet. Two and a half million dollars for each aircraft.

It was a plunge, a gamble, of such proportions that Aroni marveled at its audacity even as he doubted its wisdom. He had looked at Barney incredulously. The man who a quarter-century ago had offered him a job at ten dollars a week, was now about to spend $30 million on planes that were not only foreign-built but powered differently from any airliner flying in the United States.

"Have you talked this over with Henry McKay, or any other director?" he had asked Barney.

"No. Not with anyone in the company. You're the only one I've told."

Aroni stretched. "You might be able to sell me—*might*—but how in heaven can you justify an outlay like this to the board and the stockholders?"

"You let *me* worry about them. All you have to do is look at the airplanes. Talk to the manufacturers, the test pilots. Give me your honest appraisal from every angle. Will they be easy and economical to maintain? Will they fit into our route structure? Will we have any trouble transitioning our pilots? Will—"

"Hold it. You can stop right there. Go back to maintenance. For God's sake, we'll be three thousand miles away from our spare parts."

"That's one of the things I want you to discuss with the British—what kind of parts support can they give us."

"I can't advise you on pilot training. Maybe we should take Andy with us."

"I'll send him over later. After we buy the birds."

"*After* we buy 'em? Barney, how deep a hole have you dug? You can't sign thirty million bucks' worth of contracts without board approval."

"Anything I sign on this trip will be predicated on our directors giving me a go-ahead."

"Well," Aroni had sighed, "I was afraid for a minute that you had bought 'em mail-order. Me, I wanna see these planes first. Until then, don't expect me to give you my blessing."

"I don't expect any. That's why we're going to England . . ."

The vice-president of Maintenance and Engineering suspected the president was committed far more than he would admit. He knew Barnwell Burton too well. Barney had given him reams of technical reports, sales brochures, news clippings, and correspondence to study before they left for London. And as Aroni waded through this mountain of material, he realized how backward and deficient Coastal was when it came to long-range planning. Other carriers approached the task of ordering new flight equipment with the carefully plotted logistics of a Normandy invasion. They would closely examine all factors: anticipated traffic growth, airport compatibility, schedule revisions in accordance with aircraft delivery dates, crew-qualification requirements. There would be separate research into financing problems, additional maintenance training, and more. All this information and data had to be considered, digested, judged, sifted—the hard realities and cold facts behind the exhilarating excitement of introducing a new airliner. Integrating new aircraft into a fleet required as much as five years' lead time, a period of intensive planning by virtually all executive echelons.

And that was Barney's trouble, Aroni thought morosely. It was only fair to admit the president had done a tremendous amount of advance work, for what he had handed Larry to study represented the output of a half-dozen men on any other airline. But the product was Barnwell Burton's alone; the input from the others would merely implement a decision Larry Aroni feared already had been made, emotionally if not contractually. Here's the airplane, he would tell them in effect—you guys work it into our system. Not, here's our system—what kind of a new airplane does it need?

And what worried Aroni the most was the radical nature of what Barney wanted. The Viscount turboprop alone was a new enough concept to present problems, with its four turbine-powered engines hitched to a relatively small airframe about the size of a Convair 240. But the Comet was something completely new. A pure jet that cruised at five hundred miles an hour.

It had first flown in July, 1949, and was scheduled to go into regular passenger service on British Overseas Airlines in May, 1952. The Comet was not just another new airliner but a revolution with wings.

If one man could be called the father of this concept, it was a former Royal Air Force lieutenant named Frank Whittle. Britain's pioneering of commercial jet flight was the legacy of this quiet, unassuming pilot-scientist who in 1928 wrote a paper pointing out the deficiencies of the piston engine–propeller combination. Whittle, a lowly RAF cadet at the time, emphasized the simple fact that the higher the altitude, the less efficient the combination became. Air density decreased in direct proportion to altitude increases, and this raised havoc with both the air-cooled engine—which needed air to "breathe" as oxygen mixed with fuel—and the propeller, which got less of a bite in thinner air.

Whittle acknowledged the limitations of propeller-driven aircraft but challenged the assumption that there wasn't much anyone could do about it. In 1928, virtually every aviation scientist believed no conventional aircraft could fly faster than four hundred miles an hour nor climb higher than 25,000 feet, even with the most powerful engines imaginable. The air was simply too thin from there on up for propellers to be of much use. Why not, Whittle asked in his paper, do away with both the piston engine and the propeller and use jet propulsion instead?

He suggested an arrangement in which a gas-driven turbine could suck in air, compress it by passing it through intense heat, and then expel it out the other end at a high speed. It would make little difference how thin the air was because the compression technique would increase its density within the engine. In fact, Whittle argued, the jet engine should work even more efficiently the higher the plane climbed because there would be less air resistance to the plane itself as it flew.

Relatively little attention was paid to this paper written by an obscure flight student in the course of his own schooling. But later, Whittle became an RAF instructor and published an article in the Royal Air Force *Journal* expanding his original thesis, and it began to make the rounds in British aeronautical circles. Although his proposal for an experimental jet engine was turned down by the Air Ministry and private industry alike, Frank Whittle finally took out a patent on his own. In 1935, some bankers became interested in financing the construction of a practical jet engine based on his design, and on April 12, 1937 the angry scream of the world's first turbojet engine had sounded the start of a revolution.

Now all of Whittle's scoffed-at theories and frustrating rejections had come to magnificent culmination in the Comet. Aroni could understand and even shared Barney's unfettered enthusiasm; what nagged at him was the jetliner's viability. This was at the heart of their marathon trans-Atlantic discussion.

"The Comet's only a thirty-six-passenger airplane," Aroni pointed out. He clapped his hand down on a manila folder bearing the label *Economic Analysis of Comet Operational Modes.* "It admits right here. The plane needs a seventy-two-percent load factor to break even on segments of one thousand miles or more. About eighty percent or higher on a stage length of under a thousand. Our break-even factor on our Connies is only sixty percent. With the Comet's limited capacity and high load-factor requirements, I can't see how we can make money flying the thing."

"We'll make money because we'll be operating near or at one-hundred percent capacity," Barney said confidently.

"And what crystal ball inspired *that* prediction?"

Barney closed his briefcase and took out a cigarette. "Once people fly in a jet they wouldn't be caught dead in a piston plane. The smoothness, the total lack of vibration, the quiet. And the speed. The speed, Larry. Take this flight. Almost fourteen hours. We're both tired already with another six hours to go, and we're flying first class. A jet could cut this trip in half. Half!"

"Not the Comet. It doesn't have the range to go westbound nonstop, and even eastbound you'd need some pretty good tailwinds. Even de Havilland projects a refueling stop for trans-Atlantic operations."

"So what? Just add one hour to refuel, that's all. Anyway, the Comet's just the first of the jets. I've heard rumors Boeing's gonna build a big sonofabitch."

"We could wait for Boeing," Aroni suggested with a small grin. He knew asking Barney to wait for another dream airplane was like asking a child to wait for Christmas.

"Even if Boeing comes up with a jetliner, it's at least five years away. The Comet is on the shelf right now. Lord, look at the jump we'll get."

"That's what worries me." Aroni fumbled for matches. "We're too small an airline to go in for all this pioneering. We don't have the technical and engineering resources. We can't handle it as well as the big boys—United, American, TWA, Pan Am." He paused to light his cigar.

"Bullshit," Barney grumbled. "The size of an airline has nothing to do with imagination, innovation, ingenuity."

"I'm not talking about imagination, innovation—" Aroni waved his cigar. "I'm talking about technical facilities and manpower.

The Comet's a whole new ballgame. And so is the Viscount, for that matter."

Barney dismissed this with a grunt. "The Viscount's just another airplane with a new kind of engine. Besides, I'm buying the Viscount mostly because of you."

"Me?"

"Sure. You've been badgering me to get modern short-to-medium-range equipment. The Viscount's so modern it's almost tomorrow. Say . . . that wouldn't be a bad hook for our ad campaign."

"Now listen, assuming that this propjet is a good airplane, why do we need twenty? We couldn't fit twenty more planes into our schedules even if we added twenty-five percent more route mileage."

"I'm buying them mostly as replacements," Barney said, pulling a sheet of paper from the briefcase on his lap. "Right now we're operating a twenty-eight-aircraft fleet. I'm gonna put the four older Connies up for sale, all but two DC-4's—the pair we got configured for all-cargo—and we'll peddle five of the DC-3's. That's seventeen planes we'll be phasing out. The five remaining DC-4's will be the ones we've been operating all-coach. In other words, Larry, the Viscount fleet will take over all segments except the long-haul markets like Washington–Phoenix. Later, when we get the Comets, I'll retire the rest of the DC-4's, reconfigure the Super-Connies to all-coach, and we'll be back to a fleet with only three types of aircraft—which oughta make you happy."

"Which leaves me with a few unanswered questions, not happiness. How can you operate a thirty-six-passenger airplane over routes you've been serving with aircraft carrying almost a hundred?"

"We haven't been averaging anywhere near a hundred customers on those segments. And we can make more dough on a Comet with a full load than on a Connie flying half-empty."

"How?"

"By placing a surcharge on every Comet fare. People'll be willing to spend a few extra bucks for the privilege of jet travel. At five bucks a head, maybe even ten, we'll make up for the lack of capacity. All this is written down in that pile of stuff I gave you. Our equipment phase-out plans, the Comet surcharge proposal—haven't you read it yet?"

"In one week I just managed to cover the technical material. Selling the seats is somebody else's problem." Aroni reclined the backrest. "My responsibility is to make sure you're buying the right airplanes. And without even seeing either the Viscount or the Comet, my advice is to put a little cold water of caution on that enthusiasm you always get for a new bird."

"It's tomorrow, Larry. Think of it—Coastal Airways, the *first* American jet carrier."

"I am," said Aroni. "But you must realize what will happen if anything goes wrong—*anything*. We'll be out of business, and fast. Very fast."

Their suites were adjoining, with a small but elegant parlor sandwiched between. In each suite they found fresh flowers, a basket of fruit, a bottle of Chivas Regal, and identical notes:

Welcome to England! Enclosed is a ticket to a hit musical for tonight which I think you'll enjoy after some rest from your long flight. A Vickers car will pick you up in front of the Claridge at eight o'clock tomorrow morning. We all are looking forward to your visit.

Sincerely,

George Edwards

George Edwards, head of Vickers, was a shrewd but amiable man with a delightful, self-deprecating sense of humor. Fully aware of what a large Viscount sale to a U.S. carrier would mean to the reputation of the British aircraft industry, Edwards deftly combined tough bargaining with deference and unobtrusive courtesies, like their being met at London Airport by a chauffeured Rolls-Royce.

"Quite a greeting," Barney observed as he and Aroni were having drinks in the small sitting room.

"For thirty million bucks, they can afford it," Aroni said cynically.

The Vickers car picked them up promptly at eight, and for the next three days they immersed themselves in the Viscount. Barney concentrated on operating costs while Larry did some intensive questioning of technicians regarding maintenance support systems, power plants, and—knowing that Andy Vaughn would want full information—handling characteristics. In fact, after an hour's demonstration flight, Aroni suggested that they have the Vice-President of Operations fly over and test the propjet himself.

"I don't see any need for it," Barney said impatiently. "I was impressed by that ride and I'm a little surprised you weren't. The smoothness is absolutely incredible. And when Edwards balanced that coin on the seatback table to show the lack of vibration— What the hell more do you want, Larry?"

"A pilot's opinion," Aroni said doggedly. "That's all. Don't get me wrong. I was impressed. It's a fine little airplane. Only maybe it's too little. Forty-four passengers isn't much payload, about the same size interior as the Convairs, and the price tag is three times higher."

Barney was annoyed. "You sure are going out of your way to knock it. Every time you find something to praise, you come up with something to criticize."

"I'm just not completely sold. The airframe, for example. The wings are single-spar construction. Every American-built transport has triple spars."

"Yes, but the Viscount does meet or exceed all American structural requirements."

Aroni sighed. "I'm just being conservative. You brought me along to raise the issues and ask whatever questions I think necessary. Structural strength was one of them. I still prefer the way we build airplanes, but I don't think that opinion is enough to blackball this airplane. One thing I do like—those Dart engines. They're the best power plants I ever saw. Give us a little operating experience and I'll bet they'll go eight thousand hours between overhauls."

Barney was pleased at this, the most positive statement Larry Aroni had made yet about the Viscount. "And they'll set up a spare-parts center in the Washington area for us, too," he enthused, "plus a full-time engineer-adviser who'll work with us."

The following day, they agreed on a conditional contract for twenty propjets, deliveries to begin by June 1, 1953, contingent upon Coastal obtaining satisfactory financing arrangements.

"And if you encounter any difficulties with your American contacts," Edwards said hopefully, "I'm sure we could work out something to help you at this end."

So far the agreement was only verbal and the offer did more than pleasantly surprise Barney. It confirmed his growing awareness that the British seemed almost overanxious to crack the U.S. airline market. It was understandable. Britain had lacked the resources to simultaneously develop both transport and combat aircraft during World War II. The result was that British airlines had been forced to turn to American-built postwar commercial planes like the DC-6 and Constellation. The Viscount and the Comet represented their aircraft industry's first real chance to cut down America's civil aviation lead. Barney decided he had been playing the role of willing bride too long and suddenly switched tactics.

"That's very generous of you, George." Barney gave him his best smile. "If it becomes necessary I won't hesitate to call on you, though I think financing will come a lot easier and faster if you folks would just sweeten the pot a little."

"I believe," Edwards said with a kind of puzzled dignity, "that's a Yank poker expression, but I'm not exactly sure of its meaning."

An aide leaned toward the head of Vickers and said discreetly, "It means, sir, that Mr. Burton wants something from us in return for signing the contract. Am I correct, sir?"

"Not 'something in return,'" Barney objected gently. "I merely want to make our deal so attractive that our financing sources will regard it as advantageous in every respect."

"And what do you have in mind?" Edwards asked with wary politeness.

"Two small items. I'd like you to take four Model 049 Constellations in trade, and I'd be most appreciative if you could arrange acquisition of a Viscount simulator at, let's say, a bargain price."

Edwards guffawed. "Oh, really now, Barnwell. You might as well ask us to take in four Sopwith Camels. Those bloody 049's have a resale value of about ten shillings."

"The hell they do, George. These are like brand-new. Tell you what. If you'll take 'em off our hands at a hundred grand apiece, I'll guarantee you they'll be delivered to Vickers with zero airframe time. We can do that for these people, can't we, Larry?"

Aroni nodded dutifully.

"I might go fifty thousand," Edwards offered.

"Pounds?" Barney asked slyly.

"Good heavens, no!" Edwards laughed. "Dollars."

In the end, he agreed to accept the four Constellations in trade at $85,000 each, the sum to be deducted from the total Viscount purchase price. And Vickers promised to pay one-fourth of the cost of a Viscount simulator, also to be credited to the purchase amount.

Barney had no such success when he huddled with de Havilland and finally signed a conditional contract for a quartet of Comets, again contingent on Coastal's ability to arrange financing. Orders for the Comet were pouring in and had been since its well-publicized proving and demonstration flights that had begun in 1950. Its manufacturer was not disposed to bicker for an aircraft that promised to revolutionize air travel.

Barney was as impressed with the de Havilland people as he had been with the Vickers group. Yet with Aroni's prodding, his interrogation at de Havilland was tougher, sharper, and far more searching. Larry made no effort to hide his uneasiness about the sleek jetliner. An uneventful yet fascinating two-hour flight aboard a test Comet did nothing to allay his vaguely discomforting suspicions. While Barney was elated at his first taste of jet flying—even the Viscount seemed stodgy and pedestrian by comparison—Aroni simply stared out the small round porthole windows, feeling a little ashamed of his fears mostly because he was unable to solidify them into logical reasons, specific explanations, or even words.

Certainly he had warmed to the technicians he had met, de Havilland's chief test pilot in particular, a slim, flaxen-haired airman-scientist named John "Cat's-Eyes" Cunningham—bluff, hearty, thoroughly British, and possessing the piercing directness of a man who abhors anything faintly devious. In that respect, he was like a lot of pilots Aroni knew and respected. It was not by accident that Andy Vaughn was his closest friend. Cunningham reminded him of Andy, in that they both seemed to have emerged from the common mold of airmen.

John Cunningham clearly loved the Comet, yet he sensed Aroni's negativism long before the American revealed it in so many words. They talked for hours, usually with Barney present but silent. The two Americans trusted John Cunningham and admired him, especially after they learned something of his background. He had been a de Havilland test pilot before World War II and during the war commanded a fighter squadron that became the first to shoot down one hundred German planes in night combat, Cunningham getting twenty of them and earning his nickname in the process. He hated being called "Cat's-Eyes" but confided that the RAF had fostered it in order to keep the Germans from knowing the real reason for his success—radar. "Actually," he admitted, "I can't see in the dark any better than you blokes."

About the Comet he was poetic: "The first time I flew her, I knew she was a thoroughbred. She responds beautifully, rides smoothly and purposefully, makes turns in graceful, effortless sweeps as if she were holding to a true curve on an invisible pivot. But I don't have to tell you chaps all this. You've ridden her. You know that comparing it to an ordinary aircraft is like contrasting . . . I do go on, don't I? But, yes, she's had her troubles, I'd be the first to admit it. A slight instability at top speeds at high altitudes, for example. One problem was a violent stall buffet when the flaps were retracted, but I think we've licked that. And the prototype lacked any warning indicator to tell you when the engines lost power. That's something I'll never understand." He shook his head in a kind of sad, mild indictment of the designers, then out of loyalty to de Havilland decided on forgiveness. "But you must remember that the Comet is really an entirely different breed of airplane. Some early mistakes were inevitable."

"That's what worries me, John," Aroni said, as he paced across the pilot's office frowning. "The Comet's not just another new airplane. It's invading an operational environment nobody has tried before. Such as cruising at thirty-five thousand feet."

"Above the weather most of the time," Cunningham retorted with a touch of pride that was almost a rebuke.

"Granted," said Aroni. "But has de Havilland taken into consideration the pressurization requirements involved in altitudes that high?"

The Englishman nodded. "Eight pounds per square inch on the fuselage walls."

"Which is double the Connie's. Add to that how fast your pressurization and depressurization cycles are. The Comet's rate of climb is about three times that of a conventional transport and it comes down a hell of a lot faster."

"All I can tell you," Cunningham said reassuringly, "is that virtually every section of the structure has been tested to destruction. That includes windscreens—or cockpit windshields as you call them—windows, doors, every component subject to stress."

"How about hydrostatic testing?"

Cunningham stared at him. "Hydrostatic tests?"

"Dunking a large fuselage section into a big tank of water and then pumping water in and out to stimulate pressurization cycles. It's the safest way to determine the stress effects on structure. If the fuselage explodes, the water keeps the damage confined."

"I know what they are," the test pilot said solemnly. "No, the Comet hasn't gone through any hydrostatic tests. I have to assume our design team didn't think they were necessary. For what it's worth, I myself have complete faith in the aircraft's structural integrity, based on a completely adequate test program. I think you're being overly concerned, Larry."

"Perhaps," Aroni said abruptly, "but I found out a long time ago that assumptions are another name for aviation's mistakes."

The chief spokesman for de Havilland was Miles Willoughby, head of Sales, a blustering British type with a mustache as thick as jungle foliage. What haggling there was mostly involved spare-parts support and the amount of down-payment since Willoughby wouldn't budge a penny on price.

"We've built what you Americans like to call a better mouse-trap, eh?" he guffawed.

"An excellent analogy," Barney acknowledged. "I think I'm guilty of doing more bickering than dickering. Let's get the papers signed."

"I like the way you do business," Willoughby beamed. "By God, Barney, what did you study in college—how to get along with people?"

"Never went to college." Barney's tone was just a shade away from defiance.

"Damnation, I knew it!" Willoughby bellowed. "That's why I like you. The last American I dealt with went to Harvard and I never met such a pompous ass."

Barney was pleased. "Well, there's a saying about the Harvard man I've always liked—if you precede one through a revolving door, he'll come out ahead of you."

Willoughby actually slapped his knee as he laughed. "Have to remember that, by George. Shall we get on with it, gentlemen? We'll put that spare-parts arrangement into a notarized letter which in effect will amend the contract, if that's satisfactory."

"Fine. Where's my fountain pen?"

"Barney, could you hold up a minute?" Aroni asked. He had been riffling through the stilted legalese of the fourteen-page contract and was frowning.

"Problem?" Barney removed his glasses.

"There's no escape clause. Nothing that would get us off the hook if we decided not to take delivery."

"I don't mean to sound pedantic, old boy," Willoughby said sternly, "but de Havilland regards a contract as rather binding on both parties. And for Heaven's sake, why would you decide such a thing?"

Aroni hesitated. He did not want to embarrass Barney, nor did he want to be regarded by de Havilland as a hysteric. He chose his words carefully.

"You've created aviation history with this aircraft, Miles, but the very extent of that achievement gives me cause for concern. Maybe caution would be a better word than concern. The Comet is awesome, so new in concept, construction, and flight characteristics, it would be unreasonable not to expect a few troubles. Bugs, if you prefer the American term."

"The Comet has undergone the most rigorous test programs," Willoughby said with a tone of belligerence he could not quite hide.

"I don't question the merit of your tests," Aroni said quietly, "but I'm quite sure there isn't a manufacturer here or in the United States who won't admit that no test program can duplicate the actual conditions of day-by-day operations. No airplane ever built has been entirely free from bugs, and that includes the DC-3."

"A few . . . ah . . . technical difficulties, or bugs as you put it, wouldn't necessitate refusing delivery," Willoughby pointed out. "Airlines are still buying Constellations and DC-6's, and these were aircraft whose post-test problems were so serious as to require temporary grounding."

"Granted. But there also was the case of the Martin 202 which had a structural flaw so major that Northwest is still trying to peddle its entire 202 fleet. I don't want that to happen to us with a new airplane, a ship so new that I'd still have to regard operational service as merely a continuation of the test program."

Willoughby started to argue but Barney held up his hand. "I think Larry has a point. I'm afraid I'd have to insist on some kind of emergency clause—a reasonably worded provision, mutually satisfactory both to de Havilland and Coastal. Frankly, I don't anticipate ever having to exercise it. After all, we won't be taking delivery for another three years and I'm quite sure by then the Comet will be a thoroughly proven ship."

After a brief discussion, de Havilland agreed to add a special provision to the contract. It was quickly drafted and handed to the president of Coastal.

"Ah, yes," said Barney, " 'It is further mutually understood that the Purchaser shall have the right to terminate this Agreement provided that written notice is given to the Manufacturer not less than thirty days prior to the commencement of construction of the first of the four Comet aircraft ordered herein, said construction to be defined as the actual cutting of airframe metal. It is agreed that in the event this contract is terminated in accordance with the above conditions, the Purchaser shall not be liable for further payments and that all previous payments will be refunded to the Purchaser without interest with the exception of ten percent of all monies paid to the Manufacturer as of the date of contractual termination.' "

Barney looked up, staring over the top of his glasses. "We have a deal."

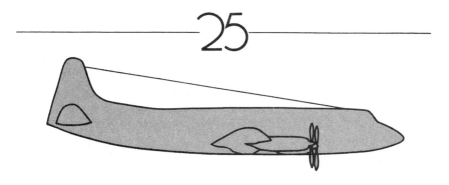

25

Their business concluded, Larry was ready to head home on the first available TWA flight, but Barney talked him into staying in London one extra night.

"We deserve some relaxation," he pleaded, "and you haven't had any chance to shop for Norma. She'll be disappointed if you don't bring her something nice."

"If I bring home the results of what you call relaxation," Aroni growled, "it'll probably be a social disease. Barney, why don't you stay on a few days and let me go back by myself?"

"Naw, I hate flying all that way alone. Tell you what, pal, I'll help you shop this afternoon, and tonight we'll hit that Avon Club."

"Barney, the Avon Club is a pickup joint for fancy hookers. Count me out."

"You don't have to get yourself a girl. Just sit with me, we'll buy a couple of the best-lookers a few drinks and have a few laughs. If I latch onto something nice, there's no law you have to play follow-the-leader."

It dawned on Aroni that Barnwell Burton was really afraid to be on his own in a foreign city, that he needed the security of a familiar companion. Reluctantly, Larry agreed. "Okay, but first we go shopping for Norma."

"Where?"

"Oxford Street."

For a man whose choice of his own clothes could have been made in a succession of dark closets, Larry had instinctive good taste when it came to women's apparel and invariably bought Norma a new outfit every time he traveled.

"Something in tweed," was what he informed the tall, dark-haired young woman who asked if she could help. Larry gave her only a perfunctory glance, but Barney was staring at her. She had somber green eyes set in a patrician face, and her tan cashmere sweater curved provocatively over her breasts. Barney whistled soundlessly and followed Larry around like an obedient puppy as he inspected the outfits she began showing him.

"Size?" she inquired.

"A twelve. She's about your height and weight, possibly an inch taller."

"That gives us something to start with. Here's an attractive tweed jacket with matching skirt."

Larry frowned. It was heavy with a masculine cut. "Excuse me, young lady, but that looks like something a dyke would wear."

Her pencil-thin eyebrows shot up. "Dyke?"

Aroni blushed. "Uh . . ."

"Oh," she said, unperturbed. "I must say, I have to agree with you. Let's find something a bit more feminine."

It took only three more outfits before Larry decided on matching slacks and jacket in black and gray, the lines so severely slim that they softened the harshness of the tweed without affecting its richness.

"That's nice," Barney admired. "Norma'll love that."

"Is it for your wife?" the young woman asked.

"Yes. I think I hit the jackpot, Barney. That outfit's a knock-out."

"She's fortunate in having a husband with such good taste," the woman said. She eyed Barney curiously. "I'm sure we could also find something your wife would like."

"I'm not married." He thought he detected a spark of interest in those green eyes. He had dated only sporadically since the divorce. He had yet to meet anyone as provocative and appealing as Vickie; inevitably, he compared any woman he met with the one he had allowed to go out of his life, and the result was always the same—a feeling of regret so sharp that it renewed his guilt. Now he was looking at this totally strange Englishwoman and sensing their similarities. A cool maturity. A frankness that was not blatant nor rude.

"Perhaps something for a girl friend?" she suggested.

"No. No, there's nobody"—he had started to say "nobody I'd spend the dough on" but realized this would sound too crass— "nobody who's that good a friend."

She nodded and gave Larry's purchase to a teen-age girl to gift-wrap in a back room. Aroni wandered over to a costume-jewelry display, and before the woman could follow him, Barney moved in like an intercepting fighter plane.

"What's your name, Miss?"

She smiled—it was half-friendly and half-sardonic. "You're an American, aren't you?"

"Yeah. I guess we don't have to wear signs around here, do we?"

"And you called me 'Miss.' It's Mrs. Mrs. Janet Leavelle."

His face showed disappointment. "Sorry. I was going to ask you to have dinner with us tonight."

"Us?"

"Larry and me. We're going back to Washington tomorrow morning."

"Then I'm the one who's sorry. I have plans for tonight."

"I envy your husband. Is he British, too? You sound British, but that last name . . ."

"My husband was French."

"Oh yes?"

"He was a pilot for the Free French. He was killed during the war."

Barney felt like applauding. "Then how about changing your mind about dinner tonight?"

"I've already told you, I have plans."

"Change 'em. This'll be our last night in London."

"I don't break dates, Mister—"

"Burton. Barnwell Burton. Barney, they call me. Look, Mrs. Leavelle, I'm not the type to push, but it would mean an awful lot to me if you'd accept our invitation."

She grinned at him in an almost girlish way. "*Our* invitation? Mr. Burton, I'll wager your friend doesn't even know you're asking me."

He smiled back, ruefully. "No, he doesn't. But that makes no difference."

"So why didn't you ask me to have dinner just with you? I'm sure he not only wouldn't mind but would prefer it that way."

"Frankly, I thought I'd stand a better chance if you knew there were two of us. But if you feel that way, okay—just the two of us."

"The answer is still no. I can't change my plans at this late hour. It wouldn't be fair."

"I'm sorry," he said honestly and simply.

"I am, too, in a way."

"And in what way is that?"

She surveyed him with a look of complete frankness. "You're rather crude, Mr. Burton. A bit too forward. Definitely domineering. But there's something about you that tells me your bark is worse than your bite. I have tomorrow night free, by the way."

"By tomorrow night I'll be three thousand miles away."

"Pity," she said sweetly, and went into the back room to get Aroni's purchase.

They didn't go to the Avon Club that night. Instead, they talked —mostly about Barney's marriage. He admitted what Larry already knew, that the breakup had been no fault of Vickie's, and for him that confession represented self-flagellation as well as catharsis.

"Barney, if she came back to you, would you change?"

"No."

"Why not?"

"Because I couldn't. Because I want both of them—Vickie *and* the airline. Only I can't have both. Not the way I am."

Aroni examined his friend with as much sympathy as reproach. "You're a big fool, you know. You don't have one logical excuse for making Coastal your whole life."

"The hell I don't! Somebody has to be the driving force. There's no autopilot on an airline. It won't fly unless there's someone in command every second."

"Bullshit. If you insist on using that analogy, you've got quite a few copilots around. Guys perfectly capable of helping you and of making some decisions on their own."

"Not final, irrevocable decisions. That's where their responsibility ends and mine begins."

"What you're describing is an indispensable man. There ain't no such animal, not even you. You only wish it was true. And that's what scares me about you."

"There's no reason to fear me," Barney laughed.

"I'm not scared of you. I'm scared for you. When a man deliberately ends a relationship that was God-given, he isn't choosing between his wife and the job. He's choosing between her and what he really loves—power, prestige. I don't think you love Coastal. You ditched Vickie because you'd rather be a corporate potentate than a husband. What you've never grasped is that authority isn't necessarily incompatible with a good marriage, not if you were only half as willing to work for the marriage as you are for the company."

"Maybe. And maybe I should remind you," Barney said, "the divorce was Vickie's idea, not mine. We'd still be married if she hadn't wanted kids."

"Having children was her last resort. Your refusal was the final straw. Being Catholic, I can't understand why you're so prejudiced against babies. But that's beside the point. What bugs me far more is why your marriage was doomed long before the possibility of a kid was ever raised. No airline needs the kind of blind, high-priest worship you insist on giving Coastal. It just isn't that important."

"Are you telling me what's important?"

"Look, Barney, if you were a medical researcher ruining your health and your marriage because you were spending twenty hours a day in a cancer laboratory, I'd say there was some justification. If you were a doctor working seven days a week because sick people needed you, I'd sympathize with your marital shortcomings. If you were an aircraft designer ignoring his family because you were slaving night and day on a device that would make flying safer, I could forgive you. But does an airline president—you or anyone else—belong in those categories? Sure you've created Coastal. You've fought and struggled and bled and you deserve a medal for what you've accomplished. Only you aren't really satisfied just with having created it and keeping it going. You've become part of it. You can't leave it any more than you can leave your own body. You honestly think you are indispensable, don't you?"

"Yes," Barney muttered. "I am."

"Well, honesty was always one of your virtues. But you've verified something for me. I asked you if you'd take Vickie back, and you said no because you couldn't change. Right?"

"That's what I said."

"Only that's not what you meant. What you should have said is that you don't want to change. You actually enjoy every minute you spend in that office because you enjoy being the indispensable absolute ruler."

Barney was silent. After a long moment, he simply nodded.

"And that's why I'm afraid for you." Aroni exhaled. "If you should ever lose what you really love . . . I'm sorry, Barney. You are a great man and a good friend. If you weren't both, I wouldn't have shot off my mouth."

Impulsively, they shook hands. Barney cleared his suddenly constricted throat. "Uh, Larry, I'm gonna spend an extra day here, if you don't mind flying back alone. I need some relaxation."

Aroni smiled. "Any messages for the troops?"

"I'll break the news when I get back Friday. Set up a staff meeting for that morning. We've done the job here. We're buying the world's most advanced airliner."

"Also the world's most unproven airliner. No, let's not argue about it. You've rolled the dice. I hope they come up right."

"Be honest," said Barney. "Can you give me one good, solid, unimpeachable reason why you're still afraid of the Comet?"

Aroni looked at him squarely. "Just one, only it's not solid. I've got a gut feeling about it."

Barney's icy-blue eyes widened in sudden understanding.

"Yeah—the same gut feeling I had about the Martin 202."

"Oh, God," said Barney Burton.

"Yes, she's a beautiful new kind of creature. Sleek, modern, and tragic, Barney. Tragic."

It was five after ten the next morning when Barnwell Burton walked into the shop on Oxford Street and addressed Mrs. Janet Leavelle without formality.

"Hi. How about that dinner tonight?"

She inspected him coolly, looking hard into his eyes like an officer at a dress parade.

"Am I the reason you didn't go home on schedule?" she finally asked.

"You are."

"Then how could I say no?"

"I hoped you wouldn't."

"I finish up at six. I'll have to go home and change. Would eight o'clock be too late?"

"Midnight wouldn't be too late if I were sure you'd come. Should I pick you up in a cab?"

"That's silly. I have my own car. Where are you staying?"

"The Claridge."

She was impressed enough to permit herself a slight smile. "Very posh. Very expensive. Would you like to dine there?"

"Any place you say. I don't know London very well."

"The Claridge is nice. I'll meet you in the lobby at eight. Now off with you. I'm working."

Janet Leavelle arrived at the Claridge precisely on time. She looked stunning. She wore a black velvet cocktail dress with a narrow but deep cleavage, tiny ruby earrings, and a single gold chain that was nearly invisible. After the maitre d' seated them at a choice table, Barney smiled in open admiration. Through dinner they talked, mostly about her. Janet's parents had died in a bombing raid, and while working as an RAF radio operator she had met her husband, Lieutenant Charles Leavelle.

"I was vectoring his squadron toward an intercept and he thought my voice sounded attractive," she recalled. "Somehow he found out where I was stationed and he looked me up. We started dating. He was very French, the kind of man you could be friends with and love simultaneously."

"And I take it you really did love him."

"Very much. Every man I've seen since has suffered by comparison. Maybe that's why I've never remarried—and probably never will."

"Never's a long time."

"I know that. So is widowhood. But I don't want to get married just for the sake of getting married. What I want most of all is some security, but marriage to the wrong person is too stiff a price."

"Exactly what do you mean by security?"

"My own shop, some day. I'm really much better at designing than selling. I'd like to have a shop for my own creations. I did the dress I'm wearing tonight." She said it with a pride that touched Barney. "Mrs. Sharon—she owns the shop—Mrs. Sharon lets me dabble at it now and then. The extra money goes toward what I'm saving to start my own business. Incidentally," she paused, "what type of business are you in, Barney? And where?"

"I work in Washington, but not with the government."

"You make it sound as if you were in something illegal."

Barney laughed. "No, nothing illegal. I'll tell you later."

"Why not now? Are you ashamed?"

"No. Very proud."

"An unsatisfied curiosity is like an unscratchable itch," Janet frowned, "but I'll change the subject. You've never been married?"

"I've been divorced for several years. Fortunately, we had no children. I've never remarried, or even thought about it. I guess you'd say I'm tied to my job. Always have been."

"And exactly what *is* your job, Mr. Burton?" she asked innocently.

"Oh, no, you don't trap me that easily. Let's just say my work requires almost full-time attention, even when I'm not at my office. Which is why my marriage wasn't a very good one."

"I'm glad you're being honest about it. Want to tell me about her?"

"Not particularly."

"Why not? I've told you all about Charles."

"There's a considerable difference. You had a happy marriage. We didn't, at least the last couple of years of it. I don't like to talk about it. She deserved far more than someone like me could give her. If she could have named my work as co-respondent, she would have been perfectly justified."

His face, so animated a few minutes earlier, was suddenly grim. She impulsively reached across the table and touched his arm. A silence fell between them.

"When are you going back to the States?" she asked, breaking the mood.

"Tomorrow. I wish I didn't have to, but I do."

"I'm sorry. I would have liked to have seen you again."

"Washington's less than fifteen hours away by air."

"You make it sound so close."

"Which brings up the next order of business. What would you like to do the rest of the evening? Take in a show? I'd suggest dancing, but I warn you, I'm a lousy dancer."

"I think," Janet Leavelle said distinctly. "I'd prefer the other."

Not for a good five seconds did Barnwell Burton grasp what she meant. He stared at her in disbelief, and she stared back, unflinching, a slight, uncertain smile on her lips.

Barney laughed, nervously and a little weakly. "I'm not sure what you mean."

"You know exactly what I mean," she said with devastating calmness. "I'd like to go to bed with you."

They rode the elevator to his suite without saying a word. Inside the room, he took her coat—noting for the first time it was rather old and almost shabby, in sharp contrast to her dress. He hung it up in the closet and turned to face her. She was sitting on the sofa, green eyes wide.

"Would you like a nightcap?" he asked huskily.

"No, thank you." She stood up and unhooked the back of the black dress, hunching forward slightly so that it fell from her white shoulders as she walked toward the bedroom, Barney following. She wore no bra. Her breasts were heavy and firm. She slipped the dress down to the floor, stepped out of the black velvet pool, and stepped into his arms.

"Take off your clothes, Barney," she whispered, breathing heavily. She broke away to remove her underpants and pull the bedcovers off. Barney undressed faster than he had ever done in his life, conscious all the while that she was watching him as she lay stretched out, her head propped on her hand. Barney slid in beside her. She looked up at him, eyes shining.

"I'd say I was a bit horny," she said very softly.

It was two hours later when they finally broke apart, so spent and relaxed that they were limp. Barney lit her a cigarette and she lay on her back, staring at the ceiling through half-closed eyes.

"Barney?"

"What?"

"You're damned good. A little uncertain at first, but great when you've lost a few of your inhibitions."

"You're quite a . . . teacher." He was on his side, facing her. "You're the most exciting woman."

"Absolutely the most exciting? Come now, tell me the truth. Oh, but then you're a spy, of course. And I can hardly expect proper answers."

"I happen to be president of an airline," he said.

"Really? A big airline like BOAC?"

"Not exactly that big. We don't have any overseas routes, but we're not small. Our fleet totals nearly forty airplanes and we've just bought twenty-four more. That's what I've been doing here the past ten days. Twenty Viscounts and four Comet jets. Or can't you tell one airplane from another?"

"I know about the Comet. On behalf of us British, I thank you, Mr. Barnwell Burton. I *am* impressed.

"I'm glad you're impressed. Is it possible you're also surprised? Or maybe pleased?"

She pondered this gravely. "Well, I'm pleased, naturally. But not surprised. You're obviously well off, so I knew you must have a responsible post. And you have an air of command about you. I rather assumed that people work for you and not the other way around. It was fairly obvious you wanted me. I think we can let it go at that."

She kissed him with a tenderness that was exciting. "All right,

Mr. Airline President, we've both made ourselves known. Now I think I'd better be going. It's late."

"No!"

It was an order, not a protest, and for a moment she felt the dominance of the man.

"Barney, I'm a working girl, and you're leaving tomorrow."

"That's why you can't leave now. God knows when I'll see you again. I want to wake up in the morning and find you here so I can kiss you good-bye."

"Darling, be reasonable. I'm wearing a cocktail dress. I can't go into work wearing this tomorrow. It's like carrying a sign that says I've been making love all night."

"You have a key to that shop?" She nodded. "Good," he said. "Leave for work a little early so you'll get there ahead of everyone else. In the morning I'll give you enough money to buy a little dress that doesn't look so sexy. Although you'd look sexy in a burlap sack. And don't argue with me. That's the way it's going to be."

And it was. He woke her at 6:00 A.M. so they could make love once more. Satiated, she mumbled sleepily, "I'd better bathe and get dressed."

Barney pulled her back as she started out of bed.

"If you're proposing marriage, the answer's no," she teased. "Maybe later, but—"

"Janet, come to America. I'm not gonna let this end as a kiss-me-good-bye-it's-been-a-nice-one-night-stand. You said you wanted security. Okay, I'll give you security, without marriage. I'll back you in starting up your own shop in Washington. If you prefer, I'll loan you the dough. How about it?"

"Barney, you're crazy. You're also implying something else— that I be your mistress."

"Undoubtedly."

"Why are Americans so boldfaced?"

"I didn't expect a decision right away," Barney said apologetically. "I want you to think about it. Before you leave, I'll give you my unlisted telephone number in the United States. All I ask is that you promise to stay in touch, even if your answer's no. I don't know when I'll get a chance to get back to England, but I don't want this to be anything but a temporary parting."

"You're a bossy bastard, darling. I do promise. Now let me take that bath."

He lay there, listening to the water fill the tub and her happy, slightly off-tune voice humming some unknown ballad, and he realized he was smiling. She came out of the bathroom draped in a towel and leaned over him to give him a brief peck. She didn't make it back to her clothes for another half-hour.

All the way across the Atlantic, he remembered her laughter.

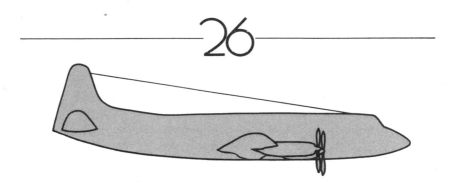

26

He thought of Janet Leavelle frequently in the ensuing weeks that stretched into months; they corresponded regularly, her own letters warm and affectionate but undecided as to his invitation.

"I want to come, Barney," she wrote in a letter he received that summer, "yet I find myself still unable to reach what has to be so important a decision. You must understand, darling. England is my home and to commit myself to so drastic a move is most difficult. I do not mean for you to give up on me entirely and I promise you I am truly weighing this dilemma daily, just as I miss you so very much every day. In lieu of my coming to the States in the immediate future, is there any chance you could get over here if only for a few days? Summer in England is such a beautiful time . . ."

There was little chance. Barney was driving the whole airline with tyrannical energy. There had been no open opposition from his executives on the Viscount-Comet purchase plan. He knew Bill Sloan and Roger Campbell had privately voiced their doubts, but that was all. However, a real fight developed among the directors. Henry McKay had questioned his judgment on the Comets—so much so that Barney suspected Aroni had been feeding him ammunition.

"I'll go along with those Viscounts," McKay told Barney at a heated directors' meeting, "although I can't for the life of me see why we need twenty of the damned things. Furthermore, they're foreign-built. And then buying Comets on top of spending twenty million dollars for the Viscounts, it's just too much."

"I'd be very happy to order American-made jets, Henry, but there are no American-made jets and there may not be any for another *decade*. We have to face up to the fact that the jetliner is the airplane of the future. And with that Comet, the future is right now. May I also remind all you gentlemen that at least two other American carriers are seriously considering the Comet, and one of them is our competitor. Namely, Eastern. Rickenbacker has said Eastern may well buy no fewer than *fifty* Comets!"

"What's the other airline?" Campbell asked.

"Pan Am. Make no mistake. Juan Trippe is known for his skill in choosing new transport aircraft. Believe me, we aren't going into the Comet program blindly and we won't be there alone."

"I'd like you to answer Henry's first point," Campbell said, leaning back in his chair. "Is the purchase of twenty Viscounts really necessary? Couldn't we get along with an order of less magnitude? Perhaps it would be best if we started out with five or six and see how well they work out."

"If we buy five or six," Barney snapped, "four-fifths of our aircraft will remain obsolete and uncompetitive. Right now we've got DC-4's and the oldest Connies butting heads with the DC-6, the latest-model Constellations, and the Boeing Stratocruisers that Northwest is operating domestically."

"So wouldn't it be better if we simply bought a few DC-6's or Stratocruisers instead of giving the British all our business?" McKay asked.

Barney shook his head. "Buying piston-engine equipment now is like ordering covered wagons for driving on superhighways. The jet age isn't over the horizon or even just around the corner. It's parked on our front step and we'd better well realize that."

McKay suddenly looked glum. "Barney, I've never really fought you before, but I can't go along with you this time. In my considered judgment, you're overcommitting the airline both financially and in the selection of equipment that is too radical."

"I have to agree with Henry," said Joe Walsh, the man from Riggs Bank.

Barney exploded. "What the hell's the matter with you guys? I've just given Coastal a chance to lead the industry into a new age of air-travel and you're sitting there whining about debts and about airplanes that are five years ahead of their time."

The latest "outsider" on the board was Galen Filmore, a retired Air Force general who had made a small fortune in Nevada real estate. He was a director in several other companies and was due to go off Coastal's board within the year, having informed Barney that his health was forcing him to cut down business activities. Barney had counted on his support but now even Filmore wore an expression of concern.

"Normally, I wouldn't let the idea of buying a rather revolutionary type of aircraft worry me," he said·with an air of regret. "After all, the Air Force ordered large numbers of the B-29 before it ever flew. But a purchase of this magnitude bothers me, Barney. As you pointed out, the Viscount and, to an even greater extent, the Comet are rather drastic departures from conventional equipment. I'd have my doubts even if there weren't any financing problems involved. Even if we could handle these, the airplanes themselves . . ." His voice trailed off, the unfinished sentence left hanging in the air like a black cloud that refused to dissipate.

"Barney," McKay said uneasily, "if someone like Galen with his Air Force background is uncertain, I would think this would be a major factor to consider."

"With due respect to Galen's aviation expertise," Barney snapped, "I refuse to accept a bunch of vague fears as proof that we'd be buying lemons."

"If you turn out to be wrong," Galen said soberly, "it could be *your* ass in the well-known sling."

"That's a chance I'm perfectly willing to take," Barney said quietly. "Larry has seen both airplanes. He's flown on them, talked to the designers, interrogated the test pilots. If he's with me I see no reason why you're all sitting there wetting your pants."

Aroni refrained from voicing his own hesitancy about the Comet; he knew Barney had the bit in his teeth and any opposition from his own officers would be regarded as outright treason. As the other directors looked at him, Larry could only nod his head. After all, they still had the escape clause in the Comet contract, he thought.

Barney sensed that the visual instead of verbal approval from Aroni was not lost on the board. He fired his biggest cannon.

"I'll tell you how sure I am. If you don't okay this equipment plan, you can have my resignation. Effective immediately."

There was shocked silence.

"Come now," said McKay, "you can't mean that."

"The hell I don't. I refuse to remain as president of an airline whose own board of directors doesn't have the guts to make American aviation history. To make Coastal the country's best airline. We have got to grow or the biggest carriers will push us out of the way."

The board voted, approving Barnwell Burton's equipment-modernization plan, subject to satisfactory financing arrangements.

Barney had $6 million accumulated in his Capital Investment Reserve Fund and he was willing to commit $5 million of this as the required down-payments on both the Viscounts and Comets. But no one bank or combination of banks was willing to loan the remaining $25 million, and even McKay struck out when he tried to enlist sufficient banking support.

It was Roger Campbell who came up with what looked like the ideal solution.

"I think I've lined up the funding for you," he said. "I've been talking to Warren Billings. He's head of Seaboard Insurance, one of the biggest insurance conglomerates in the world, let alone the United States. Seaboard will loan us fifteen million at six percent and will underwrite a ten-million-dollar stock issue."

"Goddamn!" Barney clapped Campbell on the shoulder. "Now we're in business. Roger, I'm proud of you. Go tell that Billings guy he's got a deal."

Campbell fingered the striped regimental tie that was his trademark. "There's one string attached. Just a small one. And I see no legitimate reason for rejecting what seems to be a very modest condition."

"What does he want?" Barney said coldly.

"Billings would like very much to sit on our board. Frankly, considering the magnitude of his financial help, it seems like a reasonable enough request."

"Well. I don't see any real objections," Barney said, mollified. "I would like to meet him, though."

"I thought you would. I've already set up a luncheon meeting at the Metropolitan Club for tomorrow."

Barnwell Burton disliked Warren Billings intensely right from the moment of their first handshake, which had all the firmness of gelatin and the warmth of a freshly caught fish. He was a tall, gaunt man built along the general lines of an elongated pipe cleaner. His cadaverous face might have been pleasant enough had it not been so thin, accentuating the size of a hefty nose. This, combined with hair that was sparse at the sides and bristly thick from the top of his forehead to the base of his skull, gave him the appearance of an emaciated Iroquois Indian.

Knowing what was at stake, Barney tried hard to be friendly, and he had to admit that Billings seemed to be trying, too, as he complimented Barney Burton on Coastal's progress, lauded the decision to buy jet-powered airplanes, and assured him that Seaboard wanted to be an active partner in the development of the finest air-transportation system.

"My desire to become a director is, in effect, a reflection of Seaboard's faith and confidence in your airline," Billings added ponderously.

Bullshit, Barney thought, but he said aloud: "I think our directors will welcome you as a board member, Mr. Billings."

"Call me Warren," Billings said earnestly.

The smile on his face made Barney think of a grinning skeleton, but he was in too far to back out, his negative impressions of Billings notwithstanding.

He shoved under the rug of other pressing business his feeling that he had opened his gates to a Trojan Horse. But he had had no choice.

The cause had seemed simple. The report said the elevators failed when the pilot pulled up sharply to counter a violent downdraft in a storm. When the elevators failed, the Comet pitched down so sharply that the wings failed. Aroni had brought the report into Barney, with two paragraphs he had underlined with a red pencil.

2 May 1953

It is understood that the wing was subjected to a static test by the manufacturing firm during the development of the aircraft. On the test piece, static and fatigue tests were conducted alternately. The wing failed in fatigue test, and after modifications was subjected to a static test. The wing failed again at ninety percent of the ultimate load. The failure was attributed to the fatigue test which had been made before. Modifications were carried out again and, without a retest, it was found satisfactory for the ultimate load under theoretical considerations.

The fatigue failure during static test occurred at rib number seven where the construction changes from two heavy spars to an outboard shell construction. In this accident, again the wings failed significantly at rib seven. . . .

Barney tossed the report back to the brooding vice-president of Maintenance and Engineering.

"In plain English, what is it saying?"

"That the Comet wing appears to be structurally marginal. In even plainer English, I wish it was stronger than it appears to be. And I've heard, de Havilland isn't gonna modify it further."

Barney had shrugged. "It's got an Air Registration Board certificate of airworthiness and you've told me yourself their ARB in some ways is tougher than our own CAA. That's good enough for me. Thunderstorms are bad news; they can wreck any airplane, including American-built transports."

"Just the same, Barney, I'd feel a lot better if we ordered that new airborne weather radar Bendix and RCA are offering. It'll pinpoint and measure turbulence intensity as far as a hundred and fifty miles ahead of the aircraft. A pilot could pick his way through the storm cells."

"Yeah, and we can pick our way through the bills. That's about forty thousand bucks per plane. More if we tried to put radar on a DC-4 or one of our 049's. They'd need structural modifications to accommodate all that hardware."

"The Viscount wouldn't need tó be modified. Neither would our Super Connies. At least order radar for them."

"We've been over this before," Barney puffed up his cheeks and exhaled. "The answer's still no. We're up to our assholes in capital debt already. I've never turned you down on a safety item, have I? Well, I have to this time. That radar gizmo would be fine if we could afford it. Maybe, later, if the Viscounts turn out like we expect."

In many respects, they turned out better. The first propjet was ferried over from England early in September 1953, with seven refueling stops enroute, and from then on one arrived about every three weeks. Barney did manage to fly to London for a long summer weekend, yet was unable to wrest a definite decision out of Janet Leavelle, but in her own reserved, tentative, cautious way, she was wavering. They were supposed to spend a full three days at an old inn two hours from London by train. The surroundings were idyllic, the love-making intense, the atmosphere both relaxing and stimulating. But Barney cut their stay by a full day because he suddenly decided he should head for the Vickers plant and see how his Viscounts were coming along. Oddly enough she understood the restlessness, and he was after all attentive, generous and—on the few occasions when he was willing to relax—even fun.

On his last afternoon they strolled through Piccadilly. He did not protest her indecision.

"If you want to wait until the first of the year," he said, "it's probably best for me. We'll be introducing the Viscounts in a couple of months and I wouldn't have the time. On the other hand, if you'd come right away . . ."

"No," she said gently. "I think I'll have my mind made up by the first of the year."

"Make it up the right way," he said, and slipped his arm around her waist as they huddled together against the brisk wind.

More than three-quarters of a million dollars were spent on introducing the Viscount with promotion that emphasized its vibrationless performance. The Viscount proved such a hit that Barney couldn't wait for the Comet's debut over Coastal's system. Then on January 8, Larry Aroni walked into the president's office, his swarthy face even darker-hued than normal.

"Barney, I just talked to Percy Williams, the Vickers liaison man. He got a call from London ten minutes ago. There's been another Comet accident and it's a real bad one."

Barney pushed his glasses back up onto the bridge of his nose. "Takeoff? Landing? No survivors, I suppose, if Percy says it was a bad one."

"No survivors, but that's not the only reason to worry. For no apparent reason the thing just went and blew up, at thirty-six thousand feet."

"Maybe you should go and stay over there until we get a pretty good idea of what happened. If there's something wrong with that airplane, we've still got time to cancel the order. They won't be cutting metal on our four until early next year."

Aroni made a face. He didn't want to be away from his family for what could stretch into months, although he refrained from telling Barney this. But he did point out there wasn't much he could do over there. "They won't let me take part in the investigation," said Aroni. "What could I accomplish sitting around in a hotel room waiting for de Havilland to give me periodic evasive answers?"

Percy Williams of Vickers arrived just then, quickly picked up on the argument and bluntly said it would be a waste of time and effort. "I think you're pushing a panic button, Barney. The most likely theory is a bomb. There's another possibility that a hot turbine blade flew loose and punctured a fuel tank. They've grounded the Comet fleet temporarily for modifications, y'know—installing steel shields between the engines and the tanks, plus reinforced fuel lines and extra fire detectors."

"In other words," Aroni added, "they may already have found the cause and fixed it by the time I get there."

Barney relented. A week later the Comets were reinstated and airborne once more. But two weeks later, a pale-faced Don Littlefield appeared in the president's office and wordlessly handed Barney a bulletin he had just torn from the United Press news ticker that had been installed in his office.

Barney read it aloud. " 'A Comet jetliner apparently blew up at thirty-five thousand feet over the Mediterranean on a flight from Rome to Cairo today and officials of the British Overseas Airways Corporation announced the immediate grounding of all Comets for an indefinite period.' " He took off his glasses and looked up at Littlefield. "Well, that does it."

Aroni had just walked into the president's office.

"Don't jump to conclusions," he said. "I don't deny it looks bad, but give de Havilland a break. Let 'em find the cause before you tear up the contract."

"Hell, they may never find out what happened. The wreckage is probably in fifty fathoms of water."

Aroni shook his head no. "They've already recovered a lot of the first Comet that went into the sea off Elba, plus bodies. The autopsies showed evidence of explosive decompression. And they've got six bodies from the second crash . . . same thing."

"I won't wait much longer," said Barney.

Aroni was back a few days later and gave him a full report based on what he had been told by technicians at de Havilland.

"They've solved it," he said in a matter-of-fact tone. "Explosive decompression resulting from metal fatigue."

Barney was incredulous. "Metal fatigue? On planes that new?"

Aroni slumped into a chair. "The pressurization forces on the Comet are double those on, say, a Connie: that's eight pounds per square inch. Because of the Comet's speed, the pressurization cycles have to be rapid, and this increases the stress. There's also the additional burden of the tremendous temperature on the skin of the fuselage due to heat generated by the five-hundred-mile-an-hour speeds. All this simply had the same weakening effect as bending a piece of metal back and forth until it breaks. In the Comet, the weak spot was a navigation window on the top of the fuselage. A tiny crack developed around the edge of this window frame, and after about three thousand hours of flight time the crack suddenly widened. With nothing to keep it from spreading, the whole top of the fuselage split wide open. Bingo."

"Okay," Barney sighed, "what do you recommend we do about it? I assume de Havilland will put in a foolproof fix."

"Yeah, but it'll take a long time. The whole airframe will have to be redesigned. Give up the Comet, Barney. It's a lost cause. It's got a permanent black eye, and by the time they get around to making it safe, we'll have American-built jets that are bigger, faster, better.

The British did a magnificent pioneering job. And the Comet's experience will make future jets that much safer. Every one will have metal stoppers within the fuselage so that any fatigue crack can't spread. All you'd get is slow decompression with plenty of time to descend to breathable altitudes. The Comet started the jet age . . . but a few years too soon for the state of the art to cope with."

Barney rocked in his swivel chair. "I'll have Mike Ashlock prepare the announcement. Nuts. This was our one chance, Larry. It won't come again."

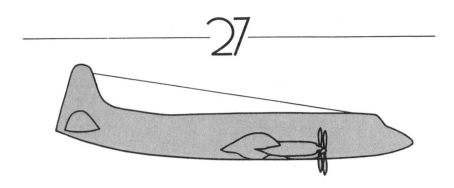

27

The dispatcher hung up, reached into a drawer, and took out a looseleaf notebook on whose black cover was inscribed the words:

DISPATCH EMERGENCY PROCEDURES MANUAL
Coastal Airlines

(CONTENTS CONFIDENTIAL)

On the first page was a list of names and both office and home telephone numbers, preceded by a single paragraph.

In the event of an accident or other serious incident involving a CA aircraft, the following persons are to be called in the order listed below.

Mr. Burton
Mr. Ashlock
Mr. Vaughn
Mr. Aroni

The list went on for two pages.

"God help me," the dispatcher said, and began dialing Barnwell Burton's office.

Barney was still in his office when Dispatch broke the news.

Aroni arrived within three minutes, his face ashen.

"Where's Andy?"

"He's on the phone trying to find out any details. He said he'll be in here as soon as he gets off."

Vaughn showed up a few minutes later but with little new to report.

"It's our Flight 28, a Viscount. Buffalo–Washington–Atlanta. There isn't much doubt it's crashed, but how bad this is, I don't know. Dennis Felton is the CAB investigator who'll be handling it, and I just got through talking to him. He says there's one eyewitness report so far that the plane was on fire when it came down. Barney, I'm afraid it's going to be a no-survivors mess."

"Shit," said Aroni. "Any wreckage spotted yet?"

"Not to my knowledge. Apparently it went down in some farm country. The only thing we know is that there was one whale of a thunderstorm in the area."

Aroni glanced at Barney but said nothing.

"As soon as they find the wreckage, I want to go out there," Barney said. "You'll both go with me, of course."

"We'll go," Vaughn said, "but there's no reason for you to be at any crash site. It's pretty rough stuff. You could do a lot more by staying right here. We'll have to set up some kind of command post at GO. The press will be all over us in another half-hour. There'll be statements to make and, with all due respect to Mike Ashlock, he's pretty young and with no experience at this sort of thing."

"None of us have had any experience at this sort of thing," Barney said with a grimace.

They talked in low tones until Dawn Sanderson poked her head into Barney's office. "Mr. Burton, there's a call for Mr. Vaughn on line two. Mr. Felton from the CAB."

"This may be it," Vaughn said, picking up the phone. "Andy Vaughn, Denny. Any news? . . . Oh, hell . . . Yeah . . . Right, Denny . . . I'd say in about an hour and a half, no more than two . . . I'm sorry, too, Denny. I'll see you out there. Thanks for calling." He replaced the receiver and faced the other two men. "They found the wreckage. On a farm near Chase, Maryland, about fifteen miles north of Baltimore. No survivors. Larry, I think we'd better be on our way. Poor Phil Haven. He was the captain."

"He married?" Barney asked.

"Yeah. I think his wife used to fly for American. Two kids—both under ten. Shit."

"Anyone called his wife yet?"

"I asked Bert Costin to go over to his house as soon as I knew it was 28. The pilots take care of their own."

"You can pass the word that if there's anything I can do for his family . . . the copilot's, too. Any family-notification problems there? I can't remember his name."

"Jimmy Pritsky. A bachelor. My office will be contacting his parents. Cathy Norris will do the same for the stews, Jane Cooper and Ruth Travers. Nice kids. What a lousy break."

"Well," Barney said, "you guys better get going. I guess you know what has to be done out there. Set up some kind of communications. I'll want to be hearing from you."

"I thought we'd take our radio-equipped station wagons," Vaughn said, putting on his rain slicker.

"You'll be too far away for us to pick up your signal," said Barney.

"We'll run two wagons out and leave one around the Baltimore area. The driver'll relay what we give him. So long, Barney."

After they left, Barney hung his jacket on a chair and unbuttoned his vest, then summoned Myler, Motts, Littlefield, Sloan, Campbell, and Ashlock to his office. Quietly, he outlined their duties for the long night ahead. "Don, you head for the terminal building. Have our agents page everyone waiting for Flight 28. Take 'em up to the Hawks' Lair. Before you go, call the gal on duty there and have her close the club up immediately. She'll probably get some static but it has to be done. I want those people to have some privacy. Jack, you and Cal get to work on the passenger manifest and, Mike, stay with them. You'll need the names for the press. Once you get the names, I'll leave it up to you as to how to get 'em out. There's a press room at the airport so you'd better set something up there. Call Blair over at the terminal. I think he's senior agent on duty. Have him make the arrangements with the airport manager. Any questions? Okay, let's get a move on."

The first contingent left and Barney turned to Sloan and Campbell. "I want one thing clearly understood: our first responsibility is to the families of the victims, including those of our own people. I want everyone handled with utmost courtesy. We're going to be vilified, accused, and threatened, but I'll discipline anyone—officer or employee—who violates that policy. Bill, I think there's a CAB rule which allows us to provide free transportation for the victims' families. Find out exactly what the regulation states and, if I'm correct, get with Myler and Cal Motts and start contacting the families. I want reservations made for them not only on our flights but at hotels either here or in Baltimore. Some of them may have to identify bodies. We'll pick up all hotel tabs. Rog, organize some kind of team to meet those people when they arrive. And I don't mean skycaps. If at all possible, use company officials, including yourself. Take along plenty of cash. I want every person arriving to be given fifty dollars for incidental expenses. Every one should be interviewed either by you personally or some other officer as to funeral arrangements, and shipping bodies if out-of-town burials are involved. Coastal pays for that expense, too. And Bill, I think you'd better call our law firm. I want them in my office at nine tomorrow morning to advise us on litigation, possible out-of-court settlements—which may be too much to hope for, because we're gonna have the hell sued out of us. Oh, Rog, you'd better contact our hull-insurance underwriters. That's it. Move."

Sloan and Coastal's law firm settled all but two lawsuits out of court. All of them would have been settled except that a New York Congressman delivered a speech on the floor of the House charging that the foreign-made Viscount was of inferior design and structurally weaker than American transport aircraft. The speech enabled the lawyers to convince the two undecided plaintiffs that their case had been made stronger. Barney's reaction was to call an immediate news conference, complete with television coverage.

"Inasmuch as Representative Othman has seen fit to libel the Viscount while hiding behind the skirts of Congressional immunity," he said with anger, "let me challenge him to repeat his charges away from that sanctuary. And the moment he does, Coastal will file a libel suit against the sonofabitch."

"Mr. Burton," a reporter asked, "what would be the amount of damages sought?"

"I had in mind at first to sue for a sum equivalent, in my estimate, to Mr. Othman's expertise—two cents. But my lawyers have convinced me we should ask for damages in line with the harm he has done this airline and the Viscount itself. Namely, five million dollars."

The "sonofabitch" was bleeped out of the television newscasts, and Congressman Othman dismissed Barney's libel threat as "grandstanding." He declined to appear with Barney jointly on a CBS talk show, much to the relief of Coastal's officers, who had a terrible time keeping Barney from going up to Capitol Hill for the express purpose of punching Othman in the mouth.

The same precautions were taken when the CAB hearings on the accident opened at the Southern Hotel in Baltimore fifty-four days after the crash. Barney sat innocuously at the table reserved for Coastal officials; he had promised attorney Tim Greene, who represented the airline, "I won't open my mouth."

Barney kept his promise, although he also kept passing notes to Greene and Bill Sloan suggesting questions to be asked. The hearings lasted only three days but for Barnwell Burton it was like reliving hell.

A great deal was known before the formal evidence was given. The traces of fire damage had been charted. The left side of the recovered fuselage sections were sooted while there was little fire residue found on the right-hand sections. Both wings were charred but the twisted cabin seats, except for one pair, showed no significant fire damage. Nor were there fire scars on the interior cabin walls. Tail surfaces and rudder had been completely free from soot —an indication that the tail section may have failed before any fire enveloped the plane.

Key structural members, such as the main wing spar, had been checked by metallurgical experts to determine whether any fractures involved metal fatigue, but the evidence was negative. In all structural areas were definite indications of failure stemming from a violent downward load. One of the Vickers engineers who had flown over to take part in the investigation remarked to Aroni, "It bears an uncanny resemblance to a Viscount that we deliberately destroyed in static testing when we applied excessive gust loads to vital structural components. There are marked similarities in the damage inflicted on the horizontal tail planes and wings."

The cabin seats had added fragmentary proof. They showed signs of having been subjected to severe loads downward and to the left. Every seat had been ripped from its floor track. The engines were found a considerable distance from the other wreckage, including the wings. Evidently the Darts had been torn from their nacelles. "Like hitting a brick wall," the Vickers man had muttered.

A lightning strike had been discounted, although two eyewitnesses had insisted they saw a bolt strike the plane. Their accounts had to be weighed against the notorious unreliability of most crash witnesses and the fact that the antistatic wicks had shown no sign of a static discharge.

As of the day the hearings opened, the CAB already was sure there had been no in-flight fire preceding midair disintegration, no fire in the pressurization and ventilating systems, no indication of defective materials, no mechanical malfunction, no structural fatigue, no sign of sabotage nor any other evidence of an explosion. The pattern of disintegration had been established: the horizontal tail planes failed first, pitching the Viscount forward so hard that the engines were torn loose from their mountings; the tail planes then severed, followed by complete failure of the right wing and subsequent buckling of the left wing, rupturing fuel tanks.

The testimony during the first seven hours pointed to the start of disintegration between 5,000 and 7,000 feet, although Flight 28 had been cruising at 14,000 feet only a minute or two before Approach Control at Washington National cleared it to start its descent. A few minutes before this clearance, there had been a sharp shift in wind direction, usually indicative of a turbulence-laden squall-line associated with severe thunderstorms.

Barney listened with morbid fascination to the testimony of a Northeast Airlines captain who had been flying just behind and slightly above Flight 28. He said he had swung somewhat farther away from the thunderheads than the Coastal Viscount. But Flight 28 did appear to be circumnavigating it.

"He was on the fringe," the captain recalled. "It was relatively clear—not as clear as where we were, and we were getting kicked around quite a bit."

The pilot was a handsome, stern-countenanced giant of a man and his very features made Barney remember the day Vaughn had shown him a picture of Phil Haven after the crash. Only there had been no face. Barney shuddered.

The next witness was a Weather Bureau expert named Leon James who resembled a pro football tackle more than he did a meteorologist. He cited several cases of vicious turbulence outside of primary thunderstorm cells.

"On the date of the accident," he testified, "our studies showed that a sharp, sudden rise in barometric pressure plus a drastic wind shift occurred in the area approximating that of Flight 28's path. These conditions pointed to extreme vertical turbulence whose severity could have existed some distance from the visible part of the storm."

The investigator stared at his notes as he spoke. "You say extreme vertical turbulence. How violent would you say it could get?"

"We measured one downdraft at one hundred fifty feet per second."

"And you'd say that could be defined as violent?"

"Enough to wreck virtually any plane ever built. I might also point out that our studies—which included examination of radar photographs—showed this extreme turbulence existed briefly at fourteen thousand feet near Chase at or about the time of the accident, and over an area of only two square miles."

"Are there any other questions?" the chairman inquired.

"I have one," Tim Greene said. "Mr. James, would it be accurate to describe such intensely concentrated turbulence as, well, let's use the word *freakish*?"

"Freakish? Well, sir, I don't know . . ."

"Freakish, Mr. James, in the sense that the violence was of such brief duration and concentrated in so small an area."

"It's not the picture of an average thunderstorm," James conceded. "It comes close to being an embryonic tornado, one that boils around at a high altitude and never touches the ground."

"Mr. James, the figures previously introduced by Vickers pointed out that a Viscount would require a downward force of one hundred feet per second to break off the horizontal tail planes. You said that one storm on record had gust forces of one hundred fifty feet per second. Would you say that the turbulence present on July twelfth would have approximated that strength?"

"Yes, sir, or close to it."

Greene looked at the hearing chairman. "I'd like to call the Board's attention once more to the previous testimony by the Vickers representative. He pointed out that a wind shear of the July twelfth velocity would not be structurally fatal by itself unless the aircraft was above maximum allowable cruise speed."

"I recall that," the chairman said. "I think what you're driving at, Mr. Greene, is that the Coastal Viscount must have been exceeding maximum cruise speed when it began to disintegrate."

"Yes, sir. And further, we know from the last communication Flight 28 transmitted to Approach Control that it had slowed to one hundred seventy knots because of turbulence. What I'm getting at, Mr. Chairman, is that a force of the magnitude required to destroy this aircraft had to have been caused by an abnormally rapid dive. It has been established that the horizontal tail planes failed first. Yet Vickers has informed us that such failure is impossible at safe cruising speed, for the tail plane structure is so designed that if it is exposed to excessive loads, the aircraft will stall before any structural failure can occur. The dive, therefore, had to have been inadvertent and resulting from forces beyond Captain Havens's control."

"An excellent point, Mr. Greene," said the chairman. "If there are no further witnesses, we'll stand adjourned."

As the hearing broke for lunch, Barney approached Tim Greene.

"I see what you're trying to do, Tim. You're getting us off the hook on possible negligence. You've been sketching an 'Act of God' situation."

"An apt phrase in this instance. The Good Lord must have goofed on this one. Phil Havens sure didn't."

"I won't argue the point," Barney murmured, "but I wish we hadn't helped the Almighty along. What's going to be the verdict?"

"My guess? Loss of control of the aircraft in extreme turbulence resulting in an involuntary dive that caused stresses beyond the plane's design limits. When Haven tried to pull out, the plane broke up. Nobody's fault."

Barney didn't wait for that report to be issued before he over-ruled Roger Campbell's impassioned objections and ordered al-most a million dollars' worth of airborne radar for the Viscount fleet and the four newer Constellations. Bill Sloan protested, too, when they confronted Barney in his office.

"In effect you're admitting some culpability in that Chase acci-dent," Sloan argued. "We got out of that mess with only two law-suits charging negligence. Wait 'til those two plaintiffs find out we're buying radar. Their lawyers will use it as a confession of guilt."

"If you and Tim Greene can't convince a jury that we're not admitting anything, you don't belong in the legal profession. There's no federal regulation requiring the airlines to install radar, so obviously we're guilty of nothing but prudence and a genuine concern for our passengers' safety."

"But Barney, in a liability lawsuit, an action like this would—"

"Drop it, Bill! I don't give a damn what those ambulance-chasing jerks jump on. One of these days the government'll make weather-warning radar mandatory and we'll be that far ahead of the game. I don't want any more accidents caused by thunderstorms we could have avoided. I don't want ever to have to look at a pilot's smashed face again, and I wish to God I had listened to Larry Aroni in the first place. Now you and Campbell get the hell out of here and take your legal whining someplace else!"

Campbell and Sloan slunk out of the office past Aroni, who was in the doorway, leaning against the jamb.

"Well, don't just stand there gloating."

Aroni smiled and sauntered in.

"You interested in a drink?" he said.

"I'm interested in what's on your mind," mumbled Barney as he shuffled through a stack of papers and withdrew one. He glanced around his cluttered desk. "Damn. Where are my glasses?"

"On top of your head," said Aroni, walking over to the window.

"Jesus, Larry, stop making me nervous and get to it. Speak. I've got a million things to do yet."

"Okay. Barnwell, there are three available jet transports—'available' meaning that airframe companies are taking orders. The Boeing 707 is way ahead of the others in production and testing."

"Yeah? Well."

Aroni stood with hands in his pockets, looking out at the runways. "You're gearing up to buy it. Correct?"

"Yes."

"Don't."

"Sit down."

"I'll stand."

Barney scratched his forehead. "Is this going to be one of those?"

"You were right, Barney. So don't do it."

"Are you speaking in tongues?"

"The 707, the DC-8, the Convair 880—they're all too big for us. You said it yourself that day we canceled the Comet order. You said it was our last chance. I didn't know what you meant then, but now I understand. You meant we'd never have another chance to jump up into the majors. We had missed and there wouldn't be anything or any way after that to catch the leaders. We would always be little. You were right. So don't do it."

"What?"

"Buy more planes that are too big for us, like the 707."

"And what are we supposed to fly our passengers in, trimotors?" Barney tossed the papers aside.

Aroni leaned against the bookcase.

"I've been talking to Jack Steiner at Boeing. There isn't a better engineer in the whole industry. Jack says they are seriously considering a scaled-down version of the 707, specifically aimed at airlines like us. They'd call it the 720. United's very interested and so are Western and American."

"How far away is it—1965?"

"The 707's due to enter scheduled service late in '58. Steiner figures the 720 would be available about ten months later."

"And you expect us to operate prop planes for a year while the opposition's flying jets? Not on your life, pal. Not while *I'm* running this airline."

"A year's delay won't kill us. United is waiting that long for the DC-8. American and TWA will be using 707's and they'll beat United's DC-7's over that period. But if Pat Patterson is gutsy enough to ride it out, then I think we could, too."

"Pat's airline is three times Coastal's size. Maybe he can afford the delay but we can't."

"The hell we can't. Boeing can't build 707's fast enough to hurt us that much over a year. That big bird is strictly a long-haul airplane, basically transcontinental. Everyone'll still be operating mostly props, particularly on route segments where they're competitive with us."

"Larry, you can bring up all these arguments at Friday's meeting. But I can tell you right now, they won't do you a bit of good."

A young woman appeared in the doorway. "Mr. Burton. There's a call from London on 254."

"London?" Barney snatched up the phone. "Hello."

"Hello darling."

"Janet."

Aroni fondled a tiny, perfectly detailed model of a Constellation that sat atop the narrow bookcase.

"Barney, all those presents—the pearls were absolutely beautiful."

"This call is the best present I ever got." He looked at Aroni, who took the hint and slipped out the door, closing it behind him.

"God, how I've missed you," Barney said softly.

"I know what you mean. Listen, this is frightfully expensive. I just wanted to tell you that I'll be in New York on the eleventh, TWA Flight 802. Darling, could you meet my flight?"

"I'll meet it in Newfoundland," Barney shouted. "Janet, is this a visit or . . .?"

"I have a one-way ticket," she said with a low laugh.

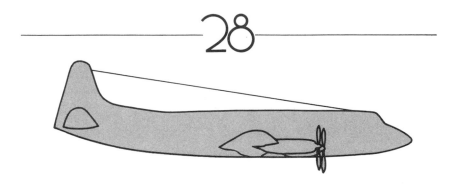

28

He found her an apartment close by, since she refused to move in with him at the Potomac house, and a month after her arrival she had secured enough of a bank loan to buy a small dress shop on Connecticut Avenue.

Their relationship was no secret around the airline, and she was quickly accepted among Barney's friends and business associates. Even Larry Aroni became extremely fond of Janet Leavelle, rationalizing his Catholic misgivings with the undisputable fact, as Aroni himself put it, that "they might as well be married."

Her presence did nothing to appease his insatiable thirst for work and his overpowering preoccupation with Coastal. Nor did she really expect it to be different nor even want it so. She had her own smaller world just as Barney had his big one; the dress shop, after a slow start, gradually built up to a clientele sufficient for her to not worry about the bank mortgage. She was a good business-woman.

She liked the airline people she met, was immensely proud of Barney, and was perfectly content to meet him in what became a kind of separate world—one they shared without ever wanting it to be their only existence.

She learned quickly to adjust to Barney's mercurial moods and the pressures of his job. She developed a sixth sense of knowing when he wanted comfort and sympathy, and when he wanted to be left alone, nor was she hurt when those occasions proved frequent. She did not really understand the airline business, but she was astute enough to realize that her arrival had coincided with a critical time not only in Coastal's life but the entire industry's.

The 1950's seemed a kind of Golden Age—the culmination of a piston-engine era that had progressed from the primitive Fords and Fokkers to four-engined giants cruising at 300 miles per hour. Nonstop transcontinental travel had finally become a reality with the development of the DC-7 and long-range Constellations, and an industry which in 1932 had bragged it was carrying 200,000 passengers a year was flying 20 million.

It was a comfortable, secure existence—almost a utopia. Flight equipment had reached a plateau of technological development, airline management had stabilized and matured, and air transportation as a whole had attained respectability. Yet Barnwell Burton was determined to have his fair share of it and more, and let the board members know it in no uncertain terms.

Aroni's was the only voice raised against the immediate ordering of four Boeing 707's. The board of directors authorized Barnwell Burton to seek new financing for the twenty-four-million-dollar contract—six million per plane. Actually Campbell had already arranged it on Barney's promise that director Warren Billings would be made vice-chairman of the board within the next two years. Barney was so excited about the prospects of flying jets that he failed to recognize Billings's growing influence on the airline. When Henry McKay quietly asked him if Billings wasn't getting a little too big for his britches, Barney just laughed.

"I'll cut him down to size if he starts throwing his weight around too much. Anyway, he won't give me any static as long as we keep making money. And Coastal is solidly in the black. Now I've got to run."

Barney waved to a lot attendant as he maneuvered the big new Cadillac past the booth and headed for home. It was a beautiful evening. And he felt himself changed. Life was more fun. Janet had brought it with her from England, he had decided, and he started enjoying himself. They entertained a lot: prominent people about Washington, football-team owners who used Coastal's charter services, fellow airline executives like Bob Six who told them stories about his flying days in China, Pat Patterson, C. R. Smith, Terry Drinkwater, C. E. Woolman. He felt himself their equal despite the difference in size between their carriers and his own. It was one of the reasons he loved the airline business; men who were the bitterest competitors were still friends, their mutual interest transcending the daily rivalry. It was quite wonderful, he was almost loathe to admit, and she had done it—brought him out somehow. At first he had suspected her interest in the airline business, but clearly it was genuine and she was such fun to explain everything to. And how they adored her. But tonight it would be her favorite coming for dinner, Don Littlefield. The three of them had become close friends, and again because of her. How did she do it?

The dinner she had prepared was exquisite, the wine superb.

"I don't understand," she said to Don Littlefield on her left. "Why did the flight manifest have an S-10 next to my name? What does it stand for, 'President's girl friend'?"

Littlefield laughed.

"Not exactly but you're close. S-10 is our code for VIP—Very Important Person. There are other codes, all for passengers who may require special handling. S-4 is a woman traveling with a small child. S-5 is a child under twelve traveling alone. Then there's S-6, a passenger who doesn't speak English. S-8 stands for passengers traveling on some emergency. Sometimes a name may have more than one code. Like S-1, 2, and 3—that's an elderly woman who requires a wheel chair that has to be raised to the aircraft door with a special fork lift. S-13 is a blind person, so the code S-1 and 13 would mean an elderly blind person. The one we also look out for is S-9."

"Why?" Janet asked, passing the salad.

"S-9 is a passenger who's been mishandled on a previous flight. The code alerts our cabin attendants to give an S-9 lots of extra loving care. The stews see all the coded manifests, of course, before departure."

He told her countless anecdotes involving Coastal personnel and those of other airlines—such as a conversation at the airport cafeteria where a group of pilots were discussing the unfortunate demise of a senior Coastal captain who had suffered a fatal heart attack shortly after taking off; the young copilot had taken over, returning the plane safely to National.

"One elderly captain was astonished that we had a first officer capable of flying a Viscount by himself. The remark carried to another table occupied by four very junior first officers. 'What I can't understand,' one of them shot back, 'is how the copilot knew the captain was dead.' "

Even Barney had to laugh.

"How many letters do you get a year?" she asked.

Littlefield thought for a moment. "Thousands. Perhaps fifteen thousand a year. Every month we tabulate them—how many complimentary and how many complaints. They help us to pinpoint areas of weakness. There isn't any doubt, for example, that by and large our stewardesses are Coastal's biggest asset and that snafu'd reservations represent the majority of the complaints. Baggage handling is another problem area, and so is flight information. Every now and then we run into an unreasonable passenger who can't be placated, but it also happens that a bad passenger often is a scared passenger. And fear can be just one factor in creating a bad-tempered customer. A man can come to the airport after a bad day at the office or fresh from a fight with his wife. We just can't expect to lock people up in a cylindrical chamber for several hours and have all of them behave normally."

Janet loved the inside view he was giving her, Barney thought. Once Littlefield had taken them into Coastal's lost-and-found room at National, where she was shamelessly curious about what passengers forgot. Barney was surprised and amused himself. There were 438 pairs of eyeglasses, 230 shaving kits, 47 cameras, 110 umbrellas, 38 pairs of false teeth, 2 portable radios, and 29 hardback books.

"It seems hard to believe," Barney had told Janet, "but apparently many passengers actually forget what they carried on the airplane. Once a five-foot steel girder turned up in my office. I was till trying to figure out who would be carrying a steel girder aboard an airliner when a guy showed up to claim it. He was a representative of some steel company and he was taking it to demonstrate to a customer. We've had to locate owners of boxing gloves, hoopskirts, and even a catalogue of crooked gambling devices."

It took Janet little time to form her own opinion of Coastal's management personnel, although admittedly her judgment was influenced by Barney's attitudes toward individuals. Her favorites were Aroni and Don Littlefield; she liked Myler and felt sorry for him, without knowing exactly why—perhaps she just sensed the insecurity mixed with lofty ambition. Motts she considered an abysmal bore, but refrained from imparting this verdict to anyone but Barney.

Don Littlefield was shaking his head when Barney resumed listening to their conversation.

"There's one big difference, Janet. If one of your customers gets mad and walks out without buying anything, you still have dresses on hand to sell. An airline seat is the most perishable product in the world. Once the flight leaves, it can never be sold. I'll grant there are rules for handling people in your business, just as any other, but I don't think any industry has to perform the high wire act we do. Maybe this will give you a better idea. Suppose you're working a Coastal counter and a passenger comes up."

"Yes?" She was intrigued.

"Okay. You've just told the passenger his flight will be delayed forty minutes because of a maintenance problem. As he turns away, you hear him say, 'I hope it isn't serious.' Now which of the following would you do? A, take care of the next person in line and ignore what he said. B, tell him 'It's nothing—they're just repairing number-three engine.' C, it's obvious he's worried so take the time to explain in detail what's wrong with the engine. Or D, assure him the mechanic will repair the airplane to the captain's satisfaction. Pick one."

"I haven't the foggiest," Janet confessed.

"The best response is D. It achieves reassurance and it also establishes the captain as a final expert—he's more impressive to a passenger than a mechanic. A is wrong because you've given him forty minutes in which to worry. B is wrong because most people don't know much about airplanes and you haven't really assured him the engine will be fixed properly. C is out because going into too much detail might confuse him and worry him that much more. These problems are part of the training we give employees who'll deal directly with the public."

"So an airline employee has to be a practicing psychologist." She made a face.

"Close to it. But that's what I love about this business—the constant challenge on virtually every level."

Barney smiled to himself. There was scarcely a facet of Coastal that did not intrigue her. She was like a movie fan who had been invited to watch the filming of a motion picture. She had learned the mysteries of scheduling—including the incredible intricacies of SC day, when the entire schedule underwent the mandatory seasonal revisions, since spring and fall were the major periods for Schedule Change, due to the beginning or end of Daylight Saving Time and the shift in weather conditions. Because prevailing westerly winds were stronger during the winter months, eastbound winter schedules could be five to ten minutes faster than the identical routes in the summer. For Coastal, SC from cold- to warm-weather operations occurred on the last Sunday in April, when Daylight Time went into effect over most of its system.

How had she managed to follow the complicated logistics? Virtually all the scheduling had the built-in hazard of a chain reaction —a fifteen-minute switch in a multistop Washington–Phoenix trip had to be scrapped because the seemingly minor change in Washington departure time would have caused severe gate congestion at Pittsburgh, ruined interline connections at Columbus, required doubling ground personnel and equipment at Wichita, and left insufficient time in Phoenix for aircraft servicing . . .

Barney realized they were talking about him.

"So you say he's decisive."

Don nodded. "Yes, and very fast."

"Impulsive?"

"Mmm. No, just quick."

"How can he decide such major things so quickly?"

Barney reached across to refill her wine glass. "Young lady, I learned after the first twenty years that I could make just as many mistakes quickly as I could slowly."

"Speaking of mistakes," said Littlefield, "I've stayed too late again. It's past midnight and Barney and I are due at the office early."

"Don't you dare apologize," she scolded. "I've had a wonderful time and I learned so much."

"Me too," said Barney. "How about some cognac?"

"No, no. I must go or I'll be useless tomorrow."

Barney saw Don Littlefield out while Janet busied herself clearing the table.

She met him as he came back from locking up, and they embraced.

"Such a nice boy," she said.

"Let's watch that, please," he murmured.

"Jealous?"

"Perhaps." He kissed her hair.

"Barnwell, I'm old enough to be his mother," she said, laughing.

"Which makes me old enough to be his grandfather."

She looked up at him, her arms around his waist. "Well, you poor old thing. Perhaps I should help you into bed and then see what I can do to help you pass the time."

"Janet?"

"Yes."

"I'm very glad you're here."

"So am I. So am I."

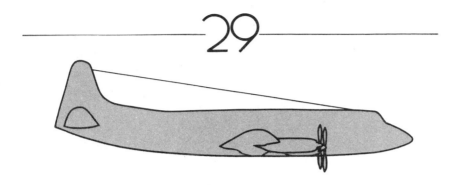

29

The year 1958 was pivotal. The Federal Aviation Agency was created—independent, powerful, and headed by a former Air Force general named Elwood R. "Pete" Quesada. For the first time, civil aviation had a tough, no-nonsense policeman who was arbitrary, abrasive, and totally dedicated. A Pan Am 707 inaugurated regularly scheduled jet service across the Atlantic—taking up where the ill-fated Comet had left off five years earlier. And the first modern reservations computer system went into operation—an electronic brain which kept a running inventory of available space and cut manual operations in half.

All of which seemed to inspire medieval reactions. It was freely predicted that jetliners would cause miscarriages among pregnant passengers, make more people airsick, give stewardesses varicose veins and more frequent menstrual problems, result in greater fatigue among pilots, lead to deafness on the part of ground crews, and create serious safety problems because the new planes would be flying higher and faster than ever before—at speeds and altitudes that amounted to a hostile environment.

The very size of the jetliners contributed to much of the concern. Too much airplane for man to handle, it was said. Too unforgiving of human error to be safe. Too complex for reliability. Too fast to fit into an Air Traffic Control system that had changed little since the days of the DC-3.

The airlines, including Coastal, were worried far more about their cost than their complexity. The price tag of $6 million for each aircraft and its parts, Myler happened to mention to Barney one day, was $2 million more than Coastal's *cumulative* profits during the first twenty years of its existence. Just the safety equipment on a 707 cost more than what the airline had paid for its first Constellation. Jack Myler, who was something of a statistics nut, read a few of the more outstanding figures at a staff meeting.

"The brakes on our 707," he recited from a recently published Boeing brochure, "will absorb enough energy to simultaneously stop 432 automobiles doing fifty miles an hour. It will have more than 1.2 million fastening devices, including a million rivets, 140,000 lock bolts and 60,000 structural bolts. There are 18,000 key structural parts and more than a half-million individual components in the 707, and the fuel load on a single flight would power the average family car for about twenty-five years."

"Very impressive," Barney said, "but I'm more interested in seat-mile costs, and they'd better be what Boeing is claiming."

"At cruising speed," Myler continued, "a passenger will travel more than a mile every time he inhales and exhales twice."

"That's just exciting as hell, Jack," Barney allowed. "Almost as thrilling as the prospect of putting one of those babies down at National, where the longest runway is only six thousand feet long."

"They won't be operating out of National," Sloan said. "Baltimore's developing its Friendship Airport to serve jets. Friendship is about twelve miles from downtown Baltimore; the CAB plans to list it as a Baltimore-Washington co-terminal."

"Twelve miles," Barney repeated. "And fifty miles from downtown Washington. Christ, a passenger will spend more time en route to Friendship than he would flying between here and Detroit."

"Not the ultimate in convenience," Sloan agreed, "but Washington will have its own jet facilities one of these days."

Jack Myler accompanied Barney and Janet around the airport, pointing out things of interest.

"Were you always headquartered here at National?" she asked as they strolled past the huge windows looking out onto the runway aprons.

"No," said Jack Myler, chuckling. "The line was founded in Binghamton then moved to Hoover Airport, then here to National."

"Hoover's long gone," Barney interjected. "The Pentagon sits there now."

"Yes," said Myler. "Swift obsolescence is an occupational hazard in this business."

"By the way, what's the status of the proposed second Washington Airport?" Barney asked.

"The site at Burke, Virginia, is out even though the government already has bought up about a thousand acres in that area. Ditto Andrews Air Force Base; the Pentagon is absolutely opposed to giving it up. Congress has just appropriated twelve and a half million for a second airport, but not one penny can be spent until Eisenhower decides on a new site. Which could very well be located near Chantilly, Virginia. That's about twenty-five miles from the White House, due west of National."

Barney frowned. "Assuming Ike picked a site tomorrow, when would we be able to use the new airport?"

"Summer of 1960, give or take a couple of months in either direction. It'll be a hundred-percent Federal operation, from original planning to actual operation, so maybe I'm being a bit optimistic."

"That's pure fantasy, not optimism. By the time those bureaucrats get through screwing everything up, we won't have that second airport before 1965. When and if the damned thing ever gets built, I think we should be prepared to move our general offices out there."

"Shut down our National facilities?" Myler asked in an incredulous tone.

"Not entirely. We'd still keep a big maintenance operation here. It's the general offices I'd want to move. The way I see it, by the mid-sixties jets will be flying at least seventy-five percent of our traffic. Propeller-driven airplanes are going to be as extinct as dodo birds. That won't eliminate airports like National because, sure as tomorrow's sunrise, Boeing and all the other airframe manufacturers will be building smaller jets with short takeoff and landing capability. National will still serve the short and medium-haul traffic. We'll probably run as many flights out of National as we do the second airport, but that doesn't mean we have to continue basing our nonflying facilities here. Air travel is going to boom and so will our payroll. There's no way to escape it. Every airline is going to need more supervisory and executive help. And I mean people with the status of assistant vice-president. We can't grow with the industry if there isn't enough space at National. Say, when am I scheduled to address the graduating stewardesses?"

"About twenty minutes," Myler said.

"May I come?" Janet asked.

Barney nodded. "Can't wait for our 707's," he said to Myler.

"I think I am much opposed to further capital expenditures," said Myler, "until we can judge the economic impact of jet operations. Those four 707's alone will involve interest payments in excess of one million dollars a year."

"So what? Those four 707's will be generating up to eighty thousand dollars a day in revenue, which adds up to . . . to . . . what the hell would eighty grand a day figure out to annually, Jack?"

"About twenty-five million," the statistically-minded Myler answered instantly.

"Thanks. Now I'll grant you my eighty-thousand estimate is predicated on high load factors. But in the jet we'll have the most productive machine in the history of transportation. A single 707 will do the work of two Connies. Once we get some operating experience, we ought to be able to bring our break-even load factor down to as low as fifty percent, maybe even forty or forty-five. That means we can start making real dough flying an airplane that's only half-full. So I don't want to hear any more of this about capital expenditures, from you, Rog, or anybody else. I'm fed up with these horse-and-buggy facilities we have at National. A major airline whose General Offices are on the second floor of a hangar, for Christ's sake! There's not only no room to move about, but no room to expand unless we expand right into the Potomac River. Jack, I want you to ride herd on that second airport. The minute you're certain where it's going, I want you to start negotiating with the government for some office space within the airport boundaries. I know it's too early for specifics, but I'm thinking in terms of putting up the dough for a new General Offices building on airport property, in exchange for something like a ninety-nine-year lease or longer for the land itself. In that one building we can put executive offices, training facilities, Reservations, Stores—the whole kit and caboodle. All we need at National is ramp space, our maintenance hangars and shops, and ticket facilities."

"What does something like that cost?" asked Janet. "Moving everything, I mean."

"Eighteen million would be my guess," said Myler.

"Dollars?" she asked with complete innocence.

Barney and Jack Myler couldn't help laughing.

Barney looked out at the smiling, expectant faces.

"Well, I suppose as the president of this airline you expect me to deliver the usual gung-ho stuff about how important your jobs are. How passengers judge an airline mostly by its cabin attendants. How you're the most direct link we have to the public and how the image you give a passenger is the image he has of the airline.

"But I'm not. I don't think I have to. If your training was worth anything, you already should know all that. I won't waste your time repeating it. What I would like to talk about is your profession —and that's exactly what it is: *a profession.* You're pros, every one of you. You're as much a part of aviation as the pilots you fly with, the planes that carry you, and the brass hats you've met in this room. You've been brainwashed these past few weeks, brainwashed into going out there and giving your all for dear old Coastal. Some of you started training when you didn't know a rudder from a girdle, and because you were mostly raw rookies and scared little greenhorns, we were pretty tough. We had to be. We had to make pros out of you in a hurry. And by doing that, I'm afraid we may have missed one very important lesson—pride in your own profession. Pride in your industry.

"I've been in the airline business since 1928, before most of you were born. I remember what it *used* to be like. When we could hire a brand-new copilot at ten o'clock in the morning and have him flying a trip by two in the afternoon. I remember when stewardess training consisted of three hours of instruction in the back room of a hangar and the training manual covered only four mimeographed pages. When a stew's first duty on an airplane was to keep passengers from opening a window and throwing out cigar butts. When stewardesses were hired for only one reason: because we figured the sight of a pretty young girl on an airplane was our only weapon against fear.

"I remember when the Ford trimotor was the queen of our fleet. When pilots had to carry forms authorizing the issuance of railroad tickets in case a flight was grounded or canceled, which was so frequent that the airlines were the railroads' best customers. When engines were so unreliable—and Larry Aroni, that guy over there who's our vice-president of Maintenance, will agree with me—when they were so unreliable, they were expected to malfunction in some way after twenty-five hours of operation. When pilots were paid by the weight of the mail they carried, and if a pilot had a mortgage due and was short of cash, he'd sneak a few bricks into the bottom of his mail sack. I remember when airline pilots stood a two hundred times greater chance of getting killed on the job than they have today.

"I remember when we had no such things as reversible props or de-icing equipment or ways to extinguish in-flight fires or even something as basic as wing flaps. When traffic was so light, the airlines ran their own air-traffic control system. When pilots weren't required to fly on instruments, which wasn't really necessary because nobody flew at night. When things were so tough financially, Coastal—along with a few other airlines—used to put advertisements on cabin walls like a streetcar, just for a few extra bucks.

"You are going to learn things about this business that we didn't teach you in class, because there wasn't time and because it's something that maybe you can't teach. You have to experience it. The comradeship. The practical jokes. The feeling of being part of something purposeful, efficient. Because all of us—president, pilot, stewardess, mechanic, agent—each one of us shares a common heritage, a single legacy—the struggle to gain respect for a form of transportation that was basically dangerous, inefficient, unreliable, uncomfortable . . . and courageous.

"There may come a time when any one of you may have to display courage, not because you're brave but because you're professionals. Like a stewardess named Mary Ruth Houghton. She was the only cabin attendant on a DC-4 that crashed on landing a couple of years ago. There were survivors. Those who did survive praised Mary Ruth for saving their lives. She got the main cabin door open, helped evacuate passengers . . . the passengers called her a heroine. But she never read all the editorials written in her praise. They found her body in what was left of the cabin.

"Now I don't give a damn whether this entire class sleeps with a different man every night, falls in love with married captains, and gets bombed three times a week. But I do care about how you do your job on a Coastal airplane, because that's how the public judges our airline. If what you do while off duty interferes with or harms your performance on a Coastal flight, you might as well get the hell out of this profession because you're not worthy of those wings.

"During your training you've had rule after rule pounded into your heads. Some of them may seem silly. But in a way, an airline is like the military—rules are really nothing but standards, to give the majority something to follow, to guide them.

"I'll give you one simple rule transcending all the ones we're burdening you with: don't dishonor those wings we're about to pin on. You can wear them in two places—on your uniform, or in your hearts. On behalf of Coastal's entire management, I congratulate you. I wish you luck and safe skies."

Everyone applauded except Janet, who was standing to the side, hands thrust into her raincoat pockets, studying him.

It was a clear, starlit night. The drapes were drawn back and they lay in each other's arms staring at the night sky.

"My, she sounds fascinating. Tell me more."

"Not much more to tell," said Barney. "She went down in the Pacific in July of 1937. There's been a lot of nonsense about it over the years. Stories about her having been executed by the Japanese for spying, but I think that's a lot of bull."

"Her having been a spy, you mean?"

"No, she and her co-pilot may well have been that in a way— skirting the Japanese bases on Truk that were forbidden to outsiders, whatever. But I think they went down for simpler reasons than that. You see, they didn't have a very good radio aboard. The civilian models weren't that good in those days and they weren't permitted a military set. The radio they had required a trailing wire antenna that was unwound when they were aloft. Well, it seems someone omitted it. Probably it was too much of a pain to reel in every time they landed. So when Amelia and her copilot reached Howland Island, the navy radios could receive them, but their plane couldn't pick up the ground transmissions and radio beacons being transmitted. It was really pretty awful, listening to them calling for help and directions as they flew around overhead somewhere until they ran out of gas."

Janet shook her head, rustling the pillow. "How awful."

"Yes. But she really had lived her life well. What a woman! Way before her time . . ." Barney chuckled to himself.

"What are you finding amusing?"

"Amelia's wedding." He rolled onto his back and pulled the blanket up over them.

"Who did she marry?"

"George Putnam, a New York publisher who had proposed to her a half a dozen times before she suddenly nodded yes one day while waiting for her plane to warm up. She was like that—casual, quick, instantly decisive. Just before the wedding ceremony—oh, she hated hats; turned up hatless and wearing a brown suit and lizard-skin shoes—anyway, just before they were married, she handed him a letter laying out her conditions. She said she was reluctant about marrying because she was so committed to flying. Also that she wouldn't hold him to any medieval vow of faithfulness and didn't expect him to think her bound by any such code."

"Really?"

"Yes. And this in 1930. No, 1931. Early in '31. Oh, and then she went on: 'Please let us not interfere with each other's work or play, nor let the world see private joys or disagreements. In this connection I may have to keep some place where I can go to be myself now and then, for I can't guarantee to endure at all times the confinements of even an attractive cage. I must . . .' How did it go? 'I must exact a cruel promise . . . that you will let me go in a year if we find no happiness together. I will try to do my best in every way.' "

They lay very still for a moment until Barney glanced over at Janet, thinking she might have slipped off.

"Awake?"

"Yes," she said very softly. "That was very beautiful, and very sensible. I'm sorry I never knew her."

"Yes, she was extraordinary. And how she loved flying and airplanes."

"What is it that's so appealing about planes? You were never a pilot but you're mad for them, too."

"They're magic. Each has its own personality. Some are male in their characteristics. Others female. There are happy planes, moody planes. Some even tragic, according to Larry. When one of them goes down it's very hard to accept. It's really like losing a person from your life; you know them that intimately."

"Even someone who's not a flier?"

"Yes. They're animate inanimate creatures. Lord, this sounds silly."

"No, I feel I understand. Charles felt the same way, I think."

"Janet?"

"Yes."

"Thank you for coming."

"You're welcome, Barney." She snuggled against his arm, her face just below his shoulder. "You're most welcome. How did everyone react to finally getting the Los Angeles route today."

"Oh, they all liked the idea of being a trans-continental airline, even with the mandatory Vegas stop. Lots of smiles today."

"And you?"

"Me?" Barney chuckled. "Aroni and I just sat there stunned when Jack announced it. We might as well have landed on Mars. It's fantastic, really. Finally. Finally."

FIVE

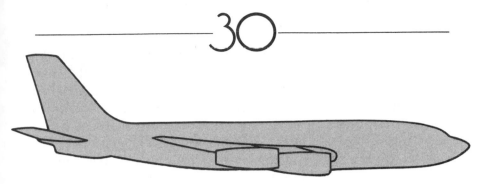

30

The clock on the wall read exactly 9:00 A.M. as the regular Monday morning staff meeting opened in the main conference room on the fourth floor of Trans-Coastal's headquarters at Dulles Airport.

There were the usual department heads: Myler, Motts, Littlefield (now a full-fledged vice-president of Advertising and Promotion, a newly established position), Aroni, Vaughn, Sloan, and Campbell. . . . Fourteen men. There were new titles held by new executives: Craig Cullenbine, assistant vice-president, Passenger Service; Ken Nash, an ex–Northwest employee, Director of Passenger Relations; and even a full-time medical director in the person of Luther Wilson, a barbed-tongued M.D. whom everyone loved despite the bedside manner of a drill instructor.

"First item of business," Barney announced, rapping on the table for quiet. "The performance record for last week." He sat with half-lidded eyes as Myler rose to deliver the operations report, accompanied by a slide projector which beamed charts and graphs onto a screen at the far end of the room.

"We had four delays of over forty-five minutes last week due to weather, with three cancellations, but only one delay of more than forty-five minutes because of a mechanical. The on-time performance of the Viscount fleet was 94.6 percent, that of the Constellations 91.4 percent, and the 707's 97.2 percent. Total mechanical delays last week amount to eighteen, four fewer than the previous week. All aircraft are in service except for Viscounts 359 and 366, which are undergoing number-two inspections but will be back in service by tomorrow. Viscount 349 will be in for a number-four inspection at midnight tonight and will return to the fleet by Wednesday morning. The weather outlook for the next twenty-four hours is favorable, the equipment outlook is adequate, and we should be able to meet all schedules—provided all present cross fingers, toes, and testicles."

"Thanks, Jack. Sully, I think you have a report on one of our outside maintenance contracts."

Fred Sullivan, Aroni's sharp new assistant, talked briefly about a private Viscount owned by a wealthy Washington woman; Coastal provided flight crews and maintenance. "We're flying her ship to Hot Springs next week. The revenue will be thirty-eight hundred dollars, which includes crew salaries. That's all—except while I've got the floor, Larry suggested I announce that modification of the 707 reading lights will begin next week; as you know, we've been getting passenger complaints."

Barney waved a piece of paper. "Jack Myler just handed me this report on air-traffic control delays for last month. I'll give you the gist of it in one sentence: we're using as much fuel on the ground and in holding patterns as we are flying between cities."

Roger Campbell sighed. "That's too bad, Barney, but it isn't our fault. ATC delays are a cost item over which we have no control."

"Exactly my point!" Barney barked. "Let's sue the bastards!"

Bill Sloan stared at him. "Sue who?"

"The FAA. According to Myler, those ATC delays have been costing us about six grand a month in wasted fuel. I want to file a suit for whatever amount those goddamned bureaucrats have cost us this winter."

"On what grounds? We can't sue them for breach of contract. We have no contract with the government for controlling traffic. The FAA supplies that service under a Congressional mandate, and it doesn't have to adhere to any minimum standards of performance."

"You're the lawyer. *You* find some grounds."

"Barney, I just got through telling you—we don't have grounds for a lawsuit. If we filed one, they'd laugh us out of court."

"Lawyers!" Barney spat. "You guys can find a hundred and fifty reasons for suing an airline but you can't find one simple logical excuse for taking legal action against the government. Okay, Roger, you got any ideas?"

"Send them a bill," he suggested, laughing. He was stunned when Barney's face brightened.

"Now *that's* one hell of a brainstorm, Rog! The delays have been particularly bad for the past month. Mail 'em a bill for six thousand dollars and we'll see what happens. Next."

Littlefield opened a folder. "Here is a list of the 'super-service' flights being offered by other carriers. American's 'Captain's Flagship,' Western's 'Champagne Flights,' United has 'Red Carpet Service' with predinner fruits and hors d'oeuvres and soft music piped into the cabin PA system. Delta's 'Royal Service Flights' with complimentary champagne, steaks cooked to order, cabin music, three stewardesses instead of two for faster meal service, and special baggage handling and identification. Northwest's gimmick— 'Imperial Service,' and TWA's pride and joy, the 'Jetstream Ambassador Flights,' featuring the most luxurious seat ever put into an airliner's first-class section—a two-thousand-dollar affair known as the 'Siesta Seat.' Padded like an expensive divan, it reclines almost full-length. Our 'Fiesta Flights' are and will remain competitive except in the area of visual entertainment."

"*Movies on an airplane?*" Barney scoffed. "You're out of your mind."

Littlefield forced a smile to appear. "Some outfit in New York is already experimenting with a lightweight projector built into the cabin ceiling. It would show films either on a large screen or on small TV sets located throughout the cabin."

"We'd be opening a Pandora's box," Barney said. "Half the passengers would eat up the movie and the other half would bitch because they wanted to read or sleep."

"I think it's possible," Littlefield said doggedly, "to fix up some kind of headset arrangement so the sound wouldn't carry throughout the airplane."

"And all of this," Barney pointed out, "would require one whale of a cash outlay: about thirty to fifty projectors, rewiring the aircraft, buying God knows how many thousands of headsets. Plus what it would cost to rent films. Let's not go overboard on entertainment. We're furnishing air transportation, not amusement. *Next!*"

Roger Campbell tossed him a page. "Figures on what ATC delays, rerouting, and noise-abatement rules are doing to our costs. Trans-Coastal is flying an average of twelve miles per route segment in excess of the minimum or direct airway mileage. It adds up to more than four thousand extra miles a day, or about a million and a half miles a year. It costs us a dollar and thirty-six cents per mile to operate a flight, so we're spending an unnecessary two million annually."

"Jesus. Bill, make a note of that. Maybe we should add that to the government's tab."

Aroni cleared his throat. "We've gotten estimates for installing a small galley for crew meals on the four Connies hauling cargo. The lowest quoted price was four thousand dollars per aircraft."

"Well, I guess we're stuck," Barney sighed.

"No, we're not. Sully just told me we could do the galley installations right in our own shop for three thousand bucks—and that's on all four planes. Some of these manufacturers and suppliers are screwing the hell out of us. We were charged a hundred and twenty dollars last week for a toilet seat on one of our 707's, and I saw the same thing in Sears for three bucks. We paid two hundred and seventy-eight dollars for an electric razor plug. My hardware store has an identical plug for eighteen cents. Last month, I asked one of our suppliers for an overhaul manual we could use to repair some air-conditioning unit. No manual was necessary, I was told, because the unit was so simple. I took the thing apart myself. It had a hundred and nineteen separate parts. Some of these bandits won't sell us individual component replacements; we have to buy the whole unit. So we're paying two hundred and thirty dollars for a small timing motor with one broken part worth not more than ten bucks."

"Turn it over to legal and hit them with a lawsuit for the two million dollars of airplane their lousy two-bit part is endangering.

Now, Jack, what about the Air Line Pilots Association demand that all Boeing 737's have to be operated by three-man crews, despite design?"

"Our pilots will buck ALPA policy but you've got to give something in return on our new contract."

Barney peered over the top of his glasses. "Such as what?"

"Better duty rigs, an extra week's vacation for every pilot with at least five years' seniority, an improved pension plan like the one United just gave its pilots, and on-duty time to include driving to and from the airport."

"Go to hell," Barney snapped. "I'll take the three-man crews. Next."

Cal Motts beamed. "We've got a new plane to christen next Wednesday—*The City of Binghamton*. Ray Dailey has made the advance arrangements. Flight 301 originates in Washington, flies nonstop to Binghamton, where the mayor's wife will break the traditional bottle of champagne over the 737's nose, and after brief appropriate remarks by His Honor, the jet will resume its regular schedule."

"Make sure it's a breakaway bottle," Barney warned. "Mohawk used to christen its planes after Indian tribes. They gave some politician's wife a real bottle that must have been made out of steel. Remember Larry? When she swung the damned thing it put a dent in the nose that cost four hundred bucks to fix."

He glanced down at the topmost sheet on the fat pile of papers in front of him. "I have a report here in front of me that it costs us nearly fourteen hundred bucks to repair two autopilot control panels because some careless sonsabitchin' pilots spilled coffee all over them. The units were out of service two months apiece. Fourteen hundred dollars wasted because a sixty-two-thousand-dollar-a-year airplane jockey hasn't got brains enough to hold a cup of coffee steady."

Larry Aroni read Vaughn's mind and broke in. "Andy's already done something about spillage, Barney. We need wider cup holders for the cockpit which we can make in our own shops. Meanwhile Andy is advising the stews never to pass any liquid over the center pedestal."

Barney just grunted, barely listening. "Three days ago we had a

720-B Phoenix nonstop with a full load that created an overweight problem. We had to offload ten passengers and half the cargo to make the flight legal. All because nobody thought of using an alternate flight plan that would have provided a higher cruising altitude at a lower Mach with reduced fuel requirements. The Phoenix flight drew a twenty-minute delay for the offloading; 603, which absorbed the ten passengers and most of the cargo, was delayed forty minutes."

Barney looked furious.

"Now listen, all of you. I've been going over these flight-delay reports. Most of them never should have happened. Here's one—" Barney picked up a piece of paper and read from it in a tone that mixed sarcasm with utter disbelief. "A first officer failed to sign in for a flight and neither Crew Schedule, Dispatch, nor the captain noticed it until two minutes before departure. Total delay: forty-four minutes. Here's another. A captain discovered the autopilot was placarded inoperative—probably the same one he spilled coffee on—so he requested more fuel enabling him to operate at a lower altitude. The additional fuel loading caused a twenty-three minute delay. Now placarded information isn't exactly a secret around this airline, is it? That additional fuel should have been planned well in advance. One more example of why we're losing customers. Now, the only man in this room who can't be fired is yours truly, so I suggest you all do some tightening up around here and get this airline back to profitability. Next."

Vaughn and Aroni returned to their offices together after the meeting. Vaughn was still shaken.

"Christ, by the time the Old Man got through with me I felt like he had shoved a proctoscope up my butt."

"You're not alone," Aroni said. "Last week it was Littlefield, the week before, Sloan. Next week it'll be somebody else's turn—probably mine."

"What bothers me the most," Vaughn sighed, "is that I deserved it. My department seems to get sloppier every day. I'm raising hell with my people, louder than the Old Man does with me, but it doesn't seem to do much good."

"It's morale," Aroni said thoughtfully. "Not enough people seem to give a damn. But part of it's Barney's own fault. He's giving us invective, not leadership. The airline's going downhill, Andy. You can scream at people just so long, and Barney doesn't seem to be doing anything but screaming. He orders enough airplanes to give us a severe case of overcapacity and then spends all his time yelling that we aren't filling up the seats."

Vaughn nodded. "He makes me wonder sometimes. A couple of months ago I showed him a plan where we could save about five million dollars a year by reducing cruise speeds. He said it would ruin our on-time performance and that delays were one of the chief reasons for poor passenger attitudes."

Aroni whistled. "Five million bucks? Did you ever take it up with Myler? A touch of more realistic scheduling would be in order."

The vice-president of Operations grimaced. "Yeah, I mentioned it to Jack. He asked if I had said anything to Barney. When I said I had, and that the Old Man didn't seem very enthused, Myler said his hands were tied."

Aroni laughed mirthlessly. "Old play-it-safe Myler. He'd rather go down with the ship than tell the captain it's sinking. Well, keep plugging away, Andy. It's like Barnwell said—he's the only one who can't be fired. One thing about him, he doesn't hold a grudge, or we'd have to install revolving doors in here."

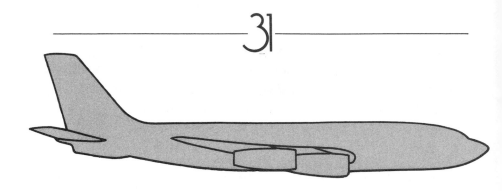

31

He was reading the Annual Report, consisting largely of Don Little-field's efforts to make past financial reverses indicate future pros-perity. Gloria Wingate, his new secretary, buzzed him.

"Someone named Vickie Doman would like to talk to you, Mr. Burton." She knew damned well who Vickie Doman was—or had been—but had phrased it in a way to elicit the maximum surprise from him and the most interesting unguarded reaction. She was disappointed.

"I'll talk to her," Barney said quietly. He wasn't about to give her the satisfaction of knowing he was shaken. Instinctively, his first thought was to wonder how he could get out of taking Janet to dinner that night as planned—and that in itself not only surprised but shocked him. The very mention of Vickie's name had been enough to loose a flash of memories, guilt, the affection he had always felt toward her. He picked up the receiver casually.

"Vickie, it's good to hear from you. How are you? And where are you?"

"In Washington. At the Mayflower. My husband had some busi-ness here and I tagged along. My name is Blake now, Barney."

She might as well have shouted that one word. *Husband*. Well, she just closed the book, Barney thought. He did not know whether to feel sad or relieved, and decided it was both. He could admit to himself that for a moment, he was taken aback, and yet when she had said it, he had felt an instant wave of relief.

"How about lunch, Vick? Like to meet your husband, if that's possible." Which was a lie; he was curious about him, but he didn't really want to meet him. The bastard might be a lot younger, handsomer, probably more considerate. "I can send a car for you. There's a nice restaurant out at Dulles close to the GO."

"Too busy to come downtown?" She was teasing, but he imagined her voice had a ring of annoyance.

"Well, I suppose I could meet you at the Mayflower. I've got a meeting with some people from Boeing at two but I'll—"

"I was just kidding. I know your time is valuable and I don't have anything else to do. I'll grab a cab and come right to your office."

"The hell you will. I'll send a company car for you. Let's see, the driver will be in front of the Mayflower at eleven-thirty. That convenient?"

"Great. I . . . I'm anxious to see you. Lots to tell you."

"Yeah. Mutual. Think your, ah, husband, can join us?"

"He already has lunch plans. You'll have me all to yourself."

The restaurant at Dulles was no gourmet's delight, but it was quiet and neither had much interest in the food. Vickie looked good—somewhat plump, but pretty as ever. She refrained from telling him he had aged more than she had expected. From the first cocktail to the last sip of coffee, they talked, nervously at first, with the embarrassed uneasiness of people turned into strangers by the passing of time. He asked her about her marriage and scolded himself when her enthusiasm disturbed him.

"Well, he's the same man I was engaged to before we got married. I was visiting some friends in Houston—his ranch isn't far from there—and one day I just called him to say hello. It turned out he was divorced, too, so we met for dinner. And I guess things went on from there. We have a little girl, Barney—Jennifer. A very small replica of Vickie Doman, I'm afraid."

"I suppose that's what you wanted," Barney murmured. "And if you're happy about the whole thing, then I'm happy for you."

"How about you, Barney? If you tell me you've remarried, I'd not only be surprised but very, very curious about your wife."

"You'll have to curb your curiosity, I'm afraid. No, I wouldn't put any woman through that. I do have a very special friend—so special I think too much of her to inflict matrimony on her. I haven't changed, Vick. She's a wonderful gal, though, and in my own selfish way, I suppose I love her. But . . ." He left the sentence dangling.

"No, you haven't changed," she said, sitting back to take a good look at her former husband. "Airplanes," she smiled. "You once told me airplanes were living creatures. Now you've breathed life into a whole company."

"Which is what an airline is—a collection of airplanes."

"And people."

He nodded. "And people. My collective family—the one I couldn't give you because I already had all the family I wanted or needed."

"I'm a little disappointed, Barney. I was hoping you had found someone by now. Someone with whom you could share your problems and triumphs."

"Vickie, if I couldn't share them with you, I couldn't with anyone. But for God's sake, don't feel sorry for me. I'm happy the way things are. And I'm glad you're happy. You deserve it."

"You don't really seem happy, Barney. You look worried. And tired. Even discouraged."

"Well, things have been a bit rough. But I'll make out."

"I've tried to keep up with you and Coastal, or rather Trans-Coastal. Oh, and congratulations on the Washington–Los Angeles route. I even made Jim—that's my husband—I even made him buy stock. It's not doing very well."

He grinned. "Tell him to hang onto it. We'll come back."

She looked straight at him. "Suppose you don't? Jim is pretty savvy about investments. He doesn't think much of Trans-Coastal as a company with a future."

"You tell him to stick to his cows or whatever the hell he raises on that ranch, and I'll take care of my airline."

"That's my old Barnwell," Vickie said. "Tell me about your lady friend."

They talked almost until two, when Barney remembered the time.

"I've got to get back, Vick. The car will drop me off at GO and then take you to your hotel. I've enjoyed this, I sincerely mean it. And I wish you luck."

She leaned over and kissed him gently. "Barney, do me one last favor."

"Sure. Anything."

"If things really get bad, try sharing your troubles with someone like Janet. Even if it means sharing your life with her."

"No way. Not if you mean marriage. One unhappy man plus one unhappy woman adds up to a couple of unhappy people. You should know that."

"There was a slight difference," she reminded him. "In our marriage, only one of us was unhappy. Me. You'd better get back to work, Barney."

He kissed her good-bye chastely in front of the GO and watched the station wagon carry her away, for some reason remembering the way she had looked, galloping along through the Potomac woods.

He could not be that cavalier about criticism of his massive equipment acquisitions. Publicly he either ignored it or snarled back, but he could admit to himself that he had overextended the airline in jet purchases. His trouble was that he had counted on steadily growing traffic to compensate for the steadily mushrooming costs of operating an airline carrier. And for a while, at least, he believed he could get away with his buying sprees.

Traffic had boomed in the mid-sixties, to such an extent that Trans-Coastal expanded from a relatively small electronic reservations setup to a fully-computerized IBM system that cost nearly $10 million. It could obtain instant data on 7.8 million flights throughout the world, providing space availability in a matter of seconds, whether on Trans-Coastal or a foreign carrier six thousand miles from Washington. It could quote fares, up-to-date departure times, meal availability, and type of equipment. It could store complete data on all of Trans-Coastal's 217 daily flights for the ensuing twelve months, order special meals, supply agents with passengers' home and business phones, and record tickets bought with credit cards, print tickets on the spot, and keep maintenance records.

Barney had resisted ordering the enormously expensive system until competitive pressures forced him into the move, but once it was installed and working, he suddenly decided that Trans-Coastal should stop catering to travel agents. A smooth working relationship with the travel-agency industry was one of Don Littlefield's top priorities, and he kept on pressing Barney for permission to take a group of travel agents on a special 727 flight to New Orleans. Barney refused, finally shouting: "We can't afford pandering to those bastards! We're already paying 'em fat commissions on every ticket sold," he announced with unexpected petulance. "Why should we give 'em a free junket?"

"Barney, you've got to be kidding! More than fifty percent of the tickets we issue go through travel agents."

"That's exactly my point. Look at the revenue we're losing. We should be getting that dough, not those agents. We can sell air transportation better than they can, anyway. You just sit yourself down one of these days, young man, and add up the amount of money we're throwing away with that five or six percent commission. In less than a year we could have paid for the whole damned IBM system with enough left over to buy another 737."

It dawned on Littlefield that Barney was more peeved—or maybe worried—about the cost of the IBM installation than the travel agencies' commissions. But that didn't alter the shortsightedness of his stand.

"Barney, fifty percent of today's traffic is for vacation and recreation. The air trip is just part of their planning. A travel agent helps in many ways no airline is really equipped to do. Believe me, we need those agencies as much as they need us."

"A necessary evil, is what you're saying," Barney insisted. "Well, if we have to keep doing business with those leeches, fine. But I'm not gonna furnish them with one of my airplanes free. Let 'em pay full fare same as everyone else. They can afford it with what we're paying for their alleged services."

"So you won't let me set up that New Orleans promotional tour?"

"No, I won't. Do you want it in writing?"

"It won't be necessary," Littlefield grated. "I'll tell you one thing, though. If we alienate the travel agents, it'll show up in our traffic volume, and you can pat yourself on the back for letting it happen."

"If our traffic drops just because I won't cater to agents, you'd damned well better start patting yourself on the back. Where's all your ingenuity? Your sense of promotion? Your gut feeling for pushing our product? There's absolutely no reason why your department can't do a better job than any travel agency. So why don't you start helping people plan vacations, arranging hotel space—all the stuff a travel agent's supposed to do?"

Littlefield barely kept his temper. "That's a great idea, Barney. Will you increase my budget by about forty percent so I can hire the manpower we'd need for turning this airline into one big travel agency?"

"I won't increase your budget by one penny. You do the best with what you've got. Heck, it doesn't have to be on a large scale, not at first. Tell your people to offer a little help when they confirm space on one of our flights. 'Can we make a hotel reservation for you?' or something like that. It may mean a little extra work but our res agents are making enough, so they owe us some extra effort. I'm not being unreasonable about this, Don. I'm perfectly willing to let the agencies have a fair share of our business, but not at our expense. Not when we can provide the same service to the public and keep the commissions ourselves. Now, I ask you, is that unreasonable?"

"Yes."

Within four months, Trans-Coastal tickets sold by travel agents dipped from fifty-four percent of total volume to just under twelve percent; word got around quickly of the deliberate effort to reduce the agency commissions. By the time Littlefield convinced Barney that the results were disastrous, the goodwill with the travel industry had crumbled. Don even went to Cal Motts for help, realizing that rapport with travel agents had been one of Calvin's few virtues.

"Barney's wrong," Motts admitted, "but I can't help you change his mind. I've known him longer than you have."

"You can try, dammit," Littlefield pressed.

"I'm sorry, but the answer's no."

"Why?"

"My new title is Assistant-to-the-President. I've been shelved. You're running the marketing department. And I'm not going to do one blessed thing that might endanger my status here. I'm pulling down fifty-five grand a year for doing virtually nothing, and frankly I'm enjoying every minute of it."

Barney paced back and forth across Don Littlefield's office.

Inflationary pressures were taking their toll on the entire industry, and the old anti-inflation formula—boosting productivity by means of larger, faster aircraft—was no longer adequate. Fuel, landing fees, and labor demands all added up to steadily mounting costs.

Slumped on his couch, Littlefield read from the Annual Report: " 'In the past, increased productivity has resulted in lower seat-mile costs—in simplest terms, what it costs Trans-Coastal to move one passenger one mile. Your Company achieved impressive gains in productivity, sufficient to produce a fifteen percent boost in revenues over 1967. Unfortunately, that increase was more than offset by a corresponding twenty-one percent hike in expenses.' Jesus." Littlefield threw the report aside. "Rough."

Revenues which might have been adequate had suffered dilution under the CAB's plethora of special fares designed to attract more people into using airplanes. They achieved that purpose to some extent, but not enough to make up for overall revenue losses created by the lower rates. The fare structure itself had grown so complex that only a computer could figure it out.

Barney halted. "Do you realize that right now there are nineteen different tariffs just between New York and Washington? This situation has gone from the ridiculous to the asinine, and you can thank those do-gooder bureaucrats at the CAB for the mess we're in. The *youth* fare, my Aunt Fanny! It's a Frankenstein fare, an industry-created monster which has run amuck. It's gotten completely out of hand. Completely."

Don Littlefield undid his collar button and tie. "I'll admit it has created problems, but basically its purpose is being achieved—filling seats that otherwise would be unoccupied, and introducing air travel to youngsters who otherwise might not have flown, except for that fifty-percent standby discount."

Barney paused and held a hand across his eyes in a pained expression. "The type of brat taking advantage of that discount doesn't belong on an airplane. Look at the cheating that's going on. A bunch of kids making phony reservations under assumed names to block out space, then show up as standbys for a flight they know isn't full. Our stews are complaining that teen-agers are demanding to be served liquor and raising hell when they're refused. One of our flights had to make an unscheduled landing the other day so the captain could bounce some snotnose off the plane after he refused to fasten his seat belt. And when he was removed, the other passengers applauded. I got a letter from a good customer of ours suggesting that regular passengers get a fifty percent discount for having to fly with those hippies. Then I get letters from parents swearing they'll never fly Trans-Coastal again because we bumped junior off a flight to make room for a full-fare passenger boarding at an intermediate stop. One of our ticket agents last week refused to let two kids board because they were obviously already flying on their own. I've had it!"

"It's possible to retain the Youth Fare without all the problems," Littlefield persisted. "Other carriers are proposing changes. Delta, for example, wants to reduce the discount to thirty percent and provide positive space, which might not be—"

"The whole thing's unworkable," Barney stormed on, unheeding. "American never would have proposed the Youth Fare if C. R. was still running that airline. That's the trouble with this whole bloody industry—it's being run by a bunch of lawyers and accountants and professors."

"Barney—"

"I'm ordering the special fare discontinued on all Trans-Coastal flights."

"You're going off half-cocked," said Littlefield. "There has to be a better way to solve the problem than throwing away sixty to seventy percent of our business in college towns." He rubbed his chin. "It seems to me the real problem is the 'no-show' problem. What are we faced with? One out of ten passengers simply fails to show up for his flight. That's what is killing us. We had one flight last week take off for Vegas with forty-nine empty seats, and the computer had the flight booked solid."

"You're right," Barney said quietly and sat against the corner of Littlefield's desk. "I suppose in the case of that flight you mentioned, the computer could have been wrong—erroneous data, maybe."

"No, I don't think it's the computer. It's our ever-lovin' public. They'll book space on two or three flights, take the one that's most convenient to catch, and leave us trying to fill empty seats with last-minute fannies. It's too bad the computer can't read some minds when . . . wait a minute!" Littlefield stopped, his eyes bright. "Why couldn't we get that electronic monster of ours to forecast no-shows?"

"You just said why. It can't read somebody's mind."

"That's not what I mean. Suppose we fed into our computers the percentages of no-shows on every flight we've operated over the past two or three years. We break the data down not only by flight number but by days, weeks, months—any factor that might have played a role in establishing the percentages. Over a long period of time, we'd not only be able to establish a percentage pattern for individual flights, but we'd actually be able to *overbook* space to compensate for the no-shows."

Barney stood in the middle of Littlefield's office, his hands resting on his hips. "Suppose the computer can't establish any pattern? Theoretically you could have fifty no-shows on 501 to Phoenix one Friday and only two no-shows the following Friday."

"There has to be a pattern," Littlefield insisted, shaking a handful of print-outs at him. "We already have a fairly steady percentage. We know from just this past year that ten to fifteen percent of our passengers won't take flights even though they hold reserved seats. What if we included the variables—travel patterns by day of the week, time of day, night, flight routing, type of equipment, even weather conditions? Look, you might have ten no-shows on a flight because of icy roads or a highway accident that tied up traffic and prevented at least some of those ten from getting to the airport on time. If the computer doesn't take *all* factors into consideration, you could wind up with a prediction that's way too high and, boy, then you've got troubles as bad as the no-show problem itself."

"Yeah," Barney agreed. "Okay, get started as soon as possible, work with the IBM people. I hate to stick you with a chore this big, but it's damned important."

In less than a month, Littlefield reported back that Trans-Coastal's no-shows would average about thirty percent per flight, meaning that on a one-hundred-passenger plane, the airline could confirm one hundred and thirty seats without worrying about over-selling.

"Jesus, that high?" exclaimed Barney. "I figured around fifteen percent."

"Thirty is the average," said Littlefield pointing to the figures on his chart. "The computer will actually tell our reservations agents the exact number of seats that can be sold. The ACP could run as low as one or two percent and as high as fifty or sixty percent— around Christmas time, for example, when so many people book space on more than one flight for protection. We're ready to put ACP into affect as soon as you give us the go-ahead."

"You got it."

"One more thing, Barney. Every airline's going in for some kind of space planning. But for the time being, I guess I don't have to tell you it's nothing we want to brag about. What this amounts to is very educated guessing. There will be times when we overbook a flight by thirty customers and all thirty of 'em will show up de-manding that we honor their confirmed reservations. Eventually, we'll have to admit we're overbooking deliberately, and also even-tually the CAB will require us to compensate a confirmed passen-ger who's been denied boarding. I'd suggest the fairest thing we can do is try our best to provide bumped passengers with alternate transportation on the next available flight. It'll cost us a few meal vouchers and maybe a hotel room now and then, but if we can lick this no-show headache, it'll be worth it."

"Amen," Barney said. "And thanks, Don."

Littlefield was surprised and caught off balance. "Don't mention it," he said and turned to leave.

"Ah . . . I . . . you might also look further into that business of movies on board our planes." Barney said this without looking up from the papers he was perusing.

Don Littlefield smiled at the ruse. "Right, Barney."

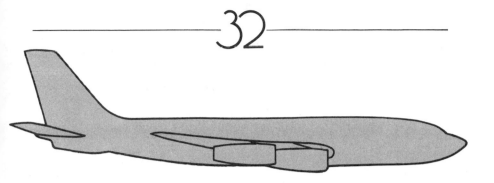

32

Barney watched the little Learjet taxi onto the apron. The engines whined down as the pilot cut the throttle. Almost immediately the cabin door folded down, forming steps for the passengers. After the flight attendant came Henry McKay, gingerly negotiating the few steps to the tarmac.

Barney stepped out of the maintenance shed into the sunlight, waving.

"Henry!"

McKay waved in return as he walked away from the plane, and the two old friends embraced halfway.

"Henry. I can hardly believe it. God, it's good to see you."

"You're not looking so bad, yourself, Barnwell."

"Come on," said Barney, leading McKay back toward the Trans-Coastal shed, his arm across Henry McKay's slight shoulders.

"Quite a little plane you've got there," said McKay. "Thank you for sending it up. I can't remember when I've been so royally transported."

"Glad you like it. Bought it last year for business trips. A spartan little ship. What's a mere nine-hundred-thousand-dollar airplane when you consider it's carrying the likes of Henry McKay?"

"Listen, you old goat. It's bad enough getting old without *your* patronizing me!"

"Hell, I'm younger than you are, Henry. What are you complaining about?"

"Stop reminding me," McKay mumbled. "Where's Janet? I need someone sensible to talk to who isn't senile."

Barney laughed. "She's back at the house getting things ready for the bash."

"Lots of people coming, I suppose," McKay grumbled in a complaining voice.

"Well, it isn't every day that I turn sixty-five, Henry."

The caterers were scurrying through the vast apartment in preparation for the evening's festivities when Henry McKay and Barney arrived. After an effusive greeting, Janet shunted them both into the study to keep them from getting underfoot.

"Drink?" asked Barney, opening the large liquor cabinet behind the bar.

"Only if you've got some milk, my boy." Henry held his side. "I've finally discovered something worse than my wife's cooking."

"What?"

"Ulcers," McKay mumbled.

Barney poured a glass of milk and brought it to him. McKay accepted it with a nod, then stopped to stare at Barney.

"Where are your glasses?" he asked. "I just noticed you're not wearing them."

"Contact lenses," said Barney, smiling proudly. "The latest in eyewear."

"Spare me," McKay waved aside the innovation. "So what's been happening? When are you going to retire? Settle down? Not work so much? And enjoy yourself? *Salut.*" McKay knocked back the milk.

"Me retire? You must be kidding." Barney eased himself into an armchair.

"Sorry to hear that." McKay suddenly looked serious.

"Why?"

"I sense trouble, that's why. That Billings character you made vice-chairman. The lousy state of affairs in the industry—Ah, what's the use. You're not going to do anything you don't intend to do. What will happen will happen."

"I know business is off. It's off for everyone. But I've had no trouble with the board."

"Also alarming," said McKay. "You've had it *too* easy with the board. Makes me nervous. Why isn't there more opposition? Don't like it."

Barney sipped his scotch. "You worry too much."

"Maybe."

The party was a roaring success, with most of Trans-Coastal passing through, it seemed. At midnight the huge birthday cake was brought out, carried overhead through the crush. It was in the shape of a Ford trimotor, with red frosting and the original red hawk insignia on its tail, and candles lining either side like runway lights.

"God," said Barney in a loud stage voice. "A masterpiece." He glanced at Henry McKay. "Remember when we had to use smudge pots to land 'em at night?"

It wasn't until 2:00 A.M. that the last guests were preparing to leave, all except Larry Aroni, Cal Motts, and Henry, who were pounding the baby grand in the living room and singing old favorites at the top of their lungs.

"Let's go," Janet whispered, and impulsively pulled Barney out of the house as the last couple drove off.

"Where are you dragging me?" Barney chuckled.

"For a ride. Air," she said, without even looking back at the large man she had in tow. When they reached the car porch she got in the Cadillac on the driver's side, Barney lurching into the passenger seat, a champagne glass still in his hand. And away they went, north on Connecticut Avenue and finally into the Maryland countryside.

Barney finished the champagne and put the glass in the glove compartment.

"What a party," he said, and slid down in his seat, enjoying the effervescence of the champagne in his system.

"Yes. A great sendoff."

"Sendoff?"

"Yes. Tribute. Farewell."

"You talk like it's going to be the last," said Barney.

"Your last as president of the line, yes." Janet glanced at him, then back to the road. "I think you should bow out."

"You do?"

"Yes. And so does Henry."

"I can't do that, Janet." Barney was suddenly sober.

"I didn't think you would," she said thoughtfully and eased the car off the road and into a small clearing cut out of the tree-lined parkway, and stopped.

"Now what?" said Barney.

"Now you kiss me, you great brute," she said and smiled as Barney slid over and took her in his arms.

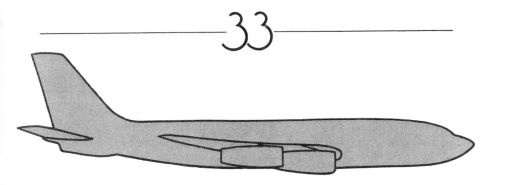

33

"That doesn't sound too bad," Campbell remarked. Barney looked pleasantly surprised and Aroni threw the vice-president of Finance a suspicious glance.

"Well," the president said with a grateful nod at Campbell, "if the chief guardian of our checking account approves, that would seem to settle it. I certainly trust Roger's, uh, conservative judgment. Wouldn't you say so, Andy?"

Vaughn looked sick. Larry Aroni turned red.

"I'd have to question Roger's judgment as being more foolhardy than conservative," Aroni said. "I'd like to ask him—and you, too—I'd like to ask if either of you have considered the cost of supporting ground equipment for these 747's. Such as the hundred-twenty-grand price tag on the only tractor capable of pulling a seven-hundred-ten-thousand-pound airplane. Or the twenty-eight hundred dollars an hour it'll cost to operate that flying hotel lobby. Or the fact that we're paying what amounts to seventy-five thousand for every seat in the 747 compared to the five thousand per seat in the DC-3. Andy seems to be too shell-shocked to oppose this brainstorm, and I can't say that I blame him. Who the hell thought it up?"

"*I* thought it up," Barney said defiantly, "and I suggest you let Andy speak for himself."

Vaughn hesitated, unwilling to leave Aroni alone at the pass, but hopelessly befuddled by Campbell's unexpected support of the 747 proposal. "I'd have to class it as a luxury at the present time," he said after a painful pause, "but if Roger says we can afford it . . ." He shrugged his shoulders in wordless surrender.

"Then that settles it," Barney said, "unless anyone else has some objections."

Nobody did. Later, Vaughn apologized privately to Aroni. "I was ready to tell the Old Man he was nuts, but when Campbell backed him up, I damned near fell out of my chair. Larry, I felt I just couldn't fight both of 'em."

"It's not the decision that bugs me," Aroni muttered, "as much as Roger Campbell's motive for going along with the Old Man. I swear to you, Andy, it's as if he were deliberately giving Barney some rope. Hanging rope."

Barney called a special directors' meeting and asked them to waive the executive retirement rule "for five more years so we can continue this dramatic comeback under leadership that has the advantage of experienced continuity."

"At the end of those five years," he continued, "I think I can turn the destiny of this airline over to a successor whom I can sincerely recommend to you as a man sharing my philosophies, policies, and deep belief in loyalty as not merely a virtue but a noble attribute. The final choice, of course, will be up to you, but I have every hope you will take into consideration my personal wishes in so vital a matter."

"I think you owe us the favor of revealing his name," Warren Billings said.

"I haven't reached a definite conclusion as of now," Barney said, smiling. "I will say, however, I believe there is enough executive talent in Trans-Coastal so that we will not have to go outside the company to find our next president."

Henry McKay chuckled. "Barney, why don't you stop acting coy. We all know it'll be Jack Myler."

Myler blushed, not daring to look directly at Barney and managing only a weak smile in McKay's direction.

"I will go only so far as to say that Jack would be one of the leading candidates. Perhaps *the* leading candidate," Barney said. "And I think that's enough speculation on the subject for now."

The vote to extend his contract for five more years beyond the retirement age of sixty-five was unanimous. Warren Billings made the motion and Roger Campbell seconded—a combination which jarred Larry Aroni, though he merely puffed on his cigar and lazily blew smoke rings at the ceiling as the meeting adjourned. Something was up and involved those two. He felt it in his bones.

When Trans-Coastal reversed course again in 1973, the first sign of trouble came not from the board but from a small group of dissident stockholders that openly challenged Barney at the 1974 annual shareholders' meeting held in Washington in mid-January.

The opposition did not come as a surprise to the embattled president, who had been getting enough angry letters to indicate adequately which way the stockholder winds were blowing. He had come prepared to fight, and fight he did, in a way that earned the admiration even of Roger Campbell.

Barney had opened the meeting with a terse, factual accounting of Trans-Coastal's current financial status and future prospects— the former admittedly gloomy and the latter reasonably, if cautiously, optimistic.

"Despite the losses of last year, which I've very frankly discussed," he declared in his best authoritative voice, "I think 1974 will be a good year and the next two years very good. I don't have to remind you that in 1976 the nation celebrates its Bicentennial, with Washington the focal point for the observance. The capital expects the greatest influx of tourists in history, and Trans-Coastal will gear the majority of its marketing and promotion efforts to that stupendous event. But aside from such gilt-edged traffic developers as a national Bicentennial, we also are carefully laying plans for sound route development, particularly aimed at markets capable of handling our 747 fleet. Now I'm not gonna give you any blarney about those magnificent but thus far unprofitable planes. Our 747 load factors for the past two years have averaged only about forty-nine percent, compared to a systemwide load factor of sixty-two and a half percent. The only thing wrong with our 747's is that they aren't serving the right places and we intend to do something about that, God and the CAB willing, although we may get more help from the former."

There were a few polite titters. "I'll now throw this meeting open to questions from the floor." Barney stepped back for a glass of water.

A dapper, slender man in his midforties rose and was passed a microphone. "Mr. Burton, my name is Travis Gillman. I'd like to ask for a bit more clarification of the route plans you mentioned."

"I'm not at liberty to disclose specifics, Mr. Gillman. I'm not trying to evade your question, but most of them are in the formulative stage and I don't want our competition to get wind of them at this point. I will say, however, that we'd like to fly into more tourist markets, particularly winter-resort areas which are not presently too well patronized but which could become very popular if they had some aggressive promotion and support behind them."

"Thank you," Mr. Gillman said.

"Mr. Burton," called out an elderly stockholder with a shock of unruly white hair. He could have been a retired coal miner except he was wearing what obviously was a well-tailored suit. "I'm Steven Webster and I own several hundred shares of what used to be a good airline. I just want you to know I'm darn tired of deficit operations, no dividends for the last six years, vague route plans that never seem to materialize, more airplanes than you know what to do with, including that white elephant you're so bloody proud of, and the general incompetence on the part of Trans-Coastal's executives. From the president on down, I might add."

"Is that a speech or is there a question buried in there somewhere?"

"The question is what are you going to do about all this?"

There was a smattering of applause, faint at first but then growing uncomfortably louder.

"Okay, I'll tell you what we're doing about it. Namely, everything humanly possible to restore this company to profitable operations. And when you accuse any officer of incompetence, Mr. Webster—including myself—you'd better be ready with some facts. I want examples of incompetence, chapter and verse. My people are working night and day, against enormous odds. You say our route plans never materialize? I couldn't agree with you more.

But whose fault is that? Mine? My officers? By God, no! Let me tell you one thing, if the Civil Aeronautics Board had granted us only twenty-five percent of the routes we've applied for in the past decade, we'd be paying you good people dividends on a regular basis!

"You say we have more airplanes than we know what to do with? Yes, we're suffering from overcapacity. So is virtually every other carrier in the United States—hell, in the world, for that matter. Now if you knew anything about ordering airplanes, Mr. Webster, you'd realize that the lead time required between an equipment decision and the actual introduction of a new aircraft into scheduled service is at least five years, and usually longer. We have always based our equipment plans on projected traffic growth. This was the case with our 747's, an airplane whose design dates back to 1965. In 1965, the airline industry was enjoying a consistent fifteen percent annual rate of traffic *growth* and there was no reason to fear otherwise. All economists—including those not directly associated with the airlines—were in unanimous agreement with their encouraging forecasts. As you all know now, the rate of growth slowed down to such an extent that the 747—a plane specifically designed to meet the expected traffic demands of the 70's—was an innocent victim of overoptimistic forecasting. We at Trans-Coastal must share the blame for some clouded crystal balls, but I'll be damned if I'll take all the blame. Suppose we hadn't ordered adequate equipment and the forecasts turned out to be on target? People like you, Mr. Webster, would be standing up in meetings like this and denouncing guys like me for not having sufficient foresight."

Barney scanned the audience.

"Nineteen seventy was a general disaster for the industry. The trunk lines lost a record $123 million. These carriers, plus the nine local-service or regional airlines, dropped $153 million. Only five trunks and two regionals finished the year in the black, and the black was more a pale gray.

"Well, the 1970 recession is behind us, and traffic has been on the upswing again. Not as fast as we'd like, but encouraging. And I can see the day coming when every man and woman in this room will be praising the management of Trans-Coastal for having the guts to continually modernize, to offer the public the finest and safest airplanes in existence, to rank progress at least equal in importance to profit, because without progress there can be no profits!

"Now, I'm not gonna stand up here and give you all a bunch of sugar-coated promises and pledges. Things have been rough, they are rough, and conceivably they could get even a little rougher. But when I look back on the past forty-six years, when I see what we've accomplished to date, and when I peer into the future and glimpse what lies ahead for this nation's most dynamic industry, I want to take the whiners, the cynics, the scoffers, the pessimists, and the doubters and shove all their heads into the history books. In less than fifty years, we've gone from a couple of Stinson monoplanes to the magnificence of the 747. It's an incredible ship. One hundred and twelve feet *longer* than the distance covered on the Wright Brothers' first flight, a tail as high as a six-story building, fuel tanks holding more than fifty thousand gallons . . . wiring which, laid end to end, would stretch one hundred miles. Its awesome strength—wing spars one hundred fifty percent of design limits, so strong that in one structural test the wings were bent thirty feet out of their normal level without popping a rivet . . . failsafe construction of such brawn that a 747 could lose two-thirds of its horizontal stabilizers and thirty percent of its rudder and still remain flyable and maneuverable. This is responsible progress, sir. The 747 *is* aviation, and believe me, ladies and gentlemen, this wasn't done entirely through Divine intervention. It was accomplished mainly by *your* management, and if the acquisition of this aircraft is what Mr. Webster would like to regard as incompetence, I'd like to tell Mr. Webster that he can go plumb to hell!"

There was loud applause and even cheers. Mr. Webster and a few others sat on their hands. Other questions were asked, including several openly antagonistic, but without much steam. Of the 598 shareholders present, at least 50 had come armed for a scrap that never really materialized after Barney waded into Steven Webster.

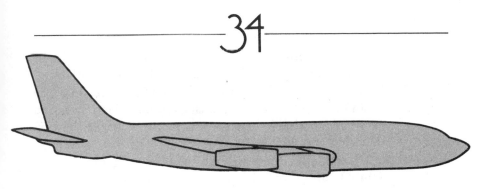

34

Trans-Coastal struggled and thrashed ineffectually throughout 1974 and then was hit by the fuel crisis in 1975—soaring fuel prices wiped out the gains of every economizing move Barney tried to make and left the budget of every department a shambles. Losses continued into 1976, mainly because Bicentennial traffic to the nation's capital fell far under all estimates.

Compounding these difficulties was Trans-Coastal's still-limited route structure; despite its imposing name, it was more of a regional carrier than a transcontinental airline. The average passenger walking up to a United or American ticket counter was handing over a minimum of $80; at a Trans-Coastal counter, the average ticket cost $40. Yet Trans-Coastal was paying roughly the same salaries to its pilots, agents, flight attendants, mechanics, and office workers as the bigger airlines.

Nearly half of its traffic consisted of passengers making connecting flights with other carriers. This led to delays, scheduling difficulties, and other factors hard for Trans-Coastal to control. And except for its western points, most of the airline's routes lay in poor weather areas where a higher rate of delays and cancellations was inevitable.

Management mistakes didn't help, and some of them could be parked right on Barney's doorstep. For example, he insisted that

Myler, through scheduling, and Littlefield, through promotion, concentrate on meeting long-haul competition head-on, with little or no effort made in developing "off-hour" traffic. And in trying to whip United and American over the plusher routes, Barney tended to ignore potentially profitable high-density markets. In the heavily-traveled Washington–Pittsburgh–Cleveland–Detroit triangle, Trans-Coastal never attempted to really compete against North-west and United, although Littlefield kept insisting those two carriers were "ripe for the taking."

As Barney's professional life deteriorated into constant bickering, quarrels, arguments, and tantrums, his only solace was an ever-deepening relationship with Janet Leavelle. She still insisted on maintaining her own apartment, but she was with him almost every night. Their favorite spot was Normandy Farm, a restaurant five minutes from Barney's home, with huge fireplaces and the finest seafood east of the Mississippi. They went three times a week, were always served by a red-haired waitress named Mary Benton, and talked increasingly about Trans-Coastal's problems.

Janet was voluptuous, her dark hair graying, but few lines on her face. She was worried about him; the tension was engraved on his face.

"Why don't you just chuck it and retire?" she asked after he had recounted a particularly painful session with Warren Billings. Trans-Coastal had faithfully met all interest payments when due, but Seaboard was pressing for reduction of the principal and had refused to underwrite a new stock issue.

"I think I'd be dead inside of a year," he said seriously. "Why is Billings being so hard?"

"No you wouldn't. We could travel, you could still be a consultant."

"Did I tell you what Cal Motts pulled the other day?" Barney chuckled. "He put out a release—"

"Barney, you're changing the subject. You can't keep going like this. Fifteen hours a day at the office, all this strain—frankly, you aren't even making love like you used to. You're just too tired."

"I wasn't aware you had grounds for complaint," he said, sounding huffy.

"I'm not complaining, darling, I'm stating a fact, and if you weren't so stubborn you'd admit it. You know what I'd like to see happen?"

"Meet a younger man?"

"No, damn you. I'd like some big airline to come along, offer you a few million dollars to merge, and maybe make you chairman of the board or something that wouldn't require much work."

"You serious?"

"Very serious."

"Janet, there isn't another airline in the country that would come within fifty miles of us . . . not with our debts. For that matter, I can't think of any airline I'd want to merge with. I'd be a traitor to every man and woman who ever worked for me. Mergers aren't mergers anyway. They're acquisitions. One of the two airlines has to die; there's only one surviving carrier. And I'll go to my grave before I let my airline be swallowed up, with only a few lines in the history books to show it ever even existed. I don't want Trans-Coastal to go the way of Mohawk and Capital and Mid-Continent and Lake Central and Pacific Northern and Pioneer. There's nothing left of 'em, except maybe a few models of their planes with their old markings—collector's items. Trans-Coastal isn't a museum piece."

"It's Mr. Hoagland of Global Airways, Mr. Burton," Gloria Wingate said.

"What the hell does he want?" Barney demanded. Miss Wingate suppressed her natural desire to ask how the hell she should know. She merely said, "Line two." Barney punched the extension button and picked up the phone.

"Dick, you old pirate, how are you?"

"Fine, Barney. I happened to be in town for a couple of days and wondered if I could see you, if you can squeeze in an hour or so. Any lunch plans today?"

"Is this business, a courtesy call, just chit-chat, or what?"

"Business." Hoagland could be just as direct.

"Christ, nobody can get anything accomplished while they're eating. Besides, I'm on a diet. Come on out here and we'll talk."

"About an hour from now be okay?"

"Fine. I'll see you then."

Normally, Barney would have been insatiably curious about Hoagland's wanting to see him; he didn't know the president of Global very well, and in their few contacts, mostly at ATA functions, he always had thought the man rather cold and distant. Yet Hoagland had a reputation for being a square-shooter, and Global itself reflected his personality—tight cost controls, competence, an almost unobtrusive manner. Someone once likened a typical Global flight to MGM movies of the forties.

Barney forgot about Hoagland's impending visit, however, amid the usual onslaught of problems, until suddenly Gloria Wingate announced him.

"I'll come right to the point, Barney," Hoagland said after a few pleasantries. "How would you feel about a Global and Trans-Coastal merger?"

Barney's answer was as abrupt as the question: "Not interested."

"Why? You've got something we want—access to cities we don't serve and which would tie in with our international routes. We've got something you want. Namely some cash to clean up all your debts."

"What the hell good would it do to bail us out and then eat us up? The only way I'd even consider would be one that left Trans-Coastal as the surviving carrier, with me as president."

"That would be a case of the minnow swallowing the whale. Trans-Coastal is the company that's in deep trouble, not Global. Merger might be your only salvation, and the terms I'd give you now would be quite a bit more advantageous than what I could offer later when you'd be forced into a merger."

"Nobody's gonna force me into committing suicide, Dick. Just for the sake of politeness, what kind of a deal are you thinking about?"

"A one-to-one stock exchange, a ten percent pre-merger dividend to all Trans-Coastal shareholders, which would give you a tidy little sum, and a ten-year personal consultant's contract for Mr. Barnwell Burton at seventy thousand a year. Global would assume all Trans-Coastal's debts, we'd guarantee the usual employee job protection in accordance with CAB merger guidelines, and we'd absorb certain of your senior officers—taking into consideration your own recommendations in that area, of course. A very generous offer, I'd say. I want you at least to think about it. I know it would be a difficult step, and I'm perfectly willing to come back and discuss it further, say, in two weeks."

"You'd be wasting your time. The answer's no."

"Don't you think you owe it to your colleagues and Trans-Coastal's directors to at least advise them of our offer?"

"I don't owe 'em a goddamned thing. Anyway, the directors do what I say and my officers are completely loyal to me and to their company. I have no intention of pushing any panic buttons. Sure, we've had our troubles, but traffic projections for this year are good, and I see no reason why I should have to discuss a merger offer from Global or anyone else, when we don't need a merger to survive."

"Well," Hoagland sighed, "I know you're the type of person who not only appreciates frankness but demands it. If Trans-Coastal's situation doesn't improve and merger becomes an attractive possibility, instead of a dose of medicine, the terms I've offered today may not be available at a later date. And that includes the benefits involving you personally."

"I'll take that chance," Barney said. "Give me a profitable 1977 and we'll make it on our own."

"For your sake, Barney, I sincerely hope so. I'd be less than candid, however, if I didn't tell you that you're whistling past the proverbial graveyard."

"We'll see, Dick. We'll see."

With the next thirty days, Barney's optimism had turned sour as the inflation spiral that had begun its invidious climb upward two years earlier continued unabated. Fuel prices stabilized somewhat, but that couldn't recover what had been lost previously. Fuel costs in 1976 had gone from a budgeted $62 million to almost $80 million, and while prices weren't going up, they weren't going down, either. And then came another round of negotiated wage boosts.

By mid-April it was only too apparent that, barring some miracle, 1977 would be another red-ink year. Desperate, Barney grounded one of the 747's, furloughed more than a thousand employees, and slashed schedules by fifteen percent. Some of his economy moves set off damaging chain reactions. When one hundred reservations agents were furloughed, the average time for answering a phone in reservations went from twenty seconds to over three minutes, while the schedule cuts simply sent thousands of passengers over to competitors with more convenient and frequent flights.

Not until an executive staff meeting in April did the Global merger offer come to light. Roger Campbell brought it into the open when he mentioned that he had heard "some merger rumors" and asked Barney directly if they were true.

Barney hedged. "There's absolutely no merger offer before us as of this moment."

"What do you mean, 'as of this moment?' Do you expect one, or has there been one in the past you didn't tell us about?"

"There was one. I didn't think it was worthy of consideration."

"Would it have been from Global, by any chance?" Roger Campbell asked.

Barney flushed. "How the hell did you know that?"

"From very reliable sources. I've also been told it was a very good offer."

"It was a lousy offer. It would have buttered my own bread for the rest of my life, but it wouldn't have done this airline any good."

"I'd like to know why, Barney."

"Because it would have meant the end of Trans-Coastal."

There was no trace of Roger Campbell's almost perpetual smile now. "I think you owed it to all of us, and the directors as well, to inform us of Global's proposal."

"You seem to know a lot about it without my telling you," Barney said bitingly. "Exactly how much *do* you know?"

"Enough for me to accuse you of being derelict in your responsibilities to our airline and to your fellow officers. And if you don't tell us what Global offered, I will."

"Go right ahead, Roger."

"An even-up swap of stock—one share of Global for every share of Trans-Coastal. Assumption of all debts and obligations. Job protection for most senior officers. The most generous provision was a ten percent stock dividend payable to Trans-Coastal shareholders before the merger. All told, a very advantageous deal which our president, for reasons known only to himself, decided to keep hidden from all of us. *Why?*"

Every head in the room turned toward Barnwell Burton, each betraying a different emotion—disbelief on Littlefield's, shocked sorrow on Vaughn's, pity on Aroni's, fear on Myler's.

Barney stood up. Larry thought he had never seemed so tall, so commanding.

"I'll ask you a question, Roger, and if you answer it honestly, I'll answer yours. Who told you about Global?"

"Warren Billings."

Barney showed his surprise. "Billings?"

"Yes. The vice-chairman of the board. He has been talking to Dick Hoagland of Global."

"Hoagland has no right to—"

"He had every right," Campbell interrupted, "inasmuch as you not only rejected Global's original offer but refused to discuss it either with your directors or your officers. He went to Billings as the second-ranking director when it became apparent this airline was heading for bankruptcy and you already had told him you would never merge."

"And I'll repeat to you what I told him—we won't ever merge! Not while I'm president."

"Then," Campbell said with deadly calm, "perhaps it's time we got a new president."

"Bingo," Aroni muttered to Andy Vaughn, sitting next to him.

"It's time we got a new senior vice-president of Finance," Barney snarled. "I won't stand for such blatant disloyalty. I could fire you right now, Roger."

"But you won't. I'm not just a senior officer. I'm also a director. If you try to dismiss me, I'll take it to the board itself."

"You can't even call a board meeting," Barney said.

"No, but Warren Billings could. As a matter of fact, it's a pleasure to inform you that within the next hour he will be phoning all directors personally, summoning them to a special board meeting for next Thursday morning. The subject for discussion will be whether to authorize the commencement of merger negotiations with Global Airways."

"There will be no merger discussions with Global or anyone

else," Barney shouted. "I won't even sit down it the same room with—"

"You won't have to," Campbell smiled. "Warren Billings is going to ask the directors for authority to conduct the negotiations himself on behalf of this company. Now about that question I wanted you to answer, Barnwell—" Barney just glared at him. "—no answer is necessary."

The directors voted nine to two, two abstaining, to give Billings negotiating authority. Joining Barney in opposing the action was Jack Myler.

Aroni expected his friend and boss to explode when he went with the majority, saying "I'm opposed to merger but we owe it to the stockholders and our own employees to at least explore the pros and cons."

Later, when he apologized to Barney privately, the Old Man merely shrugged. "Shit, you did what you thought best, Larry. I won't hold it against you. I'll need you more if this thing ever comes down to a merger vote itself."

"I hope it won't," Aroni said, "but the odds aren't exactly favorable."

"Well, even if the board voted for a merger, it still would have to be approved by the stockholders. We could put up one hell of a fight on that battlefield—one rip-snortin' speech, like the time I clobbered that Webster guy, and I'll have Billings ready to cut his own throat."

Aroni shook his head. "Don't count on it. If the directors go for merger, that's the ballgame."

Barney was silent. He knew Aroni was right, but he could not bring himself to say it out loud. He spent the next three months trying to line up antimerger support and run the airline simultaneously—not accomplishing much in either endeavor. It became only too apparent, from his written and verbal contacts with a number of stockholders, that the directors' vote would settle matters one way or the other. Of the outside directors, all of whom he visited personally, he was confident of only two: Henry, the president of a department store chain. McKay and Bob Levin. He also was sure of Motts, Jack Myler, and Larry Aroni. Six votes on a thirteen-member board. All he had to do, obviously, was swing one man over and he had the merger licked, but as of June 6, 1977, he still wasn't assured that one vote.

And June 7 was the date Warren Billings had set for the board's decision on acceptance or rejection of Global's final offer, which—as Barney learned in a coldly impersonal letter from Dick Hoagland—did not include a single benefit, concession, or remuneration for the president of Trans-Coastal. Putting on his jacket, Barney decided to go out for a walk. One more day, he thought. One more.

The old pendulum clock in the foyer struck eleven as Barney Burton sauntered into the Monocle. The maitre d' smiled and quickly strode forward.

"Good morning, Mr. Burton. Pleasure to see you."

"Thank you, Cyril. It's been a while."

"Yes, sir. It's not been the same since you moved out to Dulles."

Barney clapped the man on the shoulder. "Everything changes, Cyril. You have to get used to that, especially in our line of work."

"Barney!"

Barney squinted to see who was hailing him from the far end of the bar. "Frank Loudermilk," he mumbled, gesturing that he would stop by.

Cyril glanced back. "Not a face I know."

"Don't imagine you would," Barney replied. "He's an out-of-town reporter and a long way from home."

Barney slid by and made his way toward the end of the bar occupied by the waving figure of the Wichita *Record*'s ace reporter. Franklin Loudermilk. Barney had first met him in Binghamton. He was a happy, cherubic soul who was one of those rare drunks nobody could get mad at. The man had a glass in his hand every waking hour, yet the cumulative effect was more a state of blissful euphoria than bleary-eyed, word-slurring intoxication. The twinkle in the deep-set brown eyes seemed to increase with every swallow.

"How the hell are you, Barnwell?"

"Not too bad, Franklin. Good to see you. It must be ten years—But what the hell are you doing this far east?"

"Oh, they sent me out to cover the big airline story."

Barney wasn't surprised; Loudermilk had covered everything and everyone involved in aviation—from Lindbergh's flight to Knute Rockne's crash.

"What are you drinking, Barn?"

"Scotch, thanks. So you were up on the Hill this morning for the deregulation hearings, were you?"

Loudermilk shifted uneasily. "No. Been here since breakfast."

Barney shook his head. "I'd hate to see a technicolor shot of your liver. How the hell do you expect to file a story from here? You missed quite a session, I hear. The right honorable senators from Massachusetts and Wyoming almost came to blows."

"It's not on the Hill, Barney."

"What?" Barney looked at him, puzzled.

"The story. You're the story, Mr. Burton, and you happen tomorrow."

Something seemed to both relax and go out of Barney Burton. He raised his hand, summoning the bartender. "Make that a double scotch."

Barney knocked back the scotch. Loudermilk suddenly looked thoughtful. He raised his glass—a private toast.

"*Mañana.*"

He felt himself blossom inside her, coming in a hot spurt, his toes curling. Janet's eyes opened in surprise, not at his climax but her own. She had thought only to console him, but suddenly felt her own orgasm welling up, triggered by his.

Barney pushed up onto her, spreading her arms out with his, spreading her legs apart until they were an X spreadeagled, his body rigidly braced as she thrust against him in the last involuntary moments.

"Jesus."

He raised his head. "What?"

"Nothing. I love you, that's all."

"Why?"

She laughed. "Why do you ask so often? Why do men ask? Why isn't it enough just to love you, period?"

Barney grunted.

"But if you are referring to the fact of my enjoying conjugal intertwining with the esteemed Barnwell Burton, then I do have an answer."

"Limeys."

"However, if you persist in such references to myself and my fellow countrymen—"

"Okay, okay." He eased out of her, feeling the muscles in his shoulder vibrate with fatigue as he rolled gently off.

"Better. Actually I was thinking about it the last time we made love. It occurred to me that it always feels the same."

Barney looked puzzled, if not hurt. "Boring, you mean?"

"Hardly. No, I meant that it's always like that first night in London." She scratched her thigh, her face turned toward his in the half-light. "You know, I never thought I would ever be with someone this long, no matter how I felt about him. The thought of never experiencing anyone else for the rest of my life was always terrifying to me—like dying. Seriously. Then you came along. And not only was I madly in love, but the fear never materialized. For the longest time I wondered about it. Then I realized how strange sex with you was . . ."

"Don't stop now."

"It's quite interesting when you consider it. The first and second time with someone is deeply erotic. You've gone through all the foxing and banter and you're aching to fuck, but you also kind of savor it. It can't be too quick. When you finally undress and feel one another for the first time it's like dancing." She glanced at him, smiling. "Remember?"

"Go on."

"The skin, the folds, she fondling you, here. You caressing her, slipping inside, feeling her breasts cushioned against your chest . . . I float away, every time. Soon I'm all vagina and lips and everything is swollen and wanton. It's so silky, as if you've slid under my skin." She reached over and brushed her hand against his cheek.

"Maybe we should go back to London. For old times' sake."

"Do you mean it?" she said with that British inflection he loved. "But you can't get away from the shop, can you?"

Barney sat up, reaching for the sheet they had kicked aside. "Hon, there may not be a shop by tomorrow afternoon. I may indeed be at leisure by then."

"Well, forgive my saying so, but it has to happen sometime. And if tomorrow it is, then do it well and let's get on with our lives. You've done a hell of a job and you've worked for more years and more hours than anyone in that company and . . ."

"And?"

"And the whole thing sucks," she said, fluffing up her pillow with a punch.

And he loved her for it.

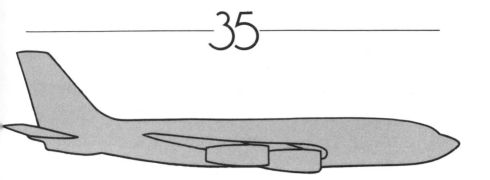

35

The man Barney Burton had wanted to be president was sitting glumly amid the trappings of an executive vice-president—an office with a decor of subdued grandeur much like the Old Man's, a Hickey-Freeman sharkskin suit on his bulky frame, and a private toilet whose paneled door was just to the right of a small bar.

John Myler wanted badly to open up that bar right now and pour himself a stiff shot of bourbon. Just the impulse to drink made him feel worse; it reminded him of Barney, who had loudly and piously forbidden the installation of a similar bar in his own office on the grounds that it would set a bad example for other executives. This admirable stand was followed closely by his insistence that Myler's office be adequately stocked for a few private belts, and the executive vice-president found himself recalling those many occasions when Barney would slip into Myler's office late in the afternoon.

Maybe he shouldn't have been so subservient all these years, so convinced of Barney's infallibility that he was unable to argue with him, to question one of his decisions, or to stand up to him. Or was it more fear than conviction? Fear of not inheriting the presidency. Fear of losing Barney's blessings. After all, Barney had promised him that some day . . .

Jack Myler loved being executive vice-president, so much so that he had deluded himself into believing the next logical, completely inevitable step was progression to the presidency. He honestly considered himself qualified to wear Barnwell Burton's shoes; he did not want to be another Barney, but he believed he had absorbed his better qualities, his goals, his strengths without his weaknesses. Myler had never grasped the truth—that during the years of subservience he had become only a smudged, pale, carbon copy of the Old Man, inheriting none of his strengths and acquiring too many weaknesses of his own making. He was more obsolete than stupid, more ineffectual than inefficient. Nor could he be blamed for his heir-apparent aspirations. Barney himself had bribed him to assure his loyalty, dangling the honor of eventual succession until it became as much an obsession as an ambition.

Far too long, Myler was now thinking. To the point where patience had turned into resentment. If Barney hadn't kept him waiting in the wings eternally, procrastinating so long in stepping aside that for his loyal lieutenant, succession was now an impossibility . . .

The buzz of his intercom interrupted his brooding.

"Mr. Myler, Mr. McKay is out here and would like to see you."

"Send him in, Shirley," Myler said, wishing he had the guts to tell his secretary he was too busy to see the board's senior director. He knew what McKay wanted to talk about—how they could save Barney Burton's scalp and block the merger. Or maybe Henry already had heard that Barney's trusted stooge had become a turncoat.

Henry McKay already had. He didn't walk into Myler's office; he marched in, his wizened face contorted with fury.

"You goddamned Judas," McKay snarled. "I just bumped into Warren Billings. He says you're voting for the merger. Is that true?"

Somehow, defiance overcame shame. "It's true," Myler bristled.

They glared at each other. Myler, only an inch shorter than Burton himself, towered over the aged banker, yet the height difference was not enough to establish dominance. It was the executive vice-president who turned away first, sagging into his desk chair.

"Sit down, Henry. I'd like to explain . . ."

"Explain, hell! An alibi is what you need—a copper-riveted, unshakable excuse for stabbing your best friend right in the back. Provided you've got one."

"I'd still rather call it an explanation than an alibi," Myler said wearily. "Does Barney know?"

"Not unless that fink Billings walked into his office and bragged about it, which I doubt. He knows Barney would have tossed him through the nearest window."

"I wouldn't blame him for doing the same thing to me. Henry, I had no choice. The war's over. We've lost. Why the hell can't you face up to that fact? Why can't Barney?"

"Because he's no quitter, that's why! He built this airline himself. He scrounged, schemed, and scavenged for nearly fifty years. For Christ's sake, Barney Burton *is* Trans-Coastal! It's his airline and nobody else's. He sweated blood to make it great and he carried a lot of guys like you on his back while he was doing it. Look at this fancy office. I remember when Barney's desk was an oil drum, and a filing cabinet was something where he hid the booze. A few lean years and everyone's ready to hang him up by the balls. You and those other smart-ass, wet-behind-the-ears vice-presidents and so-called experts and those greedy cold-blooded vultures from Global. And you of all people, Jack, cutting his throat after all he's done for you. You would have been president someday. He promised you, and Barney never went back on his word."

"And just *when* am I supposed to become president?" Myler snapped, his broad face white with indignation. "After he dies? What will I be president of—a bankrupt company? Sure, he told me I'll succeed him eventually. He's told me that a dozen times. The first time was twenty years ago. He told me again last year. But he's still around, Henry, he's still around. And I just got tired of waiting. I'm the beneficiary of his will, only there's nothing left to bequeath. You're asking me to vote for a dead man, or a dead airline. It's just like you said—with Barney it's the same thing. You're damned right he's Trans-Coastal. And they're both *finished!*"

The anguish was etched into his face; the intensity of his words had punctured McKay's anger.

"Jack," he said sympathetically, "things aren't that black. Even if you go over to the other side, it's still a close margin, and there could be some last-minute switches."

Now it was Myler whose face showed compassion. "It's four against nine."

"What the hell do you mean?"

"Bob Levin has just about made up his mind to vote for merger."

"I don't believe it!"

"You'd better believe it. Roger Campbell told me. He talked to Levin personally. He said Bob has reached the conclusion Trans-Coastal is finished. Do you blame him, Henry? He owns one hell of a chunk of our stock. Most of it he bought when it was thirty-six dollars a share; as of yesterday it was down to eight."

"That's no reason to knife Barney. I own a few shares myself and I bought the majority of it when it was a hell of a lot higher than thirty-six bucks. Damn Levin, anyway. I guess that tears it."

"It certainly does. Now can you really blame *me*?"

"In a way, yes. You're still voting against Barney, not just for merger. If he's already licked, your vote won't change a damned thing. Why not go down with him? That's what I'll do. Matter of principle, I suppose."

Myler said nothing. And in his silence, McKay glimpsed the truth. "They're paying you off, aren't they, John? Some kind of a promise to take care of you when it's all over?"

The executive vice-president could only nod and hang his head, his hands pressing his temples as if the pressure would drive out the guilt.

"I thought so. Which leads to a very interesting theory. If they have to stoop *that* low, maybe they aren't as sure about this shindig as we think. John, do me one favor." Myler looked up. "When the time comes to vote this morning, just before you open your god-damned sniveling mouth, look Barney right in the eye. Maybe you won't be able to go through with it."

The senior vice-president of Marketing and Sales sat in his spartan office, his chair swiveled around to the rear so he could look out the window behind his desk and stare aimlessly at the nearby pagoda control tower of Dulles, without really seeing it.

He was frowning and deep in thought, his right hand rubbing

back and forth across his square chin as if the very motion could conjure up the right decision. Littlefield's meditation came to an abrupt halt as his secretary buzzed his extension. Littlefield swung around, picking up his phone.

"Mr. Campbell's on the line," she said in her soft, tiptoe voice. "Also, Mr. Stein wants you to call him, and Mr. Nash is out here if you have a few minutes."

"Oh, hell," Littlefield sighed. "Tell Campbell I'll call him back. And send Ken Nash in. I'll get to Stein later."

The assistant vice-president of Passenger Relations entered, his plump face wearing its usual martyred expression. Nash lived on a diet of complaints, crises, queries, and general consumer catastrophes. He was overworked, mildly cynical, and enormously adept at a thankless task.

Ken Nash liked Littlefield, to whom he reported directly. Don was tough but fair, smart and unpretentious, informal yet a leader demanding of respect. On this occasion, however, Nash was understandably nervous. Merger had progressed from the rumor stage of four months ago to around-the-corner consummation, a distinct threat to every Trans-Coastal officer faced with reduction of rank or maybe outright dismissal once Global took over. Nash was pessimistic of his own chances for survival and wasn't quite sure how Littlefield would fare when Trans-Coastal died. Now that he was in Don's office, it suddenly seemed foolish to be bringing up a problem that would be moot in a few hours, not only for him but Littlefield as well.

"What's on your mind, Ken?" Littlefield asked.

"You wanted to be advised of passenger reaction to the meal-service changes on the Cleveland nonstops," Nash said. "We got a lot of reaction—all bad."

"It figured," Littlefield sighed. "Sixty-five minutes block-to-block time, and I suppose they're demanding full-course meals."

"Plus cocktails. We've been averaging fifteen letters of complaint for each flight over the past two weeks."

"All flights?"

"Two in particular. The one at noon and the 7 P.M. nonstop. A few gripes about no full breakfasts on the 9 A.M."

Littlefield grimaced. "So help me, I can't see why people leaving at nine in the morning can't be satisfied with coffee and rolls. We assumed most passengers already would have eaten breakfast by then."

Nash shrugged. "Ours is not to reason why, I suppose." He started to rise, then sank back in his chair. "Don," he blurted, "does it really make a hell of a lot of difference what we do about the Cleveland service?"

Littlefield looked at him, not without sympathy and in obvious understanding. His answer was soft, but touched with a trace of bitterness:

"I don't honestly know. I don't suppose so, but there's one thing I do know."

"What's that?"

"Never underestimate the Old Man."

Nash could not keep a fleeting expression of hope from his broad face. "Some of us are going nuts worrying about what's gonna happen this morning. Man, I'm not sure whether to root against Barney or pray like hell he wins."

Littlefield shrugged. "Merger will kill this airline, but without merger it may damned well die anyway. I wish I could give you some encouragement, but I can't even give myself any. And I've got a vote at this 10 A.M. bloodletting."

"It's not just me," Nash said defensively. "A lot of us are scared to death. Unionized employees have it made—they've got job protection written into the merger agreement. Christ, guys like me may wind up behind some Global ticket counter."

"I could be working right alongside you," Littlefield mumbled, then wished he hadn't said it. He knew his own future wasn't that insecure, and he admitted to himself that Nash couldn't possibly believe Global would shaft a young executive like himself, a man with a good track record despite Trans-Coastal's sagging fortunes. There were few secrets in the airline industry and it was common knowledge that at forty-two, Don Littlefield had been wooed by more than one airline. That he could resist such courtships was easily explainable in a single word: money. Barney Burton paid well, both in salaries and fringe benefits: $65,000 a year, a $100,000 life-insurance policy, stock options, free medical, and a $10,000 annual expense account. For himself, his wife, and their three daughters, there was a Class A pass—first class, positive space on all airlines, $4,000 worth of free air travel a year.

Not a bad deal. Except that all these perks wouldn't be worth a damn if Trans-Coastal crashed, which appeared highly possible and even probable. Of course, he was sure he could get as good an arrangement from Global. He already had been told that by Global's president, Dick Hoagland. Eddie Carlson of United, just before the merger talks began, also had called him to suggest talking to them.

As far as Littlefield was concerned, however, the trouble with United and Global was their size. He preferred a smaller carrier. Continental and Western, for example, and Trans-Coastal, for that matter, offered a greater challenge, more opportunity for initiative, and closer relationships within management itself and with the rank and file. And completely aside from these factors was Barney Burton. Littlefield hated him for his procrastination, blind stubbornness, his antiquated ideas. While he admired the Old Man for his honesty and devotion to the airline, he could never forgive Barney Burton for what he had done to that airline. In Littlefield's early years with Trans-Coastal, there had been a bond between them—almost akin to that of a free-thinking, independent-minded son and a strong-willed, hopelessly opinionated father. No longer. For the past two years they had fought bitterly, openly, and with mutual distrust. Littlefield had almost reached the point where he was convinced there was no longer room for both under the same roof.

". . . and there had to be a correlation between the start of merger negotiations and increase in passenger complaints," Ken Nash was saying. "Frankly, I can't blame our flight attendants for a morale situation they had no control over."

"Yeah," Littlefield agreed perfunctorily. "Look, Ken, let's talk about it some other time. I've got some things to do before that board meeting, and Campbell just called."

Nash already was out of his chair and turning toward the door before Littlefield finished. "Sure thing, Don. God, I'm glad I'm not in your shoes. Me, I wouldn't know which way to vote."

"That's my trouble," Littlefield said grimly, turning to his phone. "I do know."

Don Littlefield did not really like the senior vice-president of Finance, but he had a general live-and-let-live attitude toward anyone at Coastal who did his job competently.

That Roger Campbell was competent, Littlefield had no doubts. His syrupy voice was as irritating as a fingernail scratching a blackboard; anyone with vocal cords that oily had to possess an unctuous quality which in Campbell's case clashed jarringly with his jolly appearance.

Yet Don knew him as a coldly efficient businessman with a computer for a mind and a calculator for a heart; Trans-Coastal, Littlefield conceded, would have been in even worse shape without Roger. His personality grated, true, but in Littlefield's opinion he had done his best to compensate for Barnwell Burton's roller-coaster financial position—shortsighted economy moves in one direction and profligate spending in another. The former usually turned out to be temporary expedients—aspirin—and too often reflected the damage from some previous spending spree.

It was easy to merge two corporations; it was not that easy when it came to the people who worked for the company losing its corporate identity. Trans-Coastal ran on pride, loyalty, resilience, comradeship, and above all, a sense of being linked with the past, even when grappling with the problems of present and future. No one could kill an airline without also stabbing deep into those roots. Yet, Littlefield reflected sadly, no sense of history could make up for major mistakes; no pride was strong enough to overcome the deadly legacy of such mistaken decisions. At least, most of Trans-Coastal's rank and file would keep their jobs under Global. They would have no jobs if the airline failed, and that was the most important factor of all.

Why the hell was he so worried about them anyway? Trans-Coastal's predicament was no one-way street of blame—the greed of the unions over the past five years had been just as destructive as Barnwell Burton's egomaniac rule. Strike threats so deftly and cruelly timed—just before the summer travel season or preceding the Thanksgiving and Christmas holidays, when the airline was most vulnerable and terrified of a walkout. Excessive demands from labor negotiators, color-blind when it came to looking at the bright red ink on the company's ledgers. Let 'em deal with Global now, he thought.

He dialed Campbell's private extension.

"Don Littlefield, Roger. Sorry I couldn't take your call. I had someone in the office with me."

"Thanks for calling back," Campbell oozed. "You all set for Armageddon?"

"Your choice of words makes me want to throw up," Littlefield said testily. "Yeah, I'm ready for Armageddon. Execution might be a more appropriate word."

"You don't sound very happy about it."

"Why the hell should I? Or anyone else? I wish the old sonofa-bitch had gotten out three years ago when he could have exited gracefully."

"If he had, we'd probably be going through the same mess any-way."

"Why?"

"Because he would have shoved Jack Myler down our throats as president. And Jack would have been a figurehead. Barney Burton wouldn't have quit running this company until he was carried out of his office feet first."

"Or forced out." Littlefield's tone stopped just at the threshold of sarcasm, and Campbell didn't miss it.

"Look, Don, we're all upset about this. Do you want me to rehash the jam we're in? The worst debt-to-equity ratio in the in-dustry? The lowest cash reserves of any airline in the United States? A credit rating so bad we couldn't borrow enough money to paint one airplane? Do I have to draw a goddamned diagram for you? It's merger or bankruptcy. There's no other choice. I feel sorry for the Old Man. So help me I do, but he's the guy who dug this grave. His and ours, if we don't let Global bail us out."

"Okay, I get the message. No sermon necessary. Which reminds me, what did you call about?"

"I wanted to know if you saw today's *Daily*. They've got a story on the meeting and—"

"I read it. Seemed pretty accurate."

"Not quite." Campbell's voice took on a note of suspense. The vice-president of Finance paused dramatically before continuing. "The Old Man doesn't have six votes, Don. He has only five, and one of those is wobblier than he thinks."

Littlefield whistled. "Who's the mutineer?"

"Myler."

"Myler? Jack Myler genuflects every time Barney Burton walks into a room. He'd spit on the flag before he'd knife Barney."

"He'll vote for the merger, my friend. I happen to know Warren Billings has been talking to Dick Hoagland, and after they talked Warren had a little session with Myler."

"What did he use—water torture? Rog, nobody can tell—"

"Hold it. Let me finish. Warren didn't have to use anything except logical persuasion. He simply stated a few facts of life. The first of which is that Myler has absolutely no future with this company. If the merger goes through, he's out, along with anyone else who tried to beat it. Even if the miracle occurred and the merger was defeated, he still stands no chance of becoming Trans-Coastal's president. He's just too old—he's sixty-one and he won't get any waiver of the mandatory retirement rule like Burton talked us into. For that matter, the board wouldn't support him now regardless of Burton's recommendation. He doesn't have the brains, stature, guts, or executive talent to be president."

"That's fine," Littlefield said, "but what has he got to lose voting against Global? You said yourself he has no future no matter what happens today."

"Ah, but you're wrong. Warren gave him a very good reason for voting yes. Namely, a promise to be elected to Global's board of directors after the merger's consummated. So he'll still be something of a big shot, just as he is now—a big shot with no real duties, no responsibilities, his precious pass privileges intact for the rest of his life, and when he retires he'll still get his Trans-Coastal pension. In other words, Donald my boy, our Mr. Myler thought things over and decided he was getting a pretty good little deal. He promised to vote for the merger."

"Wait a minute," Littlefield protested. "Why is it so necessary to bribe Myler? He sure as hell isn't any swing vote. It doesn't add up. And I'll tell you another thing, Roger, I don't like what you said about wiping out anyone who's against the merger. We've got eleven thousand employees on this airline and about ten thousand of them would like to stick that merger up Warren Billings's butt!"

"Calm down," Campbell said soothingly. "I didn't mean it the way it sounded. There won't be any purge, not at the lower echelons."

"The hell there won't! Global's got more vice-presidents than we've got dispatchers. Are you telling me every officer in this company is guaranteed a comparable job and salary once we merge?"

"What I mean, Don, is that *top* officers who are against the merger can't expect to be welcomed with open arms by the surviving carrier. Myler's only human. He's just trying to protect himself."

"Who's the guy wobbling, as you put it?"

"Bob Levin."

"Aw, bullshit!" Littlefield snorted. "He loves the Old Man."

"He has been extremely critical of Mr. Burton's policies at each of the last three directors' meetings," Campbell reminded.

"He also has declared publicly and privately that this company should make damned sure corporate suicide isn't the only answer," Littlefield snapped.

"But he won't insist on Barney Burton stepping down. Don, we both know there was a time when Trans-Coastal could have been saved. Maybe only a year ago. Provided the Old Man abdicated. There was a time when new leadership might have pulled us out. Now it's too late. And I guess I can confide in you that Bob Levin is beginning to think this way, too."

"I suppose Warren's also talked to him."

"He has. No commitment, but Levin admitted he was having second thoughts. He said he honestly didn't know how he'd vote until the meeting itself. Personally, I think he'll urge us to try something that might save Barney's face, and if anyone can come up with something, he'll go for merger. And *that*, my friend, leaves the Old Man with exactly Larry Aroni, Calvin, and old Henry McKay. And himself."

Littlefield could not resist a chuckle. "I wish Warren Billings had tried to grease Larry's palm the way he did Myler's. Aroni would have unscrewed our vice-chairman's head from his shoulders."

"Warren," Campbell said dryly, "thought it rather useless to try and influence the vice-president of Maintenance and Engineering. By the way, Don, from your somewhat belligerent reactions to all I've said, I hope you're not, ah, wobbling a bit yourself."

"I've told you before, Rog, I'd be going into that board meeting with a machine gun if there was an alternative to a merger that nobody really wants, except Billings and Global. I haven't come up with any, so I'm going in with what appears to be a very superfluous vote. Does that satisfy you?"

"Eminently. I'll see you at the meeting."

Littlefield hung up, his fingers beating a tattoo on the polished desktop. Like a roll of drums before the firing squad raises its rifles, he thought gloomily.

When Roger Campbell finished the conversation with Littlefield, he was smiling—at someone else in the room.

At one end sat the gaunt figure of Warren Billings, whose answering smile resembled the cracking of frozen leather. "I feel much better," Billings announced in a deep voice that was totally at odds with his scrawny physique. He had been listening to the just-concluded exchange on an extension phone. "Littlefield worries me. He's something of an idealist, and idealists are unpredictable at times."

"He's an idealist with a large streak of pragmatism," Campbell said. "In this business, ambition is a far stronger emotion than sentimentality. Don knows he has nothing to fear from Global. Hoagland's always liked him. He could write his own ticket there after the merger."

"A ticket with unlimited possibilities—I hope he realizes that. People like you, Littlefield, Bill Sloan . . . you're all protected—you don't lose one iota of responsibility, and you won't be operating from a makeshift poverty base where you have to count the pencils every night. Frankly, Roger, I can't for the life of me see why anyone in his right mind could be against this merger."

"Except Barney Burton," Campbell said, smiling.

The time was eight-twenty-one.

The solidity of Larry Aroni and Andy Vaughn's friendship could best be measured by the fact that it stayed intact even though they were on opposite sides in the merger war.

Long ago, they had established an almost daily ritual of sharing a small pot of coffee in one or the other's office before plunging into the morning's work. Their offices at GO adjoined, a kind of physical extension of their relationship, and there might as well not have been a wall between the two rooms, for they entered each other's bailiwicks almost at will.

They were poles apart physically, yet like twin brothers in all other respects. Aroni had put on too much weight—on his face as well as his fireplug frame. His skin had the texture of aged leather, and his once-prominent Roman nose seemed to have shrunk amid his big features. Vaughn looked younger than his sixty-one years; his red hair had long since faded into an obscure gray, but he was still lean with that boyish smile. The external contrast between them was overshadowed by what they had in common. They both dealt with, and loved, the ultimate tool of every airline—the great silver birds of such strength and fragility, of effortless power and mind-boggling complexity. They both dealt with those who put life into those inanimate machines, the men who flew them and cared for them.

They had become inseparable, on and off duty. They golfed together almost every weekend, belonged to the same country club, and for years had taken joint vacations until Barney decided that the "Bobbsey Twins" could not be absent simultaneously for longer than three days.

That rule had been in effect for the past three years, and Barney refused to relent. Ironically, it was a subject that came up when they were discussing the merger during their regular kaffeeklatch. Aroni was in a bad mood. Far more than Vaughn, he knew what the Old Man was going through; for all their differences, quarrels, and clashing philosophies, he loved Barney. If his common bond with Andy was airplanes, his connection with Barnwell Burton was the airline itself.

"I feel like it's a death watch," Vaughn said miserably.

"Look at the bright side of it. Maybe when it's all over, we'll finally get to take Norma and Jeannie on that European trip."

"We've been to Europe. Several times."

"But not together."

Aroni scowled. "After today, I'm not so sure I can afford Europe. I'll probably be out of a job. My counterpart at Global is forty-eight years old."

"You still going to vote against merger?"

"Yep. I owe it to Barney. And I suppose you still think merger's the only solution."

Vaughn sipped his coffee thoughtfully. "I'm afraid I do. Unlike some of our colleagues, I don't have any real animosity against Barney. He's been real good to me. But still . . ." He shrugged, a gesture of embarrassment.

"That merger adds up to two death sentences—Trans-Coastal's and Barney's. I'm glad you're not on the board. You'd be demonstrating your gratitude in a very peculiar way."

"Being grateful doesn't mean I want to sit back and watch this airline go down the drain."

"It goes down the drain if Global eats us up. I don't want to see Trans-Coastal go out of existence, Andy. If that's pure sentimentality, make the most of it."

Andy Vaughn smiled faintly. "Nostalgia is the nonproductive aspect of this business. We turn to it when we're in trouble, but it's really just an opiate. It makes us forget what has been bad and what is bad. It even distorts the past, and it can't change the present. That's why, if I had a vote two hours from now, I'd go for merger."

Aroni eyed his friend with a look of amused resignation. "Your pilots don't agree with you. They'd welcome merger like a collective dose of—"

"Since when has an airline pilot been able to see beyond his seniority number? Same with your mechanics. Somebody always gets screwed when you merge seniority lists, namely the people on the nonsurviving carrier. Sure, most of our guys will drop down quite a few notches, but what's worse, losing seniority or losing a job?"

"It's not a case of either-or," Aroni said doggedly. "Give the Old Man a little more time and he'd pull us out of this dive."

Vaughn shook his head. "That's pure malarkey. We're in a dive all right. Anyway, don't waste so much sympathy on our beloved president. He sure as hell gave ALPA a fast brush-off when the pilots offered to freeze their contract for two years, just to help things stabilize."

Aroni stared in utter disbelief. "I never heard anything about that. When did this happen?"

"Oh, not more than a month ago. Art Granville—he's chairman of Trans-Coastal's Master Executive Council—Art told me about it. God, Larry, he said it could have been more than just ALPA if the Old Man had accepted the pilots' offer. He said the IAM, Teamsters, and the rest of the unions might have gone along, too. But when Barney turned ALPA down, the whole plan fell apart. Too bad. It might have made some difference."

"Did Granville actually see Barney? Is there anything in writing, the proposal or the rejection?"

Andy Vaughn hesitated. Something in Aroni's voice had stirred his own suspicions. "Come to think of it, no. Art never made the offer to Barney directly. The Old Man was out of town at the time—on a trip trying to line up director support against the merger."

"Who did Art talk to, then?"

"Roger Campbell."

"Did Granville ever say whether he told Campbell the other unions might go along with ALPA's plans? That it could involve more than just the pilots?"

"Larry, I'm not sure. I think so, but . . ."

"We gotta be sure! Call Crew Schedule right now and find out if we can get in touch with Granville."

Vaughn picked up a phone and dialed. "Jerry? Andy Vaughn. Is Art Granville flying today? Yeah, I'll wait."

The twenty-eight seconds it took the crew scheduler to get back on the phone seemed like an hour to Aroni. He groaned as Vaughn heard the report and hung up, a look of despair all over his face.

"He's on Flight 715, Minneapolis–Phoenix. He left Minneapolis just fifteen minutes ago."

Aroni launched himself out of his chair. "Get your ass over to Operations and try to raise him on company radio."

"Shit, we couldn't raise him out of here. We'd have to relay it through Minneapolis."

"Then set up a company frequency patch between here and Minneapolis so we can talk to him direct. I can't trust a relay. There isn't enough time and I don't want anybody talking to Granville except you."

"I'm on my way. Where will you be, in Barney's office?"

"No. Don Littlefield's."

Vaughn stopped halfway through the door. "I don't get it. Why Littlefield?"

"Even if we prove that Campbell's a goddamned liar, it's pretty late to swing any votes. I don't want Barney to expose that bastard. I want someone who's pro-merger to do the dirty work. Coming from Littlefield, the shock effect will be greater. Don will have more credibility. It won't be Barney's word against Campbell's. It'll be Campbell's against someone from his own side. It's the only way to lower the boom on our senior vice-president of double-crossing."

"What makes you think Don'll believe us? Hadn't you better ask Barney himself? It's possible Roger did tell him about the offer and that he did refuse it."

"Horse manure," Aroni said grimly. "I have known Barney Burton for almost fifty years. His airline's at stake. If he turned Granville down, the sun will rise in the west. Better get going, Andy. We don't have much time."

Aroni and Littlefield were talking quietly when Vaughn came in panting.

"I ran all the way from Dispatch," he wheezed, looking at Littlefield. "Does Don know what this is all about?"

Littlefield nodded, his face as forbidding as Aroni's.

"Fine," said Vaughn. "I contacted Granville. Yes, he did tell Campbell that if Barney bought ALPA's deal, he had indications the other unions would propose something similar. In fact, Art said IAM wouldn't go for a two-year freeze but might agree to one. Art never talked to Barney about it. He said he assumed that what Roger relayed was straight from the president. Incidentally, Captain Granville wants to know what the hell this is all about."

Littlefield swore under his breath. "Wouldn't we all. Frankly, I find it hard to believe that Roger Campbell would deliberately sabotage this company."

"It isn't hard for me to believe it," Aroni said gruffly. "I never did like the sonofabitch. The next step is to ask Barney the last question: did he know about the ALPA proposal?"

Littlefield rose from his chair. "We'd better ask him right now. Larry, I wish you'd go in with me." He turned. "Andy, the fewer people in on this scene, the better."

"Sure," Vaughn nodded. "Don, will this kill the merger?"

"I don't know. It's going to cost Mr. Campbell his job, that's for sure. Not only with us but with Global. Dick Hoagland's tough but he's honest. He'll hang Roger for pulling this stunt. *If* he did. Let's go see the boss."

"You didn't answer my question," Vaughn pressed. "What about the merger now?"

"Let's just say the odds are a bit narrower. Undressing Mr. Campbell before the board won't by itself change much. Even if the Pilots' Association freeze had been accepted, it would have been more of a morale boost than a financial one. A potential savings of a few million dollars, yes, but it would've taken a hell of a lot more than that to pull us out of this muck."

"But if IAM, the Teamsters, and everyone else went along . . .?" Vaughn was almost pleading and Aroni had to grin. Here was one merger proponent already converted.

"Helpful, but neither conclusive nor adequate. Still . . ." Littlefield's voice trailed off.

"What were you going to say?" Vaughn asked.

"Nothing. Let's go."

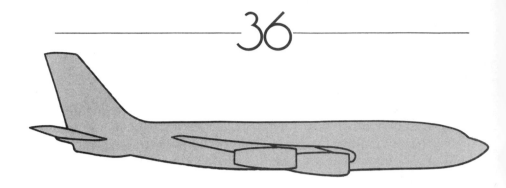

36

Barnwell Burton sighed heavily as his tired eyes finished scanning the mementoes that filled his heart as much as they did the big office. The last was a photograph of the old Jordan, which Henry McKay had restored in honor of the Silver Anniversary. There had been no place to display it publicly and it was collecting dust in a corner of the main hangar. Barney remembered sourly that he had offered it to the new National Air Space Museum only to have it rejected as "not being of sufficient aeronautical interest."

They might as well junk the car and him together, he thought. Obsolete museum pieces—but he wasn't obsolete. He was still full of fight, except there were no more weapons and he was out of ammunition. Yet he could not give up. That much he knew. Their last night in London together—what was it Larry had said? That his commitment to the airline wasn't so much that he loved Trans-Coastal, but rather what it had given him—power and prestige.

It wasn't entirely true, Barney told himself. Sure he loved the trappings. The exhilaration. The awesome responsibility. But he had loved the industry, too—that perfect combination of complex technology blended so skillfully. This was what he could not bear leaving, for he had been a part of the air-transportation miracle.

And that's what the gathering jackals, now yapping at the wounded old lion, refused to understand or appreciate.

It wasn't that he had made so many mistakes or governed unwisely. Sure, there had been errors in judgment. God, he was only human. Maybe he should have delegated more authority, controlled some of his infatuation for new planes, shown more tolerance for the views of able young men like Littlefield. But so many of Trans-Coastal's misfortunes were beyond his control, like the fuel crisis. They couldn't blame everything on him. But they were, the ungrateful bastards.

Miss Wingate's buzzer sounded.

"Mr. Littlefield and Mr. Aroni are here to see you, Mr. Burton."

"I don't know a goddamned thing about it!" Barney roared. "It's complete news to me. Why that dirty, slimy . . ."

"Save the profanity, Barney," Littlefield said wearily. "All we've done is gather evidence that Roger Campbell is a lying crook. I'll be very happy to bring this little matter before the board . . . and before the vote is taken. Whether it'll prevent the merger is something else."

"Do *you* want to prevent it?" Barney said, eagerness and hope invading his brusque tone. Aroni was suddenly alert too.

The vice-president of Marketing and Sales looked directly into the angry blue eyes of his boss. "I'm going to change my vote." He spoke with slow, deliberate force. "And I'll do my best to convince the others that this airline can survive without merger. However, before I go into that boardroom, Barney, there are a few conditions to my putting my own career on the line. Because if I fail, I'm as finished as you are."

"Name 'em."

"I want your promise that if I'm successful, you'll resign as president. And—" Littlefield's jaw tightened. "—*and* as chairman of the board."

Barney turned red. "I'll nominate you for president myself, but I'll stay on as chairman. It's my right. That's what you want, isn't it, Don—to be president?"

"Yes, I do. I'd make a darn good one and I think I could pull us out of this spin. But my own personal ambition isn't what's at stake. If you want to nominate Larry or Bill Sloan, that's your privilege. Or get a top man from the outside. I know you're not stupid enough to pick Jack Myler. We just need a new leader, and no new leader will be worth a damn while you're around. Not as chairman of the board or vice-president of the credit union or supervisor in charge of toilet-paper acquisition. If you stay in any capacity, you'll try to interfere. Anyone who's been in power as long as you have has to abdicate completely or we blow the whole ballgame. In other words, Barney, get the hell off the airplane."

Aroni expected the Old Man to have a stroke; Barney's face had gone from crimson to a deathly white. His big fists clenched and unclenched.

"So you want me out of the airline *I* built. I think I deserve an explanation."

Littlefield nodded. "You do deserve one." He ran his hand through his hair. "Barney, you've made so many right decisions— against all kinds of opposition—that you came to assume it was impossible to make a wrong decision. You once welcomed advice. Now you resent it. Sure, you've built this airline. But after building it, you made the same mistake that other airline giants made—you came to regard it as *yours*. Not even the stockholders', the directors', your fellow officers', your employees', not even the public's, but *Barney Burton's*." Littlefield made a helpless gesture. "It isn't yours, Barney. An airline, any airline, is nothing but a technological robot. What brings it to life, what gives it personality and feeling and a kind of responsibility, is *people*. Not just one—many."

"That's why you want me out."

"That's why I want you out. You consider yourself bigger than the airline itself. You still take pride in the fact that everyone says 'Trans-Coastal *is* Barnwell Burton and Barnwell Burton *is* Trans-Coastal.' A single identity. If it were that simple, I'd fight for you as well as Trans-Coastal. Only you don't deserve being fought for— the airline does. There was once a time when the company and you *were* the same person. Not any longer. What exactly is your image? I'll tell you—arrogance, stubbornness, personal glorification. And most of all, inconsistency; the customer is always right even when he's wrong, but the next day you turn around and screw the hell out of the customer with some half-baked economy move that does nothing but ruin our reputation and competitive ability. And if Barney Burton's image and Trans-Coastal's image are one and the same, we don't belong in the airline business."

Barney looked away from the man pacing the floor of his office.

"So help me, I respect what you've accomplished. I'm eternally grateful for what you've taught me, and for what you've done for me and for every man and woman in this company. You're a giant of a man, a pioneer in every sense of the word. You deserve not just gratitude and praise but a place in aviation history. Now it's over, Barney. It's all over. Try to see beyond your own ego and pride; understand *why* it's over. Look back on your mistakes as well as your accomplishments. In the past five years, you've blocked or tried to block every progressive marketing scheme that would have involved spending money. You opposed them mostly for two reasons: either you didn't think of them yourself, or you argued that we couldn't afford them. Maybe you were right about the expense, but one reason we couldn't afford them is that you consistently and deliberately went overboard on flight equipment, ordering new planes on the basis of your perpetual infatuation with new models. Think how much we could have spent on in-flight service, on ground facilities, on improved reservations, *if* we hadn't dug a hundred-million-dollar hole with those 747's which nobody else on this airline thought we needed, with the possible exception of your stooge, Jack Myler."

Barney stole a glance at Aroni. Larry was stone-faced, but Barney did not miss the almost imperceptible nod of agreement cast in Littlefield's direction. Don was still speaking, his voice a whip.

". . . your grandiose route-development plans. Applying for Hawaii when we didn't even have authority to serve Los Angeles yet. And then ordering the 747 on the grounds that we needed them in case we got Hawaii. Trying for a nonstop Washington–Los Angeles award—a market already served by three other carriers making so little money that they already had a capacity agreement when we applied. Filing for routes that made absolutely no sense other than that you got drunk with some senator and figured you had to impress him. Spending God knows how many thousands of dollars on hopeless, even ridiculous route applications and then turning me down when I asked for a hundred grand for a market survey so we could figure out some way to strengthen our route structure.

"The deadwood we've carried on our payroll. Jack Myler, Cal Motts—incompetents. But they were cronies or old-timers. Station managers who haven't done a full day's work since the last DC-3 went through their cities. I could forgive your reluctance to ditch that collection of stumblebums, but while you were paying Motts fifty-five thousand a year to do virtually nothing in a refurbished office with an empty title on his door you furloughed twenty percent of the reservations staff.

"Do I have to go on, Barney? You're a Jekyll and Hyde, only the Hyde-half has taken over. It's dominant. You were one of the greatest men I've ever known. *Were*. You can still warrant that adjective for the rest of your life if you walk out of Trans-Coastal now. The only reason I was voting for merger was because without one, you'd stay in power for another three years and then we'd be ruined. Sure we can survive without merger—if we go on without you."

"Are you finished?"

"No. Those are my terms. Accept them and I'll chew Roger Campbell into little pieces and spit 'em in Billings's ugly face. I think I can save our airline, Barney. Not *your* airline—*ours*. The price is steep. It's Trans-Coastal in exchange for your hide. All you have to do is ask youself the only truly important question: do you really love this airline? Or is it just your pride and power at stake?"

The only sound in the room was Barney's heavy breathing.

He looked at Aroni, who gently shook his head—but Barney knew it was helpless sympathy, not support. He turned back to Littlefield.

"I can't do it," he said hoarsely. "You're not just removing me as president and chairman, you're sentencing me to . . . This has been my whole life. If I leave here, there isn't anything left."

"I know that, Barney." Littlefield's own voice was choked. "So help me, I know it. But I have no alternative."

The old bombast and bluster, the fierce defiance, flared again. "The hell you don't! I've promised to work with you, to help you all I can—even stay out of your hair if you want. What the hell more can you ask?"

"I'm sorry. I've set my terms and I won't compromise."

The president's face was a mask of hatred and frustration. He was thinking of yesterday—God, was it less than twenty-four hours ago? It seemed more like twenty-four months had gone by since he had clashed with Senator Kennedy. Since Kennedy had called him an anachronism—a has-been. The very remembrance fueled his rage. "Screw you, Littlefield! You lousy ingrate! Everything you've achieved in this company you owe to me. *I* brought you out of a flunky's job in Phoenix. *I* made you a vice-president before your ears were dry. *I* taught you this business. And this is the way you repay me—stabbing me in the back!"

He was thrashing now, Aroni realized miserably, like a trapped animal. Magnificent, yet pitiful. Stubborn to the last. He's licked, Aroni thought, and so is this airline.

"I'm waiting," Littlefield said tensely. "I'll give you ten seconds to make up your mind."

"Don't you threaten me, you sonofabitch!" Barney yelled. "You can take your ultimatum and stuff—"

"Five seconds, Barney." Littlefield leaned across the desk on his knuckles, looking straight at Barney.

Aroni could hear his own heart pounding. Barney rose out of his chair. Down on the mahogany desk came the big fist.

"Then here's your answer," Barnwell Burton said and, clutching the heavy glass ashtray, he heaved it across the room with all his strength.

Barnwell Burton called the board meeting to order at precisely 10:00 A.M. He was pale and his veined hands were trembling.

"Gentlemen, may I have your attention . . . Thank you. The only order of business on the agenda today is the proposed merger of Trans-Coastal with Global Airlines."

He paused to inspect the double line of faces peering intently at him from the long, rectangular board table arranged so neatly by the efficient Miss Wingate. Pewter water pitchers spaced at regular intervals like miniature silver towers. A scratch pad and freshly sharpened pencil sat in front of each director.

How many times had he looked down at the board table and seen those faces. They changed from time to time, yet they all seemed alike. The varying expressions. Interest. Boredom. Belligerence. Cynicism. Admiration. Hope. Concern. Confidence. A little different, today—expectancy mostly, but with some nervousness. A few reminded him of vultures perched on chairs as if they were tree limbs.

To his left, as the senior director, was McKay. Aged and bent, but with eyes still alert, bright. This would be Henry's last meeting, too, before becoming a director-emeritus, which had been Barney's idea of a fitting tribute for the little banker's forty-eight years of service. Henry looked belligerent, a bantam rooster spoiling for a fight.

To his immediate right was vice-chairman Billings, his expression impatient. The hangman, Barney thought, waiting for the noose to be adjusted.

There was Larry Aroni, a quizzical smile on his fleshy face, and the look that passed between them was one of mutual sadness. Fellow conspirators.

Littlefield—he was looking not at Barney but at Campbell as a snake would transfix an unsuspecting victim.

Campbell, not noticing the senior vice-president of Marketing and Sales, had his eyes fixed on Barney, his jowls creased in a half-smile.

John Myler was rubbing his chin with one hand and doodling on the scratch pad with the other; Barney caught his eye but he looked away.

Bob Levin, wearing one of his notoriously loud ties, seemed puzzled about something. Barney had made no effort to contact him to put up an argument. He was uncomfortable.

Clark Delavan, head of the Delavan Investment Corporation of Phoenix, was frowning at Barney—one of the vultures, the latter mused. Delavan had come in with his usual ten-gallon Stetson, jade-clasped string tie, and expensive Western boots; the fact that he was only an inch or two taller than Henry McKay rather spoiled the picture.

Harrison G. Pitcher, president of the Twin Cities Canning Corporation, Minneapolis. Mr. Bell. Parker J. Thaman, board chairman of the Security & Savings Bank of Detroit. He smiled frequently, but his was a smile that seemed to be attached to a switch.

Calvin Motts. Cal hadn't said a word in weeks. He looked sick to his stomach.

Barnwell Burton's jury of peers . . .

"Gentlemen, before throwing the merger proposal open for discussion, Don Littlefield, our senior vice-president of Marketing and Sales, insists on bringing a matter of importance before this group."

Littlefield rose and nodded in Barney's direction.

"Gentlemen, it has been brought to my attention that a member of this board has committed an act I can only categorize as a despicable breach of integrity, and one that has convinced me I cannot vote for the proposed merger."

Eight heads shot up.

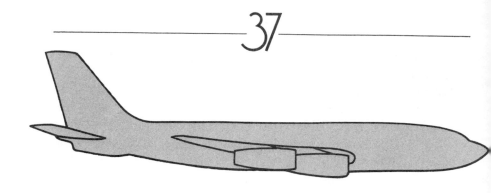

37

"Whatever Mr. Campbell's motives," Littlefield was concluding, "and apparently they stemmed from his all-consuming desire to have this merger rammed down our throats, what he has done constitutes an act of treachery, dishonesty, and—to use a more colloquial expression—dirty double-crossing. I move that this board request the resignation of the senior vice-president of Finance effective immediately."

Campbell's face was the color of raw liver. For a long minute, no one spoke. Finally Bob Levin murmured, "I so move."

"Just a minute."

All heads turned toward Warren Billings.

"I think," said the vice-chairman, "we should not turn a vendetta against Roger into an argument against merger. There's absolutely no connection. Whatever Roger did, I'm sure he felt it was in the best interest of this company. Just as merger itself is in our best interests. Let's put first things first, gentlemen. Let's not lose sight of the main purpose of this meeting. I propose we vote on the principal issue first and take up the Campbell matter later."

Barney eyed Billings shrewdly.

"I have this sneaking hunch, Warren, you're figuring that voting merger would take this conniving bastard off the hook. Am I right?"

"No, you're not right," Billings said confidently. "I have no axe to grind for anyone in this whole affair, except to save this airline from ruin. Need I remind you, Mr. Burton, that Seaboard holds liens on the majority of Trans-Coastal's fleet? If you insist on using Roger's perhaps over-zealous efforts in behalf of merger as a reason for rejecting Global's proposal, I might see no alternative except to foreclose on those liens."

Don Littlefield had never dreamed Billings would play such a trump card. But Barney was looking not at Warren Billings but at the expression on Campbell's cherubic face. There was a touch of relief, maybe, but something else. Just a fleeting, almost imperceptible, hint of resentment. And Roger Campbell was not looking at Littlefield nor Barney. His eyes were fixed on Billings.

"Warren," said the president of Trans-Coastal, "you're a goddamned hypocrite. Also a liar."

"I resent—"

"Shut up, Billings. My second hunch of this here little bloodletting session is that our boy Roger isn't the only sonofabitch with dirt on his hands. You knew all about that ALPA offer, didn't you? You told Campbell to keep it from me."

"That's ridiculous."

"Is it?" Barney turned to Campbell. "Let's have the whole story, Roger. Tell the truth or, so help me, you won't have a chance to resign. My last official act will be to fire your ass right out of your swivel chair."

Campbell flushed, started to rise, and suddenly slumped, a deflated balloon. "It's true," he mumbled. "I told Billings about the ALPA deal and he advised me to keep my mouth shut."

Billings seemed unperturbed. "A grandstand play by a union to wreck the merger, gentleman. Trying to bail out the *Titanic* with a single bucket. It didn't mean a thing as far as straightening out the company's financial mess was concerned. I readily admit advising Roger on the matter. For rather obvious reasons."

"Ulterior motives, not obvious reasons," Barney said icily. "I'll agree with one thing you said, Warren—let's go ahead with the merger vote. But I'll add this, my friend: if you don't win and then try to foreclose on our airplanes, I'll call a press conference and then let Seaboard itself try to whitewash its image. Okay, gentlemen, let's get on with the execution."

Barney called the roll.

"Mr. Billings."

"For."

"Mr. Bell."

"For."

"Mr. Aroni."

"Against."

"Mr. Motts."

"Against."

"Mr. Campbell."

"For!"

"Mr. Littlefield."

"Against."

"Mr. McKay."

"Against."

"Mr. Delavan."

"For."

"Mr. Thaman."

"For."

"Mr. Pitcher."

"For."

"Mr. Levin."

"Against."

"Mr. Myler."

A moment's hesitation. The swing vote. If Myler went for the merger, it would be seven to six, even with Barney's negative vote. If he voted against, Barney's vote would be decisive.

"Mr. Myler," Barney repeated.

"Against."

Henry McKay leaped to his feet, ran over to Myler and hugged him. Aroni whooped like a cowboy.

"My own vote is against," Barney said. "The motion to merge Trans-Coastal with Global Airlines has been defeated, seven to six."

"Everybody sit down. The final order of business," Barney announced, "is the selection of a new president and board chairman. I would like to make two nominations—Don Littlefield as president, and John Myler as chairman of the board."

"Second both nominations," McKay said promptly.

The vote was unanimous. The directors clustered around Littlefield and Myler for handshakes, but Barney stood off to one side.

When the meeting broke up, three men stayed in the room that had been the battleground—Littlefield, Aroni, and Barney Burton.

"I just want you to know, Barney," Littlefield said, "you'll have lifetime pass privileges and you'll always have an office here. We'll fix up one for you. It'll be a bit smaller than the stadium you're in now, but I promise you it won't be a phone booth."

"I'd appreciate that," Barney said. "And also your making Jack chairman. I'd like to drop in now and then, Don. And, by the way, thanks for all those things you said. Made me sound like a goddamned hero. Or a martyr, anyway."

"I had a hunch I said what you would have."

"Maybe. But you'll never know, will you?"

"I think I already do. Take your time about moving out. Actually, I'd like to talk to you at length during the next couple of weeks. Got some ideas—"

"No. I'd fight 'em. She's all yours. The power and the problems. Take care of the place."

"I'll give you the same advice," Aroni said. "One of your first problems is finding a new senior vice-president of Maintenance and Engineering."

"And just where the hell do you think you're going?" Barney demanded.

"Retiring, like you. I'll stick around to help Don another six months at tops."

"You're crazy," Littlefield protested. "I need you—your experience, your common sense, your judgment, your—"

"Six months, Don. That's all. We came in together and I think I'd like to go out with him. Wop sentimentality, I think you once called it, Barney."

"Yeah," Barney said, his eyes glistening.

"Come on, Barnwell. It's ten-thirty. The bar's open."

Miss Wingate hurried into the office of the former president and board chairman at the first sound of his buzzer.

"Yes, Mr. Burton?"

"Gloria, I want you to do two things. First, call Reservations and get me first-class space for two to London tomorrow afternoon. For myself and Mrs. Leavelle.'

Miss Wingate, for the first time, could not prevent a look of disapproval. Barney laughed.

"And second, get Mrs. Leavelle on the phone. I think I'll ask her to marry me while we're there."

Miss Wingate's jaw dropped. "Married, Mr. Burton?"

"Yeah. Might as well. I just divorced this airline."

He turned away. "Where the hell did Aroni go?" He paused in the doorway and looked back across the room. "I'm going to miss you."

"We're going to miss you, too," she said softly, but Barnwell Burton was gone.